T0283142

A NOVEL

FLIGHT
OF THE
MONARCHS

M. H. REARDON

GREENLEAF
BOOK GROUP PRESS

Published by Greenleaf Book Group Press
Austin, Texas
www.gbgpress.com

Distributed by Greenleaf Book Group

For ordering information or special discounts for bulk purchases, please contact Greenleaf Book Group at PO Box 91869, Austin, TX 78709, 512.891.6100.

Design and composition by Greenleaf Book Group
Cover design by Greenleaf Book Group

Publisher's Cataloging-in-Publication data is available.

Print ISBN: 979-8-88645-082-8

eBook ISBN: 979-8-88645-083-5

To offset the number of trees consumed in the printing of our books, Greenleaf donates a portion of the proceeds from each printing to the Arbor Day Foundation. Greenleaf Book Group has replaced over 50,000 trees since 2007.

Printed in the United States of America on acid-free paper

23 24 25 26 27 28 29 30   10 9 8 7 6 5 4 3 2 1

First Edition

For my dad.
May his stories live on.

1

Celia

C elia Lynch caught her stride. Grass tore from the earth beneath her shoes. The wings on her back, forged of welding wire and papier-mâché, dragged in the autumn wind, as did her delicate lungs. Sure, the boy was faster, but Celia refused to accept defeat.

Jeremy cocked his head back to shout, "You're just a girl, Celia! You'll never catch me!"

"I'll catch you," Celia sputtered, cheeks ablaze. "You'll see."

But the boy was right. He was impossible to catch. A fact that would be more easily swallowed if he weren't such a loudmouth about it. Celia blamed his mother. If the woman hadn't abandoned Jeremy years before, she might have hurled the filthy imp into a bath and taught him that it's impolite to gloat.

"It'll never happen!" Jeremy yelled. "You're as slow as Droopy Dog, and I'm the Flash!"

"You hush, *Germ*-y Hill! You're Pepé Le Pew!"

Jeremy Hill had only a father—a great big beast of a man with handsome green eyes and a fondness for bourbon.

Jeremy reached their destination first, with Celia well behind. Both collapsed onto a cool patch of earth near the eucalyptus tree that was shaped like an ogre with grotesque, flaking limbs.

"I touched one," he said, still full of breath.

Celia, fighting to catch hers, looked up.

Against a clear blue sky, thousands of tiny black-and-orange wings fluttered. The swarm of monarch butterflies floated peacefully by, having migrated nearly two thousand miles from their summer home in Canada to overwinter in Pacific Grove.

Celia and Jeremy, their bony, prepubescent arms folded behind their heads, welcomed the butterflies back in silence.

"*JEREMIAH!*"

At the jolt of his father's voice, Jeremy jumped to his feet and dashed toward home.

Standing, Celia shimmied the leaves off her homemade wings. "Don't be late tomorrow!" she called after him, then crossed the front lawn toward her own house.

The evening sun, as it sank into the neighboring Pacific, glowed a deep persimmon, casting wide, cottony streaks of pink and purple.

Charmed by the view, Celia trotted up the porch steps of her house—a yellow Victorian with white shutters and a wraparound porch—and got a grand idea as the mouth-watering aroma of pot roast and buttered potatoes filled her nostrils.

She threw open the front door. "Mama!" Celia shrugged out of her wings and kicked off her shoes. "Mama! Can we eat supper outside?"

"Quit your yelling," Luisa, their mother's helper, said while giving Celia's ponytail a light yank. A laundry basket was tucked beneath one of Luisa's muscular arms. "Your father's resting. He had a long day."

Celia fixed her ponytail and followed the older woman through the house. "But Luisa, it's the perfect evening to eat outside. The sunset's that bright kind, and it's not too windy out."

"That's up to your mother, *mija*. Now go wash up for dinner." Luisa's nose crinkled. "You smell like a boy."

Celia grumbled an obedient "Yes, ma'am" before darting upstairs in search of her mother.

"No running!" Luisa screamed after her.

"Mama!"

"Why are you so loud, Celia?" her big sister complained as they passed each other in the upstairs hall. "And where's Jeremy? I need to ask him something."

"Home." Celia peered into her sister's frilly bedroom. It seemed to have barfed clothing. More evidence that her *real* sister—a gangly-but-affable tomboy renowned for her well-aimed spit wads—had been taken over by body snatchers sometime in the last year. Bianca was three years older and fast becoming an insufferable snob. Thirteen now, she was practically a woman and had recently grown two unwieldy lumps on her chest. Both hovered today like twin gelatin cakes beneath a tight pink sweater. Every day since her "change," Bianca flaunted those lumps shamelessly, enjoying the reaction she got from the neighborhood boys—former spitball targets all.

But as annoyed as Celia was with her sister's newfound vanity, she sort of understood it. Bianca had become a beauty, like their mother, with eyes like emeralds and hair a rich shade of molasses. Each morning, she unrolled her curlers to expose dark, shining ringlets that bounced when she walked. But what impressed upon Celia, more than anything, was that Bianca always—*always*—painted her nails red. Blood red. According to *Vogue* magazine, red was Elizabeth Taylor's trademark polish color, and Celia was so jealous she could spit. She wasn't allowed to polish her nails until she was thirteen, too. The whole thing was terribly unfair.

"Where were you earlier?" Celia asked her sister. "Some of the butterflies came, and you missed it."

"Cool it with the butterflies, will ya." Bianca blew a huge, pink bubble from between glossed lips. "I was fixing my face."

"It looks the same as before."

Pop! Bianca rolled her eyes as her tongue collected the sticky, pink goo from her lips. She grabbed Celia's hand. "Maybe I'll paint your nails when you and Daddy come back from your walk."

Now she was talking!

"But if Mommy asks, you stole my polish. Got it?"

Celia nodded.

Bianca wrinkled her nose. "Go take a bath first. You're grody." She twisted to slip back into her room, but returned, curls bobbing deliciously. "Then I'll make you look just like me."

Celia squealed with delight. "While I'm washing up, convince Mama to let us eat outside!"

"Yeah, yeah."

———

Twenty minutes later, Celia emerged from her bath smelling of bubble soap and Lustre Crème. She wrenched on her night clothes and hurried downstairs where she found her family outside seated around the patio table.

Skipping over to join them, she kissed her mother on the cheek, then her father. "Hi, Mama. Hi, Daddy."

"And where have you been, young lady?" her father asked before his teeth sawed through an ear of corn. Thomas Lynch, to his youngest daughter, was the most magnificent man in the history of the world. He was owner and editor in chief of a small publishing company in nearby Monterey, but the stress of deadlines gave him horrible headaches. In the evenings, her mother, lead bookkeeper at Lynch Publications, would pause everything to sit with him in his study. When Celia should've been in bed, she would often spy through the slit of the door frame to watch her mother massage her father's temples while he railed about lazy employees or the contemptible quality of some new printing ink.

But then the kisses would come. Gentle, quieting kisses. His forehead, his eyes, his mouth; her mother neglected nothing. But occasionally, the kisses became more. The way her father's hands would knead her mother's breasts or the private place between her thighs, her mother's responsive moans, or worse, the whispered vulgarities that spilled from her father's sainted lips, never failed to make Celia blush and run away. The next day, she'd deliberate with Jeremy, who would request the strangest of details.

"Did he touch her there again?" he'd ask with concern. The answer varied, but it was news of her mother's keen response that seemed to trouble Jeremy most.

At the patio table, Celia took a seat across from her sister. "I was washing up for supper, Daddy."

"Where's Jeremy?" her father added as an afterthought. "I have something for him."

"Dennis called him home."

Her father blew an encumbered breath. "Well, bring him inside tomorrow afternoon. I have the plumb bob I promised him."

Celia tried not to make the ugly face that Luisa often scolded her about. Stupid plumb bob. Daddy had lit up when Jeremy requested the bizarre tool, impressed that the boy knew of it. Daddy had always wanted a son. Well, girls could like plumb bobs, too. Whatever they were.

"I will, Daddy," Celia said, forcing a smile. "Now, he can start on my tree house."

Across the table, Bianca scoffed. "You've got that poor kid building you a tree house now?"

"He wants to."

"Sure he does."

"How was school today, Celia?" her mother interjected, prying her glare from her sister.

"Oh, Moose brought a frog to school," Celia answered, grabbing a warm roll while trying to ignore the snotty look her sister was giving her. "He named him Elvis Aaron Presley. They sent him home, though, because he jumped on Patty Pierson's head."

"Moose jumped on Patty Pierson's head?" Bianca asked.

"No, stupid, the frog!"

Her mother rapped at the table. "Celia Elizabeth Lynch! Language!"

Just then, her father belched an impeccable *ribbit*, prompting giggles around the table.

———

The following morning was Friday, Performance Day at school and the day that would become one of the worst of Celia's life.

Bianca, an eighth grader, had already caught her morning bus. But Celia, in fifth grade now, was forced to wait with veiled impatience on her front porch for Jeremy.

There was a croak with each rock of the porch swing and every rise of her heels. Her fingers, now polished the deep crimson of Elizabeth Taylor, lay gracefully across her lap. The dress she wore—a red number trimmed at the waist with a belt of black-and-white polka dots—made her feel pretty and dignified. On her feet were saddle shoes to match the belt. To complete the ensemble, her strawberry-blond hair had been woven into two pigtail braids, each tied with one red ribbon and one white. On the outside, Celia was the very picture of ease and feminine poise. But on the inside, she was a tempest of angry thoughts, making not-so-nice threats on Jeremy Hill's life.

"Hey."

Celia whipped her head toward the sound of his voice and stood to see him below the porch, squinting up at her. "You were almost late," she said, grabbing her book bag.

"But I wasn't late." As she stepped into the morning sun with him, Jeremy grabbed her left hand, gave it a brief once-over, then dropped it again. "Since when do you paint your hands?"

"Since last night." Celia posed, spreading her fingers across her cheeks like the glamorous women in her mother's magazines. "You like?"

"No. It looks like a wild animal gnawed your fingers bloody."

Her excitement crushed, Celia opened her mouth, ready to bruise his unwarranted little ego, to point out the obvious disparities between them. Jeremy stunk of old sweat and cigarette smoke. He wore dirty brown slacks, two inches too short, and a white undershirt with distress holes peppered along its seams. He looked destitute, as usual, and though she knew it was hardly his fault, acid words squatted on the tip of her tongue, geared to strike.

"Daddy bought you that ridiculous plumb bob thing," she spat instead, unable to strike today. Not when his lip was split like that, his eye freshly bruised. Last night they had been nearly healed.

Flashing his battered smile, Jeremy took her hand. Together, they walked down the long dirt drive until they reached the main road leading to the school.

It was a quiet morning, aside from the sharp cawing of seabirds and the hiss of ocean surf. But having lived on the coast all their lives, they hardly noticed those sounds anymore.

"I'll get started on your tree house tomorrow," Jeremy said, rolling his tattered buck knife between his fingers, another gift from her father.

Celia frowned. "But tomorrow's the butterfly parade."

"So? I don't care about that dumb parade. Everyone prancing around, dressed like butterflies, it's enough to make a man sick."

"Good thing you're just a boy then." Celia couldn't help her flippant attitude. She knew good and well that she was too old to wear wings for the parade, but she didn't care. Neither did her best friend, Angie. The pair of them would prance around like silly, wing-wearing freaks forever. Dash it all!

The school bus passed as Jeremy rolled his eyes, but both he and Celia ignored it. They couldn't ride it anymore since the day Jeremy was barred for fighting on it (for winning was more like it; he hadn't been the only one fighting).

Even as the bus rolled past, some of the boys—the bullies!—hung from open windows to jeer at him. Celia wished she could ride it (she wasn't barred), but her father insisted she be led to school by Jeremy like an inept toddler. Protesting was of no use either. She'd already tried and gotten herself lectured on the importance of loyalty and sympathy.

Celia was positive he just loved Jeremy more.

"So, what's the getup for?" Jeremy asked, examining her outfit.

"It's Performance Day," Celia reminded him. "I have to be the prettiest. I'll die if I'm the last girl asked."

Jeremy shot her another smile. And though Celia would rather eat dirt than admit it, she liked it when he did that. It made him seem like an ordinary boy, if only for a moment. She even smiled back as encouragement.

"Celia!" At school, Angie ran over, her red ponytail swinging. "You polished your nails," she said, cutting between Jeremy and Celia. "My mother would never let me paint mine this God-awful color. Hi, Jeremy."

As he did with most people, Jeremy ignored Angie and walked off on his own.

"Come on," Angie went on, unfazed. "You need to help me with my wings."

"Wait." Celia set her attention on Jeremy's route through the schoolyard. As he walked, he kept his head down in subordination, his cagey gait resembling that of an ill-treated animal. He had to get through without rousing the attention of Kevin Donahue or any of Kevin's despicable friends.

"He made it," Angie proclaimed once Jeremy safely passed between the two giant palms that marked the end of Bully Alley and disappeared around the corner.

Once in class, Celia sat down beside Angie. Their surnames, Lynch and Martin, fell consecutively on the attendance list, allowing for the ideal seating assignment each year. They'd been best friends since the second day of first grade, when Betty Jean Finnegan, Celia's previous best friend, threw dirt in Celia's face over rights to the class recess whistle. In a brief fit of anger and retribution, Jeremy had shoved Betty to the ground. That was when Angie, playing hopscotch several yards away, having witnessed the entire ordeal, shouted something to the effect of, "That's what you get, Betty Jean!" Celia was to later discover that Betty had made more enemies than Rome in kindergarten, including one Angie Martin. Nonetheless, Celia was devastated, and while Betty ran off to tittle-tattle on Jeremy, Angie lugged Celia to the girl's restroom to clean her blubbering, muddied face.

Celia claimed Angie as her best friend an hour later during reading lesson.

A piece of chalk click-clacked against the fifth-grade blackboard. Today, they were learning how to multiply decimals.

Angie nudged Celia. "See if Fletcher has my paste."

"Fletcher," Celia whispered to the head in front of her. When the boy failed to respond, Celia jabbed her finger into the nape of his freckled neck. "I know you hear me."

Fletcher spun around, his Browline spectacles steaming over as he huffed his hostility. "You're going to get me in trouble, Celia."

"Mister Fletcher!" Ms. Pratt's voice sliced through the classroom like a freshly sharpened blade. "Is there something you'd like to share with the rest of the class?"

"No, ma'am," Fletcher muttered, turning to face forward.

After giving him a distrustful squint, Ms. Pratt returned to her click-clacking.

"Sorry," Celia whispered, sucking on the insides of her cheeks to keep from laughing. Fletcher—Thurston Halford Tiberius Fletcher, to be precise—was just too sensitive for words. But she liked him very much. A shy, awkward boy, he was frequently picked on and pushed around. Curiously, though, whenever anyone gave him trouble or called him by anything other than his requested "Fletcher," they came fist to face with Jeremy Hill, his silent but faithful bodyguard.

"Hey," a voice whispered. "Celia."

Celia felt a hard tap on her shoulder.

Oh, no.

"What do you want, Moose?" she whispered as she spun around. Anyone else, and Celia might've ignored the interruption, but she felt sorry for Moose. He was very sweet and very fat and sometimes got stuck under his desk during duck-and-cover drills. He was also half-Mexican, and the mean kids called him "half-breed," along with other puzzling names Celia didn't understand. His mother worked in the school cafeteria, and Moose spoke to her in Spanish, which got him endlessly teased. But with all that, his bright mood never dimmed, not even a little.

"Wanna see a trick?" Moose whispered to Celia.

"You're going to get us both in trouble."

"Miss Lynch!"

Wincing, Celia faced forward. "Yes, Ms. Pratt?"

"What is going on back there? Do we all need to stay in for recess and write sentences?"

The whole class groaned. Celia was mortified.

"It was my fault, Ms. Pratt," Moose announced through his agreeable smile, his dark eyes large and blameless. "Celia dropped a penny from her pocket. I was just returning it to her."

Ms. Pratt smiled. She was a homely woman. "Well, that was very gentlemanly of you, Mr. Mousseau. The next time, though, you will wait until recess."

"Of course, ma'am. Thank you."

Celia sunk into her seat and sneaked a peek over at Jeremy to weigh his reaction. But he was staring out the window, and she realized that even watching him daydream made her melancholy. It was common knowledge that she associated with him outside of school, but her chronic excuses and skillfully feigned hatred of him also made her schoolmates pity her for the misfortune. Jeremy seldom acknowledged her schoolyard betrayals, but on occasion, he would crack and rage at her for being weak, for caring so much what others thought. He would swear hatred for her until she cried, then he would bury his face in her belly, wailing that he didn't mean it, that he loved her more than steak and potatoes, more than life itself.

By gym class, Celia had forgotten her math-hour disgrace. Their class was learning to ballroom dance, and it was Performance Day. The gymnasium was lined with two distinct rows of grumbling children, divided by gender. All were on edge, especially the boys, who were required to choose partners the way a proper suitor would, to bow with an extended hand and make the genial request. The girls were far more excited, whispering and bickering over who preferred whom.

Celia's own excitement dithered, however, at the sight of Jeremy. Before gym class, Ms. Pratt had cleaned his wounded face, slicked his dirty hair, and thrown a brown tie and tweed suit jacket (many sizes too big) on him since he had not come to school in the "appropriate attire." As usual, he stood beyond the crowd, sulking in a corner, glancing occasionally at Celia.

As she dissected his strange smile from that morning, it occurred to Celia that he might be planning to ask her to dance. When Ms. Pratt gave the signal to begin, that fear manifested into reality. Jeremy's greased head and tweed chest rose. A bat of Celia's eyelids, and he was crossing the gym toward her, the first from the boy's side to brave the twenty-yard expanse. She prayed for him to change course and choose another girl, any other girl.

Celia knew she should feel sympathy for him, but she felt only sympathy for herself. Very soon, she would be humiliated. The hammering drumbeat of her heart sent her into a panic at the prospect. Jeremy, with his disheveled appearance and standoffish behavior, had made himself a pariah, and thus, every day, she spent all her energy disassociating from him, trying to preserve what little good name she had.

The gymnasium full of students, realizing what was about to transpire, began to hum with murmurs. As Celia had feared, Jeremy stopped squarely in front of her. Eyes trained on her, he drew a deep, shaky breath, then bowed and extended one filthy hand.

A whiff of his unwashed skin made her recoil.

"May I have this dance, Miss?"

He'd worded the request precisely as every boy had been coached, like the perfect gentleman.

The gymnasium fell silent. All eyes were on her.

"Go away," Celia whispered as quietly as possible.

Gasps echoed from every direction.

Jeremy straightened up. "Please, Celia," he begged softly. "I don't want to wind up with the teacher again."

"Ask someone else."

"They all hate me." He looked ready to cry. "Please."

Celia managed a step back, her nose stinging with oncoming tears. She shook her head. It was then that she witnessed what disenchantment did to a bruised face.

But Jeremy wouldn't look away, even as several girls giggled.

"*Germ*-y wants to dance," they sang.

Celia thought she might vomit. Her heart pounded painfully inside her throat.

Then Jeremy's eyes finally released her, and he fled the gym. Ms. Pratt ordered him back. But of course, he didn't listen.

Performance Day resumed without Jeremy Hill, making the gender ratio even. Celia partnered with Fletcher by accepting his trembling hand. How she could have so much mercy for Fletcher, and none for Jeremy, she didn't know. But Fletcher waltzed her round and round as she sobbed silently against him, not speaking a single word, the perfect partner.

By lunchtime, Jeremy reappeared. Forgoing food, he sat alone at the table regularly occupied by Kevin Donahue and his awful friends, a place no kid—no kid who liked the position of his own nose anyway— ever ventured. Jeremy was hunting for a fight, and Celia knew it was her punishment for hurting him. It was his way of hurting her back.

To her relief, though, Fletcher and Moose sat down on either side of him and soon had him laughing.

Kevin and his bullies left the three boys alone for no reason that Celia could see.

By recess, Jeremy seemed himself again, playing jacks with Fletcher against the wall that housed the equipment closet—"the ball wall," as it was aptly nicknamed.

It was a cloudless day. A perfect cerulean sky. The sun saturated the blacktop with heat as children played ball and joined in jump rope games. In the middle of it all, Celia made her finest attempt at beating the current Pacific Grove Elementary School Double Dutch record. Her braids soared, acting as switches against her back as they came down hard. Betty Jean Finnegan, the current record holder, would finally eat her words.

"Cinderella, dressed in yellow, went upstairs to kiss her fellow, made a mistake and kissed a snake; how many doctors did it take? One, two, three . . ."

"Fight! Fight! Fight!"

The ropes fell, and Celia wheeled around.

"Fight! Fight! Fight!"

It was the siren call only children could hear. The play yard came to a halt except for one blot of asphalt, where all energy converged into a maelstrom of chaos.

Still as a statue, Celia stood, the ropes dead at her heels. Her eyes shifted, and her heart plummeted into her stomach. The ball wall was bare. Children, rows thick, circled like vultures around the commotion. Fists pounded the air. Celia's feet began to move.

"Fight! Fight! Fight!"

Dozens of saddle shoes and hush puppies thudded against the blacktop around her.

"Out of my way!" Celia demanded as she breached the pandemonium, shoving aside her shouting classmates. "Move!"

When she reached the heart of it, she found Jeremy on the ground, wrestling with Kevin Donahue. Both were grunting and maneuvering with furious desperation, looking determined enough to kill. To make things terribly unfair, one of Kevin's fifth-grade cronies, Tommy Russo, kicked Jeremy while the crowd urged the scuffle on.

"Leave him alone!" Celia shouted. Before another boot could strike Jeremy, she kicked Tommy Russo in his knee, a move her sister had taught her. Celia found herself reveling in Tommy's pain as he doubled over. "Miscreant! Bully!"

At this, the merciless grade-school mob roared.

Then, at Celia's feet, Jeremy received a vicious blow from Kevin's fist. His head met the pavement with a crack. The crowd stopped its shouting. Somewhere amid the ferocity, a conscience had been found. Celia dropped to her knees, grasping at Kevin's arms, hoping to stave him off, but took an elbow to the face instead as he reared back to strike Jeremy again. She fell back onto her bottom and covered her stricken mouth. The pain was incredible. She couldn't imagine what Jeremy was feeling. In fact, it hurt to imagine, and she started to cry.

"Do something, you ignoramuses!" Angie shouted behind her, and it was only then that several boys, including Moose, pulled Kevin off Jeremy.

"What's going on over here?" Mr. Bennett, the school principal, tore through the crowd, which dissolved instantaneously. "Everyone against the ball wall!" he yelled. "Now!"

"C'mon, Jeremy." Celia rested her cheek on the warm asphalt next to his head. "Get up."

He was spent, his eyelids drawn. Blood stained his teeth. He didn't utter a word as he climbed to his feet alongside Celia.

"Jeremiah?" Mr. Bennett's face was wrought with concern. He secured Jeremy's chin between his fingers. "Did Kevin start this? Or was it you?"

Jeremy furnished no response.

"Answer me, young man. I'm not going to ask again." At Jeremy's continued silence, Mr. Bennett grew frustrated and, with a discouraged sigh, transferred his attention to Celia. "Miss Lynch, please escort Mr. Hill to Nurse Margaret's office."

Celia did as she was told.

When she and Jeremy rounded a corner near the front office, she stopped and jabbed a finger into his chest. "Are you happy now? Have I been punished enough?"

Jeremy scowled. "He started with me."

"Liar." Feeling a hot tear drop from her eye, Celia swatted it off her cheek. "Why can't you be normal like everyone else? I hate being your friend. It's embarrassing! I wish I'd never met you."

Jeremy gave her the wounded expression she'd been seeking, then he walked off.

"Walk away then," she cried, wishing she hadn't said those things. "See if I care!"

————

After a lonely walk home from school, Celia eventually found Jeremy lying on his side beneath a giant eucalyptus at the farthest corner of his property.

She approached, then patted the ground with the ball of her foot. "Does your face hurt?" she asked him. "I know mine does."

Jeremy plucked blades of grass from the soil.

Celia hated when he did this. The silent treatment from him was excruciating. "I got an A on my dioramas," she said lamely. "Ms. Pratt said using your toy soldiers was clever. I let her know it was your idea."

Jeremy ripped free another blade of grass.

Celia stamped her foot. "Jeremy! Talk to me!"

"Just beat it, Celia." He rolled to his other side, facing away.

Celia walked around him in a huff. "I'm sorry, okay?" She sunk down into the soft, cool grass to sit beside him. "Please stop being mad at me." Up close, he looked a fright. Dried blood snaked out of his hairline. As she brushed her thumb across the knot it welled from, hidden beneath his dark-brown hair, he winced in pain, and she did, too. He had bruises over bruises. "I hate when you're hurt."

His expression turned surly. "Why do you care what happens to me?"

"I don't know. I just do. Kevin and your dad, they're not supposed to hit you like that. I asked Mr. Bennett about your dad, and he said it's complicated—"

Jeremy slammed his hand against the ground. "Butt out, Celia! One day, I'll be bigger than them, and they won't be able to touch me. I'll kill them all!"

His mouth formed a hard line, and Celia backed down.

After several minutes of his silence, she wiggled her way into his stiff, unwelcoming arms. "Can I lay with you?"

His tone was bitter. "Sure you're not too embarrassed to be seen with me?"

She shrugged. "Nobody's around."

Jeremy narrowed his eyes at her but nevertheless allowed her head on his shoulder. Quickly thereafter, his arm curled around her, his cheek coming to rest atop her head.

Relieved, Celia closed her eyes. He never stayed angry for long.

———

Celia thrilled at this style of dream, whimsical and malleable, the kind in which her consciousness threaded illogically through bizarre scenes, where benevolent tongues spoke in senseless whispers. She could hear them now, deep and tender, urging her to wake and yet lulling her back to dream. A breeze spun a cool web through her hair, lifting the tiny strands off her neck. The smell of grass and soil chilled her nose; then a soft prickle awakened her lips.

Her eyes snapped open.

Jeremy's eyes, green and wide, were a mere inch away.

Her lips itched as if they had been touched with the lightest pressure. Had Jeremy kissed her as she slept?

Celia had never been kissed before. Her classmate, Mona Bradley, had been kissed once, but not Celia. Was this what a kiss from a boy felt like: warm and soft and tickly? Or had she dreamed it? Jeremy looked guilty, and she grew livid at the thought of having missed her own first kiss.

Celia popped onto her elbow. "Did you just kiss me?"

The fury laced within her words was intentional, but Jeremy appeared unmoved by her anger and remained silent.

Celia squinted. "Jeremiah Patrick Hill, you answer me this instant. Did you kiss me?"

Arrogantly, he assessed her. "Maybe I did."

Celia gasped. How could he?! The mongrel! "Well . . . do it again!"

"Why should I?"

Celia gritted her teeth. "Because that was my first kiss, you toad, and I missed it!" She poked Jeremy hard in his chest, drawing from him a startled look. "And since you took it from me without my permission, you will at least give me something to remember. Now kiss me. And make it good."

Without delay, Celia shut her eyes. Nervous butterflies began to flutter through her stomach. Her lips zinged in anticipation of the moment Mona Bradley had described with such superb detail: a boy's wet, squishy mouth. *Oh, let it come!* She waited and waited, her heart racing, until—finally!—a pair of lips touched hers.

Ohhh. Fleshy soft, warm, electric panic was what it was. The jarring but not unwelcome invasion that was another living, breathing mouth pressed clumsily against hers. After an abrupt flare of terror, she puckered against it, remembering every fable, every legend ever recounted in the girls' bathroom. This was what men and women did with each other. How marvelous to finally feel it for herself!

A puff of air from Jeremy's nose tickled hers. There was a faint pop, and then his lips were gone.

"So," Jeremy murmured as she opened her eyes. "How was it?"

"It was okay." Celia lowered her gaze, embarrassment stoking a fire in her cheeks. "Did you like it?"

"It was okay," he echoed quietly, his throat bobbing.

It was surprising how self-conscious she felt now, naked almost, in his presence. She lay back down against him to hide. Had she known what would happen next, she would have asked him to kiss her again. Perhaps she would have kissed him the way they did in the movies or the way her mother sometimes kissed her father, with passion and drama.

Instead, she fell back to sleep in the grass.

For the second time that evening, Celia woke with a start. Seeing only darkness, she sat up and crossed her arms to rub the goosebumps away. The crisp symphony of cricket calls and swoosh of crashing waves reminded her that she wasn't in her bedroom.

"Oh, Jeremy, wake up." Celia shook his sleeping body. "Look," she said as his eyes stretched open. "The streetlights are on. We're in so much trouble."

Jeremy sat up. "Go home."

"What about you," Celia said, growing alarmed. "Dennis is going to beat you for this. Oh, God, he's going to be so angry."

"Calm down, will you?" Jeremy stood, pulling Celia up with him. "He's probably already passed out."

"What if he's not? Come home with me." Her eyes brightened. "It'll be just like the Fourth of July."

"No," he said, his trepidation finally showing. "I should get home."

Celia took hold of his hand. They didn't have time to argue. "Then I'll come with you. I'll tell him it was my fault."

"I said, no, Celia. You'll only make things worse. Go home."

But she insisted, and after a quick back and forth, Jeremy gave up and headed for home, Celia stubbornly marching at his heels.

Once Celia and Jeremy reached his house, it became apparent that Jeremy had presumed wrong. His father was not passed out but instead pacing the house at a furious rate. The bulky silhouette behind the curtains looked like a leviathan in search of accursed sailors to eat, and it didn't take a genius to figure out who those sailors were going to be.

"You shouldn't be here," Jeremy said, watching that agitated shadow. "Go home."

"No." Celia's tone was petulant. "I'm coming with you."

Jeremy stalked toward his front door. "You never listen to me!"

Celia trailed at his heels again, feigning gallantry with her walk until a thought occurred to her. "He's not going to hit me, is he?" she asked, thinking of the bruises. "I'm going to the parade tomorrow."

"Don't be ridiculous," Jeremy said, always in perpetual defense of his father.

Celia's natural inclination was to challenge his watered-down accounts of life in the Hill household, but she decided against it tonight. On plenty of occasions, she'd witnessed Dennis Hill behave like a respectable man. She'd even seen him treat Jeremy the way a father should treat his son. On the previous Fourth of July, at the Cleary picnic, Dennis spent an hour helping her and Jeremy fill water balloons, then another hour chasing them around, pelting them with water grenades until they were soaked and gasping with laughter. He was abominably scary, yes, especially during the chase, but it was reasonable to deduce from the experience that he wasn't always a bad man.

It was the drink. It brought out the leviathan.

That same night of the picnic, after Dennis had soaked himself silly with spirits (which were illegal in Pacific Grove), he became belligerent, disrupting the festivities and upsetting the neighbors with his offensive language. Celia's father helped Dennis home and insisted Jeremy spend the night at the Lynch house. Although the night was viewed with disgrace by the adults of Pacific Grove, Celia remembered it with fondness. Once the lights had gone out, Jeremy had slipped into her bedroom and crawled beneath her covers. Brandishing a weighty, green flashlight, they told ghost stories and sneaked butterscotch candies from the foyer bowl downstairs. It was a scream. Her favorite memory.

Jeremy stepped toward her now. "Do not move from this spot." Though he was a full three months younger, he had a few inches on her, and his eyes, though light in color, could be dark and menacing, especially when he was being serious. "I'm serious, Celia."

Celia nodded.

Leaving her alone on the porch, Jeremy stole past the front door and disappeared inside the house.

The night grew frightening in his absence. Something dreadful

brewed in the air that cold autumn night, but Celia waited duti-
fully with her arms wrapped around herself. That half minute of
charged silence was followed by Jeremy's muffled voice, then Dennis's
deeper, louder one.

Seeking out a window, Celia peeked into what appeared to be a family
room. She had never been inside, but it had the typical furnishings—
a couch, a few low tables, and a small television console airing *The
Adventures of Jim Bowie*. The mess and drabness of it were depressing,
though, and she felt sorrier than ever for her friend.

Then Dennis began shouting from somewhere inside the house.
Celia's heart flew into a panic at his tone—thunderous and angry, the
words merging into a single, sloshing tirade that made no sense.

A crash shook the house.

Celia ran to another window, where a view of the kitchen and what
transpired within put a stain over everything she thought she knew.
She watched Dennis Hill shove his only son against the refrigerator
and strike him in the face with a tightly balled fist.

A sob bubbled up in her throat as she backed away from the window. She would get her Daddy. He would help Jeremy.

"Jeremiah!" Dennis hollered.

Celia jumped when the front door flew open.

Jeremy grabbed her arms, pushing her down the steps. "Go! Run!"

"JEREMIAH!"

A chill ripped up Celia's spine, while inches away, blood oozed
from Jeremy's mouth.

Catching her gaping at it, he sucked his bottom lip inward to wash
the gore away.

He was ashamed, Celia realized. But they were connected now,
weren't they? She and him. A first kiss forever binding those bloody
lips with hers.

"If I have to go lookin' for ya, you little shit stain, you're gonna get it!"

Celia gripped Jeremy's fingers snugly against her palm and ran
with all the blind determination she could muster.

To her relief, Jeremy gave no resistance and was soon ahead of her, pulling her forward.

Together, they crossed the tree line into the dark, open orchard, an earsplitting slam echoing behind them.

"*JEREMIAH!*"

"Faster, Celia."

"I'm trying." Her legs and lungs burned from her effort. But as always, she was slower, less agile than Jeremy, who had the running grace of a cheetah.

Despite her shortcomings, Jeremy handled her with patience as they plowed through both properties at record speed, her hand tethered to his. They were going to reach her house and get her daddy. They were going to escape the inescapable because in this place, on this night, dashing in vain across the playground between her heaven and his hell, they were invincible.

Up ahead, the lights of her house came into view.

"Hurry, Celia. We can make it."

It was dark, though, and Celia tripped. Dry leaves crunched painfully against her elbows.

Jeremy hoisted her to her feet. Heavy footfalls echoed in the shadows behind them, growing louder. "We have to hide," he whispered.

Changing direction, they ran for a thin shelter of Monterey pines.

Celia struggled to keep up, the sweet exhilaration of racing for fun a distant dream, replaced now by fear and the murky boost of adrenaline. The leviathan was coming for them.

"Jeremy," she whimpered, desperate for his assurances. "I can't breathe. I'm scared." Pure dread had her sniveling, and she knew she was being too noisy. But the sound was impossible to contain. All her hopes fell on him. He was so brave, so clever and strong.

Pulling her close, Jeremy hushed her and leaned back against a tree, his head falling on the bark with a dull crunch. "When he gives up, I'll take you home."

Celia pressed into him, tucking every exposed part of herself inside the warm cocoon of his protection while she fought to control her breathing. And like that, they waited. It was impossible to know exactly how long, but when Jeremy began to whisper, Celia felt like she was being summoned from another deep slumber.

"When we grow up, I'll never hit you or our kids. I promise."

There was a crush of pine needles; then a thick, calloused thumb hooked deeply into Jeremy's left cheek while the other four fingers dug into his right, forcing his jaw into a wide part, his lips into a misshapen pucker.

If Celia had breath, she would've screamed.

"Boy," Dennis Hill slurred, reeking of liquor. "I told you to stay in the goddamn house."

As the words dribbled like sludge from his father's lips, Jeremy was winched off his feet by his cheeks.

Dennis turned to Celia, who felt as though she might never breathe again. "You get on home, girl. Your dad's looking for ya."

He released Jeremy and smacked the back of his head with such force that the boy stumbled forward, nearly falling. But Jeremy caught himself and, without faltering another step, set off for home.

It was then that Dennis Hill kicked his son so violently in the back that the boy flew forward through the air before crashing chin first into the ground.

Celia's mind retreated, inexplicably, to a memory of her parents in their study, comforting each other with tender, deferential kisses . . .

"Stop it!" she screamed out, launching into a sprint. She rammed her right heel into Dennis Hill's knee as he spun around to face her. With a bellow, he doubled over, and the rush of adrenaline gave Celia a deceptive sense of power. "Stop hitting him!" she screeched, slapping wildly at his head. "Stop it! Stop it! St—"

A large, adult hand clutched her throat. Celia clawed at this new, unexpected source of distress: thick, rough fingers that wouldn't budge. Seconds passed, and she was losing her rational mind as rapidly as she was losing the oxygen from her already-troubled lungs.

The leviathan was going to kill her.

"You don't do that," Dennis growled as he rose to loom over her. He tightened his hold on her windpipe and shook. "You hear me?"

Then she was free, gasping for air from her knees. One of her palms slammed to the ground as the other moved to shield her throat. There was a racket all around that concluded with a thud.

Then nothing.

Celia twisted around. There, against a pine several yards away, clutching at his flannel shirt, sat a wide-eyed Dennis Hill. The terror distorting his handsome features instilled in Celia the very same terror, and her feet pedaled at the ground, readying to run.

The only barrier between her and the threat was Jeremy, who stood with his buck knife clutched tightly in his fist.

Celia rasped out his name, but he never turned. Instead, he dropped to his knees, one after the other, watching as his father exhaled a slow, listless breath, then slumped face-first into the dirt.

2

Angie

1967

The year had begun like every year before it. A mild winter rolled out to sea like the dependable morning fog, and when April arrived, the spring sun emerged, tepid but bright. Existing in perpetual autumn, Pacific Grove, California was a town fit for Goldilocks—never too warm, never too cold, always exactly right. Yet, in one straightforward way, it was like any other place: filled with life's surprises. For there was no telling what each new season would bring.

"It's gonna rain," Angie said, gazing out the diner window. "I can smell it."

"It's not going to rain." Moose bit into his cheeseburger. "Stop being such a drip all the time."

"I'm a drip because it's going to rain?" Angie turned to watch her oldest friend. Grease trickled down his fingers onto his new, brown suede vest, darkening some of its fringe. The vest was ill-fitted, too tight and short, against his portly frame, but she didn't have the heart to tell him. He seemed to love the silly, beaded thing.

"No," Moose explained, "you're a drip because you see that as a bad thing."

"I have to walk home after work," she reminded him.

"No date with Roger tonight?" Moose took another bite of his dinner, then shoved several ketchup-coated french fries into his mouth.

"Nope." Angie kissed the crown of her friend's shaggy head, its scent a heady mix of pot and Prell shampoo. "Back to work I go."

Still occupied with his meal, Moose mumbled a distracted goodbye. The diner where Angie worked was two blocks from his bar in Monterey, the town neighboring Pacific Grove. On paper, the bar belonged to his father, but Moose, who was starting to insist people call him by his God-given name, Curtis, managed the daily operations now at the ripe age of twenty-one. The September prior, he'd enrolled at Peninsula Community College to study accounting so he could take over the family business someday—but more importantly, he enrolled to classify himself with the Selective Service as a 1-S, Student Deferment. Not doing so was too risky while the war in Vietnam continued to escalate.

That same classification protected their friend Fletcher, who was currently attending California State University in Fresno as a Pre-Law, majoring in theater of all things (though he swore his end goal was to become a civil rights attorney). Berkeley, his father's alma mater, had been his college of choice, and he'd been accepted easily, being valedictorian for Pacific Grove High's class of '64. But his beloved Celia had chosen CSU Fresno for its theater program, and everyone quietly agreed that she shouldn't go off to college alone, not with her asthma and depressive episodes.

Thus, Fletcher's decision had been made. Celia and Fletcher, thick as thieves, now lived in Fresno nine months of the year, returning home for only summer, spring, and Christmas breaks. It had been this way for nearly three years, and Angie found herself simultaneously missing them and hating their guts for leaving her behind.

To be fair, most of their graduating class had spread its wings and left Pacific Grove in the last few years since high school. There were surely more interesting places than the tiny beach town.

Fortunately for Angie, Moose had stuck around. Not that he'd had much choice.

Getting to his feet, Moose waved to Angie and dropped a bill on the table. "Swing by after work," he said with a wink. "I'll give you a lift home."

She winked back. Her nights at Moose's bar provided a little excitation from the status quo, which meant home with her mother and younger brothers when she wasn't "out" with Roger.

"Angie."

Angie sighed. There were a few other stragglers, classmates who had remained in town after graduation. One of them happened to be the daughter of Angie's boss.

"Earth to Angie!"

Closing her eyes to Betty Jean Finnegan's grating voice, Angie quietly cursed her life and craned her neck around to smile hatefully at the famed blond scourge of Pacific Grove. "What now, Betty?"

"There's a run in your stocking," Betty said.

"What do you want me to do about it? I'm in the middle of a shift."

"You don't have to get lippy. I was just tryin' to help. But I can see now that you're completely hopeless." Betty retied her apron. "So, you're goin' out after work?"

Taking a deep breath, Angie blinked. "What?"

"Moose told you to swing by. He meant his bar, right?"

Angie's eyes narrowed. "Yeah . . . ?"

"Well, can I come along?"

"No."

Betty snorted. "You don't have to get your panties in a twist, Angie. It's Friday night, and I . . ." Glancing around, she lowered her voice. "Look, I don't have a date, okay. I can't show my face at home right after work. My mother will know I lied. I told her I was going out with Max Moriarty. You know him? His father's as rich as they come, and my mother spent a fortune on a dress for tonight."

Angie knew Max all right. He was a pervert. "Interesting. I thought you always have dates, Betty." Oh, this was too good. Angie smirked as she set her dish bucket down. "Weren't you lecturing me—what was it, Monday?—on the importance of a girl's dating status? *Always have a date on date night, Angie, or you'll wind up a spinster.*"

"Oh, stick it where the sun don't shine, *Angela*. You're taking me with you."

"Am not," Angie said, incredulous. "Celia would have my head. She still hasn't forgiven you for making out with her prom date."

"Well, Celia's not here, is she? She's busy making new friends in college, having a marvelous time with her boy toy Fletcher, while you're here, serving greasy fish to stinky fishermen. With *moi*." Betty smirked. "Besides, you know I'll get my way in the end. Why fight it?"

Angie let out a groan. "Fine. You can come, but I still detest you," she said. "Let's make that crystal clear."

"As you should. Because if you don't take me, I'm telling my dad it was you who stole this five-spot from the register." Betty wore a devious grin while she waved a crisp five-dollar bill under Angie's nose.

Most likely, the blond was bluffing, but you could never be too careful around Betty. You could wind up with mud on your face.

At a quarter after nine, Angie Martin—with her entourage of one—strolled into Moose's bar, the Blue Pelican. The Friday-night crowd was subdued. Aside from Fishbait Fred (a town drunk who sat rambling incoherently while nursing his gin), the patrons consisted of the customary mingle of locals and tourists from the hotel across the street. Two familiar young men played pool in the back. One of them, a local fisherman named Tom, smiled shyly at Angie. He'd been a senior when she was a freshman, and she'd always had a teensy-weensy bit of a crush on him. Nowadays, though, she ignored his attention. The last thing she needed was to get knocked up by a local. She'd never get out of here.

Angie and Betty chose adjacent stools at the bar, where Moose stood pouring a Schlitz from the tap. He frowned when his eyes fell on Betty.

Angie savored his reaction: disbelief and disgust with a juicy tinge of fear.

Addressing Angie, Moose feigned a smile for professionalism's sake and leaned over the bar toward her: "What are you up to?"

Angie spread her arms wide. "Happy Friday!"

"Moose!" Betty yelled, seemingly over the jukebox music that was only moderately loud. "Can I get something fruity? Maybe a Shirley Temple or something with a little umbrella in it!"

"It's Curtis," he corrected her, grabbing an empty glass. "And you don't need to yell. I can hear you."

Betty nodded. "Gotcha!"

Angie leaned forward. "I'll take everything you've got, mixed in a dirty glass because I don't care to remember this night."

"Are these peanuts?" Betty asked skeptically, poking at the contents of a wooden bowl on the bar. "Blech! No one's touched these, have they?"

Moose watched Betty with incredulity, then turned to Angie. "What did I do? Are you punishing me for something? Is this because I said Elvis is a dead ringer for Lady Liberty?"

Angie popped a peanut into her mouth. "She blackmailed me."

"Again?"

"Is that milk he's drinking?" Betty pointed to the farthest corner of the bar, where a young man sat alone.

Angie had never seen him before.

"Yes," Moose answered, snatching the peanut bowl from Betty. "It's what he ordered."

"Is he some kind of fruitcake or something?"

"For ordering milk?" Angie asked.

"It's a bar," Betty said, her blue eyes thorny on the milk-drinking stranger.

Angie ignored her, asking Moose, "You sell milk here?"

"Of course," he said as he worked on their drink orders. "Milk's a groovy liquid, Ang. Lots of cocktails call for it. You should get out more."

Angie stuck out her tongue, then snickered at her own thoughts. "So, did he say, 'Milk. Straight up,' when he ordered?"

Moose faked a laugh. "No, dipstick. He just ordered a glass of cold milk. Said he doesn't drink liquor."

"Well, what's he doing in a bar then?" Betty sneered, her volume increasing. "Hello! This isn't Pacific Grove! You can drink alcohol here!"

Angie pushed her. "Betty, for Pete's sake, stop."

"Oh, go suck an egg, Angie. I'm standing up for Moose here."

"He's a paying customer," Moose told Betty through clenched teeth. "I couldn't care less what he orders. So long as he isn't botherin' anybody."

"Well, he's bothering me," Betty said.

"So, did you talk to your dad yet?" Angie asked Moose as he handed her a drink. She tossed it back, cringed at the burn, then chased the fire with a handful of peanuts. "He gonna give you the summer off?"

"Doubt it," he said, refilling her glass.

Still watching the stranger with the milk, Betty hopped off her barstool. "I'm going over there."

"Betty, damn it, leave the guy alone." Moose's eyes widened at Angie. "What were you thinking bringing her here?"

"I told you. She blackmailed me."

"Ahem." Betty tapped the young man on his shoulder, then gave his half-drunk glass of milk a poke. "What is this about?"

Surprised at the intrusion, the young fellow gave Betty a quick once-over. "What's it to you?"

"I'm asking because it's not normal to come into a bar and order milk." Narrowing her eyes, Betty studied the stranger. "There's something fishy about you."

"Because I like milk?"

"Everyone likes milk. That's not it."

"I don't like milk," Angie said, now seated two stools down from the stranger.

Moose, too, had moved closer.

"Fine," Betty said, returning her attention to the stranger. "The redheaded weirdo doesn't like milk. But this is a bar, and you're not following the rules."

The brown-haired young man looked to Moose for assistance. "Who is this chick?"

"Never seen her before," Moose replied. "I can call the cops. Just say the word."

Rolling her eyes, Betty pointed at the stranger. "The real question is: Who are you?"

"He asked you first," Angie reminded Betty.

"Fine!" Betty thrust out her hand for the stranger to shake, but he only stared at it. "I'm Betty Jean . . . Betty Jean Finnegan. My father owns the most successful diner in Pacific Grove. Just over the town line there."

The young man nodded, "Neat," and returned to his milk.

Betty's hands flew to her locally famous hips. "Well?"

"Well, what?"

"What's your answer?"

"What's your question?"

Angie's head volleyed back and forth as she watched a total stranger beat Betty at her own game. The night was turning out better than she'd hoped.

"I told you my name," Betty explained, as if to a child. "Now you have to tell me yours."

"I don't have to do a damn thing," the young man replied calmly. And it was then, as Betty and the stranger glowered at each other, that Angie felt a spark of recognition. She knew this guy from somewhere.

"You know what? I change my mind." Betty sat down beside the stranger with a huff and looked at Moose. "One milk, please. *Pronto.*"

Confused expressions bombarded her from every angle, but Betty remained resolute in her request.

"With a straw," she added, her expression haughty but refined as she folded her hands atop the smooth surface of the bar. "And lots of chocolate syrup."

Moose snorted. "One chocolate milk, coming up." He mixed her drink together in under a minute, adding a tiny paper umbrella and everything. "That'll be twenty-five cents," he said, setting the frosty glass down in front of Betty.

Angie wondered what Betty was up to. The stranger appeared equally suspicious—a suspicion that quickly turned to irritation when Betty motioned for him to pay.

Begrudgingly, and to Angie's horror, the guy sighed and then placed a shiny quarter on the bar to cover Betty's tab. Then he watched with bemusement—they all did—as she dunked her straw into her chocolate milk a few times, then began slurping it down. She even winked at the stranger as she drank.

Nobody said a word.

When Betty finished her beverage, she placed the glass down gently and smiled at the stranger, bringing a beguiled grin to his face.

Angie shook her head. The moron had actually been charmed by the cutesy little act.

Men.

"Now will you tell me your name?" Betty asked him, her voice full of sugar and silk.

"Jeremy," the young man said with an easy smile that softened his expression all the way up to his green eyes.

Angie's jaw fell.

That was it!

"Moose," she whispered hoarsely as Betty began to flirt with her newest victim. "Moose!"

"What?"

They whispered at the other end of the bar. It couldn't be. But it was. But it just couldn't be!

"Hey," Moose called out to the stranger. "Can you help me out with something? My goofy friend here thinks she knows you. What's your last name?"

The stranger took a deep breath before saying, "Hill."

Angie gasped. "I knew it!"

"Jeremy Hill," Moose recited. "We were friends in elementary school."

Jeremy nodded, though he seemed unhappy about being recognized.

At his side, Betty's jaw dropped. She pointed an accusing finger. "You shoved me in the dirt in first grade!"

"I also just paid for your chocolate milk."

Betty shoved the cloudy glass away and folded her arms.

Moose looked as dumbfounded as Angie felt. A million questions flooded her mind, but it was Moose who was brave enough to ask those questions first.

"So, Jeremy," he said, "wow, what happened to you, man? I mean, if you don't mind me asking."

"Yeah." Angie leaned forward. "Where've you been?"

"And why are you back?" Moose added. "Is it for good? Are you staying at your old place?"

Betty twisted sideways to face Jeremy. "Have you been in prison this whole time?"

That one surprised Jeremy. "Prison?"

"You know, for killin' your dad," Betty said.

Angie could see the gossip wheels churning behind those bright-blue eyes. His answers would be used against him later.

"Why'd you do it?" Betty went on. "Was it Celia's idea? I've never trusted that girl."

"Betty!" Angie scolded.

"What?"

"Some people said you were sent to a secret jail for kids," Moose explained to Jeremy. "Celia said it wasn't true, but with our government, you never know, you know? Everyone figured the Lynches were threatened into silence by the CIA or something."

Jeremy tilted his head. "Why would the CIA get involved?"

"It's what they do, man . . ."

Her thoughts jumping from one concern to another, Angie wondered if she should even tell Celia about this. How would she react?

Celia had made herself sick over this boy for years, to the point of long, unexplained absences from school, psychotherapy, and even hospitalization after a nearly successful suicide attempt that had the whole town's tongue wagging.

"Do you remember us?" Angie asked Jeremy, thinking perhaps she was getting ahead of herself. "I'm Angie, Celia's friend."

"I know. I recognized you right away. Moose, too." Jeremy turned in annoyance toward Betty. "Not you."

With racy flare, Betty squinted her eyes and flipped her bright blond hair from one shoulder to the other, an action that had him grinning again.

Angie rolled her eyes. "Celia's in Fresno with Fletcher," she said, interrupting the disturbing little flirt session between the two. "They're in college there. They were here about a month ago for spring break."

His attention still on Betty, Jeremy said nothing.

"I could telephone her," Angie continued. "If you want. Tell her you're here."

"No, thanks," Jeremy said, his eyes growing softer the longer they rested on the blond beside him.

"Wow," Betty cooed as she pinched Jeremy's chin and turned his head from side to side. "You don't look anything like you used to." A finger moved to twirl at her hair. "You're all grown up now, aren't you?"

Moose leaned toward Angie and said, "Am I stoned, or did he start acting weird when you mentioned Celia?"

Equal parts appalled and fascinated, Angie spoke discreetly through the side of her mouth. "Yes."

3

Jeremy

Caroline Mitchell stood before him, a nervous wreck. The whites of her eyes were a spider web of ruptured blood vessels, her nose cherry red. She'd been crying for months. And now her thin, over-worked fingers were brushing doughnut crumbs from his shirt.

Jeremy eyed her maternal activities. "Good thinking," he said. "I wouldn't want to fly to California with crumbs on my shirt. They might not let me in."

"Don't be smart." Caroline's puffy eyes tightened. "You know I don't want this. I don't need the money. I'd rather you spend these last few months here with me. This is your home."

"You'll need the money when I'm gone," Jeremy said. He was tired of arguing about this.

She looked much younger than her thirty-six years as her chest convulsed with the warning of fresh tears. Her impeccable brunette bob fell a little behind her ears as she peered up at him. "Promise you'll think about college while you're in California. You can still enroll, get a deferment."

"Caroline—"

"Mom."

"Mom," Jeremy corrected himself, squaring his shoulders against her. He had a good seven or eight inches on his mother but recognized her advantage. It was entirely psychological—all guilt. "I told you, I'm not cut out for college." He said it with the sharpest conviction possible for probably the hundredth time, even though he knew any attempt to persuade her was made in vain. "But I promise, the minute the house is done, I'll catch the next flight back, long before I need to report for boot camp. I don't want to be in Pacific Grove any longer than I have to be."

"Promise me you'll really think about college," she choked through a sudden gush of tears. "Boys are dying in Vietnam every day. And those who don't die—"

"I know. 'Lose a limb or worse,'" he recited. "Look, I'll worry about that landmine when I come to it."

Caroline lightly smacked his chest. "That's not funny, Jeremy." Nevertheless, she laughed along with him. "Do you have the billfold I gave you? With the deed and the will?"

"Yes, ma'am."

"And the little green phone ledger?"

"The little green phone ledger, too."

"And your father's—"

Jeremy cut her off. "I have everything."

Overhead, a voice, pleasant and docile, announced the boarding of United Flight 5984.

Grabbing his duffel bag, Jeremy hugged his mother again. Before she could say another word to try and change his mind, he walked away, tossing her a parting hand as he stepped onto the tarmac to board his red-eye flight.

———

When his plane landed in Monterey, California, nine taxing hours later, the midmorning sky was overcast into a dark gray panorama. In his washed-out memories, the California sky had always been a serene, cool shade of blue.

The light drizzle of rain quickly turned into a downpour as Jeremy trotted down the plane's portable stairs with the other passengers, then jogged toward the cover of a canopied walkway. He had to remind himself that his purpose here was not to mull over the color of the damn sky. It was to get in and out of this hellscape as quickly as possible with enough money to leave his mother.

Jeremy trudged through the airport, collected all his baggage, then flagged down a taxicab. Its driver, an older gentleman with a friendly face, stepped out and opened the back trunk while Jeremy chucked his suitcase across the backseat.

Before Jeremy could stop him, the driver tried to lift the steamer trunk by himself and immediately dropped it with a grunt.

"Whatcha got in here?" the man said, scratching his scalp with his hat. "A dead body?"

"Tools." Together, they heaved the trunk onto the cab's cargo rack, as it wasn't going to fit in the trunk. "Lots of tools."

Inside the car, the driver set his meter. "Where to, young fella?"

"Sunset Drive in Pacific Grove."

"You got it."

The driver took a route along the foggy Pacific coastline. The overcast sky shrouded the interior of the cab in drabness, and regrettably, compelled its driver to chitchat.

"It's too bad," the man said, peering upward. "Not the best day to visit California for the first time."

"What makes you think it's my first time?" Jeremy asked, a touch peeved. The driver's assumption had struck a nerve, though he wasn't sure why. Maybe it was jet lag.

The older man laughed. "You look too uncomfortable for this to be home."

"Tennessee is home. But I've been here before."

The driver's right hand doubled as a white flag. "My mistake. It's still a shame. Yesterday, there wasn't a cloud in the sky."

"Doesn't matter," Jeremy said, slouching in his seat, trying to relax. He crossed his arms over his chest and dropped his head back. "I'm not here for the weather."

"Well, hell's bells, you look too young to be here for business." The man's seasoned but jovial eyes sought Jeremy out in the rearview mirror. "Too serious for pleasure."

Jeremy didn't answer, nor did he try to hide his irritation.

The man cleared his throat. "So, what's the address then?"

"Oh, right." Jeremy rummaged through his duffle bag for the green phone book, then read off, "One nine seven five Sunset Drive."

"That beachfront?"

"More or less."

His driver grinned. "Well then, pleasure it is."

As they moved from Monterey into Pacific Grove, the skyline grew fringed with dark-green Monterey pine and eucalyptus trees. The wall of fog crept closer to the rocky shoreline. Streets narrowed, so much that by the time they reached the city line of Pacific Grove, there was barely enough room to drive without hitting the tourists who strolled the tiny downtown shopping area.

Jeremy felt claustrophobic as the cab snaked deeper into the heart of town. Rolling his window down, his senses were instantly assaulted by the heavy stench of seawater and fish, the sound of seabirds cawing at each other, and the cold, wet mist of the air. The houses appeared older and smaller than he remembered and were bunched more tightly together. Jeremy wondered what he was getting himself into, coming back to his father's house, to this place he hated.

Five minutes later, the cab pulled onto the dirt driveway at 1975 Sunset Drive.

Both men cringed.

"You're sure this is it?" the driver asked, scrunching his nose.

"Positive."

The deterioration was worse than Jeremy had imagined, the house smaller than he remembered. It was an ancient pile of dog shit covered in rotting, moss-slathered wood siding and bricks that were chipped to near powder. The roof would need replacing, and the siding, too.

Jeremy glared at the house, and the house seemed to glare right back. A dreadful sensation crowded him as familiar shapes began to detach from the structure itself—a corner window, a stretch of porch railing—like a belt being cinched tightly around his chest. He sucked in a deep breath, trying to shake the shitty feeling off.

"What a dump," the cab driver muttered, then caught himself. "Oh, no offense, son. Someone you know live here?"

Jeremy didn't reply. His mind was already imagining, sketching, calculating. Without specialized training, he questioned his ability to accomplish this undertaking, and he hadn't even seen what rot waited inside. Back home, he'd handled all the major home repairs for his mother and now-deceased grandfather. And he was handy. To the point of arrogance. But glowering over this heap that his father (whom he refused to think about) had willed to him, Jeremy realized he might be in over his head.

He had only four months to secure a home improvement loan, get the proper permits, renovate the dump—mostly by himself in order to maximize profit—then list it for sale. From there, his mother would take over. Once he was sworn into the United States Army, her executorship over his affairs would activate, and she would receive the proceeds from the sale. Then he could die in the war guilt-free, knowing his mother would be all right.

Four months.

"Hey, kid," the cab driver said. "You gettin' out?"

"Not yet." Jeremy slapped several bills down on the man's shoulder. "I need to get to First National Savings and Loan. I think it's a few blocks from here."

"I know it."

After dropping Jeremy's luggage onto the rotting front porch of the house, they set off for the bank.

Jeremy sat forward as the cab picked up speed. Beyond the tangled weeds and unkempt brush of his father's yard stood a neat row of buck-eyes, and beyond that, a small grove of thriving fruit trees. It was like driving into another world, so dramatic was the visual improvement. Past a stretch of manicured lawn, a driveway appeared between two low thickets of well-maintained vegetation. It was much longer than his father's short driveway. The yellow Victorian sat farther back.

And there it was.

He wondered if the Lynch family still lived there. It stung to think that life had gone on so effortlessly without him, as if his presence hadn't mattered at all. And now it seemed like fiction, the life he remembered. Something was off, too. There was too much light filtering onto the Lynch property. Gone was the lean wood of pines and eucalyptus, where, if he was remembering correctly, his father's face had collided with a patch of pebbled dirt. Someone had removed it all, perhaps hoping to remove the memories along with it.

Jeremy wondered about the girl whose face he could no longer recall. What he could recall was that he had been abysmally in love with the little monster.

His most fervent wish for the summer of 1967 was to get in and out of this place without running into her.

The cab curved around a bend, where the state beach met with winding road. Even on this cloudy day, cars lined its edges. People milled about with surfboards and other beach gear. Then, as if to contradict him, the sun revealed itself, its hazy light stealing through a break in the cloud cover, making the deep-blue water glisten as it crashed against the massive rocks.

As the taxi moved through town, memories crystallized, and Jeremy realized that not much had changed. The pharmacy with the bulbous blue lettering across the window, the park with the half-moon playground, the gas station where his father had picked a fistfight with a teenaged greaser . . . they were all here, just a little busier and worn.

"We have arrived," the driver announced as he pulled into a parking lot. "First National. Shall I wait?"

"Yeah, why don't you wait around back? And keep the car running."

With a stunned blink, the older man parted his lips, then blinked twice more.

"I'm kidding, man, relax." Jeremy chuckled. "You can go. I'll probably be a while."

"Oh," the driver laughed. "All righty then. Well, good luck to you, young man."

Jeremy handed the man his fare and stepped out, reevaluating his jest. Maybe he should hold up the bank, maybe make a run for the border. It was a decent alternative to what lay ahead.

Instead of committing bank robbery, Jeremy spent an hour pouring over the paperwork that told his life's story—his birth certificate, his father's rock-solid will, his father's death certificate, his deed to the house, an updated market report that his mother had ordered through the mail, his Tennessee driver's license, as well as construction plans with structural blueprints, schematics, and drawings—seeking to convince the loan officer inside to take a chance on a walking dead man with no cash and no collateral, other than a run-down, cottage-style Victorian across the street from the Pacific Ocean.

The land alone was worth a pretty penny, the loan officer informed him while trying to convince him to sell the property to the bank "as is." But Jeremy insisted he could maximize its value with his tools and a little hard work. All he needed was money for supplies.

With a lien securing the bank's interest, Jeremy's home improvement loan was approved. He walked out of First National Savings and Loan with $7,400 in his new passbook savings account, a free set of stainless-steel flatware, and a thin stack of cash, which, added to his previous billfold (what remained after plane fare and breakfast), made $172.

After treating himself to a basket of fried clam strips from a stand he didn't recognize, Jeremy decided to walk back to the house on Sunset Drive. He was in no hurry to return, and Monterey's rain had never reached Pacific Grove. The afternoon sun now shined, revealing more of the gleaming blue sea he remembered from his childhood. For the first time in months, contentment wormed its way inside his chest. Step one of his plan—upon which all other steps were contingent—had been accomplished, and he'd been in California less than a day.

He wasn't about to rely on that scrap of good luck, though, or trust it. Bad luck was bound to find him eventually. And even if everything went right, he was still likely to be maimed or die violently sometime in the next two years.

That thought never failed to shit on his good mood.

When Jeremy reached Sunset Drive, a location that housed the most prevalent of all his demons, he took a hesitant step into his father's—legally, his own—yard. And though the sun had set long ago on his past, that past seemed to beat evocatively back to life with every new step forward. Jeremy tried like hell not to think about any of it. It was just an old, ramshackle house. A meaningless, soulless object.

"Screw you, old man," he muttered, letting his eyes trail over the property, listening carefully to the silence that answered, then chuckled at himself for being such a pantywaist. Ghosts didn't exist. Pasts didn't return to haunt. He was all alone.

Jeremy walked up the porch steps, praying that the key, mailed by a lawyer a decade prior, still worked. He shoved it in the keyhole, and the knob turned, but when he pushed, the door refused to budge from its frame. It took all of Jeremy's weight to force it open, thrusting him into a cloud of dust and debris.

Pulling the neck of his shirt over his mouth and nose, he walked farther inside the foyer, waving the dust and cobwebs away.

First, the house was going to need extensive cleaning. It reeked of a decade's worth of grime and mildew. It would be an unhindered task, though, since the place was mostly empty of furnishings. The small room to his right, dark from the boarded-up windows, contained only dust, while the larger room to his left appeared to contain a couch (covered with a dusty sheet), two small tables, and a seashell lamp.

His father's cousin, Ray, had cleared the house back in the winter of 1957—to help Jeremy and his mother, he maintained. They hadn't received anything other than a stack of crinkled photos and a yellowing wedding gown, a dress Caroline had never worn. The teenaged mother had been beaten unconscious and dumped onto the lawn, without her toddler son, by a drunk Dennis Hill, before any weddings could take place.

Jeremy dragged his steamer trunk into the house and opened it.

First things first, he dug out his maternal grandfather's tattered Stetson—for good luck—then placed it on his head, ready to get to work. With his claw hammer, he proceeded to pry every wood slat from every window on the first floor. His skin and clothing were covered in muck by the time he was done.

When the dust settled—and when he finished forcing its particles from his lungs and casting every window open to welcome in the cool, salty air—Jeremy was left standing in the middle of the kitchen with an uneasy feeling.

The refrigerator was in its place. The stove and oven, too. Two intact bowls, two rusty spoons, and a pair of drinking glasses rested inside the stained ceramic sink, still waiting to be washed. The stiff, mangy remnant of a dish towel hung faithfully from the rack on which it had been hung back in the fall of 1956. All these insignificant items Jeremy was suddenly remembering with an unnerving level of clarity. The wall of indifference he had maintained for years threatened to crumble. He could hear Dennis calling for him, hollering his name from the other room. He could remember the fear, could feel it pinch and prod at him, and yet he felt able to laugh about it at the same time. The noise existed only in his head now. His father had been silenced long ago.

Jeremy poked at a ceramic bowl in the sink, verifying its existence, then headed up the stairs to disentomb the second floor. His heavy tread on the old wood slats incited so much dust that he had to remove his shirt and tie it around the bottom half of his face in order to breathe.

Coughing and blinking the dust from his eyes, he located his childhood bedroom at the far end of the hall. It was completely empty. A memory urged him toward the far corner of the room, where he used his claw hammer to lever free a window board for light and then a strip of floorboard that came up far too easily.

After fishing around inside the floor for a beat, he found it.

"Ha!" Jeremy grinned as he liberated the Roy Rogers watch he'd hidden thirteen years before. Stolen from a local department store in a moment of despair, this watch had once been his most cherished possession. No way would his father have purchased it for him. And though he'd never worn it, for fear of it being taken away, the comfort and thrill of knowing it lay below his feet had always been worth the crime. Unfortunately, the police had hauled him away before he could retrieve it.

Now Roy Rogers and his horse, Trigger, were barely visible beneath the layers of grime. Jeremy rubbed his thumb across the glass, removing some of the filth, then gave the watch a quick wind. He touched it to his ear, thrilled to hear it ticking.

It was too small to wear now, so he stuffed it inside his pants pocket and gave it a pat.

Looking around, Jeremy tried to remember his last night in this room. He was sure it hadn't been pleasant or warm. Nothing about this house ever was.

He walked over to the window and yawned, finally feeling his jet lag and lack of sleep. From this vantage point, the Pacific was visible between the buckeye trees in wide, gleaming pools, as was the large, yellow Victorian he'd spent his childhood longing after.

He let his eyes drift down below the windowsill at his waist and acknowledge the wall there, the hand-carved manifesto of his pathetic upbringing, complete with pocketknife etchings of Superman, the Lone Ranger and his horse, Silver, and the blond devil who lived in that yellow Victorian.

Unnerved by the images, Jeremy turned away, determined to ignore these embarrassing reminders. They weren't why he was here.

Jeremy spent the first few days sweeping, scraping smoke-stained wallpaper from plaster, dragging up polluted, threadbare carpeting, and patching fist-sized holes in walls, among other necessary fixes. He only left the house to walk to the hardware store or catch a ride to the lumberyard, the dump, or the place with the clam strips. He spent several afternoons at the library reading up on structure maintenance and repair and specialized drafting techniques.

He was grateful nobody recognized him those first two weeks, and even more grateful that the house had given him few surprises. He'd nearly sunk to his knees with gratitude upon professional confirmation that there was no evidence of a termite infestation. With cautious planning and budgeting, and with no company other than his transistor radio, everything was proceeding as planned.

Until the night he stepped into the Blue Pelican for a glass of cold milk.

4

Fletcher

It was called *Lysistrata*. Fletcher had auditioned twice, and though he had given the director his soul in the first audition, it was his second, more blasé attempt that secured him the minor role of Cinesias, the unfortunate, sex-starved husband of Myrrhine, a woman who pledged, with all the women of Greece and Sparta, to withhold sex from their husbands in hopes of ending the Peloponnesian War.

"Take off your glasses," Celia had whispered moments before Fletcher stumbled—was shoved!—out into the spotlight at that second audition. The rest was history. It was a distinguished role, despite the character being erect (a stuffed sock would be positioned inside his tight-fitting costume pants once previews began) and soliciting sex throughout his entire scene.

"Ah, how the dear girl loves me!" He delivered the line boldly, from his gut, as trained in his drama class.

Myrrhine, played by Celia, widened her eyes as she placed a cot before him. "Come, get to bed quick; I am going to undress," she recited, flitting across the stage with dramatic flair, exactly as assigned in blocking rehearsals. She spun around to face him, her strawberry-blond hair glittering like gold under the severe lighting. "But, oh dear, we must get a mattress."

Fletcher's eyes darted to his script. "A mattress? Oh! No, never mind about that!" He crossed the stage as she did.

"No, by Artemis! Lie on the bare sacking? Never! That would be squalid."

"Kiss me!" he pleaded.

"Wait a minute!"

"Good God, hurry up!"

Celia blinked vacantly at him, his sweet, darling Myrrhine. Damn it.

"Here is a mattress," Fletcher prompted in a whisper.

"Oh!" Celia's eyes finally registered. "Here is a—"

"That's enough!" their theater professor called out. "This is a good place to stop. We'll pick up this scene tomorrow. Good work, everyone."

The students of the theater department at CSU Fresno began to disperse in every direction, murmuring among themselves.

"Shoot," Celia spat, gathering her things into her bag. "I completely spaced."

Fletcher grabbed his book bag and hers. "Don't feel too bad. I'm still using my script."

It took them fifteen minutes to cross the dark campus and reach Celia's off-campus housing. The brownstone bustled with girls heading out for the evening. Not a single one questioned Fletcher's presence as he walked alongside Celia. It was routine—even if it was officially against the rules—to sneak boyfriends up to the resident floors. Everyone assumed Celia and Fletcher were dating. And why not? He was a boy and she was a girl, and almost every night, Fletcher slipped into her room with her, not to be seen again until morning.

Celia's roommate, Gwen, a fantastically inhospitable troll of a girl, eventually accepted the arrangement. Back at the beginning of the year, when Gwen's boyfriend got an apartment of his own, her things started slowly disappearing from her side of the room. After a week of watching her bed linens go untouched, Fletcher began to commandeer her bed at night, and that was how the rumors got started. Neither he nor Celia bothered to refute them because they made life a lot easier. And it wasn't a complete falsehood. Fletcher *was* terribly in love with Celia. It just wasn't the kind of love pervading those sordid rumors, like the sexual sort or even the romantic sort that had every female coed cooing whenever they pressed Celia about him. It was another sort entirely, the less intriguing sort (or more intriguing, depending on the outlook). Fletcher adored Celia and relied on her for the most basic of things: company, affection, support. She was his sweetheart in almost every sense of the word, his best friend, his shield.

Without her, college would have been a far more dreadful place for Fletcher. He hated his housing and loathed his housemates and the expectations they entertained about university life. They were constantly getting sick-stinking drunk, seducing foolish girls, or playing aggressive, violent pranks. He couldn't relate at all. But burying his nose in textbooks, like some students, did not fully interest Fletcher either. He yearned to interact. He'd made a few friends in his government course, but they were acquaintances mostly, study buddies. It was in his first drama course that he'd found a few kindred souls, and of course, Celia had been there with him. It had been her idea, back in their junior year of high school, to sign up for drama class, and then audition for *Arsenic and Old Lace*.

Where Celia had dredged up the courage to audition in the first place, Fletcher couldn't say, but she'd positively glowed on stage. With nothing but a spotlight in darkness, she was her former self again, before life had beaten the shine out of her.

Acting had been an outlet for Fletcher, too—a means to breathe, rage, and release. It was freeing. And he liked being around the others. He liked the camaraderie and enthusiasm that seemed unique to the cast and production crew of a theater group. Most of all, he liked the excitement of performance nights, especially opening night. The air felt electric. There was nothing like it.

When they reached Celia's room on the third floor, Celia shoved her key in the lock. "Did you see Chrissie O'Connell tonight?" she asked Fletcher as she popped open the door to her room. "Not a brassiere in sight. And under the stage lights . . ."

Before they could step inside, they heard the hysterical sobbing of her roommate, Gwen. Quietly, Celia re-shut the door and shot a questioning glance at Fletcher.

"Common room?" he suggested, and she nodded.

"I hate when they fight," Celia complained during their trot down the stairwell. "First Gwen cries, then she yells."

"Then she throws," Fletcher muttered, rubbing the faint scar where his head had once interfered with the trajectory of a flying stapler.

Downstairs, about a dozen young women, all residents of the dormitory, lounged in the common room—studying for midterms, watching television, rolling their hair into curlers. Fletcher kept quiet so as not to rouse too much of their attention. When the group of them got bored, they liked to give him the third degree about his relationship with Celia. Most were genuinely curious, some sought something juicy to gossip about, while one in particular—going by her fluttering eyelashes and beckoning smile—seemed keen to steal him away.

The first to notice him and Celia, a girl seated cross-legged on the floor, surrounded by linguistics textbooks, looked up and pulled the pencil from between her teeth. "Gwen and her boyfriend fighting again?"

"Yep," Celia sighed, taking Fletcher by the hand to direct him around the heap of textbooks and toward the couch, where several girls sat glued to the black and white television set.

As Fletcher plopped down with Celia on one of the sofas, he caught the tail end of a story about a man being beaten with bricks by his own father.

"What on earth are you watching?" Celia asked one of the girls, then grabbed a fistful of popcorn from a bowl on the coffee table.

"A special news report on homosexuals," a fellow junior named Lydia said as she tossed a kernel of Jiffy Pop into her mouth. "It started a few minutes ago."

Fletcher and Celia exchanged a loaded glance.

Fletcher settled into his sofa cushion, engrossed immediately as the man on the television, his face obscured in darkness, began to detail his problematic life as a homosexual, which he blamed on an overbearing mother and issues with weight. Was that indeed what caused homosexuality? His own mother was a doormat, and he'd been rail thin his entire life.

Again, he glanced over at Celia, but she was transfixed with the news report.

"In fact, recent surveys have shown that a majority of Americans feel repulsed by or fearful of homosexuality and homosexuals," the moderator reported to his audience. "Because of these disapproving attitudes, homosexuals have developed secret enclaves, often in bars or clubs in big cities like New York and San Francisco, where they can gather and indulge in their widely despised pursuits."

"What is this world coming to?" Lydia asked no one in particular, her expression sour. "Men with other men."

"It's disgusting," a psychology student named Mary remarked.

"Vile," a nearby brunette added.

All three turned to Celia, seeking her input.

"Yeah," Celia said on cue. "Gross."

Fletcher felt Celia's hand slip into his and squeeze. He squeezed back, knowing she hadn't meant what she'd said. And the experimental acts she performed on him proved she wasn't disgusted by him. Nor he by her. In fact, those calculated experiments had been quite successful. His body had responded as any man's would when taken into a warm mouth for a long, vigorous sucking or into a baby-oiled fist to be stroked and milked. What separated him, Fletcher suspected, from the straights were the masculine images that flashed behind his closed eyelids as she did it—Mitch, the school's track star, or Rowland, the gorgeous sophomore cast as the magistrate in *Lysistrata*.

The experimentation had been at Celia's insistence, so his guilt, while genuine, was minimal.

"You're probably not gay," she'd said after an exhaustive discussion, one of many they'd had in the years since he confessed his secret to her, since the night of the spring dance that would change them both forever. "I'll bet it's just a phase, and I'll prove it."

She'd been somewhat correct in that he was probably not *all* gay, if there was such a thing. He'd opened his eyes once, to watch her fellate him, and the view had galvanized him so much that he grabbed her head, thrusted several times into her mouth, and came. But he knew for certain he wasn't "straight." He'd been fantasizing about boys for as long as he could remember. And yet, as Celia had proven, he could have sexual relations—fruitfully—with a woman, which meant he could perhaps live an ordinary life.

With Celia.

With only Celia.

On the television a psychiatric expert was now being interviewed on the psychology of homosexuals, and the question came up of whether it was possible for a homosexual to be happy. Having asked that very question a million times himself, Fletcher sat forward, setting his elbows on his knees.

Celia began to rub his back.

"No," the psychologist replied. "As homosexuality is a psychiatric disorder, it's a complete impossibility."

Fletcher sulked back in his seat, and Celia hugged his arm. He'd finally gotten his answer. By a psychologist, no less, an expert on the human condition. How could he argue with that?

"I can't believe they're airing this," Mary said. "Children could be watching."

Beside her, Lydia nodded. "We should contact someone and complain. Write a strongly worded letter demanding they stop airing this type of filth. I mean, really."

"You know what? That's exactly what we're going to do," Mary announced. "We'll create a petition and get the entire school to sign. Then we'll organize a walkout and notify the papers."

The TV program droned on without the full attention of the girls—protest committees were being formed and duties assigned—but Fletcher remained rapt. He listened carefully as a federal judge provided figures and data and sober warnings to the show's audience. "The United States has held a long tradition of imposing legal punishment for homosexual acts, including use of the death penalty. Currently, most states have sodomy laws that criminalize any sexual behavior between two males. In some places, it's possible for a homosexual to incur a sixty-year prison sentence . . ."

"Sixty years for being gay?" Celia asked. "That's a life sentence."

"Should be more," Lydia said. "They should be taken off the streets and kept away from the rest of society forever."

As Fletcher felt his heart rate increase to a steady, echoing thud and his stomach churn with a nauseating mix of shame and fear, the television hummed along, casually reporting about homosexual witch hunts, mental institutions, and lobotomies. Sweat began to bead along his brow. His eyeglasses slid down his nose.

Pushing them back up, he glanced once again at Celia.

Recognizing his distress, she leaned closer. "Do you want to go?"

Fletcher thought about it. Did he? Sitting there, his heart felt as though it might burst from his chest, but he had to know. Was there a cure? A solution? A way out? He shook his head in answer, and Celia squeezed his hand for a second time.

On the TV, another man was now being interviewed, his faced obscured. "I'm a lawyer and am involved with our city council. I have a wife and children. And I'm a homosexual."

The girls of the common room collectively gasped, exchanging wide-eyed glances.

The man continued, "I love my wife, and I think it's impossible to ever find that same emotional connection with another man."

"That poor woman," one of the girls said. "Married to a fiend. How awful. They have children."

"Why would she put up with such a thing?"

"Well, what can she do?"

At its conclusion, the news report affirmed its prognosis for homo-sexuals, predicting a grim, difficult future, full of scorn and exile, without any possibility of love or even contentment. If it hadn't been clear to him before, Fletcher knew now with absolute certainty that he was destined to be alone forever if he didn't secure his future right now, before it was too late.

As the credits began to roll, he pushed himself off the couch, taking Celia with him. "Let's get out of here," he murmured, using every acting skill in his arsenal to sound casual and unaffected. "Good night, ladies."

"Good night, Fletcher," the women sang in unison, gawking and giggling as he walked off with Celia in tow.

"Where are we going?" Celia asked him.

"I heard someone talking about an anti-war speaker off campus. At Teddy's." It was a small hole-in-the-wall in the north end of Fresno. "I thought it sounded interesting. Is that all right?"

Celia gave him a false smile. "Sure," she said.

His instinct was to defer to her discomfort, but he couldn't tonight. He needed a distraction, or he might break down and scream.

As they walked briskly toward his car, Fletcher pulled the cool night air into his lungs and then turned to Celia. "Wait," he said, set-ting his palms on her reddening cheeks. Without another word, he kissed her, pushing his tongue deep into her mouth.

It was in moments such as these, when his best friend softened in his arms and kissed him in earnest, that he felt like a fraud, like an actor cast in his own life.

And in his fear and selfishness, he had made her a fraud, too.

Pulling away, Fletcher looked at her. Without a doubt, she was lovely. How effortless life would be if they were physically attracted to each other. Or he to her, as he sometimes thought her attraction to him might be genuine. It was hard to distinguish anymore what was reality and what was wishful thinking. Celia, too, was a talented actor.

"It's going to be all right," she told him, reading his thoughts.

"I promise. We'll fix this." She shook her head. "We shouldn't have watched that. It only upset you."

"No, I needed to see it." If he allowed his desires to guide him, he could be incarcerated for life, shunned, beaten, institutionalized, disowned by his family—and for what? Romantic thoughts? Sexual cravings that he had not yet acted on? Celia was right. The two of them were both intelligent people and devoted friends. Together, they would overcome this complication.

Grateful for her devotion, Fletcher gave Celia's lips an affectionate peck, then leaned his forehead against hers. "Cee?"

"Hm?"

"If I asked you to marry me, what would you say?"

"I've already told you. I'd say yes. You know I would."

Squeezing her tight, Fletcher smiled and said, "Imagine it. Big Sur, overlooking the water. All those wildflowers. You'd make a beautiful bride, even prettier than Priscilla."

"Would that make you Elvis?"

"Uh-huh," he answered in his best Elvis impression, making Celia giggle.

Her laughter settled into a loving smile. "You feel better?"

"I think so."

Without another word on the matter, they drove to Teddy's bar, and even after such a grim start to the night, Fletcher began to feel inspired. A disheveled, fanatical man screamed of rebellion through peaceful defiance and an end to the war in Vietnam. Johnson could not ignore the piling bodies for another term.

Fletcher and Celia had tucked themselves inside a dark corner. Intently, he listened as the candle flame on his table appeared to lick dotingly at the boots of the orator, while beside him Celia daydreamed and carved her name, beneath a dozen others, into the tabletop with her metal nail file. But his own focus only lasted so long. Marijuana smoke had rolled through the small nightclub like the morning fog in Pacific Grove, and Fletcher wasn't sure if he was stoned or tired. He'd never been stoned before. He certainly felt . . . delayed and more introspective than usual. All mind and no body. He'd get lost in his own thoughts, not meaning to, and then "wake up" after what seemed like an hour-long cognizant doze. Still, he was glad they'd come. He and Celia too often sheltered themselves inside a self-created bubble, where both were perfectly content to watch the world turn without them.

Back in their freshman year of college, Celia had tried wandering from the bubble to attempt dating. But time and again, the young men could not accept her close friendship with the "four-eyed pretty boy"—what one of her callers had so eloquently christened Fletcher. One by one, they demanded she choose between Fletcher or them and always managed shock at the outcome. They never comprehended how amenable she was to being lured away from her four-eyed pretty boy. All it would've taken was a little unbridled passion, what she craved most and lacked with him. But all they ever seemed to give her was grief. The jealous fools.

By the beginning of June, both the play and finals were over. School was out for the summer of 1967.

Suitcases in hand, Celia squealed as she darted for Fletcher's car. "Hurry up, slowpoke!" Her head was shaded with a paisley scarf. Large, white, square-framed sunglasses hid her eyes but not her red-painted smile. "Let's speed all the way home!"

Adhering to her wishes, Fletcher gunned it all the way back to Pacific Grove, three hours west, throwing the top down to let in the heat of the sun and salty ocean wind as home drew nearer. He was grateful to be going home, where Angie and Moose were, where Celia's home was (though her mom was visiting family in Denmark for the summer). His own family, consisting of just his two biological parents, had moved three years prior, as he was entering college. They'd sold the Fletcher family home in Pacific Grove and purchased an outlandish spread up in Sacramento. His father had conquered for himself the title of partner in a revered law firm adjacent to the California State

Capitol, earning the income that allowed his mother to retire early and become the proper snob she'd always dreamed of being. But if anyone asked, Fletcher regretfully informed them that his parents had been arrested in India while protesting British colonialism and were shot blindfolded for their insolence. But they died together, challenging the establishment, so no condolences required.

Nobody need know that his parents were run-of-the-mill, wealthy elitists who thought of only themselves. How original. How dismal! To be the fortunate son. To be such a cliché. Let people think of him as the sole creation of witless rebels. Let them think he was on the level and dating the mysterious ingenue with the beguiling, brown eyes. Better than what he truly was: a disappointment to his parents, a disgrace with a dirty little secret that only the ingenue held.

And with the ingenue, it would stay.

"Angie!" Celia hopped out the moment the car's wheels came to a stop in front of Celia's home.

Pleased that Angie had come to welcome them, Fletcher smiled and grabbed their luggage, but before he could make it to the front porch, Angie's legs were wrapped around his waist, her arms like a boa constrictor around his neck.

"Oh, thank God!" the redhead shouted to the sky, her arm reaching out to Celia. "I missed you jerks!"

Fletcher took the kiss she offered and laughed. "Nice to see you, too."

"Oh, look at you!" Angie smiled like a doting mother, cupping his cheeks when he set her down. "You get more good looking every time I see you. There's a new girl at work I want you to meet. I've told her all about you!"

"Well, let me get inside the house first before you marry me off." Fletcher shot Celia a wary glance, and she laughed.

"So, so, so . . . talk to me!" Poor Angie, she was so lonely with only

Betty and Moose to keep her company nine months of the year. She bounced on Celia's bed, watching as Celia unpacked. "What happened with your roommate? Gwen, is it? Did you pass your philosophy test? How was the play? Spill everything. It's so boring here!"

"They're back together," Celia said regarding Gwen as she flung out a wrinkled dress and grabbed a hanger from her closet. "Ugh, I have so much ironing to do."

"I aced my philosophy final." Fletcher fell back beside Angie, ready for a nap. He yawned. "So, what's going on tonight?"

"We are going to a bonfire at Lovers Point," Angie replied with an odd grin. Lovers Point was a tiny stretch of state beach, shaped like a cove, with the addition of a park and Olympic-sized pool. At night, however, the young claimed it to drink and make out.

Fletcher groaned. "Oh, Angie, my maven cynic, have you gone conventional on us? The Point? Really?"

Angie's expression sobered. "Well," she said, a frown snapping her brows together. "There will be someone at the Point tonight that I . . . okay, I might have kept a bit of news from you both in my last letter."

"You're not dating someone new, are you?" Celia asked, half-occupied by her clothes. "What about Roger?"

Fletcher gasped. "No, I bet she's PG. The bunny died. You slut!"

"I'm not pregnant!" Angie stood up as Fletcher laughed and turned her attention to Celia, her palms poised defensively. "And I'm still with Roger. Now keep in mind that I only did what I thought was best for you."

By now she had Celia's full attention, but Fletcher lay with his arms folded behind his head, unimpressed. If Angie wasn't knocked up, then the issue was a bust. Nothing could be this important.

"If Celia had known," Angie continued carefully, glancing sidelong at Fletcher, "she might have come back early and missed her finals and that great, great play, which she was probably so . . . great in. And I . . . I thought to myself, you know, that it was probably best if . . . well, if . . . you know . . ."

Fletcher crept upright, his eyes narrowing. Angie—voted in high school as Most Likely to Take a Vow of Silence—was rambling now. Not good.

In clear agreement, Celia shot him a dubious squint.

"And I figured school is more important, right, because I know that if Celia had known, she would have dropped everything, and that would have been—"

"Oh, for the love of Fabian," Celia snapped. "Out with it!"

"Jeremy's back." Angie winced.

Celia froze, blinked, then after what seemed like ages, said, "I'm sorry, what?"

"Jeremy."

"Jeremy?"

"Yeah. Jeremy."

Taking two steps forward, Celia tossed the dress she was holding onto a nearby chair. "As in *my* Jeremy? Jeremy Hill."

Angie nodded.

Celia's mouth popped open. "Angela Lorraine Martin, this had better not be some kind of practical joke. Because it's not funny."

"It's not a practical joke. He's been back for over a month." Angie pointed toward the window. "He's fixing up his father's house, so he can sell it. He's right over there."

Riveted, Fletcher's eyes bounced between the two girls.

"No."

"Yes."

Celia brought her palm to her mouth, a smile shining through moist eyes. "If you're pulling my leg right now, I will tell everybody about you and Donald Weiner."

Fletcher flinched at Angie. "What happened with you and Donald Weiner?"

"You quiet your mouth," Angie snapped at Celia, clearly feeling herself again, the previous apprehension gone. "I'm not pulling anybody's leg. Jeremy is back."

A laugh burst through Celia's fingers. "You swear it?"

"Swear it on George and Paul."

"Oh!" Celia threw herself at her friend, hugging her fiercely. "Tell me everything!" she screeched, visibly shaken. "What's he like? Where's he been? How does he look? Did he ask about me? Oh, tell me every little thing!" Celia sat down, then stood up again to pace. "Oh, my gosh. I feel like I'm having a panic attack, but a good one! So, tell me, tell me, what's he like?"

Angie smiled. "He's still a little rough around the edges, but he's grown up, like the rest of us."

Again, Celia spilled over with anxious giggles, a tear streaking down her cheek as she hugged Angie again. "Did he . . . ?" Backing away, she steered Angie to sit down. Celia knelt before her, bouncing on her calves. "Did he ask about me? Did you tell him where I was? What'd he say?"

Angie tucked a piece of Celia's hair behind her ear. "I haven't really talked with him about you, but I did tell him that you were away at school." Angie's nervous glances toward Fletcher had him concerned, especially as he watched Angie give Celia fishy answers and even fishier smiles. "He remembers you."

Celia returned a bright smile. Wiping the moisture from her face, she nodded and stood, picking her dress up off the chair. "I need to get ready. I can't believe this is happening!" She disappeared into the closet. "And he'll be at the Point tonight? I have nothing to wear."

Fletcher turned his full attention to Angie, giving her a skeptical but meaningful look. There was more she wasn't telling Celia. "Does he really remember her?" he whispered.

"Oh, yeah," Angie said. "He remembers. He just . . . I don't see him much, but I'm getting the impression he doesn't want anything to do with her."

Fletcher deflated. If Jeremy Hill ruined Celia's progress . . . He quickly dismissed that thought. Angie was almost certainly misreading things. It was in her nature to see the negative, more cynical side of things. She was a glass-half-empty sort of girl. Still, Fletcher trusted her judgment when it came to Celia. So, he would temporarily contain his own excitement about this apparent return of Jeremy Hill, who was practically legend now, his story all but a parable, as if he'd never existed except as some terrible lesson to all wayward children of his generation.

Fletcher barely remembered him. Only traces of that time remained, and not all the memories were pleasant. Red rubber kick balls, jacks and green chalk, bruises and swollen lips, and the aura of anxiety that surrounded Jeremy's gaunt, cheerless face. But what the departure of those things had done to Celia . . . He could still remember the day Jeremy Hill left Pacific Grove forever. Fletcher felt the tension of it all over again, of watching from the school bus as Celia sobbed in her father's arms, of watching Jeremy get taken away. From that dreadful day forward, Celia experienced long bouts of depression, experiencing one terrible setback after another, and never reverted to her former self.

Whatever trepidation gnawed at Angie began to gnaw at Fletcher, too. This visitor was not good news. But telling Celia that would be futile. His fanciful friend was already daydreaming, ready to blow through the ceiling and float away. He and Angie watched her dance and spin around the bedroom, pressing dresses to herself with the hopeful whimsy of a cartoon princess.

By the time the three of them arrived at Lovers Point that night, the parking area was already packed with cars. A fire roared on the beach below, the crackling audible between the recurrent swish of waves. The chatter of Pacific Grove's youth filled the spaces between.

Standing beside Fletcher, Celia leaned against his car and dug through her purse.

"It doesn't have to be tonight," Angie reminded her. "He'll be here all summer."

"No." Celia inhaled deeply. "I don't want him to think I don't care. I do feel anxious, though, and I can't find my inhaler."

"I put it on your nightstand after you used it earlier," Fletcher said, frustrated with himself. "We can go back. Do this tomorrow. He's right next door."

"No, no, we're already here." Celia fixed her dress and squared her shoulders. "Do I look all right?"

"You look amazing," Fletcher said for about the twelfth time. "It's going to be fine, Cee. Just say hello. It's all you have to do right now."

"Say hello." Celia nodded, satisfied with the directive. "I can do that."

Together, the three of them followed the stone steps down to the beach. Celia reached the sand first and stopped. Fletcher moved in beside her as Angie stepped onto the beach, slipped off her sandals, and pointed at the raging bonfire.

"Right over there. That's him."

5

Celia

1956

The morning after Dennis Hill's death, nobody could offer Celia a straightforward answer for Jeremy's whereabouts or a time for his return. He missed the monarch parade (as did she) and then school for two weeks thereafter. And as she'd always wanted, Celia rode the bus with the rest of her classmates. It wasn't as thrilling as she remembered. She stared out the window, watching for Jeremy, ignoring the mindless chatter around her. Since the night of his father's death, the entire school had taken a sudden interest in Jeremy Hill. He was the new, exciting mystery to gossip about.

"He killed his own father, didn't you hear? Stabbed him right in the chest!"

"No! He saved me!" Celia would scream at them, sending herself into hysterics until she was sent to the nurse's office, then eventually home to shed her tears where the rest of the town didn't have to watch. They could all disappear for all she cared. It was stinky, crabby ol' Jeremy Hill she wanted, and nothing in the world could alleviate the pain but him. Had he really murdered his father? Was he in jail, as her classmates claimed? Her parents would only say that he was in the "custody of the state," which left Celia even more confused.

"Why can't he come live with us?" she'd asked a dozen times, only to be brushed off with patronizing ripostes, as if her young mind couldn't be expected to understand. They would take him if they could, they'd said, leaving Celia frustrated.

Each confrontation ended the same, with her dashing to her room in tears.

Every night, she scrambled off her mattress and dropped to her knees. "Please, God," she'd pray, pressing her palms together while her eyes besought the ceiling. "Give him back. I promise this time, I'll be nicer." An angel now, that's what she would be. She would show Jeremy every day how much he meant to her.

The following week, on the bus ride home, Angie thrust a home-made card penned messily in crayon at Celia. The inside declared that their best friendship would last forever and ever.

"Thanks," Celia muttered as she put the card in her book bag. She propped her head against the window. A quick side glance told her that her classmates were staring. All of them were treating her with kid gloves, as though at any moment she might shatter.

In the seat in front of her, Fletcher turned and got on his knees. Behind his glasses, his blue eyes shimmered with sympathy. "You know, I'll bet Jeremy was probably adopted by a rich family with a mansion and a dog."

"Rich people don't have dogs, goofus." Moose chortled from across the aisle, and then immediately wiped the smirk off his face upon noticing Celia. "I mean, sometimes they do. Like fluffy, fancy ones. But those aren't real dogs."

"Sure, they are," Fletcher argued. "They have tails, don't they?"

"What does that matter? Cats have tails."

"Well, cats don't bark."

"Neither do fancy dogs."

"Yeah-huh!"

"What are you two kettle heads even talking about?" Angie reprimanded. "Leave Celia alone. Can't you see she's shook up?"

Moose folded his arms. "Jeremy liked dogs. That's all we're saying."

Gazing out the window, Celia tuned them all out. As they had been doing for the last two weeks, they were referring to Jeremy in the past tense, as if he no longer existed.

She felt like sleeping suddenly but would have to wait another minute or two. The bus was rounding the corner onto her street. Soon, she could curl up beneath their ogre tree and wait for Jeremy in peace.

As the bus completed its turn, Celia spotted several people gathered outside her house beside a candy-red Chrysler she'd never seen before. The smallest figure was unmistakable, though. Chocolate hair, scrawny shoulders, sulking on her front stoop.

"Jeremy!" Celia pushed past Angie and stumbled into the aisle, making a crazed dash for the exit, nearly tumbling as the bus came to a halt. Her heart raced as she hurled herself at the bus doors. "Jeremy!"

She shoved at the doors with all her might, but they wouldn't budge. She felt like a caged animal, rabid and afraid she'd never be set free.

Celia spun around to face the bus driver, a droopy, ill-tempered woman. "Well, open it, you cow!"

The driver grimaced but sent the doors shooting open with a hiss.

Celia jumped free and took off running, dropping her book bag at the edge of the lawn. Her legs had never labored so hard, not even on those summer afternoons when she'd raced Jeremy for supremacy. A smile stretched across her lips at the clearer sight of him. The nightmare was over. Life could return to normal. Oh, she had so much to tell him! They had so much to do!

"Jeremy!"

He sat alone, dressed handsomely in a black, fitted suit and tie, his head down and his hair clean. In his lap, a golden canister rested on its side.

Celia didn't bother to catch her breath as she came to a sharp stop in front of him. "Oh, you're really here! Where've you been?"

Jeremy looked up. "With my mother," he snarled, then stood. "They're making me go live with her in some other state."

"That's your mother?" Celia glanced over her shoulder at the young woman standing by the red Chrysler who noticeably shared his features. She was striking, with flawlessly pinned sable hair and brightly painted lips. The black dress she wore was so swanky that Celia thought she could be a movie star. "She's lovely."

"She's a two-timing whore!"

Celia gasped. She'd never heard such profanity from Jeremy's mouth, which she now realized bore no cuts, his face no bruises. His cheeks looked plump and rosy.

"My father hates her," he hissed through healthy, pink lips, "and so do I."

Celia lowered her voice, speaking to him softly. "But Jeremy, your father's dead."

Jeremy backhanded her across her cheek, knocking her to the ground. As her palms caught asphalt, the force of the landing stung her wrists, hurting far worse than the pain that blasted across the right side of her face.

With red, watering eyes, Jeremy bent over her. "I wish it had been you."

Celia clutched her cheek. The flesh there was flaming hot. Tears burned through her nostrils as she stared up at him in shock.

The four adults in the yard—Celia's parents, Jeremy's mother, and an unfamiliar woman—all dressed in black, ran over. Jeremy's mother took him by the shoulders to berate him.

Her own mother was quickly at her side, inundating her with questions.

As Celia was helped to her feet, Jeremy was whisked away toward the red Chrysler. His mother urged him inside the back seat, then shut the door. "I'm so sorry," she said to Celia's father. "We're leaving."

"No!" Celia dodged her mother's arms and ran for the car, pressing her palms to the back window as the car started. "Jeremy?"

His head was down as he sobbed, his tears cutting shiny tracks down his cheeks. Two suitcases lay in a neat stack next to him.

"Please don't leave." Celia rested her forehead against the cool glass. "I'll dance with you." As the car began to roll slowly backward, she walked with it, pleading with him to look at her, until her father caught her by the arm and pulled her away. "I'm sorry!" The Chrysler picked up speed down the driveway. "Don't leave!"

"That's enough, Celia," her father said. "There's nothing we can do."

"Let go of me!" Squirming free, Celia darted after the car. It was nearing the bottom of the long dirt drive by the time she reached a respectable sprint. "Jeremy!" Midway there, Celia tripped over an exposed tree root and fell, smacking her chin to the ground. Her mouth throbbed with pain, but she scrambled to her feet, noticing that all her classmates were watching from the road. The bus driver struggled to corral them back inside the bus.

The red car backed onto the road, pivoting to face eastward. "I'll dance with you!" Her speed increased, her legs pushing beyond their limits. "Don't leave!"

Out of air, Celia dropped to her knees at the edge of the road, wheezing and sobbing.

Her father lifted her off the ground, the bus pulled away, and the candy-red Chrysler vanished behind the eastern horizon.

1967

When the beach ceased its spinning, dark blue remained. It was in the shifting ocean, in the sky overhead, and in the dye of the shirt he wore. Its fabric rippled with a gust blowing in from the north, clinging here and there to boast a shape that had not previously existed in Celia's mind. It had never even been considered.

Bare forearms leaned on denim-clad knees, and then his back, long and broad at the shoulders, straightened. He was home. A grown man.

The boy Celia remembered was gone, and in his place sat a stranger.

As the bonfire's flames rose high, bucking and snapping wildly against the night, Celia's gaze stroked his unfamiliar silhouette, then stopped on something remembered. A deep, rich, chocolaty brown. The color of his hair. That hadn't changed.

Celia smiled with her whole face. If he only knew how terribly he'd been missed, how irreplaceable he'd turned out to be, how many nights she'd cried and prayed, wishing on star after star to bring him home so she could tell him how sorry she was. She still didn't know how she was going to make it up to him, but she was going to try.

First, she would need to call the little clothing shop at the Cannery where she'd spent the last four summers working and put in her notice. The stranger would be her priority now. There were plenty of local girls dying to work at the cute shop, so Ruthie, the owner, would be fine.

Celia was still trying to find something familiar in his silhouette when shock hit her like a sucker punch to the gut. Lean, feminine fingers rode the long valley of the stranger's spine. For the first time, Celia noticed the pale blond occupying his side. A familiar blond.

It couldn't be.

"In the dark shirt?" she heard Fletcher ask Angie. "Is that Betty he's canoodling with?"

"Yep," Angie confirmed with contempt.

Celia's mouth fell open.

Betty Jean Finnegan?

But Betty hated Jeremy.

Jeremy hated Betty.

Celia shook her head. It didn't make any sense, but she would sort the situation out—if Betty truly qualified as a situation—later. She'd been dreaming of this reunion for years, planning every detail, rehearsing every word. Like the denouement of a stage play, the tragedies of the past would finally be put to rest, and all would be right with the world again. No way was she going to let Betty Jean Finnegan ruin it all with her bony fingers.

Fletcher reached around Celia to pinch Angie's side.

"Ow! Hey!"

To Celia's relief, Fletcher was equally as unsettled. "Did you teach him nothing about the dating etiquette around here? Nobody in their right mind takes up with Betty Jean Finnegan."

Celia felt sick. "They're dating?"

"What did you want me to do?" Angie asked Fletcher. "In case you don't recall, he's not exactly a sponge for sage advice."

"Offer yourself up as a saner alternative." Fletcher got a slap on the arm for that one. "Ow. Take mercy and bludgeon him to death. Anything, woman."

"Oh, give me a break," Angie huffed. "Does he look to be suffering to you?"

"Yes." Fletcher grabbed Celia's hand. "I'm going to say hello. Let's go."

Rooting her toes in the sand, Celia watched from behind a crimson sheen of dread as Betty whispered something in the stranger's ear and dipped her hand beneath the hem of his shirt to rub at his back.

"Why didn't you mention this before?" Celia asked Angie, feeling a little betrayed. The bitter, grainy tang of first-grade mud still lingered on her tongue. "I wouldn't have come."

"I didn't know she'd be here," Angie said. "I'm sorry. Look, I can't believe he made it with her either, but it's not like—"

"HE HAD SEX WITH HER?!"

Celia clapped a hand over her mouth. Now she'd done it.

The mood at Lovers Point changed in an instant. The crowd on the beach transferred its attention to the bottom of the stairs where Celia stood, compelling her heart to all but fibrillate on the spot. At that exact moment, Betty took hold of the stranger, the so-called Jeremy, driving him to his feet while he patted Moose (who Celia was only now noticing) on the shoulder.

Moose was condoning this sacrilege?

And now, Jeremy was protectively steering Celia's archenemy toward the stairs, causing the wretched mudslinger to giggle as he touched his lips to her ear. It was the sound of puppies dying and Satan grinding rust-marred metal between brittle teeth. *Down, thou climbing sorrow!*

Celia shut her eyes. She would not let anyone, including herself, ruin this crucial moment. It had taken four years and four unspeakable events to make her see that Jeremy Hill was the key to her happiness. His departure from her life had signaled the beginning of a curse. It was when fear and anxiety had begun to torment her. Making things right with him was the only way to undo it all.

In those early days, when she'd tried to forget him, the universe had chosen to remind her in stark, horrible ways, ensuring that she never dared forget him again.

"He's coming over here," Fletcher announced, sounding composed as always. But she knew him well; he was nervous, too. "This should be interesting."

As they waited, Celia struggled to breathe, panicked suddenly over how to approach this new, adult version of Jeremy Hill. Once upon a time, they had been bound together by proximity, and then by a pinky promise. But all of that was now locked in a past that he may or may not remember with fondness. Her preplanned script sounded ridiculous now that he was actually here, walking straight toward her.

She pulled in a deep breath and felt the air glide smoothly into her lungs, easing her some. Perhaps she would start with a simple "hello," as Fletcher suggested. Several possible scenarios cycled through her head. A few minutes of nervous chatter, a traded smile or two, and they would be reminiscing, reconnecting deep into the night.

Another full, satisfying breath entered Celia's lungs. She could do this. She just needed to get through it without seeming too flustered. Nonchalance was key. But at the same time, she felt compelled to tell him how much he'd been missed. She owed him at least that, didn't she?

As this new Jeremy approached, passing through a shadowed stretch of beach, Celia prayed that he'd become hideously unattractive in the last decade (it would make him much easier to talk to). But she could see that he was not. He still had a nice face. And he was much taller, with a lean but no longer scrawny frame. He'd filled in well. Celia could appreciate the way his shirt clung to his chest and shoulders. An urge struck her to hug him, to confirm his body heat, to assure herself that he was real and not the ice-cold, silent version of him that visited her in dreams.

Celia moistened her suddenly dry lips. Details became clearer the closer Jeremy got: the straight slope of his nose, the hard angle of his jaw as his lips parted to kiss Betty's cheek, lips upturned slightly at their edges, contemplating a smile.

The pair came to a halt directly across from Angie, and Celia could remember herself inside his arms beneath the cool canopy of a eucalyptus tree, watching as he talked to the sky, plotting their great escape and charming her with knowledge no child should ever have.

He was better than attractive, Celia realized.

His was a face she had loved.

To her right, Angie grinned gracelessly at Jeremy while completely disregarding Betty, who had her arms cinched around Jeremy's waist, as if at any moment he might discover her true identity and make an encore of the recess whistle fiasco of '52. But the blond smirked boldly at Celia, and though Celia held her composure, jealousy frothed like acid in her veins.

Beside her, Angie's voice sounded phony. "Hey, Jeremy . . . Betty," she added tartly, giving the blond a once-over. "Looky who. I told you I'd bring them by."

Jeremy acknowledged Fletcher first. "Fletch," he said, extending his hand. "It's good to see you, man."

The depth of his voice leveled Celia completely. It, too, was that of a stranger, and yet somehow familiar. It clouded her head with disjointed memories, things she hadn't thought of in years.

"You remember me?" Fletcher asked.

Jeremy gave him an easy smile. "Of course."

Celia's insides liquefied at that smile, but her throat turned a fallow desert. Rich, echoing booms thundered against the center of her chest and inside her ears. What would she say? Would Jeremy smile and hug her, too, as he was hugging Fletcher now, punctuating the gesture with a firm slap on the back? Or would he embrace her gently, kiss her cheek the way he had kissed Betty's?

Angie peeked over at Celia with a reassuring nod. But the red-head's expression quickly transformed into concern when she saw the look on Celia's face.

"What's wrong?" Angie mouthed silently.

Shaking her head, Celia risked a backward step, but the retreat was foiled as Angie seized her hand and held on tight. She wished Angie would let her flee. Preparation was what she needed, more time. She had no idea what to say to him.

Jeremy and Fletcher chatted as if not a minute had ever passed between them. Then Jeremy reclaimed Betty's hand. "I don't have a phone so just swing by," he told Fletcher, before finally setting eyes on Celia.

Her heart pounded. It was now or never.

"Hi." Her voice betrayed her desire to exude cool, sounding feeble and pathetic as his gaze addled like a spotlight, scalding her face and trapping her eyes so that the rest of the beach disappeared into the surrounding void. Human eyes never change, never grow, and her memories of Jeremy's held firm. He'd been teaching her to duck-dive beneath the waves of the Pacific. When she'd resurfaced on the other side with him, her dive successful, he'd smiled proudly, his green eyes, framed by dark, wet lashes, bright in the summer sun.

These eyes.

"Hey," Jeremy uttered back through a mild frown. He moved ever so slightly toward her but then twisted to address Fletcher. "Actually, why don't you make it the day after. I've got to go into Monterey tomorrow for materials."

"Oh." Fletcher glanced at Celia and then again at Jeremy. "Yeah, sure."

"Okay. Well, night." Jeremy stepped around the group of them, taking Betty with him.

"Nighty night, Celia," the blond sang.

It felt a little like clinical shock. There was a sloshing noise in Celia's ears. Any second, the moment would come into focus. The scene would transition into something identifiable. Her disorientation, a feeling like submersion, was already dissipating but far too slowly.

Fletcher and Angie stared up the steps after Jeremy and Betty. Celia stood still until a dizzying shudder arrived, making her wobble on her feet. "Are my legs moving?"

"What? No."

Celia closed her eyes. "Oh, that's better."

She felt Fletcher's hands settle on her waist. "Are you all right?"

"Oh, I'm great," she replied sarcastically, opening her eyes, finding solace in Fletcher's blue eyes. Her shoulders drooped. "What just happened?"

"I haven't the slightest idea," he said.

"Maybe he didn't recognize you," Angie proposed. "I mean, I never actually said your name. Maybe he thought—"

"Stop." Celia breathed, her heartbeat finally slowing. "Can we go? I don't want to be here anymore."

Curious thoughts took rise during the car ride home, dormant memories that bobbed to the surface of her mind. Beneath a vast shadow—the shade of a pier or a rock cliff perhaps—he cleared sand and other debris from a scrape on her foot. She could still recall the rapture, the warm sensation of security that filled her. There were a million trivial memories like that, varying merely by time and place, in which he had bewitched her with doting, comforting regard. The consequence of his spell still loitered within the darkest depths of Celia's subconscious. Even now, she hungered for the little boy's assurances, his outrage at this betrayal. How could he overlook her, like she'd meant nothing? The little boy, a principled tyrant, would have demanded vengeance. It was lucky for the grown man that Celia hadn't the proclivity or the guts to exact any.

"He was smashed," Celia declared while pacing her bedroom floor hours later. Her two friends shared a dubious look. "What? No good?"

"He didn't look drunk," Fletcher said. "And he didn't sound drunk."

Celia huffed. "Well, what would you know about being drunk anyway?"

"What would you know about it?"

"Enough," Angie interjected. "I know lots about it, and he wasn't drunk. He doesn't drink liquor. Whenever he goes to the Pelican, he orders milk or a soda."

"Really?" Celia asked, intrigued. "Well, why was he acting like that then? Do you really think he's still angry with me?"

"What does it matter?" Fletcher said. "Who cares if he hates you? To hell with him."

Celia froze. "You think he hates me?"

This conclusion that Fletcher had so casually drawn was one of her greatest fears. Unrequited love. The beloved who refuses to love back. It was at the heart of every tragedy ever written or performed. Was there anything more painful in the world?

But *hate*? Hate went even further.

Evidently, Fletcher caught the swing in her disposition because he promptly began to backpedal. "That came out wrong." He detached himself from her beanbag chair to sit forward. "Maybe he doesn't remember you like you remember him. It has been a long time."

Celia plunked down on the floor at the foot of her bed, opposite him and Angie. That was worse. At least hatred signified emotion, a passion, albeit negative, for something significant. A lack of memory equaled nothing at all.

"I remember everything about him," she said, proving it to herself with a flood of assorted memories, ranging from the pleasant to the downright miserable. She wanted to hate Jeremy Hill suddenly, wanted to smack his stupid, disinterested face until his eyes flickered with recognition. "He sure remembered you," she muttered resentfully at Fletcher.

Angie shot Fletcher a disapproving glare. "Why are you listening to him?" she asked Celia. "He doesn't know what he's talking about. He's a boy. They're notoriously unobservant. Watch." She shut her eyes. "Fletch, what color are my eyes?"

"Brown," Fletcher answered straightaway. "But there are little yellowish-green specks all around the iris, so when you wear green or yellow, they can look hazel."

"Oh, for the . . ." Angie growled. "Fine, Mr. Green friggin' Specks . . . Keep your eyes closed." She smirked darkly at Celia, winking as her expression grew overconfident. Celia shook her head. Angie was fated to go down in a ball of flames messing with Fletcher. "What are Celia and I wearing right this second?"

"Celia's wearing her new, paisley shift dress, and you're wearing those ratty, cut-off shorts I told you to throw away with a mint-green button-up . . ."

"Oh, forget you." Angie sat back with folded arms.

Fletcher beamed. "Don't feel too bad. Not everyone can be as gifted as *moi*."

Angie rolled her eyes.

"You really think he hates me?" Celia asked Fletcher again.

Dropping the smug attitude, he said, "I don't know, Celia. Maybe he feels guilty or embarrassed over what happened the day he left. Maybe he's still angry. I mean, let's face facts, you weren't always very nice to him when we were kids. And you were kind of involved in his father's death. Either way, he won't be here long, so try not to let it bother you too much."

Celia knew it was too late for that. She'd wondered for years if Jeremy's father would be alive had she gone home as Jeremy had insisted. She wondered if it was karma itself that had come for her own father three years later, when a white Oldsmobile struck and killed him. An event that, in her mind, led to a handful of other punishing events. She had caused them all with her selfishness, her weaknesses. She sometimes questioned, late at night, if making things right with Jeremy was the key to redemption, to the dissolution of the curse that seemed to follow her.

Fletcher waved his hand for her attention. "Why don't you go ask Jeremy?" he suggested. "He's right there. What's the worst that could happen?"

Angie groaned. "Why'd you have to say it like that?"

"Like what?"

"What's the worst that could happen?" she mimicked. "That's the kiss of death." Her gaze settled on Celia. "I say, stay away from Jeremy Hill altogether. He's bad news."

Disheartened, Celia sat back. She already knew what Jeremy would say. It couldn't have been more apparent than had the words been decreed on his forehead in flashing neon letters.

He hated her.

"She should talk to him."

"No, she shouldn't . . ."

Celia let her head fall against the mattress. The very idea of going to the Hill house to talk to Jeremy sent her body into a cold, nauseated sweat, and she began to chew on her thumbnail. Funny how she could command a stage, entertain a crowd of six hundred fastidious undergrads, yet some rude boy calling himself *Jeremy Hill* could give her such a terrible case of stage fright.

6

Celia

The next morning, Luisa plopped down a large platter partitioned with fruit, *huevos con chorizo*, fried *papas*, and handmade tortillas. "Eat," the older woman commanded.

Seated around the breakfast table, Celia, Fletcher, and Angie all eyed the display of food like zombies, near dead from their late night, and whirred a harmonic, "Thank you, Luisa."

Luisa sat down to eat with them, a welcome rarity.

Fletcher handed her the Styrofoam tortilla warmer, then began filling his plate with food. "Why don't you both come with me when I go over to his house tomorrow?" he asked the two girls, then yawned. "Strength in numbers."

Angie shook her head, popping a spicy cube of potato into her mouth. "I've got work."

"I wasn't invited," Celia mumbled through her food.

"I'm inviting you," Fletcher said. "And if Jeremy Hill doesn't like it, he can just kiss my—"

"Jeremy Hill?" Luisa said, her accent making the "j" sound more like a "y." She perked up. "*¿Dónde?* Celia, what's going on?"

"Oh . . ." Celia wiped her mouth with a paper napkin.

Luisa—who a year before had moved to the new Hacienda Carmel community twenty minutes away—didn't yet know of Jeremy's return. Neither did her mother, Celia realized. She was going to have to send a letter out.

"Jeremy's back." Celia peeled a tortilla from the warmer. "I guess he's here fixing up his dad's house. We saw him last night."

The fork that Luisa had been clutching clanged against her plate. "Why, Celia? Why would you not tell me?" In a flash, the old woman was on her feet, moving like lightning across the dining room. She blustered into the kitchen as Celia, Angie, and Fletcher exchanged befuddled glances. When Luisa returned a moment later, she was carrying a kitchen towel that held two metal casserole pans capped in aluminum foil. "This was your dinner," she spat before bolting into the entryway and out the front door.

"Where is she going?" Fletcher asked.

Celia gasped. "Oh, my God . . . Jeremy." All three disappeared into the sunlight behind Luisa, chasing her across the yard in bare feet. "Luisa, come back!"

"No!" None of them had ever seen Luisa so furious. "I go see Jeremy!"

"Luisa! Please." Celia trotted alongside her. "You can't! Not yet."

"*¿Por qué no?*"

Fletcher threw Celia a confused look. "Yeah, why can't she?"

"I don't know!"

"I go!" Luisa charged onward.

Celia groaned.

"I guess we're all visiting Jeremy then," Fletcher said, stifling a giggle as they trailed Luisa. To be helpful, he took one of the pans from her.

"Super. Say hi again for me since it worked *so* well the first time." Celia spun around, charting a beeline for her house. It was a commendable attempt at escape, but Fletcher nixed it swiftly and pushed Celia along with them. "I look terrible," she complained as they approached the thin wood of trees that screened Jeremy's yard. "My hair's a wreck."

"Oh, pish." Fletcher put on the silly voice that usually made Celia laugh. "You look scrumptious, darling. Very Ann-Margret in *Viva Las Vegas*."

"Oh, pish you."

"No, it looks nice," Angie agreed. "You look just like her when it's all loose and wavy like that. I'll bet Jeremy loves Ann-Margret."

"Fletcher hates Ann-Margret," Celia reminded her.

"Only because I've taken Priscilla's side," he reminded her. "We've talked about this."

"Speaking of," Angie chimed in with atypical excitement. "Jeremy has been living outside Memphis, Tennessee. This whole time, he's been a thirty-minute drive from Graceland!"

Fletcher gaped. "Get outta town! Does he know Elvis?"

Having a thought, Celia stopped walking. "What if Jeremy has Betty over?"

"Buck up, Celia," Fletcher ordered, nudging her to move faster. "You're boatloads more appealing than Betty, even with that hair. We're going."

Celia wanted to trip him suddenly, but her resentment fell away upon sight of Jeremy. He was seated on his roof, astride its highest pitch, with a hammer in his fist.

"Aye, Jeremy! Jeremy!" It was Luisa's energized voice, more cheerful than usual as it settled into a steady flow of Spanish exclamations, which caught Jeremy's attention.

Startled, he looked down at his visitors and grabbed a tattered hat from his side. Setting it on his head, he rose to his feet. With balanced steps, he hopped from one part of the roof to another, then ambled down the precipitous slope of the lower roof to reach a ladder that was propped against the house.

Celia covered her mouth. "Oh, God, he's going to fall."

Fletcher cupped his hand above his eyes to block the morning sun. "He's fine."

"Aye, no, *mijo*. Get down." Luisa made the sign of the cross. "It's too dangerous."

Fletcher held out one arm, a gesture for Jeremy. "I'm sorry about this. I tried to stop them, but Celia insisted we come."

Celia gave Fletcher a quick shove, which only made him laugh. "Traitor."

"You have to break the ice somehow."

Once Jeremy reached the ladder's third rung, he hopped to the ground and walked over. Before he could say anything, Luisa had him locked inside her fierce embrace, muttering Spanish terms of affection and planting rough kisses all over his cheeks.

Celia looked on in astonishment at Luisa's fervent response. The two of them had never discussed Jeremy after his departure from their lives. Luisa had remained quiet on the subject. Though now that Celia thought about it, Luisa had maybe been too quiet. And Celia had been so focused on her own pain that it never occurred to her that Luisa, too, may have been devastated at his loss. As she had looked after Celia, Luisa had looked after Jeremy from the time he was a toddler.

Today, the woman pinched his face and rubbed his arms, doting on him like a mother welcoming home a long-lost child, checking him for injuries or protruding ribs.

Sweetly, Jeremy smiled and returned a kiss to her cheek.

Luisa, a notorious hard-ass, gloried in the minor show of affection. She may have even been blushing. "Oh, you're so handsome, *mijo*," she said, fawning some more, palming his cheeks.

Celia found herself envious. Perhaps she had approached Jeremy unwisely the night before, expecting him to react rather than leading with a reaction herself, the way Luisa had just done. She clearly still had a lot to learn from the older woman.

Luisa muttered something in Spanish, snatched the pan from Fletcher, glided joyfully past everyone, and walked straight into Jeremy's house as if it were her own.

Wearing a stunned but delighted expression, Jeremy simply watched her go.

"Yeah, that's pretty much how we wound up here," Fletcher said, shrugging.

"It's a good thing I remember her," Jeremy replied, laughing a little. Again, Celia marveled at this new adult voice. "That could've been awkward."

Angie leaned forward. "Then you do remember people."

Jeremy tilted his head at her, clearly confused. "Yeah . . ."

An uncomfortable silence followed, then Fletcher and Angie nodded at each other.

"Holy cow," Angie blurted in a voice that was not her own, then looked at her invisible wristwatch. "Would you look at the time? I forgot I have a thing to do. I should go."

"I should go with you, though, right?" Fletcher nudged her. "To do that thing?"

"Well, I can't do it without you, Crazy!" Angie faked a laugh. "Let's go!"

Celia glowered at them. "What are you two talking about?"

"Can't chat now!" Fletcher pushed Angie toward the tree line. "Gotta jet. Pressing business ahead. You understand. Call me. We'll do lunch."

In their lame attempt to be crafty and cute, her so-called friends slinked into the daylight shadows like ghouls, leaving only tension in their wake. Not even the loud clanging of pots through the open window of Jeremy's house could pierce through it as Celia and Jeremy stood alone, looking at everything but each other.

Celia sighed, then attempted a smile. "They're always doing stuff like that," she mumbled, fidgeting with her hands. "You know, sometimes, I don't even like them."

Pinching his lips together, Jeremy rocked on his heels before drawing in a deep breath. "Okay, well, bye." He pivoted toward his house.

"What?" Waking from her nervous stupor, Celia followed him. "Jeremy?" When it became evident that he wasn't going to acknowledge her again, the nervousness yielded to anger—a much more productive emotion. "So that's it? That's all you're going to say to me? 'Hi' and 'bye'?"

Contributing further to her fury was the indignant chuckle Jeremy produced as he spun back around to face her, the move so abrupt, she nearly crashed into his chest, which was covered in a sweaty, white T-shirt. She anticipated the unwashed stench of the boy but found only a pleasant mixture of soap and . . . lemon oil?

"Did you think I had a speech prepared in your honor or something?" he said.

"Of course not," Celia replied, stepping back. "I didn't think you'd be rude, though."

"How was I rude?" By the looks of him, he honestly didn't know. But in her hesitation to come up with a concrete example, one he might or might not listen to, Celia lost the battle before it even began. His lips slanted in annoyance, and he turned on his heels again.

"You're pretending like you don't know me." Celia followed him as he made his way toward the house. "That's rude."

"I *don't* know you," he said. "But what I'm starting to know of you, I don't think I like."

Celia gasped and trotted up several steps behind him. "You *are* still mad at me!"

"No." Jeremy spun back around, startling her again.

Celia skidded to a stop against him, accidentally touching his cotton-clad stomach, a firm, warm, *verboten* thing. She quickly clasped her hands together behind her back.

"I just don't like being called rude," he said. Against his palm rested a new screen door secured to its hinges. Measurements still tagged its edges. "Now, if that's all, I have work to do." His body language was crystal clear. She wasn't coming inside.

Or so he thought.

"No, that's not all," Celia said. "I'm coming inside, so if you don't mind." She gestured for him to step aside. "Luisa's in there."

"Since when does Luisa need a chaperone?"

"She doesn't. But she'll need help carrying the pans back." Celia raised her eyebrows. "So, if you'll just . . . you know, move."

"I'll help her with the pans." Jeremy stepped inside his house, attesting to his own impudence by letting the door spring shut with Celia still in its path.

"Ow! Hey!" Swinging the door open, she followed him inside to where the sound of clanging pots and pans partnered with the sight of swirling dust bunnies. Celia let out a cough and almost collided with Jeremy's back.

"*¡Ay dios mio, esta cocina!*" Luisa stood in the middle of his kitchen. "*¿Dónde están las placas? ¿Y los tenedores?*" She slammed shut another empty drawer and continued to shoot rapid questions at Jeremy like missiles. "*¡No puedo encontrar nada en aquí! ¿Cómo tú comes? ¿Que comes? ¡No tienes nada!*"

Celia crossed her arms over her chest. "She's asking where all the—"

"I know what she said." Peeling his glare from Celia, Jeremy offered Luisa a sugary smile. "*No necesito mucho, Señora,*" he said to her surprise. "I get by just fine."

Luisa shook her head. She muttered something under her breath, smiled at Jeremy kindly, then sighed. "You look hungry, *mijo.*"

"I just ate." He directed her to a frying pan glazed with grease and meaty bits of bacon or maybe sausage.

"That's not enough," the older woman said. "Sit. You're a grown man. You need to eat."

"Really, I'm not hungry. I need to get back outside. I have a lot of work to do."

Luisa ignored him and began to scoop warm piles of rice and beans onto a cast iron skillet, using it as a makeshift plate for him. Trying to stop Luisa from feeding a man, especially one she loved, could cost someone a finger or two.

"I would sit if I were you," Celia mumbled behind him. "She's not going to stop."

Grudgingly, Jeremy planted himself at the small Formica table in the center of the kitchen and slapped his hat down.

Luisa pointed her serving spoon at the seat across from Jeremy's. "Celia, sit."

"Luisa, just give him the food, so we can go. He doesn't want me here."

"Of course, he does," she said. "He loves you. Now sit."

Jeremy snorted.

Taking a seat, Celia watched Jeremy, stunned by what she saw. In the stark light of morning, wearing that stubborn scowl, he was identical to the person she remembered—the angry little boy with folded arms and puckered lips.

Half-humiliated, half-amazed, she accepted her forced breakfast in silence. Across the table, the irritation rising off Jeremy was all but tangible. Never in her life had she felt so unwelcome, and yet still, she felt at home, his presence an inexplicable comfort.

Luisa passed her the other pan. "Serve him the rest."

Her own mood plunging into disgruntlement, Celia gritted her teeth. She obeyed, nonetheless. Arguing would only make her look like a bigger fool.

Cautiously, as if she were reaching into the darkest of tide pools, Celia placed an enchilada onto Jeremy's skillet. How utterly degrading. Thankfully, Jeremy said nothing to make it worse. He simply watched the food pile up from behind the armor of those angry, folded arms. How fascinating they suddenly seemed, firm and bronzed, awash with earth and sweat.

Luisa kissed the top of Jeremy's head and, following the example of the other two double-crossers, skulked out of the house, leaving Celia and Jeremy to themselves to dine on cheese-and-onion enchiladas at nine o'clock in the morning with a giant serving of tempered silence. Jeremy consumed every bit of it.

Several chilly minutes later, Celia tried again. "Jeremy, I—"

Jeremy slammed his spoon down and scooted back from the table, the chair producing a screeching thrum as it scraped across the old wood floor. "You can leave now," he said with subdued fury. "Tell Luisa I'll bring her pans back later." He stalked out of the kitchen, carving a cold gust through the air that made Celia shudder.

A moment later, the screen door slammed shut.

Celia sat frozen in disbelief, unable to sensibly track the development of this incomprehensible situation or of his level of anger. Yes, maybe she had been a rotten little girl. Maybe she was partially to blame for his father's death. And maybe she had made presumptions about their reunion, thinking Jeremy would receive her with happiness. But here she sat, humbled and punished. In fact, it was starting to feel like a continuation of the day he left. He had humiliated and punished her that day, too, with a smack to the face. She had every right to be furious as well. She had every right to an apology from him. But all she'd wanted was his time. The chance to talk things over. Was that so much to ask? For a little civilized to-and-fro? They were adults now, for crying out loud.

Incensed, Celia rose to follow the loud, grinding noise coming from the unattached garage behind the house.

The garage itself was in quite the state. Slats of wood, varying in size and shade, lay scattered like pick-up sticks across the dirt floor. Tools, big and small, dirty metal gadgets that could have substituted as alien artifacts or devices of torture, spilled from everywhere. She could only identify a screwdriver and hammer that sat on a decaying workbench.

Jeremy stood by the far wall with his back to her. His profile was visible, his expression severe behind the pair of safety goggles strapped to his head. Gingerly, he pushed a slat of wood through a noisy metal contraption, slicing it in two. The sound grated almost unbearably.

Celia's objective was to reach him, to shake him and scream in his uncaring face—why was he being like this?!—then tell him how considerably he'd been missed, even with his surly little attitude, how hollow the days had felt without him. If he only knew.

But the ground under her naked feet was only visible in peppered increments. The rest presented like a garbage dump, where unknown hazards lurked beneath the surface. Trying not to think of the tetanus shot she would surely need later, she took a step.

Jeremy's arm flew out. "Don't!" he yelled over the machine, not looking at her as he finished cutting another strip of wood. "There are metal and wood shards everywhere! You'll cut yourself!"

"I don't care!" Celia screamed over the horrible sound. "I need to talk to you!"

The machine shut off.

Jeremy sighed and ran his palms up his face, removing the goggles. The tension of his posture accentuated the muscles of his back and arms, and it struck her hard and fast—a reckless, sophomoric desire to hold him and be held by him. It was overwhelming.

"Well, I don't need to talk to you," he said, letting his hands fall to his sides.

"Clearly," Celia said as he turned to face her. "You never wrote. Or called. And I had no way of contacting you. Your mother left us no information, not even her last name."

"Celia . . ."

It was the first time he'd uttered her name in the new grown-up voice. It shocked her senses. Her concentration centered on replaying the sound, comparing it to that of the boy. Where was he now? Wasn't he in there somewhere, some sliver of him that still cared?

"Come on, you hated me," Jeremy continued rather affably, then tossed his goggles to the table behind him. "We did nothing but fight."

"I never hated you, and we did other things besides fight."

"Whatever. Look, it was nice of everyone to stop by, but I've got shit to do and only so much time to do it." His scathing edge had all but vanished. As far as he was concerned, the conversation was over. He grabbed his goggles off the table, readying to return them to his head. "Watch your step on your way out."

"You're hurting my feelings, Jeremy."

Celia immediately regretted her words. She sounded like a petulant child. But he was treating her like an insignificant nobody, and it hurt somewhere deep and fundamental.

Jeremy pinched his eyes shut, and when he reopened them, Celia saw a vestige of remorse. "I'm not trying to," he said, pensive as he watched her. "And you know what, you're right; there is something I should say . . . I'm sorry I hit you."

Her throat catching, Celia gulped. She hadn't realized how much she had needed to hear him say that. For years, she'd devalued the incident, deeming it "no big deal," then later pretending it hadn't happened at all. In truth, giving it its due weight hurt too much. But more significantly, he was being the considerate Jeremy she remembered. Maybe he wasn't completely gone.

"It was wrong and inexcusable," he went on, "and I'll always hate myself for doing that."

"You were a child," Celia said softly. "I forgave you the instant it happened. You were sad and scared, and I knew you would never hurt me on purpose."

His brow furrowed. "I don't need you to make excuses for me."

"I'm not. I just want us to be able to talk to each other. I missed you." Celia smiled even though she was exhausted—from this conversation, from the night before, from life in general. She needed first to break through this barrier of his and remind him that there *were* happy times.

Selecting a memory at random, she said, "Do you remember when we were going to run away to Scotland and get married because you heard they gave out dragons as wedding gifts? But we didn't have any money, so we started that lemonade stand and everyone got sick?"

Jeremy's expression turned wary. "No."

Not the response Celia had been hoping for, but she held her smile.

"And I don't know what you thought was going on between us back then," Jeremy said, looking at her like she was a madwoman. "But if I gave you the wrong impression, I apologize."

"What?" Celia's thoughts skittered. Her smile fell. "No, that's not—"

"I really think you should leave."

"What, why—"

"I don't want you here. I don't want to talk . . ."

"Wait, but I just—"

"I'm asking you, as nicely as I can . . ."

"Jeremy—"

"I'm begging you." Jeremy said each word in earnest, a desperate entreaty. "Please leave. Do not come back. You're not welcome here."

Returning the goggles to his head, he hesitated a moment, wiping his mouth, then turned and restarted the table saw.

Celia felt as though her stomach was being sawed in half by that raucous machine. How had the conversation taken such a grim turn, so fast? The words of protest died in her throat, and she had no choice but to wander away. Her mind clung to the last image of the stranger named Jeremy Hill. There had been no anger, no malice in him as he so casually erased a vital piece of her childhood. If anything, he seemed sorry to be doing it, looking at her the way everyone else in town did, with pity and contempt. And it had the intended effect, casting shadows over memories as she dazedly made her way home. The past seemed imagined somehow, dreamed up by a silly girl who believed with all her heart that a boy had once loved her so absolutely that he kissed her awake before slaying a monster to save her wretched life. Like a fairytale. Like make-believe.

7

Angie

"We're going to the Pop Festival this weekend!"

Startled, Angie grabbed her heart. "For the love of God, Moose." He was always doing that. His big, booming voice was like that of God in the burning bush, except Moose never had anything of significance to announce. "What the heck is a Pop Festival?" she asked, returning to her meal.

"You yankin' my chain?" Leaning toward her, Moose slapped his hands on the table between them. "The Monterey International Pop Festival. Have you been listening to anything I said?"

"Mm. Not really, no."

He sat back. "Why do I hang around you?"

"For the free food," Angie said through a mouthful of fries.

"Fork it over." He took a few french fries from her plate and crammed them into his mouth. "Like thirty bands. The Byrds. The Who. The Mamas and the Papas. It's going to be major! Nuclear! The musical version of the Human Be-In. Music is evolving, Ang. It means something now."

"Swell." Angie swallowed, then grabbed another fry and dunked it in ketchup. "And you expect me to go to this pop thing with you?" Attending one of Moose's wacky love fests was not on her list of things to do. Please say no, please say no . . .

"Well, no."

Yes! She wouldn't have to feign a mysterious case of the black death after all. Angie grinned and popped the ketchup-y fry into her mouth.

"It's just Jeremy, Fletch, and me." Moose winced apologetically, stealing another fry. "The revolution can't risk your presence. You'd hex all the good mojo with your pessimism."

Angie nodded. "So, Jeremy's going, huh?" she asked skeptically. "He said that?"

"Well, not yet, but when I tell him about the half-naked chicks, he'll want to go."

"What half-naked chicks?"

Moose shrugged. "There might be some. It's a concert."

"You're a pig."

"I'm a paragon of virtue. I've decided to invest myself—selflessly, may I add—in the pursuit of Free Love. Women have started their own sexual revolution, and I want to be supportive."

"Of course you do," Angie said wryly. "And how convenient that revolution is for you."

"Hey, I'm not gonna pretend it's inconvenient." Moose stuffed another fistful of fries into his mouth. "Come on, Ang. Join your sisters in the rebellion. There's too much happening right now to ignore. And this bullshit war . . ." he said with much more hostility than usual. "People are dying in Vietnam while we sit here, twiddling our thumbs, doing nothing to stop it. People are out there talking about world peace. Equality, Ang. Even for women. You can be something. You don't have to marry some creep and have babies for the rest of your life like your mom."

"And why would I want to," Angie said, cocking one brow, "when I can be at outdoor concerts, dancing half-naked for the sake of the revolution?"

"Now you've got it."

Angie rolled her eyes. "Well, you'll never get Fletch to go. He hates crowds."

A smug smile flitted across Moose's face. "He already agreed."

"He'll back out," she sang in return. "Like he always does."

His smile gone, Moose swung out of the booth, taking her fries with him. "Always ruining the mojo!"

———

"Oh, what hooey," Celia said the following afternoon as she and Angie lay out on her lawn. It was their usual spot beneath the largest elm on the west side of Celia's property, where the tree split the ground into a perfect yin-yang of sun and shade, Celia taking the sunny side, Angie the shade. "It's not about music. It's about the minuscule possibility of meeting easy girls."

"I can't even imagine Fletch there," Angie said.

Celia laughed. "He's going to hate it. You should see him when we go out. He's a total square and not the slightest bit sorry about it."

Angie tossed a few blades of grass at her friend. "Like you're not a square."

"I'm not! I'll try anything once. That's the opposite of a square."

"Really? You'd try this Free Love business? Marijuana? LSD?"

"I might," Celia said, her demeanor turning coy. "It can't be so bad if people our age are getting into it. They say marijuana transcends your mind into this whole new level of consciousness."

Angie sneered. "So does every episode of *The Twilight Zone*, according to Moose."

"And Free Love could have its benefits," Celia mused, then wrinkled her nose. "Depending on the situation."

"Oh, don't you get started on that, too."

Celia had a strong proclivity toward the dramatic, and it always got her into trouble. "Why not?" she said. "Wouldn't it be nice to live a little before settling down? Love a little? Men get to do it all the time, and no one says a word about it. In fact, they're praised. Aren't you curious at all?"

Angie shrank back a little, feeling bad. Now would probably be a good time to confess losing her virginity to Roger (two years before), but she was still too chicken, even though she was pretty sure Celia would understand. So instead, she said, "Free Love is something guys made up to give girls a free pass to behave like tramps. Don't be fooled. It doesn't exist. Nothing is free. Especially not love."

"Anyway," Celia said with a side eye, "I'm surprised Fletcher agreed to go. He hates crowds."

"That's exactly what I said!" Cheerfully, Angie sat back. "Well, at least he'll have Moose and Jeremy there to protect him in case any half-naked concertgoers try to force a little fun on him."

With a gasp, Celia sat up. "Jeremy's going?"

Before Angie could respond, Celia was sailing through another one of her Jeremy fantasies, which had increased exponentially in the nearly two weeks since their disastrous reunion. Her eyes glazed over in her attempt to find hope. "This might be my chance," her blond friend muttered. "If it's just the three of them and me . . ." The last word drawled salaciously from her lips as she plotted. "He won't be able to escape. He'll have to talk to me."

"And then you'll be miserable for a week because he either won't talk to you, or he'll be an absolute jerk when he does."

Disappointed silence followed, then a burst of new energy seemed to strike Celia. She settled on her calves, her brown eyes wide. "What if you and I go on our own adventure?" At Angie's questioning tilt, she went on. "We can pack a bag, get in Fletcher's car, and just drive."

"To where?"

"To wherever! We'll choose a direction and drive until we find something interesting."

The utter excitement on Celia's face confused Angie. So many things could go wrong. "What if the car breaks down? What if we get lost?"

"Then we get lost."

"I don't have money."

"I have some. And if the car breaks down, we'll fix it . . . Oh, come on, Ang! It'll be fun! We never do anything, just me and you. Go on an adventure with me. Please?"

"Be serious, Celia."

Celia's smile fell slightly. "I am being serious."

"Then . . . no. You know I can't leave."

In the hush that followed, Angie watched her friend sulk and peer through the tree line to Jeremy's house. Above the swaying branches, the sun was positioning itself center sky, the time of day, lately, when Jeremy took his work back outside after a short lunch break.

"He's not there," Angie told her gently. "He's on the beach with Fletcher and Moose."

Her face aglow again, Celia got to her feet and took off running toward her house.

Angie groaned and fell back into the grass.

"I'm going to burn," Angie complained thirty minutes later as Celia dragged her over the dunes of Asilomar State Beach. The afternoon had grown bright, and the soft, white sand warmed the soles of her feet. "I haven't been out yet this summer. I'm pancake batter."

"Well, you look phenomenal in my bikini. Why's it so crowded today?"

"Don't try and butter me up," Angie said, adjusting the too-small bikini top over her sizable breasts, noting to herself to keep a bathing suit in her mom's car from now on. "I'm not talking to Jeremy for you."

"I didn't ask you to. I'll deal with him myself." Celia faced Angie, rubbing cherry-glossed lips together, her honey hair falling in loose waves around shiny, sun-kissed shoulders. She palmed the sides of her small breasts to try and create cleavage one last time. "How do my boobs look?"

"Friendly," Angie said. "Like there's a big ol' flashing sign on them that says, 'Grab us, Jeremy, we're yours!'"

Celia beamed.

They found the boys, damp and lounging, near the high tide line, and Angie sighed happily. It was the rare day that they were all four together like this (plus Jeremy, but whatever).

Moose sat in a folding chair, holding a vividly colored flier that shook in the wind. He was trying to show it to Fletcher, who sat in a similar chair wearing a long-sleeved, button-down dress shirt with his swim trunks, but Fletcher was too distracted by something in the water to pay Moose any mind.

On the other side of Fletcher, perched on a blue metal cooler a few yards away, Jeremy chatted with a pretty pair of brunette locals competing for his attention. He was still the exciting new talk in town, and the coquettish smiles being hurled in his direction were nauseating even to Angie, who could only imagine the hellfire that had to be blazing through Celia's retinas right now.

"Afternoon, boys." Her disposition brighter than that mid-June sun, Celia came to a stop in front of Fletcher, plunking down her beach tote and raising her Wayfarers to the top of her head. "We didn't know you'd be here." A passing glare scorched through the two brunettes before Celia's smile returned. "What luck."

Yep. Undiluted hellfire. Angie loved to be right.

Moose frowned. "But I told Angie—"

Using her toes, Angie flicked sand at him. The two exchanged a few wordless words, reaching a silent agreement for Moose to button his mouth, and in return, she wouldn't smack him for gawking at her bikini top. "Hey, champ, my breasts are down here."

Moose shot her a guilty grin.

As that was happening, Celia cordoned off a section of beach for herself and Angie. To no one's surprise, she positioned herself directly in front of Jeremy and his groupies.

Angie leaned toward Celia as she spread her blanket over the sand. "Subtle."

"Can it."

Dissuaded by the new female presence, the two brunettes began a slow, reluctant retreat from Jeremy. Without uttering a word, Celia had made it perfectly clear that he was already (albeit unknowingly to him) spoken for. She may as well have peed a circle around him in the sand. Most of the town was aware of her and Jeremy's past anyway. And yet, while his reputation cut him a dark and intriguing figure, Celia's made her a pariah.

Still, the local girls weren't leaving fast enough.

"Scram already!" Angie barked at them, hastening their evacuation. Let them say what they would about her. Angie welcomed gossip from the chinwaggers as long as they left her friend alone.

Artfully, Celia conveyed to Angie a very specific and lauding look, and Angie, understanding completely, replied with the same. The two of them—one a reported lunatic, the other antisocial as the day is long—were an unbeatable pair when the need arose.

The unworthy focus of this minor skirmish among the women merely sat there, shaking his stupid head. Angie would never understand Celia's infatuation with Jeremy, but Celia was her friend, thus Celia's problems were her problems. And he was definitely becoming a problem.

Angie took a seat on the blanket, stretching her legs out in front of her, as Celia began to slather herself with baby oil.

"I figure," Moose was saying, "we can walk to the fairgrounds from the Blue Pelican and avoid any parking troubles. There's a lot to carry, but—"

"I can help carry stuff," Celia interjected as she oiled her arms. "I might not be big, but I'm pretty strong." She flexed a reedy bicep, grinned proudly, then rose to kneeling to tactically shimmy out of her shorts, leaving her clad in a racy yellow bikini, the bottoms tied loosely at her hips.

Angie stared with incredulity as Celia dallied on her knees, raising her arms to ruffle her hair for no good reason, lolling her head to draw attention to her throat and décolletage as she oiled her skin to glistening. Angie had come to realize that her oldest and dearest friend had no shame, no decorum whatsoever when it came to this boy. She'd never seen Celia behave in such a way, like a skilled temptress on a life-or-death mission. College had really changed her.

It wasn't until Angie caught the drowsy flicker of interest in Jeremy's eyes, lingering on her friend's hips and breasts before darting away, that Angie could appreciate Celia's strategy. It was unlikely to succeed in the long term, but it proved nicely that he was more aware of her than he was willing to admit.

"Um," Moose made a face at Celia. "You are aware you're not going, right?"

"Oh, I'm going."

"No, you're not," he said. "You'll spoil the good vibrations."

Angie rolled her eyes. This again.

"What good vibrations?" Celia asked.

"It's a guys' trip."

"Why? So you can pick up girls? I thought the Pop Festival was about music and women's liberation and world peace. Isn't that what you told Angie?" Celia turned to Angie. "That is what he told you, isn't it?"

"Pretty much," Angie confirmed, looking pointedly at Moose, whose mouth hung open. "There was definitely something about women's lib and equality or some crap."

Celia clicked her tongue. "And yet you're going to subjugate us further by making us stay home," she said, shaking her head in disgust. "Typical."

"Oh, not *us*," Angie corrected Celia. "You. I have no interest in being a half-naked go-go girl because I can be anything I want now . . . Right, Moose?"

Moose pursed his lips. "Curtis." The defeat in his expression was undeniable, though he was clearly more displeased with this method of persuasion: the two-fronted assault, using his own principles against him. "Jeremy, what do you think?" he said.

"Why are you asking him?" Celia snapped.

Moose turned mopey upon sight of her anger. "It's not just my decision."

"I couldn't care less if she goes," Jeremy replied to Moose, speaking about Celia as if she weren't kneeling half-naked right in front of him. "But I'm not babysitting her."

"I don't need babysitting, thank you!"

The two glared at each other, but there was the barest hint of a smirk behind Jeremy's facade. He was enjoying the rise he'd gotten out of Celia with that single remark more than he should have if he was truly indifferent to her.

Angie sighed and committed her attention to Fletcher instead. He was still in his own universe, surveying the ocean. He was the only person on the planet, it seemed, who hadn't surrendered his good mind to the institution of love—neither the free nor the costly variety.

But maybe she was wrong.

Angie tracked his eye line, and it led her to a young couple bouncing playfully in the waves. The male of the pair was irrefutably attractive, his body muscled, his dark skin glistening. In his arms, a black-haired beauty reached up for an embrace, receiving a zealous kiss instead. Together, the pair sunk deeper into the water, looking like a scene out of a Frankie and Annette movie. It was lovely to witness, but Angie wondered why Fletcher was so captivated by the pair. Everyone knew he'd been in love with Celia since high school. Though Angie guessed it was possible his eyes had finally begun to wander. He was a man, after all—an intelligent, kind, absurdly attractive man who had an endless array of options. Women regularly chased after him, but up until now, he'd seemed oblivious to anyone other than Celia, which, funnily enough, made him even more attractive to his admirers.

Celia's new infatuation with Jeremy had to be bothering Fletcher. The two, Celia and Fletcher, were close, but just how close had become a hot topic of debate for Angie and Moose in recent years. What boy and girl—both attractive and both romantics at heart—spent all their time together, got so cozy, and didn't fall in love? And if they had, why not admit it or make it official? Any time Angie asked, they each found a way to avoid answering, and the mystery continued.

"Earth to Fletcher," Angie said with a wave, while the others bickered over details of the Pop Festival outing. From what Angie could gather, there were going to be ground rules, and Celia already wasn't cooperating. "Are you all right?"

"Fine." Fletcher smiled faintly, his fingers moving to unbutton his shirt. "I'm going to take a dip. Want to come?"

"The water's freezing."

"It's always freezing," he laughed, standing up with an outstretched hand.

Gratefully, Angie took it.

And that was the way the summer of 1967 had unfolded thus far. An endless cycle of embittered jabs from Celia and Jeremy, avant-garde sermons via Moose, hollow conversations with Fletcher, daunting reports from the war front in Vietnam, copious signs of a sexual revolution in the making, and now, as rumor had it, God was dead.

So much for the Summer of Love.

————

That evening, while doing her best impression of a baked lobster, Angie ambled gingerly into her kitchen, where her mother stood elbow-deep in dishwater. "Hey, Mom."

"My stars in heaven, Angela." Her mother shook the bubbles off as she examined the blisters forming on her daughter's skin. "Go take a cool oatmeal bath. I'll get the aloe from out back."

"Do you need help?" Angie asked, referring to the housework.

"No, I've got it tonight."

Angie scanned the house for her young brothers. It was too quiet. "Where are the boys?"

"Sleeping." Her mother appeared cheerful tonight, and though Angie was glad to see it, she couldn't help but be suspicious. For Rosemary Martin, happiness was the exception, never the rule. Not in the last few years anyway. "I'm going to the show with a friend."

"What friend?" Angie asked, becoming even warier of her mother's overzealous smile.

"Connie." An old high school pal that her mother hadn't mentioned in years. "I ran into her at the market."

"Hm."

Her mother's strange mood didn't matter, Angie decided twenty minutes later as she sunk into her milky bathwater. She wasn't going to get caught up worrying about her parents tonight.

The stinging of her flesh began to ease and the tightness loosened. More than anything, it was a relief to finally be alone. Angie loved her friends; they were like family. But their lives were chock-full of agitation. Privately, she thought they brought these problems on themselves. They were endlessly pursuing something—love, objects, experiences—and by doing so, each struggled to find contentment, creating unnecessary friction in a world bubbling over with it. Resistance and revolution, discord and war, desire and obsession . . . Where did peace, a word voiced constantly nowadays, fit into any of it?

The world never seemed further from peace than it did right now.

Angie had to admit that every now and then, she longed to feel the kind of passion her friends and family pursued, longed for something substantial to move her, to render itself so essential that it made her crazy with self-serving desire. Angie tried to imagine craving something so much. And if that something was unattainable, be it a lover or a calling, would she lavish it with devotion anyway? Would she chase after it? Fight for it? Die for it? Which type of individual was she? The pacifist or the fighter? The diplomat or the rebel? Angie sank beneath the water, fearing she may never know.

8

Jeremy

What he was doing was probably tantamount to spying, but Jeremy didn't care. He liked it up here in the cool shade of twilight. He liked guzzling orange Tang while listening to the surf crash against the rocky coastline. There wasn't much else to do here after the sun went down.

Over the past week, he'd relegated these late evening hours to sitting on his new rooftop, resting and watching shadows undulate across the windows of the Lynch house. No, it wasn't spying, he told himself. He had no idea if the room he gazed into still belonged to Celia Lynch or if the shapely silhouette he occasionally caught glimpses of was even hers. And it was natural, Jeremy told himself as he sipped from his sweating glass, to wonder if Fletcher slept in there with her.

He hated, though, that it dogged him with such vehemence, Celia and Fletcher's relationship—whatever it had become in his absence. He had hoped to get out of here without getting caught up in the minutiae of this place. The many years away from Pacific Grove had

freed him completely from his own pigheaded grip on the girl next
door. Letting her go had required a massive internal struggle and a few
external ones, but once he'd done it, he'd never looked back. It was why
seeing her face at Lovers Point had thrown him. He'd almost forgotten
her in his self-discipline. Then the next morning at his house, she'd
thrown him again with her behavior, with her affectionate declarations
and wide, teary eyes. That wasn't the Celia he remembered. But she'd
looked an unkempt mess, and he was grateful.

He was even more grateful for her opening reaction. It reminded
him, right away, what an imperious brat she'd always been, expecting
his fealty and worship. It helped him remain steadfast in his rejection. The pathetic kid he'd once been would've fallen over himself to
please her. Anything to make her love him. It never mattered what
she'd done to hurt him. To lonely, untrained eyes, she had appeared
infallible, beautiful, and so soft and clean that he'd once believed her
to be an angel sent to warm his bitter insides. Devotion to the girl had
kept his heart and mind alive through the hellish days and nights of his
life here, and for that, he would always be grateful to her.

But those nights ended long ago, as did his devotion. He'd made
it out, alive no less. And here she was again, trying to reel him back in
with her egotistical recollections. The past had been so fine and dandy
for her. But it wasn't how he saw it at all, and he doubted she was
even capable of seeing it from his perspective. He would give her the
benefit of the doubt, though. Maybe she had grown up. Maybe his
arrival had thrown her, too, and she hadn't handled it well. He couldn't
be too angry; he wasn't acting much better. But he couldn't be around
her either. He wanted to finish his work and leave. There were more
pressing things to worry about than his wretched childhood and its
uncaring sweetheart—shapely and grown or not.

Below him, somewhere near the front porch, there was movement. Silently, Jeremy waited, listening, hearing the snap of a twig and
then, "Jeremy?"

Jeremy scooted to the rooftop's edge to find Betty wandering his
front yard, huffing to herself. He grinned. Betty was cute. A little

stuck-up and demanding for his taste, but cute, and an enjoyable way to spend his downtime when he wasn't hanging out with Moose.

He especially liked the dress she wore tonight: red and low cut.

"I can see down your top."

"Oh!" Polished fingertips spread across her cleavage, shrouding the view. "You scared me," Betty said, angling her head. "What are you doing up there?"

"What are you doing down there?"

"Come out with me. We're having a bonfire at Lovers Point."

"Again?" Groaning at a volume she would hear, Jeremy walked toward the ladder to climb down. "I'll pass."

Betty, now with both hands secured to the ladder, wedged her high-heeled shoe on the first rung. "I'm comin' up then."

"No. You'll kill yourself with those shoes. Move." After a few speedy movements, his boots were on the ground, where he caught Betty by the waist and pulled her in for a kiss. The sweet flavor of her lip gloss blended with the Tang on his tongue, and he was happy.

"Where've you been?" Betty asked, pulling free. "I haven't seen you in over a week."

"Right here." Jeremy pointed up with a smirk. "New roof. See?"

"Every time I stop by, you're nowhere to be found."

"Well, I don't know what to tell you then. I've been here."

Taking her hand, Jeremy headed for his front door, but Betty yanked her hand free. He ignored the moody gesture, a thing he was learning to expect from her, and kept on walking.

"I heard from Dina Derby that you were on the beach yesterday," she said accusingly, shadowing him.

"Yeah?"

"With Celia Lynch."

"Okay."

"Why?" Betty demanded, still following him.

"Why what?" Jeremy held the door open as she stormed inside ahead of him. He looked out into his yard for witnesses to this absurd conversation, finding none before heading inside.

"I also heard she's going with you and Moose to the Pop Festival."
Betty continued to trail him through the house, her voice reaching
panic level. "Is that true?"

Jeremy shrugged.

"You know why she's going, don't you?"

"I think I have an idea."

"I'll bet you do, seeing how you're the one encouraging her unseemly
behavior. Don't think I haven't heard about the two of you. I'm not stupid, you know! I've got your number."

Betty was growing hysterical, and Jeremy wheeled around to face
her, at last taking full inventory of her conniption in the bright, fluo-
rescent lighting of his mostly refurbished kitchen. Her hands were on
her hips, her face beet red, and her glossy lips pursed. She was furious
but still cute. He was more than a little confused, though. She had
seemed fine when she'd first arrived, and now this.

"What are you gettin' so worked up about?" Jeremy opened his
fridge and, realizing he was out of Tang, reached for the half-empty
carafe of milk. "Get to the point."

"As if you don't know."

Jeremy sighed. "Betty, spit it out or go home. I'm not in the mood
for this crap tonight."

He left the kitchen without her.

Sounding like an agitated gorilla in heels, Betty clomped across
the freshly restored hardwood behind him. As she fumed and ranted
about something involving Celia Lynch, Jeremy took a swig of milk
and flicked the dining room light switches. Nothing happened. "Damn
it." Why weren't they working now? He couldn't afford to call the elec-
trician back in.

"Everybody's talking about it, how I can't hold onto my man! I'm
a laughingstock! The other day, Marcie De Luca had the nerve to ask
me if . . ."

In the front room, Jeremy switched on his transistor radio, then
fiddled with its antenna. A ball game was on. The Giants were losing
to the Astros. The Giants had been his father's team, and among the

contents of his head was a memory of getting smacked in the face with the hard bill of a Giants cap.

Jeremy was rooting for the Astros.

"The least you could've done was end it with me before you moved on to someone else. Especially *her*. I'm humiliated!"

At that, Jeremy faced Betty again. "You and I aren't going steady. We've talked about this."

Her eyes narrowed into dark, menacing slits, making him recoil. "I knew you'd wind up a snake," she spat. "You were a snake then and you're a snake now!"

"All right." Jeremy slammed the carafe down on the coffee table (harder than he'd meant to), causing a geyser of milk to erupt. "What the fuck are you talking about?"

Betty gaped at him icily. He realized then that he'd cursed in her presence, consequentially damning the night's plan to try and get his hands under that red dress (not that he'd had much hope left for that). It was an unfortunate habit of his, cursing, and he'd made an honest effort to watch his language around her. But she was presently pissing him off, cuteness be damned.

"Don't you swear at me," Betty commanded with one rigid finger. "And don't you dare play dumb." She hurled the words at him the way a prizefighter threw punches—with precise, skilled blows. "I've heard all about you. How you've been slinking around town with Celia Lynch and going into her house late at night, to do God knows what!"

Jeremy blinked back his surprise and crossed his arms over his chest. A genuine smile of intrigue replaced his frown, his disinterest momentarily forgotten. On several occasions, and from virtually the entire town of Pacific Grove, he'd received warnings and riveting, cautionary tales about the notorious Betty Jean Finnegan. He remembered—sort of—the terror she'd been as a child. But fast-forward a decade, and he merely found her amusing and fun to make out with, so he ignored the foreboding caveats her name tended to inspire.

But this . . . this was just cuckoo.

"So . . . you found out about us, huh?" At his words, the totality of her face, from ear to ear, flushed a bright, shining, blotchy pink, and Jeremy wondered if it was possible for a person's head to explode given enough internal pressure. For a moment, he felt guilty for taunting her, but then she opened her mouth again.

"I always knew Celia was a whore." Her tone had become vicious, hateful. "She's spread her legs for half the boys in Pacific Grove. I just didn't think she was a boyfriend thief, too. And you, you're a pig just like her."

Jeremy lowered his arms to his sides. "Time to go." Taking Betty by the shoulders, he steered her body toward the door.

Her mood swung once again. "Robby Faulkner asked me on a date this weekend, and I said yes."

"Good for you."

"Aren't you jealous at all?" She sounded near tears. "Even a little?"

"I might've been, but definitely not now."

"Wait." Betty tried to out-muscle him, to weasel herself around, but he stopped her easily and continued to drive her toward the front door. "We should talk."

"Isn't that what we just did?"

"I can forgive your indiscretions with Celia. I know I haven't been a very good girlfriend."

"You were never my girlfriend, Betty."

Betty squirmed out of his hold and wriggled around to face him. Her hands flew to his chest. "You know what I mean," she said, unfastening the third button of his shirt. "I didn't put out—and I'm still not going all the way without a ring on my finger—but I've been thinking, and I can attend to your . . . needs, if necessary." Defeat glinted in her eyes, but still, she undid another of his buttons and then another. She raised an eyebrow. "Way better than Celia."

Glancing down at his half-open shirt, Jeremy scowled. He found this kind of desperation revolting, and what little he felt for Betty Jean Finnegan immediately dissolved away. Though he had not been a fan of her chastity, having attempted several times to coax it out of her, he had at least respected her choice to protect it.

"You're out of your mind, you know that?" he said, undoing the grip she had on his shirt and placing her hands back at her sides for her. "Sweetheart . . ." He looked at her with all seriousness now. "I was never sneaking around with Celia."

Betty's shoulders drooped, her chin trembled, and again, he felt guilty. Until she said, "Then take me upstairs."

"What?" Jeremy blurted. "You're going to put out just to keep me around?" In fact, the more he thought about it, her goal was not to keep him around so much as it was to keep him away from her oldest rival. "Have some self-respect, Betty, Christ."

It wasn't that her proposal didn't interest him. It did. As he stood before her, his body warred with his mind in favor of letting her take a stab at reconciliation, batshit crazy as she was. Her current psychosis might even heighten the fun. But he knew better than to take advantage. He knew from experience that she would come to her senses tomorrow and hate him.

Jeremy bent and kissed her cheek. "Have fun on your date. I'm sure Robby Faulkner will be thrilled to have you attend to his needs."

Spinning her around, he nudged her over the threshold onto the porch.

Betty turned, then gawked as if appraising him for the first time. "I always hated you."

Jeremy gave her a weak smile. Though Betty had lived up to her dodgy reputation, her contempt still stung. But only a little. "I'll give Celia your regards when I see her tonight."

Betty's blue eyes tightened with fury. "Murderer."

Jeremy released the door, slamming it shut.

⸻

The morning of the pop festival, after pondering his ceiling a while, Jeremy climbed out of bed with a purpose. He was going to have a little chat with Celia Lynch later because, unless Betty was a complete headcase, someone was spreading rumors. Normally, he would ignore dumb shit like this. But in this instance, he felt ready to snap a particular strawberry blond's meddling neck. Celia was continually ruining his good time, chasing every interested chick away for some reason, and he'd grown tired of it. He had two months of freedom left, of life maybe, and he wanted to enjoy it.

Jeremy entered Moose's bar, the Blue Pelican, at around four that afternoon, wearing jeans and a burning glower for his childhood's deepest wish and greatest antagonist, who sat solo at the bar as Moose and Fletcher chitchatted behind it.

Beside her feet rested two folding chairs, and Jeremy's gaze skimmed up her bare, tanned legs until they disappeared beneath a short skirt; then he reminded himself to which pain-in-the-ass those pretty legs belonged.

Celia turned to smile gloriously at him, faint dimples parenthesizing full, rosy lips. It was how she'd fooled him when they were young, with a misleadingly sweet face and a smile.

"Hi, Jeremy."

Without a word, Jeremy took her by the arm and pulled her around the partition near the bathrooms. "Spill it," he said, setting her against the wall. "Why did Betty's head about explode last night?"

Dark, chocolate-colored doe eyes blinked up at him. "Oh, Betty's crazy."

"I realize that. But this has to do with you. What are you up to?"

"I don't know what you mean." Celia wore a blameless expression. He couldn't tear his eyes away from her lips, though—like plump little berries he wanted to sink his teeth into—until her tongue darted out to moisten them, breaking the spell that wanted so desperately to make camp in his jeans. She was just like Betty—cute but crazy.

He leaned in and said, "People think you and I are getting it on."

"Oh. Yeah. That."

Jeremy started. "That? You know about it?"

"Oh, sure. Everybody in town knows about it." Celia leaned in this time, her teeth pressing into a wide, culpable grin. "It is pretty big news, after all. You and me. Together again."

Jeremy took a backward step. What the hell was wrong with the chicks in this town? They were nutcases, every last one of them.

"Relax." Like she had not a care in the world, Celia shrugged. "I tried to set everyone straight, but the more I said, the less they believed me. So, I gave up. Does it bother you?"

"No . . . I don't know," he said, incredulous. "It should bother you, though."

"It doesn't. But I've been dealing with this kind of thing for years. It's a small town. People talk. You have to ignore it, or you'll go crazy." Celia touched his upper arm. "Anyway, I'm sorry about Betty. Is she very mad?"

"You know what?" Jeremy said, shaking her hand off. "It doesn't matter."

He walked away. Talking to Celia had been pointless. And he needed a cigarette.

Celia caught up with him. "I could try and talk to her for you. I doubt it would help, though. She'd probably—"

Mere strides from the door, Jeremy cornered Celia against another wall, drawing in close to whisper to spare her any humiliation. It took him a second to realize that her breathing had picked up pace. An excited little gleam appeared as her gaze dropped to his mouth. She thought he was going to kiss her. Then his mind considered doing it, his own attention flying to her lips again, parted and waiting.

Jeremy retreated. "Look," he said, pointing, feeling like a complete idiot stick. "I'm sorry I even started this conversation. You stay away from me, and I'll stay away from you, all right? This weekend doesn't have to be a complete bust."

Celia didn't respond right away, giving his initial anger some time to subside, time for his shame to react to the look in her eyes, to the unfathomable sorrow there. Memories pursued him in turbulent strobes. He could see her as he once had—inviting and soft and everything painful in the world lain upon a deceptively angelic face. But this warm, foolish feeling toward her never lasted. It always darkened and twisted into bitterness, something mirroring hate, and he couldn't remember much about why.

Celia swallowed. "If you really want me to stay away from you, I will."

"I really want you to stay away from me," he said with far more disdain than he felt.

In the last second before she withdrew, her expression buckled in anguish, making him feel like the meanest bastard in the world.

Jeremy watched her retreat until she disappeared through a swinging door behind Fletcher, who stood glaring at him with reproach.

Of course, Fletcher had been listening. He was Celia's friend, maybe her lover. Jeremy no longer wanted to know. But he was reminded with this look that he was the outsider here, that these "friends" had lived a short lifetime without him, as he had done without them. They were essentially strangers, and frankly, it surprised him that none of them had expended much energy defending Celia from him this summer. For whatever reason, they were holding back.

———

En route to the fairground, Jeremy enjoyed brief stretches of tranquility, and then it would happen again: hollowed aluminum clattering across the concrete, then across his nerves, slicing through his brain and obliterating all thought. All he could process anymore was the timbre of her breath, which came in dainty puffs as cheap metal was retrieved from the ground behind him. A minute of uninterrupted walking—two, if they were lucky—then another racket loud enough to disturb the entire population of Monterey's east side would strike. More breathy grunting. More walking. Another crash, and Fletcher turned.

"I'm fine," Celia blustered for the umpteenth time before the cycle repeated itself. She wouldn't allow anyone to help her, and it was slowly driving them all bananas.

The afternoon sun taxed as it inched farther west. The ice chest began to feel like a ceramic bathtub packed to its brim with bricks. Jeremy thought his right arm might give at any moment, along with his wits.

Fletcher slowed and shot Jeremy a weary look. "Switch?"

Jeremy nodded, asking Moose, "What's in this damn thing, anyway?"

"Ice, beer . . . more beer. Hey, you need a hand, Celia?"

Another loud crash. "I said, I'm fine!"

"That's all?" Jeremy asked, referring to the cooler and its arduous cargo. "Just beer?"

"Oh, and a couple pounds of bologna. Some cheese. Oh, and another layer of light beer beneath that. For the chicks." Moose spun to walk backward, a rueful grimace crossing his face. "Aw, crap, man, I'm sorry. I may've packed too much beer. I forgot you can't drink alcohol."

"I can," Jeremy explained. "I just don't."

He and Fletcher lowered the cooler to the sidewalk to exchange sides. That was when Jeremy caught his first real glimpse of Celia since setting out from the bar. Her skin was moist and flushed a deep pink from heat and frustration. The brown paint on her eyelids had melted. Unlike the guys, her arms were full, albeit with less weighty items, and she was foolishly dressed in an extremely short, mint-green mod dress that hindered her movement, along with flimsy, white sandals. A geyser of breath erupting from her bottom lip boosted a tuft of wavy hair that had fallen loose from her ponytail. Though it had probably not been her intention, the girl made for a dismal sight.

Lifting the cooler, this time from opposite sides, Jeremy and Fletcher continued to follow Moose's lead toward the fairgrounds. For an entire block, there was quiet. Until they turned onto 10th Street and another grating racket exploded across the sidewalk. Jeremy let his side of the ice chest slam to the ground. "That's it." He stalked back to a chasm in the sidewalk where Celia knelt to recover the troublesome, green lawn chair, then snatched it off the ground himself.

"Hey!" Celia rose upright, smoothing a chunk of loose, damp hair back against her head and straightening her dress. "I said I was fine."

"You're not fine." He yanked the second chair out from under her left arm. "You're a goddamn butterfingers is what you are."

"They're awkward to carry. They keep opening. Give them back."

"Not a chance."

Celia opened her mouth, but before she could protest, Jeremy raised a finger to her. "Say one more word, say you're fine again, and I'll hurl these damn chairs into the street to get run over."

Her eyes watched him darkly, her lips pressed tightly together, and that was when he saw it: the slight twitch of her nose. Celia heeded his warning and spoke not a word, which only served to further unsettle Jeremy. He had seen this expression before, this subtle, foreboding spasm of her nose, the stony eyes, and the cool silence. A memory clawed its way back from oblivion, like a newly animated corpse from its tomb.

More than a decade before, waves had swelled and crashed into foam behind her head. She'd demanded that he build her a sandcastle, and when he refused, she became irate, needling him relentlessly, then throwing sand in his face. He told her off and threatened to bury her if she didn't shut her trap about the doggone sandcastle. Then that dour look assailed him, and the unconscious tic that he now realized reminded him of Samantha Stevens from *Bewitched*. That's what little Celia had been, a spoiled witch who had compelled him into servitude with a cute, freckled nose and rosebud lips. He had been a chump for both.

Jeremy found himself intrigued by the memory and by the grown woman standing before him. He hated these pounding reminders of the powerlessness he had felt as a child, yet the anger that accompanied the memories made little sense to him. So, she had been a brat when they were kids. So what? Was that really why she infuriated him now, all these years later? If the answer was yes, then he was crazier than she was.

He pondered his threat to her chairs, briefly regretted it, then walked away before this incomprehensible anger could settle over him completely. He handed one of the chairs off to Fletcher, grabbed his end of the cooler, and continued on.

No one spoke for three blocks.

As they neared the entrance to the fairground, the street grew more populated—vendors, musicians, attendees, and a large gathering of bikers—becoming a spectacle of sociable energy. The love crowd was scattered throughout, some carrying bunches of wildflowers, dancing to the erratic rhythm of street traffic, preaching of flower power and peace on earth. A flighty brunette with hair past her ass, wearing a colorful sari, pushed a purple orchid through Celia's hair and kissed her cheek.

Celia smiled for the first time (that Jeremy had seen) since leaving the bar, and he was glad to learn that he hadn't completely ruined her day with his temper. After their brief argument, he had tried to ignore her, but it was difficult with the expanding crowd.

Up ahead, Moose radiated pure joy, greeting everyone with a two-fingered peace sign. He dispensed cold beers to the thirsty, and people responded in kind, offering their own tickets to transcendence while striking up conversations about achieving peace through music and the groovy vibe in the air. Some of the people he knew from his neighborhood, others from his community college courses. A handful knew him from his bar. But the majority were strangers from out of town. It didn't seem to matter to Moose, though; everyone he encountered instantly became significant and worthy of his undivided attention. He was truly the friendliest person Jeremy had ever known.

Jeremy, Moose's polar opposite, was approached by at least a dozen strangers in the span of a single block—strangers offering help with the cooler or illegal gifts that might help Jeremy better bear the weight of it. Gifts that he refused. He felt a deep need to stay alert today. He trusted no one.

"Hey, Celia," Jeremy called over his shoulder. "Walk in front of me."

"Why?" she asked, readjusting the bag she was carrying.

Just then, someone passed her on the right and accidentally nudged her forward. Her bag flew to the ground. The young man at fault picked it up for her and apologized profusely before moving on, but the incident only confirmed for Jeremy that he was doing the right thing.

"Because there are too many people out here," Jeremy answered her. "And you're . . ."

"I'm what?"

"A girl."

"Wow. You are perceptive."

"Just walk in front of me. Smart ass."

Moose laughed. "Man, you've gotta relax. Everyone's just here for a good time."

"Yeah, that's what I'm afraid of," Jeremy said. "Celia, come on. Walk in front of me. I can't keep an eye on you when you're behind me."

"I can see her," Fletcher cut in. "She's managing fine now without the chairs."

Celia frowned at him. "I can answer for myself, thank you."

"Why are you fighting me on this?" Jeremy asked Fletcher. "You asked me earlier to watch her. You said she panics in large crowds."

"I do not panic," Celia hissed, widening her eyes at Fletcher. "Why would you tell him that?"

"I said that in private," Fletcher reminded Jeremy, gritting his teeth.

Jeremy was unrepentant. "Wouldn't it be better to just keep her between us?"

"What's the difference?" Fletcher asked. "We're right here."

"Hello," Celia called out. "Do I get a say in this? Could everyone stop talking about me like I'm not here?"

Jeremy waved Celia forward. "Get in front of me. Now. I'm serious."

"Oh," she said. "Well, that changes everything. See, I didn't know you were *serious*."

Celia tilted her head at Jeremy and appeared happy to discover that her second round of sarcasm had been heard loud and clear.

Jeremy rolled his eyes. "Forget it."

Still grinning from ear to ear, Moose spun around to address him. "Look around you, man. There's nothing to get in a twist about. We're all here in harmony to experience the music and brotherhood. Did you see the lineup?"

"There's at least thirty thousand people here," Jeremy said. "She gets separated from us . . . there's always some dirtbag who'll take advantage. Look at her in that damn dress."

"What's wrong with my dress?"

"Not a thing, dollface. You look beautiful as always." Moose shifted his attention back to Jeremy. "Come on, man. You're coming at this all wrong."

Jeremy shrugged. "Better wrong than sorry."

Moose was an optimist, believing everyone to be inherently good, and while that rose-colored lens worked well for Moose, Jeremy found it dangerous. He'd seen the way his father had treated women, the way many men treated them, like objects manufactured for their personal use.

And young, naive women like Celia, without a father or brother to look after them, usually topped their list of preferences. Jeremy could remember one young woman with a taste for vodka, who his father regularly brought home from the bar. She'd looked a lot like Celia, in fact, blondish and sweet-faced. Except this woman had more demons beneath the surface and a deep, heavy sadness that never left her eyes. The sounds the woman made had scared him as a kid—rasping, choking sounds. Peering from the dark bedroom hallway, Jeremy would watch his father's large, damp body repeatedly slam into her petite frame, his hands, like baseball mitts, locked around her slim neck as he called her abhorrent names, slapping her, biting her. But what bothered Jeremy most at the time (though he understood a lot of it now) was that this woman appeared to enjoy the abuse, begged for it at times.

One night, Jeremy sneaked downstairs to the kitchen to get a glimpse of her as she prepared his father a snack. She caught him there and, after asking him a few questions about school, made him the dinner he'd missed. Grilled hot dog sandwiches were her specialty and became his favorite. The nice lady, her bruises matching his own, would smile and hand him his hot sandwich, never forgetting to give him a glass of cold milk and a hug before heading back upstairs. She had been the most enchanting thing to ever enter that house, but she left one foggy morning after a loud argument, her nose swollen and bloody, and never returned.

To Jeremy's surprise, Fletcher said, "He's probably right, Moose. We should stick close. There are a lot of people here."

Moose shrugged in mild defeat. "Fine, but mark my words, this festival, like the Be-In, is going to prove that peace is not just some radical notion. You'll see." He was pondering his own statement even as he spoke. "And besides, if anyone messes with Celia, the three of us will turn 'em into lunch meat."

They reached the parking lot of the fairground, and though it was crowded, it was not yet full. "I see a lot of parking spots, Moose," said Fletcher.

"So do I," Jeremy seconded. "What the hell?"

Moose had Celia at his side. "I really ought to kill you," she said to him. "My hair's a wreck, I'm covered in sweat, and we could've driven in?"

Moose wound an arm around her. "Aw, but you look so pretty with that flower in your hair."

"Don't fall for it," Fletcher said. "He's trying to make you forget that we still have to walk back tonight."

Celia's expression hardened. "You're lucky you have the tickets, Curtis."

"What happened to our harmonious vibe?" he laughed, flicking the flower in her hair.

"Oh, shove your harmonious vibe," she said. "This crap is heavy."

Moose's attention was suddenly elsewhere. "Holy shit." He slowed his stride. Everyone did.

"You think those guns are loaded?" Fletcher asked, nodding toward the hundred or so police officers lined up on either side of the fairground entrance. Donning blue helmets and riot gear, each man stood several feet apart, expressionless. It was an undeniable show of force intended to dissuade anyone considering disobedience. It seemed peace required more than simple faith; it required a hundred double-action rifles.

"They wouldn't really shoot anyone, would they?" Celia asked.

"If pushed, they would," Jeremy answered.

Moose resumed his stride. "Well, let's hope no one pushes them."

It felt peculiar to walk through such a barbaric display. It quieted even the most exuberant in the crowd. Peace required trust, and the trust, evidently, would need to be earned.

Beyond the hawkish gates of the fairgrounds, the crowd had swelled to nearly fifty thousand. That was the rumor anyway. Everyone was grateful suddenly that Moose had offered to help man a booth. It would serve as shelter from the sun, as a rendezvous point, and as a place to stash their stuff.

The four of them strolled past colorful rows of nearly identical booths. It was a flea market of vendors selling fresh flowers and home-made crafts, cocktails, and cleverly marketed drug paraphernalia.

"There's my girl," Moose called out.

"Curtis!"

"Who's that?" Fletcher asked Celia as a stranger threw herself into Moose's arms.

Celia shrugged, so Jeremy filled them in. "Some chick he met at a festival in San Francisco. Her name's Peggy, but she wants to be called Delilah." He shrugged. "She's cool."

"You guys." Moose spun around. "This is my friend, Delilah . . . Delilah, this is Celia, you know Jeremy, and that's my good buddy Fletch. I've known 'em all since kindergarten."

Moose liked this girl. It was evidenced by the goofy grin on his face.

"Groovy. Welcome." Delilah flashed two fingers at them. "Hey, you brought chairs," she exclaimed, relieving Fletcher of his. "Far out."

Sitting between a dozen others, the cubicle in which Delilah worked stood canopied with an ill-advised aluminum roof, closed in by three walls that kept away the brunt of outside elements. It was cool out with the breeze coming in off the Pacific, but after carting a cooler of beer, more beer, and two pounds of bologna and cheese, the air felt sticky and thick.

On two rectangular tables, rows of bracelets and necklaces made of hemp, beads, and feathers lay ready for purchase. A variety of home-sewn garments—hats, bags, dresses, and tunics with chaotic patterns in flamboyant colors—hung on racks and hooks, covering any hint of wall. But it was all junk to Jeremy. What interested him was the brunette who lounged beside one of the display tables, chatting with Delilah.

He'd never seen this girl before. Shining, caramel skin with limbs for miles and long, black hair. A sheer, white, cropped blouse clung to her breasts like wet tissue, leaving her belly and shoulders bare. Even barer were her legs as she drew them toward her chest, letting her flowy skirt slide higher up her thighs, revealing smooth brown skin all the way to the taut pleat of her hip. She was a goddess in homemade clothing. The mere half-naked sight of her filled Jeremy's head with thoughts of sex and every crude act that composed it. He would do every one of those things with and to this girl if given the chance. His thoughts sunk even deeper into his jeans as her pouty, pink lips began to suck water from the rim of a sweating glass.

"Jeremy."

"Huh?" He didn't have to look to see that it was Fletcher yammering something at him.

"Put your tongue back in your mouth, man."

Jeremy smirked. "You see her too?"

"Yeah, she's all right."

Jeremy managed to turn his head away from the girl. He gaped at Fletcher as though he had tentacles growing out of his eyes. "All right? Man, are *you* all right? That chick's a knockout."

Celia snorted, reminding Jeremy that she was even there, behind him. "I guess," she said, folding her arms, "if you like that glamourous, Amazon type."

Jeremy handed her back her green chair, figuring she could surely manage the four steps into the booth without destroying the thing. "If that's what that girl is," he said and pointed, "then that's my type." But in reality, this girl was not his usual type, only because the planet was not teeming with a plentiful array of her kind. Any man would be a fool to declare this sort of girl his type and then settle for nothing less. Loneliness and the destruction of the species were all that would result from such a blunder.

In the meantime, he needed to pull himself together. Be cool. Fletcher was right about that part.

Beside him now, Celia huffed as she ripped the rubber band from her head. Disgust set her mouth into a taut line, and her shoulders drooped. The pucker that formed between her eyebrows heightened her attractiveness, even in her melancholy, and Jeremy supposed, if he was being straight with himself, that Celia was his type, too. Had that face not inspired so many ugly memories, had he no more than stumbled upon it this summer—on the beach or at the drive-in, having no knowledge of the maddening girl who accompanied it—things might've been different.

Movement caught Jeremy's attention. The leggy brunette was scanning the crowd, looking for something or someone, and her eyes found his. She smiled a great smile and bent her neck seductively away. Italian. Greek. Mexican. Brazilian. He couldn't tell. He didn't care. An electric guitar was being tuned somewhere. Moose popped open a beer and hollered his excitement. The brunette tossed Jeremy another smile. And for the first time all day, he was glad he'd come.

9

Jeremy

Her name was Antonia. She was raised in Portugal but spoke perfect English and was as tempestuous as she was beautiful. The fervor with which she spoke, her contemptible beliefs, and the things she'd done in the name of those beliefs had Jeremy hypnotized and wondering if she took all that fire with her into the bedroom.

Antonia smiled as though she could hear the lustful commentary of his head. "I don't buy it," she said with an accent that Jeremy found incredibly sexy, responding to something he'd said (though, for the life of him, he couldn't remember what it was). "It's the social establishments of this world that breed anarchy. It's human nature to challenge authority. It is not part of the natural order." Her teeth nipped at her lower lip as it spread into a smirk. "The humanity you see around you was born from the loins of rebels. People want to be bad, and rules provide the perfect opportunity to disobey."

It was Jeremy's turn to smirk. The girl was out of her damned mind, but he was sold one hundred percent. "I guess it depends on your definition of bad," he challenged her. "What might be bad to you could look like a good time to me. You've gotta draw a line somewhere."

"Why? If there were no municipal laws, no social or religious establishments, then who's to say what's good or bad? There would be no such thing."

"Theft, rape, murder . . ." Jeremy suggested. "Those are bad. Our establishments didn't decide that. Humanity did."

"Those are extremes," Antonia said dismissively, sitting back in her seat. "Government uses those extremes to enslave us all with archaic, fascist rubric. It's the desperate, constrained by rules and propriety, who resort to violence when they find no other recourse. As for theft, how many times have we been told that possession is nine-tenths of the law? No possessions, no crime." She shrugged, as if to say, "Problem solved."

"And you think if we all dance around naked, screwing and listening to acid rock, all crime will vanish?"

Antonia laughed. "Something like that." Her index finger, elegant and unpolished, made circles on his forearm. He liked where this was going. "I'm beginning to think you're not interested in sexual freedom," she said softly. "The death of consequence. Free Love doesn't appeal to you?"

"Oh, it does," he said, tearing his eyes from her lips to trade gazes. "But nothing's free."

"Love can be free." Then she grinned. "Unless, of course, you're loving a streetwalker."

Silently, Jeremy chuckled. "Ah, see, that's where your cute little theory goes south," he said. "Love is expensive as hell."

"How do you figure?"

"People sacrifice everything for it, right down to their sanity."

Antonia rolled her eyes. "You're talking about love as perpetuated by the establishment."

"Huh?"

"Love," she explained, shifting closer to him, "as defined by the patriarchal dictatorship that you and I both live under, the one in which women must relinquish their freedom, their dreams, their very names, in order to take a lover. Meanwhile, men relinquish nothing and reap all the rewards. As a society, we claim human beings like chattel—sign a dotted line, brand our bodies with blood diamonds, and force another human being to love, honor, and obey us until we're rotting in our graves. And we have the nerve to call that love. It's slavery, nothing more."

Jeremy sat back in his chair and studied Antonia for a few seconds. She was dead serious. He thought about this grim picture she painted with such zeal. He wondered what man had burned her. A boyfriend? Her father? Whatever the case, to this girl, uninhibited sex held more value than traditional bonds. Jeremy decided right then and there to quit arguing with her.

"I know your type . . ." she accused gently, forgivingly.

Jeremy barely caught her words, because as she said them, she swung from her seat to his lap. For the first time, he looked around to note that they were completely alone in the back of the poorly lit booth. Everyone had taken off to watch the concerts.

Antonia spread her legs to straddle him, and her fingers slipped into his hair, causing white-hot sensations to flare in his belly and groin. "You're a good boy who thinks he's bad," she murmured softly, sliding her hands down to his jaw. The pad of her thumb slid across his bottom lip as she studied his mouth. His chest ballooned with desire, the feeling sinking low as he pushed her skirt up to her hips to get a grip on her, to seek pressure and friction, and put an end to this pointless conversation. "You think you're a rebel . . ." Her voice was almost pure breath now. "But at the same time, you hope to have a pretty wife someday, to make pretty babies with, and live in a cookie-cutter house with a white picket fence and a porch that has one of those quaint little wooden swings." Her eyes were bright with ridicule. "Am I close?"

"Maybe," he said, conflicted. He wasn't exactly into being mocked by know-it-all academic chicks, no matter how perfect their tits were. "What's wrong with that?" He moved to kiss her, but she dodged his mouth, still playing her little game.

"It's an expensive dream," she chided, using his words against him. "Maybe it's worth the price."

"Don't be dull. How can you be sure what you want at twenty-one is what you're going to want at forty-one or sixty-one? Humans weren't intended for monogamy. And you," she said, letting her mouth drift hotly over his, "were built to spill your seed in as many—"

To shut her up, Jeremy gripped the back of her head and forced her mouth down on his. Their tongues met hotly, and Antonia's hips rolled, hitting just the right spot on his lap. He let out a gratified moan, and kissed her harder, deeper. At that, her hips bucked more forcefully, and he realized, the rougher his kiss, the more enthusiastic she became. It had probably been her intention all along to provoke him. She wanted to be handled forcibly. He could feel it in her posture, hear it in her whimper, the desire for violence. He knew it well and was beyond willing to oblige.

Jeremy wound her dark hair tightly around his fingers and made a fist, wringing a sexy little cry from her lips as he yanked her head back. He gripped her exposed throat with his other hand, squeezing just enough to startle and excite her. "My belt," he told her, testing his theory. "Now."

With pure carnality, Antonia complied, and he slanted his lips over hers. A choked-off moan and her tongue filled his mouth while her fingers went to work unfastening his belt.

A sharp gasp tore Jeremy's attention away. He and Antonia broke apart to look at the tent's entrance, where Celia stood, breathing as erratically as they were. Dark, devastated eyes questioned Jeremy, and a heavy weight of guilt fell over him, as though he had been caught in some infraction. He had no ties to Celia, no commitments. And yet, a sense of betrayal flowed freely between them. An apology hung on his still-tingling lips.

Grabbing her beach bag, Celia took off before Jeremy could say a single word to her. But what was there to say? He hadn't done anything wrong. Still, he squeezed his eyes shut. "Shit."

"Your girlfriend?" Antonia asked, somewhat amused by the prospect.

Shaking his head, Jeremy replayed the pain in Celia's eyes. Sharp enough to pierce. "She's nobody," he said. Then something occurred to him. "Hey, was there a guy with her?"

"A guy?" Antonia laid a soft kiss on his mouth, then his cheek and under his jaw.

"With glasses." Jeremy lifted Antonia off his lap and stood to refasten his belt. "Light-brownish hair, cut short, and a blue, or maybe it was beige, turtleneck . . . Come on. The guy who was here earlier with her, with the glasses." He was getting frustrated with Antonia, who had clearly grown bored of his questions.

"I don't remember that girl or any guy," she said. "Come sit. Let me take your mind off her."

Jeremy drove his own fingers into his hair, though it didn't feel as good as when Antonia had done it. "Was Moose with her?"

"Moose?"

"Curtis!"

Antonia hooked a finger through a belt loop in his jeans and tugged him closer. "I didn't see Curtis, no, and I'm really sorry about your girlfriend, but can we get back to our discussion?"

Moving her hand away, Jeremy paced. Celia had taken off into the crowd alone, doing exactly what he'd warned them all about—what he'd made a huge fucking deal about on the walk over. "Damn it," he bit. "I have to go find her."

Sighing, Antonia stood and fixed her skirt. "Why don't you come find me when you're free."

Jeremy approached her. "I won't be long." He took her face, kissed her deeply, and left.

10

Fletcher

Fletcher called on all his strength—on every brave thought he'd ever had or wished for—and before he could talk himself out of it, shoved Jeremy as hard as he could into a rack of tunics.

Recovering swiftly, Jeremy shoved him back much harder.

A table laden with beaded jewelry caught Fletcher, and he went tumbling over.

"You two, out!" Jeremy's tall brunette shouted. "Imbeciles, fighting like cavemen over a silly little girl. Get out!"

"Sorry," Fletcher uttered as he climbed out from the mess of trinkets and textiles.

He followed Jeremy out of the booth. He knew Jeremy could pulverize him, break his face into a million pieces if he so chose. But at the same time, Fletcher had faith that Jeremy would fight fair. Therefore, he had no excuse to back down from what he'd started.

"What did you do this time?" Fletcher demanded to know. "Why did Celia run out of here in tears?"

Twenty minutes before, when The Association (the first band on the set list) had started to play over the loudspeakers, everyone had left the booth to watch. Everyone except for the dark-haired woman selling homemade wares, and of course, Jeremy, her drooling admirer.

"I can't leave him alone with her," Celia had groused, trying to tear her hand from Fletcher's.

But Fletcher hauled her through the market, refusing to let go.

"Moose left with that other girl. Nobody's there. Fletcher, stop! He's alone with her!"

"Yes!" Fletcher had hollered, his frustration with Celia getting the better of him. "He is! He doesn't want anything to do with you, and you need to get over it already."

The cold, disillusioned look he'd gotten for that comment had never been aimed at him before. Until now, her face had only ever been a source of love and affection. Still, he didn't regret his words. She needed to hear them, and he loved her enough to bear the consequences.

"You would know a lot about that, wouldn't you?" Celia had said then. "Men don't want anything to do with you either. Next time you complain, I'll be sure to tell you to just 'get over it.'"

She'd walked away then, and Fletcher had wandered alone for a while, thinking about what she'd said, brooding and agonizing until he saw her run out of that booth in tears. He'd tried to follow but lost her in the crowd. The next familiar face he'd encountered was Jeremy's.

"How the hell should I know?" Jeremy said now in a calmer tone than Fletcher had anticipated. "She saw me kissing that girl and took off. Where the hell were you? Why weren't you watching her?"

"I'm not her keeper."

"You sure about that?"

Fletcher stared at Jeremy's face in disbelief. There was no sentiment there for Celia, only annoyance at his interrupted romp. "She really doesn't mean squat to you, does she?" Fletcher fixed his vision hard on Jeremy, as though, if all else failed, he could scoop the answer right out of those dead green eyes. Eyes that, alive and warm, might have driven him to obsession, too. For they once had. When Fletcher was a boy of about eight or nine, he'd developed his first crush—on Jeremy. He'd made him feel protected and safe, in an environment that otherwise left Fletcher feeling terrified on a daily basis.

More than a decade later, Jeremy showed none of that earlier nobility.

"Just stay away from her," Fletcher said.

"She stalks me."

"So, shoo her away."

"What do you think I've been trying to do?"

"You really want me to answer that?"

Jeremy tilted his head like a bemused collie.

Could this be their first honest conversation? Back in school, Jeremy rarely spoke. Instead, he communicated with capable, assuring eyes. "You're safe with me," those eyes would promise. "I'll protect you." Instantly, Fletcher felt his anger with Jeremy fade. All that remained, if he could fully relax and let himself acknowledge it, was disappointment in the person Jeremy Hill had become. Jeremy owed them nothing. He'd long ago paid more than his due.

Jeremy waited. "Say what you gotta say, Fletch."

Fletcher took a deep breath, losing the vehemence he'd felt a minute earlier. "I think you're spiteful," he said gently, sadly. "I think you haven't got the slightest idea what Celia went through after you left. And even if you did, you wouldn't care. And before you go thinking it was only you they hated, you should know that the other kids called her a murderer, too. And a witch. And a lunatic. They tormented her for years. But after her dad died, a few of them—" Fletcher shut his mouth. What was he doing? It was none of Jeremy's business. He had no use for these details other than to scorn and reject her like the others. "How about the next time you feel like being a cruel bastard to her, you instead pretend to be a decent human being, just for a minute, and give her a damn break?"

"Wait." Jeremy's frown deepened. "Say that other part again."

"What other part?"

"The part about her dad."

Fletcher was confused. "What? About after her dad died?"

And there it was, finally—a human response. Jeremy's cold eyes thawed. "Angie told me the Lynches were in Europe," he said.

"Mrs. Lynch is in Europe. In Denmark, visiting her sister. Mr. Lynch died years ago."

Backing up, Jeremy leaned against a chain-link fence. "Oh."

A small commotion erupted behind Fletcher, and he turned to look. The beautiful, dark-haired girl, while shooting them a furious glance, retrieved baubles from the ground.

"Sorry about that," Fletcher murmured to Jeremy. "She seems pretty mad."

The mask of indifference returning to his face, Jeremy pushed himself off the fence and browsed the area. "All right, you go that way," he told Fletcher, pointing westward. "I'll go this way. Cover the entrance and booths, in case Celia comes back. I'll take the rest."

"Okay, but if you find her—"

"I know, I know, pretend I'm a human being."

11

Angie

Summer nights in Monterey, especially Friday nights, were seldom so quiet. At the very least, people were visible, cruising or strolling the boardwalk, building up appetites. The diner should have been teeming with tourists and hungry locals by now. Angie should have been sweating and cursing her job—which began as a temporary summer gig six years before—shaking her fist at the grease-splattered ceiling before plastering on a toothy smile for customer rounds.

Instead, a few old fishermen dined, murmuring to each other about town hall meetings and catch quotas while silverware clinked inside coffee mugs. It had Angie shifty-eyed and anxious. It was like *Invasion of the Body Snatchers*, except that the bodies were missing, too—so it really wasn't like that at all. Aliens, Angie hypothesized. Aliens had abducted the entire town, snubbing the old, the smelly, and her.

That or everyone was at the music festival.

"Angie!" Stan—her boss, Betty's father—barked from the kitchen. "Table six. Snap out of it."

"Oh, shove table six up your ass, Stan."

"If I thought it might improve your waitressing skills, I would."

Moping nearby, Betty sighed. "I wish I was at the festival, too. Better than being here."

"I don't wish I was there," Angie countered as Stan stalked past her with a bag of trash. She eyed him threateningly. "I like how quiet it is. It's like my grandpa's rest home or the morning after an H-bomb blast." She tossed down her towel with a grimace and finished out her shift.

After her last customer paid his tab, skimping on the tip, Angie grabbed her bag and ducked into the employee restroom. There, she washed her hands and face, yanked her thick mane of red hair from its rubber band, kicked off her work shoes, then shimmied out of her stinking uniform. A shake of her head and her hair was done—"done" meaning it was rid of crumbs, which would have to do. She brushed her teeth, spackled her lips with gloss, spritzed on perfume to veil the remaining stench of fried fish and money, and glanced at the clock.

Nine fifteen. Roger would arrive any minute.

Roger Flowers. The name alone was marriage material. *Mrs. Angela Flowers*, she recited in her head while giving her face and hair a final once-over in the mirror. By name, at least, she would be charming and soft.

Roger was twenty-seven and lived five miles away in Seaside. He was an apprenticing marine engineer, which meant he built machines for ships. He was also kind, generous, and handsome, though he didn't look one iota like Elvis, the man she'd planned on marrying since she was ten.

A lot of the things weren't panning out as she'd hoped.

After adjusting her brassiere and slipping into one of Celia's hand-me-down dresses, Angie sighed and stepped back to pose. The chest area was tight, pulling around the buttons, so she undid the second one, exposing cleavage and the full upper swells of her breasts. She eyed the result with an approving grin. That would take his mind off the fried fish smell.

A knock on the door startled her. "He's here!" Betty announced from the other side. "Finish stuffing your bra and come on. He's waiting."

Angie opened the door. "I don't stuff, bottle-job. I don't need to."

"Sure, you don't." Betty's cool, blue eyes swept down Angie's body and then back up. "That dress is tragic."

Angie blew out a surly breath. She should have seen it coming. Betty positively knew whose dress this had originally been. Celia had worn it to Marcie De Luca's shotgun wedding to Brian Simmons three years earlier.

"Good grief, Angie, haven't you ever heard of makeup?" Stepping forward, Betty pinched Angie's cheeks and then slapped them hard to draw a blush.

"Ow!" Angie drew back in surprise.

"You're going to have to put out. I'm fresh out of ideas." Betty spun, her hair whipping Angie in the face, and strutted away.

Rubbing her stung cheeks, Angie followed Betty down the hallway that led to the main dining area where Roger waited. It was where he usually picked her up for dates. He'd asked on several occasions to pick her up at home and be introduced to her family, but Angie vehemently refused. It was a miracle that he loved her as it was. And he did love her, to the point of foolishness, Angie believed. He didn't seem to realize how handsome he was or how out of her league he had always been. And tonight, to make it worse, she felt filthy and crabby and tired. Her feet hurt. Her head ached. She wanted to walk right past Roger, out the front door and all the way home, where she could shower and watch *Carson* in her nightgown. A date sounded like more work.

She enjoyed Roger's company, but they were hardly close. Rather, he was in love with her while she was too suspicious of that love to bother deciphering her own feelings.

For days, they'd go without speaking and even longer without saying anything meaningful. Then, when they finally came together, they often spent their time fooling around in his car. Though that wasn't by Roger's choosing. Angie was a private person. Companionship and romantic affections, physical or otherwise, were not necessities in her life, nor was finding a husband. Her parents had long ago destroyed those notions for her. Love and marriage were just another part of life that looked like work without compensation. But of course, her mother encouraged her relationship with Roger. He was a "nice man" who would be a "good provider" who tolerated her "difficult" personality. The expectation was that someday they would marry. As a woman, she would eventually need to latch onto a man for survival. That seemed to be the message she was getting.

Standing up as Angie entered the dining area, Roger looked like a doting groom awaiting his bride. "That dress," he said appreciatively. "It's stunning on you. My God, you're gorgeous."

Angie felt her cheeks flush under his scrutiny. She hated compliments. She never knew how to respond. He was the gorgeous one, with his Robert Redford hair that felt like silk between her fingers and his vibrant blue eyes with those weathered commas at the edges. When he talked about his work, she would trace those crinkles, noting how they changed and deepened as his excitement dithered or grew. His skin, bronzed from long spells at sea (he'd made his living as a fisherman while in college), was somewhat leathered by the elements. But when he smiled, it was pure magic.

"I thought you'd like it," she said.

Roger seemed surprised. "You wore it for me?"

"No, I wore it for Stan."

He frowned at her sarcasm, but it was too calculated. As always, he was trying to hide his happiness from her, his love, knowing how skittish it made her. For that, she felt a pang of guilt.

"We have a dinner reservation in fifteen minutes," he said. "Afterward, I thought we'd go to the drive-in."

"I already ate," Angie said. "Let's go for a drive and park somewhere."

Roger moved closer, taking her hands in his. "What's wrong?"

"I'm tired."

Roger watched her a moment, deliberating, thinking—always thinking. He was too considerate of her, of everyone in general. While she was becoming the complete opposite in response—selfish, thoughtless, distrustful—not knowing how else to react.

He blew out his next breath. "All right. We'll go for a drive. If that's what you want."

They didn't drive far. They "compromised" by parking beneath the shadow of a huge pine near Angie's house, where Angie climbed onto his lap to initiate the one activity that could dispel the day's tensions.

"Angie, baby, talk to me," Roger said while she attempted to silence him with kisses. He wasn't cooperating at all tonight. "I know something's wrong."

Angie groaned. "If you love me, you'll stop talking and kiss me."

"Can't we do both?" He set a light peck on her mouth. His strong arms snaked around her waist and squeezed her close. "I'll kiss," he said as Angie sunk down on his lap, relaxing into the closed-in, intimate feeling of him. "While you talk."

He pushed a hot, open-mouthed kiss into the base of her throat, and it felt so good that she couldn't help but shudder. Oh, he was good at this. He was good at everything.

"All we do is screw in my car," he said through another kiss. "Come home with me so I can make love to you properly in my bed. I feel like I'm disrespecting you."

"Ohhh, but you're not." Panting now, Angie grabbed his face and kissed him deeply. It was in these moments, exclusively, that she felt love for Roger. He was the one sane, clean part of her life, and his kisses made her heart awaken with a ferocious stir.

"Angie," he tried again, dodging her next kiss. "Angie." His fingers gripped her upper arms and jerked her back, ruining the moment. "Angie, enough. I want to know what's going on in your life. Please. Talk to me."

Angie shrugged his hands away. "My life is none of your damn business."

Shock and disbelief flashed in his eyes.

That was when Angie heard it.

Roger's eyes widened. He heard it, too.

Coming from inside her house.

Yelling.

No, not yelling. *Screaming.*

Angie and Roger scrambled from the car and ran toward her house. The screaming intensified. Porch lights came on. Neighbors emerged. Then a hard crash sliced through the warm evening air, and instantly, Angie knew—her father was there.

Roger brought his arm down like a pass gate when they reached the front door. "Maybe you should get behind me."

"Oh, get out of my way!" Batting him aside, Angie stormed into her house. "Mom!" Most of the commotion was emanating from one of the bedrooms, while in another, the baby wailed bloody murder. "Dad!"

Once upon a time, her parents had been madly in love. "Mad" being the central word, for they had each played the antagonist in their own love story, turning every disagreement into an outright battle. Nothing physical. Rather, they had tormented each other with cruel comments and persistent threats of divorce, then basked together in the high of reconciliation. This, however—what was happening right now—was the result of three turbulent years of pain, distrust, and betrayal. This was different, Angie realized, as she entered the bedroom her parents had once so passionately shared and found her father trying to kill her mother.

Back in the spring of 1964, Nathaniel Martin had solicited an affair with a woman named Elise, who lived on his mail route. His excuse was that he had fallen in love with the artsy blond from Wayland, Texas, unable to help himself. Soon after, Nathaniel moved out of his home to be with Elise, leaving his wife of seventeen years a deflated, broken mess, and causing Angie (his then eighteen-year-old daughter) to assume the role of responsible adult, breadwinner, and caregiver to her grieving mother and two—later three—younger brothers.

While her father spent his paychecks on his mistress and their new life together, and while her mother wasted away beneath still-warm sheets, Angie tried to pay what bills she could with her meager compensation from waitressing and ensure that her brothers were happy, clean, and fed.

Both tasks she botched miserably.

The eldest of her younger brothers, Robert, had been fifteen when their father left. He grew angry with the entire world and ultimately ran away from home. But Angie couldn't blame him; the boy had admired their father, loved him blindly. He was the only child besides Angie old enough to remember a time when Nathanial Martin had been a decent man who loved his wife and children.

The two younger boys, midlife accidents both, would never know anything but the madness. The oldest of them, Ben, had been only two when robbed of his father, while the youngest—Michael, now one— was conceived in the aftermath.

Their mother could never shake her high school sweetheart, nor could he seem to truly shake her, despite his mistress—wife now. Only a year into his new marriage, Nathanial Martin started coming back around late at night, having sneaked away from the home he shared on the other side of town with Elise. On his knees, in the darkness, he would cry into his ex-wife's lap that he missed her, loved her. Angie's mother would sob with him, cradling him, professing the same. Angie had never witnessed a more pathetic sight in all her life. Somehow, her father had managed to turn her mother into the mistress, the homewrecker. And her mother, sick in her own right, reveled in the notion that she remained the love of his life, the prime focus of his erratic and beleaguered desire. Nine months later, Michael was born.

In that very same month, across town, Michael's half sister, Maggie, also entered this dysfunctional equation. "We'll need to keep those two apart in the next few decades so they don't commit incest by mistake!" was her father's running joke. Angie didn't find him funny. In fact, she wanted to massacre him every time he showed up drunk, yearning and crying for her mother.

In the years since their divorce, Angie had come to lose all respect for her parents. Like most children, she'd grown up believing them infallible. In reality, they were weak and selfish and undeserving of all they had despite those things. While they licked their own self-inflicted wounds, she worked fingers-to-bone to raise their babies, to locate her disgruntled, runaway brother, all to save a family that no longer existed, headed by parents she could never again respect.

They were at each other's throats now, literally. Her father's meaty hands were wrapped tightly around her mother's neck. A usually pale woman, Rosemary Martin had swollen to a frightening shade of purple, her terrified hazel eyes a crimson map of burst vessels.

"Dad!" Angie shouted, lunging to separate them. "Stop! Get off her!" She yanked and pulled, but he was fixed in his intent to wound. Every muscle in his body was impossibly locked.

A muscular, suntanned arm wound around her father's neck and wrenched him away from her mother, who dropped to the floor with a rattled gasp.

Roger dragged her father out to the front lawn while Angie trailed behind, screeching at him, the hatred inside her exploding outward. "Get out of my house!" she bellowed, her authority final and true. The moment Roger released the man, Angie shoved him toward the road. "And don't ever come back here! Or so help me God, I'll kill you! I'll bury you where no one will ever find you!"

Roger's arms closed around her. "He's going," he said in her ear. "He's going." He hushed softly until Angie realized she was sobbing. The soft sounds Roger made and the warm imprisonment of his arms were soothing, but she refused to let it lull her completely. Breaking free of his embrace, she spun to face him and cleared the tears from her eyes.

His handsome face radiated sympathy. "Should I call the police?"

Angie shook her head. "Go home."

"What if he comes back?"

"He won't."

Roger reached out to touch her face, but she backed away.

"Your cheek is bleeding," he said. "Let me help you."

"Go home," Angie said more forcefully. It was probably only a scratch, a surface wound that would heal. "I don't need your help. I don't need anything from you."

"Angie." Roger's features conveyed frustration suddenly. It made him even more handsome, and Angie considered going home with him, to let him soothe her the only way he could. "I'm not your father," he said evenly. "I'm not going to hurt you."

Angie laughed. "Like I haven't heard that before."

"What does that mean?" Roger shook his head in dismay. "I don't—" Rubbing his hand over his face, he wandered away, then turned again to face Angie, staring at her before saying, "You don't love me, do you?"

"No. I don't." Angie felt almost nothing, and it was beginning to scare her. "Now leave."

The pain in his eyes was too much to stomach, so Angie left him on the lawn and stalked into her house where the baby continued to cry his heart out, his chubby cheeks stained with tears. Angie lifted the inconsolable boy from his crib and went looking for little Ben, finding him in their mother's arms on the master bedroom floor.

Angie stood over her mother, bouncing the baby. "What happened?" Her voice sounded lifeless to her own ears.

"We got into a fight."

"Yeah, no shit. About what?"

In pleasanter years, her mother would have corrected such language, but she had no right to parent anymore, and she knew it. "I told him we had to stop. I started seeing another man. I told him to go home to Maggie and Elise."

Angie watched her mother, feeling a deep sense of relief at her admission, then handed the baby over. "Good," she said. "Now break it off with the other one, too, or I'm leaving."

ANGIE | 135

Tearfully, the broken woman who gave birth to her nodded and hugged her youngest son to her chest, kissing his fine, red hair.

Angie returned to the front yard and slumped down on the porch steps. She scanned her quiet street. No Roger. No father. No disapproving neighbors.

Feeling like a guard dog, she pulled a cigarette from the secret compartment in her purse and lit it, dragging in a deep, shaky, smoke-filled breath.

12

Celia

1960

C elia was fourteen years old on that first day of her all-too-brief
voyage into womanhood, having spent the school year (like countless girls her age) in a fanciful mating dance, flirting with her eyes,
blushing like hell, then turning to giggle with her friends.

A freshman at Pacific Grove High School, she was beginning to
feel normal again. The year before, after her father's death, she'd barely
been able to get out of bed, and now she could hardly contain her
excitement over the upcoming Swinging on a Star dance.

It was a welcome change. And it was all due to a boy.

Beneath a bright spring sun, Celia poked at her school lunch, a
dry hamburger and soggy fries, while her friends—school gossip
Marybeth Hackleman, the audacious Dina Derby, and of course,
Angie—coached her on the habits of the newest beast prowling in
their midst: the teenaged boy.

Glen Pelletier was nice looking but several inches shorter than
Celia, so he was not an option right now as she had plans to wear heels
to the dance.

Bill Renwick, on the other hand, stood tall and strong and could have been a real looker had it not been for his acne. It got so bad once, his chin began to ooze a snaky little river of blood-tinged pus while she was chatting with him about their biology homework. Celia shuddered at the thought of putting her mouth anywhere near that chin.

Seated cross-legged on the grass a few feet away, Angie cringed. "Ew, you're right. What about Kenny Parks? He's not completely awful."

"He already asked Betty," Dina chimed in before taking a very unladylike bite of her Elvis-inspired fried peanut butter and banana sandwich.

Angie whipped her head toward Dina. "How do you know?"

"Kenny told Harlan in gym." Harlan Matisse, Dina's steady. Everybody in school knew they were making it. To Dina's dismay, though, nobody seemed to care anymore. "Harlan told me that Kenny told all the fellas that he's got a good chance of slipping Betty Jean Finnegan his summer sausage after the dance." Dina wiggled with delight.

"Dina!"

"His words, not mine."

Celia harrumphed. "What a sleazeball."

Angie could only nod. "Kenny is a whiz at statistics. I graded his last exam."

"Well, one of us needs to find a date," Celia said to Angie, frustrated. "We can't both go with Fletcher."

"Fletcher doesn't want to go, and neither do I," Angie said. "Why don't you go with Moose?"

"Oh, didn't you hear?" Marybeth snorted, adjusting her new designer eyeglasses. "Moose asked Yolanda Rodriguez to the dance, and she said *yes*." Yolanda Rodriguez, a pretty but quiet girl, was the only other Mexican in school besides Moose. Celia didn't get the joke but laughed along with Marybeth and Dina anyway.

Angie elbowed her.

"Ow." Celia rubbed her arm. "I'm going to be dateless. My social life is ruined."

"What social life?" Angie scoffed. "We have no social life."

Dina rolled her eyes and twirled her shiny, black hair around her index finger. "We'll find you a date, okay? Don't have a bird about it." Then Dina gasped. "Holy guacamole! Stop the presses!" Her eyes grew massive and her arms rose like the uprights at Homecoming as her licentious gaze switched focus to a solitary location across the school quad: Boy Central. Dina was suddenly in her element. Celia could tell because her voice got all sing-songy and snotty. "Don't look now, Celia Bean, but I think someone's taken a shine to you."

Celia followed Dina's eyeline to the infamous picnic table that crawled with freshman boys and met eyes with the loathsome Kevin Donahue. Her breath came to a halt in her throat. "Kevin?" Celia hissed. "Are you demented? We hate him!"

"Why on earth would anybody hate him?" Dina had moved to Pacific Grove the year prior and was not well versed in the playground politics of the old-timers, veterans like Celia, Marybeth, and Angie. "He can float my boat any time." Dina slung a wink at Kevin, but he didn't notice.

His gaze remained glued to Celia.

Celia blockaded his ocular advances with the back of her hand. "Stop staring at him, Dina!"

"Yeah, down, girl," Angie agreed. "You have a steady."

"I can look."

"Not at Kevin Donahue," Celia bristled, swatting at Dina's thigh. "I told you. We hate him!"

"It's true," Angie said. "We took a vote in third grade. It was unanimous."

Marybeth nodded. "That was a dark lunch period."

Dina remained unconvinced. "But why do we hate him? He's an eyeful and a half. He plays baseball like a dream. Have you seen his brothers? And in case you haven't noticed, this town isn't exactly heavy on the pickings."

"Because he's a lowdown, dirty toad," Celia said with conviction.

She could still recall every fight, every taunt, every cruel prank Kevin had launched against Jeremy Hill in elementary school. She could still hear Jeremy's head smacking the asphalt after Kevin punched him. Still feel the resulting knot on her fingertips. That particular fight, that memory, was from the afternoon of Dennis Hill's death. Kevin would always be a part of that awful day.

Celia set a hard glare on Boy Central. None of those boys had done much growing up since then. "All those creeps over there are toads."

Marybeth leaned forward and lowered her glasses. "I heard through the grapevine that Marcie De Luca dumped Kevin for Brian Simmons. But nobody knows why."

Dina soared at this news. "He's free?"

"As a bird." Marybeth grinned.

Both girls swung their grins toward Celia, who folded her arms. "Big whoop."

Meanwhile, Angie studied the enemy with fascination. "He's still looking over here."

"Because you're gawking at him," Celia complained, tossing a crumpled napkin at her oldest friend.

"Hey, I'm just reporting what I see."

"You're rubbernecking."

"I wouldn't mind doing some necking with him." Dina was just so stinking pleased with herself. "But it's looking like he's got the hots for Celia."

"Well, he can just sit on his hots." Celia huffed, then crunched emphatically into her apple to express the finality of her statement. But as she chewed through her private unease, she peeked over at Kevin. Sweet juice filled her mouth. She hated to admit it, but Dina was right. Kevin had grown rather handsome over the years and was unabashedly watching her. Only her.

———

"Hi, Celia."

Startled, Celia screamed and whirled around, dropping her schoolbooks.

Kevin hurried to collect them.

Celia watched him with astonishment. She was two blocks from home. Kevin's house was on the farthest western edge of Ocean View Avenue, across town. What was he doing here?

Despite her horror at his presence, she couldn't help but admire the healthy, sun-kissed glow of his arms, corded with new muscle as they gathered her books from the sidewalk. Or how nicely he'd grown into his face since their last summer vacation. Most striking were his eyes, which swirled with every earthy color. They were hypnotizing, and her heart began to dance.

At the same time, she thought of Jeremy and wondered what he would have to say about these treacherous observations.

Plenty, she was sure.

"You scared me," she accused.

"I didn't mean to." His expression uncharacteristically shy, Kevin straightened and, instead of handing her books over, he clutched them to his chest as though they were his.

Still dumbfounded, Celia did and said nothing.

Kevin braved a step forward.

Celia stepped back.

"So, um . . . can I, maybe, walk you home?"

Walk her home? WALK HER HOME?

Celia snatched her books from his clutches. "Get lost, Kevin!" Spinning on him, she stomped away, leaving him standing alone at the edge of the road. "And stop staring at me all the time!" she hollered back. "You're being a real creep!"

But Kevin didn't get lost. And he didn't stop staring. Rather, in the weeks that followed, his fascination with her grew, and the ensuing tension between them rocketed to unfathomable, heart-stirring heights.

Finding herself more inquisitive by the day, Celia began to stare, too, making them both look to the outside world like a pair of moonstruck lunatics. They stared from across crowded gymnasiums, through hushed classrooms and bustling hallways, waiting for something—anything!—to happen, and soon found themselves in full pursuit. Following, hunting, scheming, searching, staring . . . always with the staring. Anything for their daily dose of whatever the other was offering.

One day, worried she'd been forgotten in the hour since their last stare-a-thon, Celia put on a famously dramatic performance for Mr. Mooney, her third-period English teacher, to get her greedy hands on a hall pass that she used to make an "accidental" appearance past the windows of Kevin's history class.

To her relief, she hadn't been forgotten. The smile Kevin gave her, first-rate in its delivery, sent her heart skyrocketing into the stratosphere. Oh, the joy and delicious ache of it all. It was disorienting and yet exhilarating. Though Celia had no idea what was happening to her (or to Kevin Donahue for that matter), and though she knew it was probably wrong to feel this way about a once dreadfully mean boy, she also knew that it felt wonderful to be wanted by him and to want him so desperately in return.

Meanwhile, Kevin, unlike her, didn't shy from their predicament. He didn't care who knew that this madness had consumed them. He wasn't ashamed or afraid or even deterred by the constant ribbing he got from his friends and brothers. Celia couldn't help but become smitten with the audacity and nerve that took. She was spellbound by his bravery, by the storm that brewed behind his persuasive hazel eyes, by the lovely outline of his smiling mouth, and by the warm golden-brown shade of his flawlessly cropped hair. She often wondered what it was about her that captivated him. Her eyes, too, perhaps? Her smile? The coy demeanor she put on around him? It didn't matter, so long as he was feeling what she was feeling.

Some fight she'd put up in Jeremy's honor, though. Some friend she was, pining after the one person she'd pledged never to forgive. The thing was: she no longer cared. Not really. No matter how sticky she and Jeremy's past or how many pinky pacts they'd made, Celia wanted Kevin Donahue. Awful, terrible Kevin Donahue. And she would have him. She would let him have her.

With her guilt neatly dispatched to the furthest corner of her mind, the staring was able to progress into more energetic activities. After school, she and Kevin began exiting the school bus a good half mile from her house, making a run for the woods there. Kevin would chase her in, swearing her capture as she screamed in delight. They dodged Monterey pines until the afternoon sunlight could only spear their skin in thin shards, then he would bring her down to the ground to kiss her breathless.

In those moments, Celia felt alive. Even more so than the new breasts she'd sprouted or that monthly demon that had destroyed all her favorite underpants, rolling around in the dirt and foliage with Kevin Donahue made her feel like a woman.

Forget baseball; Kevin kissed like a dream. The day of their first kiss, they'd met in those woods after school to talk.

"I can't stand your brothers," she'd admitted after exchanging awkward pleasantries. It was their first private meeting. Seated cross-legged, their fingers plucked anxiously at the sparse blades of grass between their knees. "One of them broke my sister's heart, and the other teases me all day at school because you like me."

"I'm sorry about that," Kevin muttered, lifting his eyes to meet hers. "I hate my brothers, too."

"You hate your own family?"

"You would, too, if you had my family."

Celia got the sense that he wasn't going to elaborate, and she didn't have the courage yet to push. But she did manage to admit, "I used to hate you, too."

Kevin lowered his head again. "I know."

"You were so mean to Jeremy. He was my friend."

Kevin supplied no response, but his slumped shoulders and downcast expression told Celia that he wasn't proud of his aforementioned behavior. Not in her company, at least.

She deflated at the sight and took his clammy hand in hers. "Please don't be sad. I don't hate you anymore."

That was when he straightened up, pondered her face a moment, then asked for permission to kiss her.

Her belly doing somersaults, Celia nodded.

Kevin leaned forward to stamp her lips with their first kiss. That kiss, swift but tender, turned into two kisses the following day, then three and four, and then into lengthy French kisses.

Lost on a heady trip of youthful experimentation, the two of them blazed uncharted trails with curious adolescent hands and mouths, whispering silly accolades sure to make the other smile as the long afternoons slowly drifted into weeks. And while that ordinary forest became a love nest of sorts, Kevin Donahue became Celia's first real boyfriend. And she loved him for it. She loved him instantly.

On a cool April afternoon at school, two weeks into their "secret" relationship, Kevin quietly asked Celia if he could escort her to the Swinging on a Star dance. Losing all composure, she threw herself at him and planted an enthusiastic kiss directly on his smiling mouth.

In front of everyone.

The gossip mongers went wild. They were officially Kevin-and-Celia and—ecstatic at the turn her life had taken—Celia floated on through her own private version of heaven. Magic seemed to permeate the air. Love was everywhere, in everything. Yet, in the middle of it all, that voice emerged again to reprimand her. It sounded suspiciously like Jeremy Hill's, with weeping and the gnashing of teeth. What kind of friend was she? How could she betray him this way? Words like traitor and liar were thrown around. But Celia shut that tiresome voice out. To heck with Jeremy Hill.

Kevin Donahue was here.

Kevin loved her.

Kevin would never hurt her or wish her dead.

Would never *ever* leave her.

In retrospect, she should have listened to that voice, should have remembered why she'd made all those sunset promises to her sad, bruised friend in the first place. But it had all gotten so far away from her so fast.

The night of the dance, Kevin showed up on foot in a suit jacket two sizes too big. On his left palm rested a corsage of yellow carnations that didn't match Celia's royal-blue dress. But it hardly mattered. She relished his offering, and after he pinned it carefully to her breast, she kissed his hot, rosy cheek.

Her mother had insisted on photographs, thrilled to see Celia smiling again, to feel life finally returning to normal after the death of the family patriarch the year before. Helena Lynch had no real knowledge of Kevin before that night. In her eyes, he was an angel come to restore what remained of her daughter's damaged childhood. It was Celia's father who had known about Kevin's ruthless torment of Jeremy. Her father would have turned Kevin away, would have rehashed his lectures on loyalty. Celia knew this, and so for one disconcerting moment, she found herself glad he was dead.

Her mother, in contrast, adjusted Kevin's tie and fixed his hair. She clasped her hands together as Kevin ushered Celia down the long driveway. They must've looked to her like they'd stepped out of some charming scene from a Norman Rockwell painting.

What a lie it all was.

In Celia's memory, the gym floor shimmers with a million tiny orbs. The band plays its rendition of Johnny Mathis's "Chances Are" while the crowd cheers for Celia's sister, Bianca, the new spring queen. But Kevin only has eyes for Celia. He holds her closer than he should as they dance. The chaperones gesture and frown, but Kevin pulls her closer, making her giggle. He confesses his love, and swearing the same, Celia kisses the lips undeniably sent by heaven to make her feel healthy, beautiful, and strong again. One of the female chaperones forces their impetuous young bodies apart—arm's length! They dance and dance.

Her recollection always sputtered and stopped there, then picked up again, like a dream, during their walk home, forever injecting that wretched Johnny Mathis melody into both the best and worst moments of her life, the tune trudging on as they walked hand in hand through the dark, desolate school campus.

Why her mother had let such a young boy walk her home alone so late at night, she'd never know. But in fairness, it was 1960. It was Pacific Grove, California. Butterfly Town, USA. Norman damned Rockwell.

Kevin looked so handsome to her, even seven years later in memory. Celia could still see him through her fourteen-year-old eyes, smiling in his ill-fitted suit, so gentle with her, so sweet. He had been a perfect gentleman as they stopped on the other side of the school's sports field to slip the fence that would put them on the small street behind the school. He didn't want to take the main road. He wanted privacy, he'd said. He wanted to kiss her. She looked so pretty tonight.

She'd felt pretty. For the very last time.

As Kevin had reached his hand out to help her, his splendid face fell. "Come on, Celia. Hurry."

But Celia hadn't comprehended at first. She'd played coy. How foolish she must have looked to him, grinning, swinging her hips like a dumb, oblivious child while he tried to protect her from the truth of the world, from the ugliness hidden in plain sight.

Kevin caught her wrist, but she yanked it away. She wanted him to chase her. She wasn't ready for this perfect night to end. But when she turned and ran smack into a hard chest, she finally understood.

Celia raised her head to see Kevin's oldest brother, Will, grinning down at her. His king's crown was still atop his head. She'd never noticed before how tall the popular senior was. Behind him stood Kevin's other brother, Dean, a junior, along with Kevin's best friend, Tommy Russo. They must have been smoking and drinking behind the high school, a rumored Friday night activity of the tough kids. She could smell the liquor on Will's breath.

"Where are you two crazy kids going?" Will asked with an air of playfulness, and Celia relaxed a little.

"I'm walkin' her home," Kevin answered quickly. "I'll be right back."

"Nah, it's too early to go home," Will said to Celia. "We're celebrating my ascension to the throne." The two boys behind him snickered. "I was hoping to celebrate with my queen, but the little slut ditched me." His smile fading, he took one of Celia's curls between his fingers. "Lucky for me, there's a next-best thing."

Celia took a backward step toward Kevin, but Will captured her waist and pulled her close to his adult body, so different from Kevin's.

"Hey, where're you going? I'm not gonna hurt you. I just want my dance." Together, they started to sway like a grotesque imitation of her and Kevin's dance from earlier. "This isn't so bad now, is it?"

"Kevin," Celia squeaked as she tried to wriggle away.

"*Kevin,*" Will mocked.

As the other boys laughed, Kevin stood in rigid silence, his severe stare pointed at his oldest brother.

"Relax, will you?" Will told Celia, his voice easy. "It's a celebration." His breath touched her ear in humid puffs. "I like your dress. I can't wait to see what's underneath. I wonder if you look like your sister. The prettiest pink I ever saw."

Her earlobe clipped by teeth, Celia gasped and fought harder to get away. Her next breath came in shallow, the next even shallower.

"Cut it out, Will," Kevin finally said.

Will tsked. "Come and make me."

Gasping and wheezing, Celia continued to struggle. What happened next happened fast. Kevin slammed into them, bringing both his brother and Celia to the ground with him. Will, a grown man of eighteen, exuded little effort in disabling Kevin with a series of very unbrotherly punches.

Celia watched with horror from the grass nearby. Will was laughing at Kevin, razzing him, noogying his scalp, as if he were wrestling his twerpy little brother in the yard at home. It all seemed so ordinary. Until she noticed that Tommy Russo wasn't laughing anymore. His expression was a pendulum of conflict and fear. A can of beer in his hand, he didn't budge, only watched, his pendulum swinging as Kevin groaned in pain and struggled to get up.

Once on his feet, facing his brother who now stood at full height, Kevin grew composed, grave, his head bowed with a new air of obedience. "Let me walk her home," he proposed calmly, though his voice quaked. "I'll come right back and make a beer run for you guys. I won't chicken out this time. I swear."

Terror quickened inside Celia. What was transpiring before her eyes? It appeared as if her right not to be violated was being negotiated with stolen beer. He was talking, bartering, as if she wasn't standing right there, gasping for breath, a free human being.

She screwed her eyes shut against the view. It wasn't happening. She was at home, dreaming of movie stars and monarch butterflies, safe in her bed.

When Celia reopened her eyes, a teardrop was making its way down Kevin's cheek. "Please, Will," he pleaded now. "Not her."

Will regarded his little brother, and Celia recalled how the girls in school worshiped Will Donahue. How many times had Dina Derby remarked on his rep as a "grade-A dreamboat"? On how many afternoons had he winked at her friends and sent them into a fit of giggles? How many nights had her sister cried herself to sleep over him?

"Sorry, Kev," the "dreamboat" said now. "It's what you get for getting attached to one of these Lynch sluts. Better you find out early, like I did." Will patted Kevin's shoulder remorsefully—as if to say, "nothing can be done, little brother; these wheels are already in motion"—and pushed him gently aside, heading again toward Celia.

It was then that she snapped out of her fog and began to pedal backward toward the fence.

As she got to her feet, Kevin charged his brother again but was easily cast aside. His other brother, Dean, caught and restrained him, for whose benefit she didn't know.

Tommy, her classmate since kindergarten and Kevin's best friend, did nothing but sip his stupid beer.

Celia hated them all.

Will took hold of her, ignoring her shouting as he pawed and kissed and laughed at her pitiful attempts to fight. "Ooh, you're feisty, like your sister." Gripping her harder against him, he continued to make comparative, incestuous commentary on parts of her body that she hadn't ever let Kevin near, that she'd never even explored herself. Celia had the additional, sickening feeling that this wasn't a first for the Donahue brothers. Kevin's countenance was that of inevitable doom.

Nevertheless, he exhausted himself trying to break free of the arms that held him, while the sweet lips that only an hour before had kissed her so lovingly now spat depraved, vain threats of murder.

Eventually, Dean released his hold on Kevin, but Kevin, exhausted and vacant now, never again tried to help her. Instead, he wandered in the distance as Celia begged his help. He was supposed to protect her. All these boys were supposed to protect her.

She squirmed and pushed and used all her strength to dislodge a rough, merciless hand that had forced its way inside her underwear. Her dress was hoisted to her breasts in trade.

Thirty yards away, Kevin plopped down on the grass and cried, covering his ears while his best friend, Tommy, took a seat beneath a tree and nursed his beer, staring at nothing.

Celia couldn't have weighed more than a hundred pounds, but big, weighty swaths of anger swelled up from deep inside her. As did a stronger impulse to fight. She pulled in a deep, satisfying gulp of oxygen, and didn't question it. She would thank God later for her breath. For now, Celia tried to hone and simplify the frenetic, muddled thoughts pinging around in her head. She had to focus. She thought about her daddy. What would he tell her to do? She thought of her sister and recalled a story Bianca once told her about a date she'd abruptly ended. The word "tease" kept coming to mind. Some boy, some handsy jerk, had gotten angry at Bianca for refusing to go all the way. He'd called her a tease, and she'd hit him for it. No . . . No, she'd stomped his foot with her heel. Celia remembered how powerful Bianca had sounded as she told the story, how courageous. "After that, I kicked him where it counted," she'd said with such confidence and grace. "He went right down."

Celia drew power from the recollection. The skin of her neck was wet from Will's saliva, and he was angling her toward the ground.

Time was up.

Feral in her frustration and anger, Celia screamed in Will's face and stomped her left heel downward, again and again, as her right shoe was missing, having come off in the scuffle. It wasn't until the third or fourth attempt that she finally made contact. Will shrieked and hopped onto one leg to clutch his aching foot. "Bitch!" Disbalanced, he reeled and fell to the ground.

That's when Celia noticed that the pig had begun to undress himself. His pants were unzipped, his genitals exposed and roused—by her fear, by his own brother's torment . . .

Celia growled at the sight. "You sick pervert!" Slamming her heel down hard on his exposed erection, she felt the pop, like a high heel piercing firm, wet lawn. To her dark delight, Will screeched a noise like death as he rolled into a fetal position. She cared for none of his wailing, though. "Shut up!" Tearing the bloody heel off her foot, she aimed it at the other boys like a switchblade. "If any of you follow me," she snarled, "you'll get it right in the nards, just like him!"

Backing away, Celia glared at each of them, lingering on Kevin, who regarded her retreat with astonished relief.

As Will howled like a dying animal, Celia slipped the fence and ran until her lungs burned.

When she neared her house, she changed directions. There was no way she could face the dilapidating Hill house tonight. That ghost would be vengeful and unforgiving. It would crow and scorn her, for she'd gotten what she deserved.

Stumbling down the back roads of Pacific Grove, her body ached everywhere—her legs, her throat, her lungs. But going home, even from the other direction, was not an option, not disheveled like she was, wearing a torn dress and missing a shoe. Her mother would be horrified to discover that her daughter had been assaulted in such a way. Celia had been hanging on by a thread as it was, even with the psychotherapy. Her mother would blame herself like she always did. But Celia knew the truth. It had all been her own doing: Dennis's death, her father's death, and now this.

Celia considered looking for Bianca, but the thought of ruining her sister's night stopped her. She thought of going to Angie but found herself traveling down Fletcher's street instead.

Barefoot and cold, still clutching one shoe, she curled up on the grass in his backyard, trying to calm her racing heart and her erratic breathing. When the downstairs lights finally went out in the house, she went to the flowerbed beneath Fletcher's window and tossed a few pebbles up.

Fletcher opened his window with a squint. He put his glasses on. "Celia?"

A minute later, she was sobbing in his arms. After several failed attempts to question her, Fletcher helped her up to his bedroom and locked the door. He peeled her fingers from the blood-crusted party shoe, then inspected her body. He saw the marks, the dirty, ravaged dress . . . "Kevin did this?" he asked, horror-struck.

Celia shook her head.

"I'll walk you home," he said after she told him everything, his expression equally doleful and doting. "We'll tell your mother together."

"No! I can't go home like this. Just help me."

His face turned indignant. "We need to tell the police, Celia, and they're going to tell your mother. They'll have to."

Celia blew up at him. Telling the police, telling anyone, would only mean more ridicule, more hatred! She didn't want anyone knowing. They wouldn't believe her anyway. They all thought her a scourge to begin with. And they'd seen her running into the woods with Kevin every day for a month. The Donahue boys were local sports stars, their father a respected member of the community, a baseball coach, and volunteer firefighter. She'd be called a liar, a troublemaker, a whore.

Reluctantly—very reluctantly—Fletcher agreed to keep the secret and help clean her up. But first, he handed her one of his mother's Valiums and a glass of water. Then he used his mother's sewing kit to do a quick repair job on her dress (enough to get her past her own mother and up to her bedroom), then fixed her hair. To conceal the bruises developing around her mouth, he filched his mother's expensive makeup.

"There," he said when the deed was done, plainly unhappy. "Your mom shouldn't suspect anything as long as you say you're tired and get quickly to your room."

During the walk home, in an attempt to soothe her and show her that she wasn't the only one with shameful secrets, Fletcher confessed his homosexuality, revealing his crush on Brian Simmons. Thoroughly medicated, Celia barely reacted to the revelation, leaving Fletcher pleased. They were a pair now, two safeguarded secrets bonding them like glue.

Fletcher waited beneath her bedroom window, and when Celia peered down, after being reprimanded for arriving home past curfew, he blew her a kiss and then disappeared into the darkness.

13

Celia

1967

The Monterey International Pop Festival was in full swing. On a dark stage, ringed in a spotlight, two young men performed the last song of the night with nothing but the whisper of their voices and a single acoustic guitar.

Seated on a chair some thirty feet away, Celia raised her knees to her chest to make a pillow of them. She was no more than a fleck in a bottomless sea of strangers, all together heralding a symphony with their silence. It made her think of Moose. If anyone was going to appreciate this peaceable gathering and the beautiful, profound music, it was him.

After catching Jeremy and that ridiculously pretty girl, she had run as far as her asthmatic lungs would allow, crossing the fairgrounds in minutes.

Taking deep drags off her inhaler, she hid inside a toilet stall until her breathing returned to normal. Then, with cold water and a restroom napkin, she scrubbed her face clean of sweat and makeup. It had been a complete waste of time, preening for a boy who wouldn't notice or care.

Comfortable in her skin again, Celia reemerged and hunted for something more appropriate to wear.

In another restroom, she put on a new pair of Capri pants and a handmade embroidered blouse she bought from a teenaged vendor, a kind, easygoing girl with kinky hair and a baby boy named Dancer. The time spent cooing at his dimpled, smiling face had worked wonders on her mood.

Feeling more like herself, Celia bought a cherry soda and wandered the grounds, wading through the immense crowd of strangers and listening to music as the sun warmed her skin. Returning to Moose's booth was not an option. In fact, crawling back to Pacific Grove on her hands and knees, alone, in the dark, or hitching a ride with a pack of snarling wolves sounded more appealing. Anything to avoid *him*, or worse, him and her together.

Perpetually masochistic in its worldview, Celia's imagination presented to her, in all its twisted splendor, the prospect of Jeremy and that girl seated together in this very crowd, embraced as before, listening to beautiful music as they kissed and fell eternally into love. The fictional development alone weighed Celia's chest down with a heavy dose of exaggerated, self-inflicted anguish.

The reality would be torture.

Despite her peevish mood, Celia had managed to make a few friends over the course of the day. People were so welcoming that her usual fear of strangers seemed a silly, embarrassing pastime, an arbitrary lapse in her already thin ability to cope. She made a mental note to get out more this summer and socialize, to stop obsessing over Jeremy Hill. Because consenting to the idea that she was a weakling, the spineless, blubbering scourge of feminism itself, did not sit well in her stomach tonight.

She ordered herself to focus on the festival, the music, and the potential in the smiles of new friends. She learned that Moose had not been embellishing (something he often did); this event was truly monumental, the music candid and meaningful. The shared sense of goodwill among the youthful crowd was invigorating. It was not dangerous or seedy as the papers had predicted.

That night, as Celia watched the day's final performance, the young man seated to her right, a wiry college sophomore named Daniel from Oregon State, took her hand into his with such tenderness that it hardly occurred to her to recoil from his touch. The girl on Daniel's other side, a round-faced waitress named Darlene from his hometown—who, Celia suspected, had a huge crush on Daniel—accepted Daniel's hand into hers in the same gentle manner.

It prickled at Celia at first, being emotionally vulnerable with strangers. She wondered why they were being so kind to her; then she retreated from those thoughts using coping strategies Dr. Frank had taught her. She took a deep breath in order to center herself and began to list all the ways she could take responsibility for the situation she was in, all the ways she could retake control . . .

She felt somebody drop down onto the empty chair to her left. His scent gave him away first, a soap or laundry detergent she couldn't identify. Her heart betrayed her and leaped for joy.

"You changed clothes," Jeremy said. "Clever."

Taking a deep breath, Celia turned her head to look at him. She was waiting for him to fly into one of his tirades, to curse her for whatever asinine reason he found suitable tonight: for spying on him, for interrupting his spit-swapping session, for existing at all.

His eyes bounced between hers. His lips parted, then resettled into a hard line.

While Jeremy struggled to speak, Celia couldn't help but marvel in the fact that he was here at all. His presence pleased her to no rational end, and she was angered by that suddenly—by the fact that even now, she wanted him. Even now, she wanted him to want her. The desire had become so potent in recent weeks that it felt beyond her control, well and good beyond any coping method she could think to apply.

"Do you even realize what you put everyone through today?"

he finally said, his tone fatherly, which mercifully added more fuel to her anger.

Celia returned her attention to the stage, folding her arms to punctuate a silent message—*get bent.*

"Celia?" Jeremy let out a huffy breath. From her peripheral, she watched him hang his head, then set his eyes on her again, his gaze scratching at her like the prickly wool blanket that trimmed the foot of her bed back home. "Are you all right, at least?" he asked.

"Stellar." She stared at the musician Darlene had called Garfunkel. "Now get lost."

His voice was even more mulish than hers, though. "I'm not going anywhere."

"Stop talking, will you? You're ruining the song."

To her surprise, he did stop talking. Patiently, he waited to resume his interrogation until Paul Simon smiled, Art Garfunkel waved, and the crowd cheered.

"Where are your shoes?"

There was that fatherly tone again, the silent "young lady" inherent within.

Celia snapped her head in his direction. "An unruly mob of flower children mugged me, then disappeared into the night. Thank God you're here." She flipped her eyes away. The memory of him kissing that girl and her own juvenile reaction to it came screaming back. She feared she might cry at her own stupidity. Then he'd really win. "Go away, Jeremy."

"No."

"Why are you here? Why aren't you off with your latest conquest? Aw, is she in a restroom stall somewhere, cleaning up for the next fellow? That's too bad." Shooting him a mock pout, Celia gathered her bag and began to rifle through it.

"Ouch," Jeremy replied. Wearing a faint smile now, he scrutinized her with interest, and she hated that she liked it, that she felt such an overwhelming attraction to him. She was sick! That's what she was. Sick over a stupid man. She'd loved the boy with the sweet simplicity of a child's heart. But then the grown man had waltzed into town and flipped that love upside down, turning that sweet, innocent affection into something lurid and grown. The physical desire for the man had taken root almost immediately. But *that* she could manage.

What she couldn't manage was the intense longing she felt for his love, because when Jeremy loved, she knew, he loved absolutely. It had intimidated her as a little girl, his attentiveness, his possessiveness, his boundless devotion . . . She hadn't known how to handle it. But when he'd left and taken all those things with him, she realized that she'd come to prize those things, need them. And with every subsequent, painful experience, she required them more and more. Inside their young, naive world, he'd promised to love her forever. A guileless child, she'd believed him.

By the time she was a young woman, his promises were all that remained, and they were a comfort. She'd convinced herself that he was out there somewhere, still loving her, still fighting to get to her—that one day he'd return. He'd hold her and take it all away, the pain, the fear, and the emptiness. She'd carried that belief somewhere deep and unconscious until the night she saw him at Lovers Point, the night she discovered that his love, too, was gone. And she felt immense pain over that, while he felt nothing. She was little more than a nuisance to him. Yet, here she was, pining, overjoyed at his mere presence. There was nothing in the world more frustrating suddenly.

"If you must know," Jeremy said, "Antonia ditched me for a guy who wasn't wasting his time looking for a spoiled brat. And I can't say I blame her." He stared pointedly at Celia, daring her to retort.

But she only turned to stare back in equal measure, internally rejoicing at his "bad" news. Outwardly, she remained cool. Of course, he would take this opportunity to insult her. Since day one, he'd gone out of his way to shower her with contempt, belittling her at every turn.

Well, enough was enough.

"Daniel." Celia twisted right to face Daniel, who had at one point during a Lou Rawls performance offered her his half-smooshed peanut butter and jelly sandwich, worried that she was hungry. "It was so nice to meet you. You, too, Darlene. Would you please tell Serenity that, if I come back tomorrow, I promise to stop by her booth and buy that gorgeous paisley blouse she made?"

"Of course," Darlene answered, glancing warily at Jeremy. Celia had explained everything to her hours before. "Will you still need a ride home?"

"No, but thank you . . ." Celia explained that she had to meet up with some friends, then stood, letting her bag rake across Jeremy's face as she passed him, hoping like heck that it hurt.

The first day of the three-day festival was over, and all around them, people rose to their feet.

Jeremy stood, too. "Where are you going?"

Ignoring him, Celia moved briskly into the growing crowd. She heard him call out her name in exasperation. He was following, and that brought her a sordid sense of vindication, another disappointing reaction to add to her list of self-destructive behaviors. But for that, she could scold herself later. Right now, she would drink in the feeling of his impassioned presence at her back, closing in. The sound of her name steaming off his heated lips made her feel seen, wanted, even if in some misguided, chauvinistic way. Truly, she was sick.

"Celia! Damn it! Get back here!"

And, oh, was he mad.

Tickled by this smallest of victories, Celia picked up her pace, inhaling the charged evening air as she slipped and dodged her way forward.

It all made her glad to be alive suddenly—Jeremy enflamed and determined at her back, the stadium lights that surrounded them, the endless ocean of warm bodies, the deepening night that seemed to crackle with energy.

Celia ducked a few confused strangers. Her heart pounded wildly, sensing the mounting urgency at her back. Then the multitudes parted, and she slipstreamed into a full run.

"*Celia!*"

A glance back confirmed it—he was chasing her—and she laughed, unable to help herself. "Not so fast anymore, are ya?" she yelled back.

His footfall padded harder behind her, and Celia screamed in anticipation. When he snagged her, not far outside the watching crowd, her entire body exulted, and she didn't fight it. She let him have her, sinking back into his familiar shelter, breathing the long-overdue sigh of relief. He was furious and had no idea that his fiery condemnations were falling erotic on her ear. If there was any doubt before, it was now salt against the Monterey wind. She was insane, and she would surrender to it as long as he never let go.

Spinning her around, Jeremy held her out in front of him. "Why the hell did you run from me? You're acting crazy, you know that?"

Celia smiled.

"We're leaving," he said, gripping her hand and pulling her eastward toward the booths.

"Let go of me." With a yank, Celia freed her hand, stumbling backward.

Jeremy twisted around, his every facial feature rigid. "We're going back to the booth to meet up with everyone so we can get the fuck out of here."

"I'm not going anywhere with you," Celia said, aware of the curious eyes around them. "I left for a reason."

"Yeah, and what reason was that? To get my attention for yourself? Well, congratulations, you've got it. Let's go!"

Darkly, Celia laughed. "You think I orchestrated all of this? You think I made you kiss that girl, then took off for seven hours so you'd chase after me? Oh, I'm good, Jeremy. Pretty risky strategy, but boy, did it work out in my favor." Her false smile fell. "You're as crazy as I am if you think I'm going back there with you."

"I told you, Antonia is gone!"

"I don't care!"

Celia could see the attempt he was making to subdue himself—eyes closing for longer than necessary, inhalations deep and purposeful, hands stretched out as if he needed them for stability.

"Will you please come back with me," he said. "I'm tired, and I want to go home."

"Sure." Celia folded her arms. "If you tell me something first."

Jeremy eyed her with suspicion. "What?"

"Why you hate me so much." She swallowed down her nerves as his temples and the corners of his jaw balled and flexed. He seemed so close to answering, to spilling his guts or unleashing his disdain, the words only a lightning strike away. She would suffer all of it for a little clarity.

"You don't know when to quit, do you?"

"I don't quit," Celia said. "And you refuse to talk to me, so here we are."

"I don't want to talk to you. I can't stand the sight of you, if you want the truth."

Celia ignored the buckle in her chest and raised her chin slightly. "Well, aren't you sweet. And here I missed you while you were gone."

"Knock it off, Celia."

Celia shook her head, hell-bent on not crying. "It's the truth. I missed you." She found his green eyes comforting, soothing, even as they scorned and rejected her words. "I still do. I was terrible to you when we were kids, and I'm sorry for that. If I could take it all back, I would. I would do anything. If you'd just talk to me."

Jeremy looked away, swallowing hard. "Why are you apologizing?"

"Because I need to."

"Well, stop it."

"Or what? You can't hate me any more than you already do."

His eyes settled on hers again, and to her relief, they softened. "I don't hate you."

"Well, you certainly act like you do."

Sighing, he lowered his head. "I know, and I'm sorry for that." His eyes bolted back up to hers, full of ire again. "I didn't mean it when I said I couldn't stand the sight of you, but I don't know how else to get it through to you."

"Get what through?" He turned to walk, but she grabbed his arm and held it firm to herself. "Why do you do that? Why do you say awful things one minute, then take it back the next? I don't understand you, Jeremy. Please just answer me, and I'll walk back with you and not say another word." She hooked his pinky with hers. "I swear it."

Snapping his finger back, he frowned, but instead of anger, it was pity she saw now.

"Why does any of this shit matter to you?" he asked. "We were dumb kids. You don't need to apologize, and you shouldn't care what I think."

"But I do," Celia admitted. "I can't help it."

Jeremy didn't seem to have a good response to that. "Look, can we just get out of here?" he asked, noting the curious eyes around them.

Celia watched the way he fidgeted, the way his eyes settled on nothing, on anything but her. It was extraordinary, really, how one face, how one single set of human eyes could vault her into another lifetime, into a past so bona fide that it tumbled over her in broad waves of perfectly preserved scent and sound. All by himself, without even trying, Jeremy Hill had become the most surreal experience of her life. He was past and present, love and hate, joy and grief. She loved him, for better or worse, and he'd done it to her long ago, then left without realizing what he'd done.

"It's time to go," he said, clearly uncomfortable with the way she stared at him. In that instant, a stray wind lifted a posy of dark hair at the nape of his neck, behind his earlobe, and awakened in Celia a warm, salty memory. They were children, and high above in the silvery sky, a thunderstorm loomed. On a rock, black as granite, she and Jeremy had clung precariously, their bellies cold and wet as they bent over the edge with their arms submerged in the frothing Pacific. Its surf relentlessly veiled the family of starfish trapped below. The purple one was hers, but her arms lacked the necessary length it would take to grab it. Jeremy could reach—he'd already retrieved his own orange sea star. But she wasn't a baby anymore. She wanted to take hers for herself. So Jeremy, risking the might of the sea, anchored her to the slick rock so she could stretch safely and grab her own prize. Successful in her pursuit, she'd kissed the purple sea star and named her Celia. Jeremy teased her the whole way home. "Only a lunatic would name a starfish after themselves." But his smile had betrayed him that afternoon. He loved her for it.

"What happened to you?" Celia asked him now, more than a dozen years later, doubtful he would respond in any meaningful way.

Jeremy's gaze landed on her. "I grew up," he said.

They stood silent for another moment before Celia took the opportunity to say, "I'm sorry about your dad. I'm sorry for my part. I never got to tell you that."

"I don't want to talk about my dad."

"Are we ever going to talk about what happened?"

Jeremy shook his head.

Desire struck her, twisting and straining against the unease in his eyes. She wanted to wrap her arms around him and absorb into herself all his pain and fear and insecurity and whatever else it was inside him that made him regard her, even now, with so much anger and weight.

Celia shouldered her bag and took a deep breath. "All right," she said. "I think I understand why you don't want to talk to me. I probably wouldn't want to talk to me either. But please try to understand why I can't give up. It's not in me, and you're too important."

With a discomfited huff, Jeremy walked away but stopped to address her after a few steps. "Are you coming or not? Fletcher and Moose are worried about you."

Celia sighed. "I'm coming."

Midway back to the booth, as they walked side by side, Jeremy asked again, "Where are your shoes? Without being a smart-ass this time."

Celia stifled a smile. "In my bag."

"Are you hungry?" He asked the question like she was some alien being with habits unfamiliar to him. Was he making small talk?

"A little."

"I'll get you something to eat then."

Celia tilted her head. "Is this your version of an apology?"

"Apology for what?" he asked, looking legitimately confused. "For kissing that girl? Hell, no. I'm not sorry for that. You said you were hungry, so I'll buy you a burger. No strings."

"I'll pass, thanks." It came from a place of spite. As Celia felt her stomach rumble, she knew she was only hurting herself, but what little dignity she had left would be tastier than his pity-burger.

"Suit yourself."

"Hey," Celia said, having a thought. "Do you remember our sea stars?"

Beside her, Jeremy grimaced in question.

"Jeremiah and Celia," she prodded. "Remember? We took them from the water, but the next day my dad told us to put them back, so they wouldn't die."

Jeremy shook his head, his expression revealing the barest hint of contrition.

"That's okay," she said, smiling. "It was a good day is all."

If Celia thought Jeremy was the worst of her troubles, she'd been sorely mistaken. Fletcher was the real hornet's nest. He was livid. And not in a good way, like when Jeremy had rumbled low and hot in her ear, but the cold, spine-shivering way that had Celia recoiling. He grabbed her by the shoulders and exploded, unleashing every frustration he'd ever had with her. He'd been worried. He was about to call the police and her goddamn mother. Had she any idea what she'd put everyone through? Put him through? Did she realize how selfish and childish she was being?

Moose had only bear-hugged her and walked away. He was upset, but yelling wasn't Moose's style. It was rare for Fletcher as well, but when he did finally blow, his temper was a firestorm.

Well, so was hers.

"I am a grown woman!" Celia countered, her blood boiling over after the long day. "I have every right to go off by myself! If a man disappeared, no one would call in a search party. None of you chauvinist jerks would care. But I do it and, 'Oh, alert the press! Call in the National Guard! The *girl* is walking around without a sitter!' It's a rotten double standard, Fletcher, and you know it!"

Jeremy snorted.

"You stay out of this," she snapped at him, then turned back to Fletcher. "I'm sorry I worried you. I really am. But I will not apologize for needing to be alone."

Fletcher was not so amused with her outburst, though, and ignored her after that, denying her even the satisfaction of a retort.

They left immediately. No one spoke on the walk back to the bar. No one made eye contact on the drive back to Pacific Grove. Fletcher didn't even say good night before retiring to Bianca's old room for the night.

Celia went to bed alone, trying not to think about the fact that she and Fletcher were drifting unusually far apart, and that he seemed to be spiraling into another depression. They would make up by morning, she told herself. They always did.

The next day, Fletcher forwent the concert, as did Jeremy, who resumed renovations on his father's house.

Moose returned alone to the Pop Festival for both Saturday and Sunday's performances.

And Angie was behaving strangely. Her voice was distant over the line when Celia called. Angie swore she would explain "everything" later, then hung up.

Rather than mope, Celia spent the remainder of that unfortunate weekend on the beach with Martha and the Vandellas, the Marvelettes, the Supremes, and, her favorite, the Beach Boys.

———

In the days and weeks that followed the Pop Festival, foggy mornings progressed into clear afternoons, and then into radiant, multicolored evenings. Gulls sang their wistful song. Leaves swung playfully from their trees. The exceptional weather had Celia outdoors most days, but the solitude left her feeling lonely and blue.

The worst part was that Fletcher was avoiding her. After a silent breakfast, he'd head to the library or the Cannery in Monterey, or to the town center's little movie theater to catch the latest flick alone, flouting all her requests to come along.

Her mother wouldn't be returning from Europe for another month. Rarely did she call, but she wrote once a week. She was seeing the world with her sister, Florence—traveling by train from Denmark to Belgium, to Holland and Germany, and on a whim once, to the south of France. Celia was happy for her. Her children were grown, the love of her life long gone. It was her time now.

Helena Lynch remained a worrywart, though, and kept Luisa on her payroll to make sure her daughters had someone solid, someone who loved them, to turn to if need be. Celia was almost certain Luisa would've done it for free. But even the older woman's visits had dwindled in recent weeks and were only to make certain the house was still standing. She'd bring dinner dishes—one for her, a second for Jeremy—and money to pay the milkman and paperboy, then vacate. Her granddaughter (a pudgy baby girl with a festooned tuft of hair à la Pebbles Flintstone) kept her happily occupied.

"Behave, Celia," Luisa would instruct on her way out the door, laying a rough kiss on Celia's cheek. "Your mother doesn't need any more grief."

What sage advice Jeremy received with his casserole, Celia didn't know, but she often wondered.

Moose was also preoccupied, though he did take the time to swing by and show off his new car before vanishing from Pacific Grove. A social butterfly, he was always on the move. Before he left, he'd kissed her head, saying, "Keep your chin up, dollface. He'll come around."

Celia regretted not asking Moose to whom he was referring— Fletcher or Jeremy.

Angie's work schedule had become grueling. "I need the cash," she groaned one day over the phone. "I'm not on summer vacation like you."

Celia assumed her best girlfriend was having more troubles at home, but Angie was remarkably secretive, and Celia had learned long ago not to pry; it only made Angie clam up more. The prideful girl never accepted help anyway. Moose had learned that the hard way the day he'd snuck five twenty-dollar bills into her knapsack upon news that her electricity had been disconnected, spoiling all the food in her icebox. Wildly offended by the gift, Angie had flipped her lid. But Moose refused to take the money back, so all five bills wound up in the Pacific Ocean. The two friends didn't speak for a month, and nobody dared force charity on Angie Martin again.

Beneath the shade of a large pine, Celia lay with her cheek smashed into her arm. These summer days felt long and lonely without a summer job to keep her busy and without Fletcher to romp around and gossip with. Tired of the beach, she'd started spending more time on this spot of grass, where she ate warm plums and read playscripts, listening as Jeremy tacked away at mysterious objects across the yard. He was like a worker ant, his assignment all that mattered in the world.

Tack, tack, tack.

Pound, pound, pound.

Celia longed to walk over and talk to him, get to know him again, but his tireless rebuffs had finally started to whittle away at her resolve. Not to mention, the tree line deterred her like a castle wall. But it also provided great cover for spying, if one were so inclined (and knew precisely under which trees to crawl).

One day, she sat up and decided to collect apples from the orchard, in lieu of plums, with a plan to bake an apple pie. It didn't seem that difficult a recipe. And Fletcher liked apple pie. Maybe it would persuade him to stick around for dinner, if he came home at all before bedtime.

Grabbing her basket off the porch, Celia set out for the orchard between the Lynch and Hill properties. It wasn't large, by any means, but it was an inviting area, shady and secluded. Beyond it, the seamless line of buckeyes separated the two yards.

Tack, tack, tack . . .

Bending down to collect a fallen apple, Celia made a lame effort to peek into Jeremy's world, seeing nothing.

Pound, pound, pound . . .

She huffed, shuffling past another few trees, then crouched lower, where the noise pierced.

TACK, TACK, TACK . . .

As covertly as possible, Celia crawled between two of the thickest, low-lying yellow buckeyes, angling for a better view. A loud curse startled her, and she froze.

High on a ladder propped against the side of his house, Jeremy leaned with a thumb in his mouth. "Son of a bitch," he muttered, then picked up a hammer.

The pounding resumed.

Celia watched, rapt. He was driving strange nails into a wide, white slat, then attaching the slat to the house. One after another, he hooked on more pieces. Celia lowered her belly to the ground, sinking her cheek back into her arm. After completing a stack, Jeremy stopped to wipe his damp face with his T-shirt before climbing down off the ladder to light a cigarette.

Celia watched the meticulous way he toiled around the yard, picking up wood scraps and nails, tossing them into a tidy pile as he smoked. An empty bucket got in his way, its handle snaring his left foot, and he crossly kicked it aside, almost falling onto the seat of his pants.

Celia silenced a chuckle with her hand. Then she got an idea and ran all the way home, stopping only to tug a few lemons off the tree beside her house.

In record time, she whipped up a batch of lemonade. Her mother's glass pitcher set with the raised grapevines would look the nicest, she decided.

With the pitcher full of sugared-just-right lemonade in one hand and a matching glass in the other, Celia headed back outside.

Saying a little prayer, she breached the buckeye line and walked straight into Jeremy's yard.

It was empty.

"Hello?" Slowly, Celia continued forward. She reached his porch, with its patchy mix of old and new wood slatting, then carefully set the empty glass down and filled it with ice-cold lemonade. She garnished it with a few mint leaves fresh from her mother's garden before setting down the pitcher.

Satisfied with the presentation, she turned around to leave.

Startled, Celia jumped. "Oh, my God."

Balancing several long planks of wood on his shoulder, Jeremy stood—stopped dead in his tracks, it seemed—only a few yards away.

He eyed her coolly.

Feeling unwelcome, Celia lowered her hand from her heart and uttered a weak, "I made lemonade," before retreating into her own yard. She felt like a fool but floated home on a cloud of pure bliss. He had his lemonade, and knowing that she might have improved even a small part of his day made it all worth it.

Hours later, after another solitary dinner and mediocre dessert—she'd burned the apple pie crust—Celia made her way back to Jeremy's house to retrieve her mother's pricey glassware.

The pitcher sat on his porch, exactly where she'd left it. Untouched. The glass beside it brimmed with warm, watered-down lemonade, its mint leaf a green glob at the bottom.

"You." Celia cut through Jeremy's yard and grabbed the pitcher and glass, undaunted by the fact that Jeremy was loafing on his porch, watching her. "Why?"

Jeremy didn't respond. Instead, he took a drag from his cigarette and watched as she marched out of his yard rumbling with displeasure.

The following morning, Celia returned with the same pitcher, filled with a fresh batch of lemonade and a slice of burnt, day-old apple pie. Making eye contact, she dropped her offering on Jeremy's porch with a decisive thud before spinning on her heels to stalk off.

Again, he ignored the offering.

"What a creep," Celia groused into her sink that night as an entire batch of rejected lemonade whirlpooled away. He was ridiculous! He wouldn't even drink her lemonade!

Celia kept up her lemonade campaign for several more days, and each day, her efforts were spurned.

On day six, Celia opened the garden shed and ferreted out her mother's Radio Flyer wagon—purchased to haul heavy items. She took the hose to it, lined it with a towel, then filled it with as many drinking glasses as it would hold. In her right arm, she cradled a large, glass jug of freshly squeezed lemonade.

"What the hell are you doing?" Jeremy said as she maneuvered the wagon around him and through his yard. This time he followed her closely. "Celia?"

Oh, *now* he was speaking to her.

"Celia!"

Celia arranged the glasses, one by one, at the top of his porch steps in a wide, zigzag pattern. She poured lemonade into each glass, then settled herself into the lawn chair she'd also carried over—and not dropped!

Wearing her most dignified expression, Celia flipped down the hand-painted sign she'd fastened to the wagon: "10 cents," it read.

She watched Jeremy try to hold back a smile. "You're charging me now?" he said, crossing his arms.

Celia merely raised her eyebrows and an upturned palm.

"You're out of your mind," he said.

"Maybe." Slipping on her sunglasses, she grabbed one of the full glasses and pulled a long drink from it, gasping emphatically at the end. "But I'm not thirsty."

"Get the hell off my property, Celia." Jeremy stalked back over to his day's work. "Before I call the cops!"

"You don't have a telephone," she sang.

Jeremy was openly vexed but managed to ignore her presence and return to whatever it was he was doing. He seemed to be sanding something, more wood planks maybe. She couldn't tell from her vantage point. But no matter. She spent her day sunbathing on his overgrown, weedy lawn, reading *Valley of the Dolls*, and manicuring her nails.

It wasn't until late that afternoon that Jeremy, flushed a beet red, approached the porch steps. He hadn't hydrated himself enough, and the effects were showing.

"Why are you still here?" he asked, his disdain halfhearted.

"You're going to get sick."

"I'm not going to get sick." Even his voice lacked energy. "I'm just beat. I've been out here working since before six. Unlike you. How are your nails coming along, princess?"

"Quite nicely, actually," she said, giving them an appreciative glance. "Thanks for asking."

Once his eyes were finished rolling, they darted to the porch stairs.

"The ice is melted, but it's still good," she told him, setting her book down on her lap. "It doesn't mean I win if you drink it. It's just lemonade. I promise not to gloat too much."

Jeremy yawned and threw his weight onto the porch steps beside her. He put his head in his hands, forcibly rubbing at his face. "How does it look?"

"How does what look?"

He raised his head wearily. "The siding. I'm finished."

"Oh!" He was asking her opinion, Celia realized with astonishment. She got up and walked to the edge of the yard to give the house a proper inspection. "It's amazing," she said. "I can't believe it's the same house." The clean, white facade was welcoming and light. She could imagine green grass and porch furniture, overflowing flowerpots swinging in a breeze. "You're really good at this."

Jeremy let his head come to rest against his hands and yawned again.

Returning to his side, Celia poured a fresh glass of warm lemonade from the jug and handed it to him. "Stop being stubborn and drink it."

"*I'm* stubborn?" Jeremy took the glass and chugged the lemonade so fast that Celia had to wonder if he'd even tasted it. "Thanks," he said, eyeing the bottom of his empty glass.

"You're welcome."

He placed the cup down at his side, but he did it so sulkily that Celia knew she was going to have to assist the process along.

"Would you like some more?" she asked gingerly.

Faintly, Jeremy nodded. They sat in silence while he drank a second glass. When he was done, he lay back, his forearm over his eyes, and fell asleep.

Quietly, so as not to wake him, Celia gathered her belongings and left Jeremy on his porch.

The following morning, a little after dawn, Celia returned with the wagon of lemonade, now also stocked with food stuffs (sandwiches, cookies, and fresh fruit). Over the course of that long day, Jeremy worked up such a thirst and drank so much lemonade that she was forced to make three more batches. The food was devoured. Not much was discussed. He asked her opinion on a varnish shade, and she commented on the superb weather, but mostly he worked while she read.

On the tenth day of her campaign, Celia closed her book and raised her sunglasses to ask Jeremy what he was doing.

"Taking surface measurements of the yard," he said as he took long, even strides over his patchy, pitiful lawn.

"Why?"

"I need to know how much grass seed and fertilizer to buy."

"Aw, shit," she blurted, then immediately slapped her palms over her mouth. It wasn't ladylike to swear. Her mother and Luisa had drilled that notion into her brain since birth. But it was practically sacrilegious to swear in front of a man. Slowly, she lowered her hand, folding it gracefully over the other on her lap. "I meant to say, shoot." She wrinkled her nose. "It's going to stink out here now."

Jeremy chuckled, and Celia had to smile. It'd been eleven years since she'd made him laugh. He'd laughed! And it sounded delightful to her ears. It sounded like home, and Celia thanked God for lemons.

14

Jeremy

For an entire month, Celia Lynch loitered in his yard, shaking him down with lemonade and tasty snacks. He'd been much easier to break than he would've previously thought. That or she was less annoying. And he was lonely.

Each morning around six, she would appear from between the buckeyes in short shorts or a leggy little skirt, her red wagon piled high with temptation—homemade cookies, finger sandwiches, sliced fruit, and ice-cold lemonade.

And each damn morning, he was gladder to see her than he'd been the day before.

In the beginning, she'd kept to herself, reclining in her little chair, reading or listening to music on his transistor radio. He'd been standoffish and rude, largely because she'd ignored his demands to leave, instead plopping herself right in the middle of his business. It had always been her way, though, and he learned quickly—as he had as a kid—that it was easier to just let her have it.

On sunny days, Celia sunbathed in one of her colorful swimsuits. The yellow bikini had become Jeremy's favorite. Naturally, he found her sexy, the half-naked college girl stretched out on his front lawn. He wasn't a simp. Her smooth, sun-kissed skin left his mouth watering for a taste. Her slender curves were so tantalizing against her frame that his hands itched for a feel. The girl knew exactly what she was doing. When she'd catch him stealing a glance, she'd swiftly present him with a treat from her wagon. It began to feel like Pavlovian conditioning: ogle like a good boy, get a treat. That part was irritating, but she was appealing in so many other ways that it became harder and harder to stay irritated.

He started to look forward to her cutesy little games, to the subtle flirtation, the "accidental" touching. It gave those long, hard days some zing. He had to admire her tenacity, particularly on those days when she offered to help. Never once did she complain or give up, no matter how difficult a task he assigned her. Like the day he agreed to let her stain the front and back porches. Celia spent that humid morning sweating and mopping varnish into the slatted wood flooring, inadvertently staining herself into a corner. When she'd called out to him, he'd put his wooden swing project on hold, left the garage, and hopped onto the outside edge of the front porch.

Leaning over the railing, he had to laugh at the sight of her crouched in the corner, splotched with lacquer. "Stuck, princess?" he asked.

"Seems so. Get me out of here."

Reaching in, Jeremy lifted her over the railing, then helped her down to the ground.

"That was a lot harder than I thought it would be," she admitted, pulling the rubber band from her head. "Come to the beach with me to rinse off."

Jeremy glanced around. There wasn't much left to do outside, and he couldn't go inside for another few hours. "Okay," he said, bringing an enormous smile to her face.

"Really?" she asked. "You will?"

Jeremy had to laugh. "Don't get too excited. My company's not that stimulating."

"It is to me."

It unnerved him when she did that, when she said incredibly kind things with that sentimental glint in her eyes. His heart stirred for her in those moments, and he couldn't maintain eye contact.

Turning away from her, he headed toward the road. "C'mon. Make it quick."

Celia followed a few paces behind as Jeremy crossed Sunset Drive, which was congested with cars, putting them on the dirt path that led to the dunes, a path he'd traveled with her countless times. As kids, they'd used it daily—racing over the bridge, past the private golf course, through the scant woods, gunning for the ocean.

Once his shoes sunk into the softest sand of the dunes, Jeremy kicked them off. The beach below had a decent crowd today, a Saturday in mid-July.

"I reek of shellac," Celia complained beside him as she undressed down to her swimsuit—a conservative, black one-piece today—looking like she stepped straight out of an episode of *Gidget*, her body made for the beach. "What?" she said, reacting to his gaze.

Jeremy smiled. "I didn't say anything."

They dropped their shoes and clothing in a pile and headed for the water. The wind was strong and the water cold. Celia yelped when it rushed in over her knees.

"Don't be such a baby," Jeremy told her, wincing as the icy surf soaked through the lower half of his jeans. "It's bath water."

Celia let out a boisterous laugh. "Well, jump on in then, tough guy. I'll be right behind you."

"No, no, ladies first," he said, throwing an arm around her waist, relishing the scream it got him. He cut a path through the incoming waves and tossed her in, then hurled himself in after her. The frigid seawater pierced his skin like raw electricity. Every muscle in his body stiffened. "Jesus," he sputtered as soon as he emerged. "Shit, this is cold!"

Beside him, Celia panted through the pain and slicked her hair back. He grinned, ducking futilely when she splashed him.

"I should've known you'd do that," she said, then shoved him back into the water. "You never could help yourself."

When Jeremy emerged again, spitting salt water from his tongue, she was scrubbing her skin and hair, working to remove the sweat and lacquer. Jeremy wondered why she hadn't simply gone home to shower. Why jump in the freezing ocean? Was it to show off the new bathing suit? He did like this black one better than the others, even if it covered more skin. He'd never seen anything like it. It had a wide slice cut out of each side, from her breasts to her hips, leaving one black strip of material to run down her belly. If she knew what vulgar thoughts it triggered in him, she might not have bothered.

Back on dry sand, Celia couldn't speak. They'd stupidly forgotten towels and were forced to use their clothing, chattering and shivering as they sorted everything in the coastal wind. Her once-alluring skin was now purple and cloaked in goosebumps.

They hurried home, and without a goodbye, Celia trailed off and disappeared into her house.

The following morning, she showed up on cue with her wagon and a tray of egg salad sandwich squares.

Starving, Jeremy scarfed half of them down immediately, leaving her the rest.

"You didn't come back yesterday," he said while unwinding the hose to water his budding lawn.

"Oh." Celia settled into her chair. "Yeah, I jumped in a hot shower, then fell asleep. I figured you'd be thrilled to have me out of your hair."

She'd figured wrong—he'd watched the trees for her for the remainder of the day—but he wasn't about to cop to that.

Later that week, as Jeremy installed the wooden porch swing he'd constructed from excess lumber, Celia lolled on the porch steps, reading to him a novel called *The Outsiders* that she'd checked out from the library. He dug it so far and had taken an interest in the characters, especially Ponyboy. He could relate to the dumb kid. He could also relate to Dally, the impulsive hothead.

"What did he go and do that for?" Jeremy grumbled the moment she finished a chapter in which Dally was shot and killed by police. "What did pointing an empty gun at the cops prove? All he got was dead."

"He was angry," Celia said.

Tightening a screw, Jeremy shook his head, then dropped his arms to look at Celia. "The police don't give a shit how he feels. Nobody does."

"I think that's the point. Dally was fed up with being . . . outsiders. They're poor and uneducated and nobody cares about them, and now Johnny's dead. He snapped."

Jeremy grunted. He understood, but he didn't have to like it. It's why he didn't read. Stories where underdogs stayed underdogs, where winners win and losers lose pissed him off. It was too much like real life.

Tossing his screwdriver into his toolbox, he hopped off the step stool and moved it aside to give Celia a better view of the mounted swing. "What do you think?"

"You're done?" Celia climbed to her feet and walked over. "Oh, it's perfect!"

"Give it a try."

With clear excitement, Celia turned and backed gingerly over the seat. Then she paused, hesitant to set her weight down.

"Go on," Jeremy said, laughing. "Don't you trust me?"

"I do." Setting her bottom down, Celia lifted her feet. The swing creaked. Shooting him a smile of relief, she patted the empty spot beside her. "Come on, sit. It'll hold both of us, right?"

"It should." They both eyed each other, faces tense, as Jeremy lowered himself onto the slatted seat. The chair creaked and chirped when he lifted his work boots off the porch floor. Then he and Celia were swinging freely, grinning at each other.

"And you were nervous," Jeremy teased.

Celia laughed. "Was not."

Relaxing, he threaded his fingers at the back of his head and watched her merriment ease into contentment, her brown eyes tranquil on something in the distance.

"Want to go watch the sunset from the dunes?" she asked him.

"Nah, I'm beat. I'll catch the view from my roof."

"I was going to ask about that. Aren't you afraid of falling off?"

"No. Haven't you ever sat on a roof before?" Jeremy couldn't believe his eyes when she shook her head. With a disgruntled huff, he stood and trotted down the steps of his porch, waving her over. "C'mere."

Reluctantly, Celia stood. "I don't think—"

"Come here."

She pointed. "Where? Up there?

"Yeah. You're coming up with me."

"But—"

"No 'buts.'" Jeremy grabbed the ladder lying against the side of the house and heaved it up against the edge of the roof. "Up you go."

When Celia reached his side, they looked up toward the lowest section of the roof, above the porch. She shot him a dubious squint. "I thought you use your bedroom window."

"I do," he said, thinking of the wall of shame in there that he still hadn't painted over. "But you don't. Start climbing."

He watched Celia look up with a deep scowl and wondered what she was thinking. Her lips bunched and twisted. Her brow furrowed. Was she angry with him, nervous?

"Would you be right behind me?" she asked.

Jeremy smiled. "If you want me to be."

"Okay, but . . ." Celia inched toward him and lifted her eyes to him, whispering, "I've never climbed a ladder before either."

Realizing she was scared, he almost caved and offered his window. But how to explain the blindfold she'd have to wear . . .

But then Celia stepped forward to wedge one sandaled foot on the bottom rung of the ladder, casting him a wary glance before beginning her climb.

Jeremy moved in directly behind her and secured the ladder with both hands.

On the third rung, Celia's hand flew down to press her dress to the back of her thighs. "No looking up my dress," she said, making Jeremy laugh and the ladder shake. "Oh!" She stiffened. "It's not going to tip, is it?"

"It might wobble some, but it's sturdy. Just take your time. I'm right behind you."

Rung by rung, Celia climbed, but when her chest came even with the edge of the roof, she looked down and tensed. "I can't," she said, then started to climb back down.

Halfway beneath her, Jeremy didn't budge. "You're not going to chicken out now, are you?"

"Of course not," she blustered, turning back to the roof. "Now what?"

"Keep climbing till you can crawl onto the roof. Keep your center of gravity low. Then sit down till I get up there."

Jeremy stuck to her as closely as possible as she followed his instructions.

Seconds later, he stepped onto the roof. "See? You did it, and I only had to look up your skirt twice."

Celia smacked him playfully. "It's just my bathing suit underneath. Degenerate."

"Scoot up here." Jeremy walked toward the pitch of the roof. "The view's better." He sat in his usual spot, resting his elbows on his knees.

With ladylike prudence, Celia mimicked his movements until she was seated likewise beside him.

"Pretty nice, huh?" he said.

Celia nodded, taking in the vista. "Hey, you can see my house from here." After several minutes of watching the sun dissolve into the Pacific, she nudged him. "Would now be a good time to finally talk?"

"We've been talking," Jeremy said, feeling trapped suddenly.

Celia made a face. "Not about anything important. I know you don't want to talk about your dad, so I thought, maybe, we could start small, get to know each other, like . . . What's your favorite color?"

"My favorite color," Jeremy mimicked, chuckling at the juvenile question. "That's what you consider important?"

He was on the verge of teasing her more when he realized she was being serious. There was a pure, hopeful quality to her expression that he couldn't bring himself to crush.

Jeremy sighed. "I don't know, I guess blue."

Her shoulders rising to her cheeks, Celia smiled. "Blue is my favorite, too," she said. "I think it's because of the ocean and the sky. Otherwise, it'd be yellow." She rocked a little on her bottom. "This is nice. What's your favorite food?"

With a grin, Jeremy shook his head. "Probably steak and potatoes."

"Still? Well, mine," she said, pressing a hand to her chest, "is chocolate milkshakes."

"That's not food." Jeremy watched the swift downturn of her mouth with fascination. Her lips looked fuller than usual today, lusher, and he was pretty sure he would disintegrate into dust if he didn't taste them soon. Over the weeks, what had started as a simple, neanderthal desire had grown into an ugly, stinging demand. It was one he'd never encountered before because with every other girl, he'd made his move (with either success or failure) and gotten it over with, sparing himself this senseless torture. But he'd decided weeks ago that that kind of cavalier attitude would be unwise with Celia. He had no idea how her kiss might affect him. It could send him hurtling back to a place he had no business going. Or worse, make him want to stay there.

Better not to kiss her at all. There were other girls to kiss, other lips to fetishize.

"Sure it is," Celia said in response to him. "It's milk and fruit. Some even argue that chocolate is a vegetable . . . Your turn. Ask me anything."

Clearing his head of the image of her lips sucking milkshake through a straw and trying like hell to ignore the fact that her arm was brushing lightly against his, giving him tingles, Jeremy asked the only question his gutter-born mind was capable of conjuring. "Uh . . . I don't know, what's your favorite television program?" Damn, he was an idiot.

"Oh, that's easy. *Bewitched*," she answered, then cocked her head at his response. "What?"

Jeremy appraised her, transfixed on her face. He recalled, as he had the day of the Pop Festival, that her nose twitched like Samantha Stevens's whenever she was upset. He wondered if she was aware of it. Surely, someone had told her by now. Her nose was perfectly still now, though, which told him she was happy, if not a little confused by the way he was staring.

Jeremy forced himself to blink. "Nothing."

"All right . . . Oh, I thought of a good question. How did you know what Luisa was saying that morning in your kitchen? How did you learn Spanish? Luisa rarely spoke it to us as kids."

Jeremy found himself enjoying her intense interest in him. "My granddad—my mom's dad—had a few ranchers working for him. Mexican guys. They'd talk about me, right in front of me, calling me *pendejo, cabrón*, saying *que la chingada* and *vales verga*. I couldn't figure out what the hell they were saying. It drove me so nuts that I went to the library and checked out a Spanish-to-English dictionary. But none of those phrases were in it. Then I met a woman at our county fair who spoke Spanish. She helped me with the cuss words, and I started talking their shit right back to them."

Celia's eyes widened. "Were they mad?"

Jeremy snorted. "No. They thought it was hilarious, me trying to speak Spanish. We got along fine after that. I'm not fluent, but I can hold my own with those guys now."

A warm, sweet smile illuminated Celia's face against the orange glow of sunset, and Jeremy once again fought back the urge to kiss her.

She turned her attention back to the horizon, asking, "Are the sunsets pretty in Tennessee?"

It took Jeremy a second to snap out of his trance. "Yeah." Taking a deep breath, he rubbed his face, then rested his back against the roof. "My mom took me to visit her cousin in Virginia Beach once, though. They have killer sunrises there. I think it's the water. It makes the sunrises better on the east coast and the sunsets better on the west."

"I'm glad I'm on the west coast then," Celia replied. "I'm not normally a morning person." She straightened her legs out in front of her. "I've never even been outside California. My mom almost took me to Copenhagen for my cousin's wedding a few years ago, but I caught the flu and had to stay home with Luisa."

"Copenhagen. That's where your parents are now, right?" Jeremy knew full well her father wasn't in Denmark, but it bugged him that she still hadn't told him herself about her father's death. Not one damn word. "Celia?"

She stared at the disappearing sun. "My . . . um . . . my mom's there. I told you that."

"And your dad?" he prompted, popping onto his elbows, intently watching her face. "I'd like to talk to him."

Jeremy caught the thick roll of Celia's throat as she pulled her knees back up to her chest.

"He would've loved to talk to you." She pressed her palms to her eyes. "He missed you."

Sitting up fully, Jeremy set his palm to her back. "Celia, I already know—"

"It's getting late," she said abruptly and stood. "I should go."

"Wait." Jeremy reached out, alarmed that she was standing, not paying attention to her footing as she scurried toward the ladder. "Slow down. You can't—"

As Celia turned to face him, she slipped, fell, and went sliding on her belly with a yelp, feet first, toward the edge of the roof.

Lunging forward, Jeremy tried to grab her hand but missed, his heart leaping into his throat as her legs disappeared over the edge.

But then, astoundingly, she stopped herself. Her body, from her hips to her head, lay flat against the shingles, her hands clasped low at her sides.

Sliding down, Jeremy helped her swing her legs back up onto the roof and then collapsed beside her.

"Holy shit," he breathed at the sky, his heart pounding. "Are you all right?"

Celia lay beside him, hyperventilating. "I think I got roof burn."

Trying to calm his aching heart, Jeremy shut his eyes. "Fletcher told me about your dad."

Celia continued her rapid breathing.

Jeremy rolled his head to frown at her. "Why didn't you tell me?"

Her red face soured on him. "When exactly was I supposed to do that? When you were threatening to call the cops on me or when you were pretending I don't exist?"

Jeremy sighed, feeling like a real *pendejo* now. "What happened to him?"

Celia opened her mouth but closed it again, then sat up. "Help me down."

"No. You wanted to talk. Let's talk. What happened to him?"

"I'll figure it out myself then," she said, reaching for the ladder.

"Damn it."

Muddled by her rapid shift in demeanor, Jeremy helped her down the ladder, which turned out to be much harder than helping her up. He reached the bottom before she did and relieved her of the last few rungs, lifting her to the ground.

Instead of releasing her, though, he wound an arm around her and tugged her close. "Please, will you just tell me?"

Freeing herself with a shove, Celia muttered a terse, "Good night, Jeremy," then vanished through the buckeyes.

The next morning, she was there with her wagon, wearing a long, flowing skirt and behaving as if nothing out of the ordinary had happened the evening before.

"Cookie?" she offered with a bright smile.

"For breakfast?" Jeremy asked, happy to chase a subject matter that wouldn't scare her off. If nothing else, he wanted her to stay.

And if that meant talking cookies and favorite colors, that's what he would do.

"Sure, why not?" Celia waved the cookie in front of his nose. "Mmm. It's chocolate chip."

Accepting the cookie, Jeremy took a bite. It was warm and chewy in his mouth. He watched her perfect, hope-filled face with a smile and ate cookies with her until it was time to work.

15

Fletcher

It was late afternoon, and Fletcher sat on Celia's old tire swing, patting the soles of his shoes against a watery, top layer of mud. Life as he knew it seemed to dangle by a thread, swiveling and whirling like the twin ropes of that swing, keeping him disoriented. Several yards away, a ray of sunlight caught his eye as it splintered against the tips of her fingers. Water ricocheted into a shower of iridescent light while she braced herself against the aquatic siege and screamed Jeremy's name.

Fletcher winced at her delight. It physically hurt.

He couldn't see Celia fully. Her back was to him. But he could see Jeremy, who was dressed in his dead father's checkered gardening shorts and a straw fedora, grinning triumphantly, his expression growing stern as he released the crimp in the hose, his thumb pressed to its nozzle. Water shattered once again in every direction, the radiance of the evening sun kicking off the droplets like a thousand tiny mirrors. Celia screamed his name again, her body and clothing soaked, her fair hair dark and in wet chunks against her cheeks.

A safe distance from the deluge, Moose's eyes shined with intent.

Though bulky in stature, he took off like a ninety-pound sprinter and, within seconds, had Angie by the waist, swinging her body around to face the others, triggering another concerto of high-pitched shrieks. "Spray 'er!" he commanded Jeremy. "Do it!"

"No!" Angie screeched. "My hair! I have to work later!"

"No, you don't, liar," Moose said. "Get her, man, and get her good!"

Happy to oblige, Jeremy rereleased the hose, dousing Angie this time (and, thus, Moose) with the freezing-cold spray.

"Celia!" Angie screamed, trying to block it. "Help!"

Celia did as her friend asked, seizing the hose Jeremy held in order to execute a perfect alligator roll, twisting against his grip, using the awkward angle to her advantage. Her back was to him now, his arms stretched around her, his fists gripped to the hose, caging her.

Then Jeremy whispered something in her ear and made her laugh.

Fletcher felt his heart drop into his belly. He wondered when their relationship had changed. Last he knew, Jeremy and Celia weren't speaking. Then again, Fletcher had spent the last month distancing himself from them both. He watched them now, captivated by the thinly veiled bliss on Jeremy's suntanned face. With Celia pressed against him (while they pretended to wrestle over the hose), Jeremy nuzzled her neck, then shook his head for a tickle, making her squirm as laughter bubbled out of her. They were enjoying the physical contact. That much was obvious.

It shamed Fetcher to be this excruciatingly jealous. He wasn't even sure of whom he was more jealous: Celia or Jeremy. What kind of friend was he to feel this way? He used to think himself a good person. A friendly, thoughtful, selfless (most of the time, anyway) kind of fellow. But it seemed he was *this*, a bitter, spiteful lump on a tire swing. And nobody liked a bitter lump. Nobody.

Fletcher watched Jeremy regain control over the hose and douse Celia. When she should have been running away—the hose was stretched to its limit—she futilely blocked and shrieked instead.

The entire scene may as well have been playing at the drive-in for as far as it was from him. He couldn't relate at all, not in its current manifestation. First, there was Jeremy, who could not stop touching Celia whenever an opportunity presented itself, a girl who had, only a month before, been his sworn enemy. Then there was Moose, whose eyes lingered shamelessly on Angie's breasts and hips without so much as a reproachful side-eye from her. In fact, she seemed to revel in the attention. Friends were friends, but in the summertime, in the after-noon heat, the sexuality of people rose like a mirage off a blacktop. It flowed so readily between them, and not one cared to hide it. If they only knew how fortunate they were to live with that kind of freedom.

As another symphony of glass-shattering squeals rang out, two tee-ny-weeny, crystal-clear droplets of water landed on the right lens of Fletcher's eyeglasses, directly in his line of sight. Miffed, he removed the glasses, sightlessly buffed the water out with his shirt, then hooked them back over his ears, deciding that this was the universe's way of telling him it was time to go.

He pressed his shoes into the watery mud and stood.

Trying to ignore the cold splashes against his sock-covered ankles, he headed across the yard toward Celia's house.

"Where ya goin'?" Angie shouted. "Fletch!"

When Fletcher looked back, she was jogging toward him in her soaking wet clothes.

"Getting my keys," he said, still walking. "We need a few things from the market for dinner."

"Are you all right?" she asked as he trotted up the porch steps, kicked off his shoes, and opened the screen door.

"Never better."

After grabbing his car keys, Fletcher went into the linen closet and grabbed four towels. When he returned outside, Angie was still on the porch waiting for him.

He handed her a towel, then hung the remaining three over the railing before slipping back into his damp shoes.

"I want to know what's going on," Angie said, drying herself off while she followed him to his car. "Why aren't you and Celia talking?"

Fletcher opened the driver's-side door and twisted around,

propping his elbow atop the door frame. "There's no talking to her right now. She's too fixated on you-know-who."

"You can talk to me. I'm a good listener. There's a reason I get the best tips at the diner. And it's not by shaking my ass like Betty."

Fletcher snorted. "I know. I'm just used to talking to Celia when I'm down. She knows what to do. What to say. But I can't talk to her anymore. She's—I don't know, maybe I'm just feeling sorry for myself."

Angie appeared hurt by his response. But she was trying to hide it, and he felt awful. "Well, what does she say to make you feel better?" she asked. "What does she do? Maybe I can help."

Fletcher nearly choked on his own spit. "There's no one thing," he said, clearing his throat. He was lying. But the truth was far worse than the lie. The truth was: Celia enabled him. She sheltered the coward inside him. She supplanted his perilous lust by kissing, stroking, and sucking him until he convinced himself that he liked it.

Fletcher loved Angie, but like a sister. He wouldn't want her to do such things. How could he explain that to her? Confess to the unspeakable acts that he and Celia had carried out in the name of experimentation? Admit that it was boys he preferred? No, not boys . . . Men. Rugged, physical men like the sinewy, sun-kissed surfer who frequented Asilomar Beach in the summertime or the strong, curly haired stock boy from the grocery store—or Jeremy Hill. And not girls like Angie or even Celia. He could barely admit those truths to himself, let alone her. Angie would never speak to him again. He had no doubt about that.

"Do you want me to talk to her for you?" she asked him now.

"No." Fletcher kissed her cheek, then ducked into the driver's seat of his car. He smiled as Angie raised a single hand and then tightened the towel around herself. He set the gear in reverse and backed down the driveway.

From the sparkling wet lawn, Moose threw a hand up to him, while nearby Jeremy continued to hijack Celia's attention. Both were in high spirits, poking at each other, still wrangling over the hose.

Tired of looking at them, Fletcher backed onto the road. His beloved shelter had blown away with the summer wind, leaving him exposed, bitter, and terrified beyond belief. Crying about it would not bring her back. He was going to have to figure this out on his own.

Minutes later, Fletcher pulled into the parking lot of the spherical Purity Market building. Folded inside his pocket sat Celia's grocery list: a head of lettuce, three tomatoes, two cucumbers, five sirloin steaks, five large potatoes, bread, flour, sugar, two bottles of Diet Rite, toilet paper, and toothpaste.

Inside the store, the aisles were busy with shopping homemakers, stocking up for their weeknight dinners of pot roast, Salisbury steak, and meat loaf. In the "oven ready" section of frozen foods, the Swanson TV dinners were on sale—"2 for a dollar!"—so Fletcher grabbed two: a fried chicken dinner with mashed potatoes and mixed vegetables and the chopped sirloin beef with peas and fries. He thought about how annoyed Celia would be when she saw them and smiled to himself, dropping them in his basket.

Though tempted, he'd refused to eat her homemade dinner offerings for a month now. She was trying to have it both ways, using food of all things. She fed Jeremy daily, luring him in like a stray cat, while she tried to pacify Fletcher, presenting him with all his favorite crumbs: fresh, fried fish, chicken à la king, her mom's famous lamb stew, apple pie à la mode, freshly baked cookies—the bribery went on and on. But he'd denied her the satisfaction of watching him eat it.

He wondered when he'd become so spiteful.

As Fletcher left the frozen foods aisle, he saw *him* (the reason he'd chosen this market and not another) stocking the "Oriental foods" display. Tightly curled, black hair with natural, sun-bleached highlights; smooth skin as dark as Moose's, maybe a shade darker; eyes that pierced in honied gold. He looked magnificent as usual, stacking cans of teriyaki sauce and chicken chop suey in perfect symmetry, labels facing out. His hands—manly, calloused, with bulging tendon and bone—could've been displayed in a museum somewhere, knocking vacationers back with their excellence. "Gorgeous," the gawkers would whisper to each other. "Virile. California truly has it all."

But his arms, Adonis-like in their potency, put his hands to shame. His physique, his face, his mouth, the intensity of his concentration . . . Fletcher couldn't help but be drawn in. And since he couldn't approach Charlie T.—his name, according to the name tag—Fletcher could only assign a personality to the boy who seemed unaware of his own allure or of how appealing his lips were when they parted or folded inward, shining like a beacon in the middle of this lackluster grocery.

The summer before, Fletcher had composed a modest fantasy, starring himself and Charlie T. Alone in Bianca's old bed, he would close his eyes and imagine driving past the market in the evening hours after closing . . .

The handsome, curly haired clerk walks home as he usually does, but on this imaginary night there's rain, and Fletcher, who is fearless and bold in his fantasy, seizes the opportunity. A regular white knight, he pulls to the side of the road, leans over, rolls down his window, and offers Charlie T. a ride. Charlie accepts, thanking Fletcher profusely. Soaked to the bone, he slides into the passenger seat, apologizing for his wetness, for ruining Fletcher's leather seats as he shuts the passenger door. But Fletcher isn't bothered. He's a gentleman, a gracious host, and offers Charlie T. a towel (he would need to remember to keep one in his car from now on).

"Where are you headed?" he asks Charlie T., and Charlie directs him to a small, humble house, where he lives alone (because that suited the fantasy best). Pulling into the driveway, Fletcher sets his car in park and politely smiles. Charlie T. returns the gesture, expressing gratitude for the ride, and then everything goes quiet, except for the gentle pelt of rain and the electricity that sizzles between the two of them, a sensation that burns as hot and bright as a fleet of meteors passing though the atmosphere. Oh, the awkwardness, the cascading rain, the sweet anticipation . . . Does Charlie T. feel it, too?

"Would you like to come inside for a drink?" Charlie asks, sending Fletcher's heart spiraling.

"Sure, why not?" Fletcher responds, playing it cool.

Inside, Charlie picks up a few messes, dishes and dirty laundry, his nervousness charming. He hadn't expected company, he says.

Fletcher's sure he's seen this in a film once, though he can't recall the name. Charlie T. plays his part flawlessly. He's even more remarkable in this light as he moves toward Fletcher, their eyes meeting. *Will he?* Fletcher wonders. *Oh, God, please.* Charlie T. gives him a smile, then leans close, and shuts his eyes. Fletcher shuts his own. The mouth that presses against his is so soft and warm, so vital to his existence suddenly, that it breaks his heart. If Charlie T. could only read Fletcher's mind and understand how perfect Fletcher finds him, how utterly relieved Fletcher feels at his kiss. In time, they move into a bedroom, onto a plush, welcoming bed, where Fletcher spends the hours showing him, loving him, feeling restored and alive until the morning arrives to remind him that none of it had been real.

It was a whimsy Fletcher returned to often, in some form or another, and each time, the high was worth the inevitable fall back to reality.

As Fletcher approached "Oriental foods," Charlie T. turned from his display to face him.

Fletcher froze.

Setting down the last of his teriyaki sauce cans, Charlie T. said, "Can I help you?"

"Uh . . ." Fletcher fumbled with the grocery list. Clearing his throat, he shoved his glasses to the bridge of his nose. "Toothpaste," he read, then looked up at Charlie T.'s exquisite face. "Toothpaste."

"Aisle three," Charlie T. said, his tone professional, before grabbing his pushcart to walk away.

Fletcher mumbled his thanks and headed for aisle three, admonishing himself the entire way. Toothpaste. What an idiot.

After snatching a tube of Gleem from the bin, then finding the remaining items on the list, he sulked his way to the front of the store. Why couldn't he put a coherent sentence together around this guy? Even a simple 'Hello, how are you doing today?' would work, something to start a conversation, to establish, at the very least, a passing acquaintance. How did people do that? How did Moose do it with such ease?

At the register, as Fletcher handed the cashier a twenty-dollar bill, Charlie T. walked over to bag his items, then handed him the overfull paper sack with a trained, "Thank you for shopping at Purity Market."

While Fletcher waited for his change, Charlie T. moved to another line to bag more groceries. Fletcher tried like hell not to watch him but was unsuccessful, glancing over once, then twice, and then for a third, lengthier bit of time. The boy noticed with a scowl, and Fletcher lowered his head, mortified.

He took his change from the cashier and shoved it in his pocket. "Thank you." He absentmindedly searched out his crush once again, triggering Charlie T. to approach as Fletcher walked out.

"Hey." Charlie T. seized Fletcher's arm. "You got a problem with me, Poindexter?" His voice was tense, his expression bitter. "You come in here every day and stare. What's the deal?"

Behind him, the shoppers, all locals, tried to decipher the quiet exchange.

"No. No problem," Fletcher said, holding back vomit as his eyeglasses slid down his nose and his heart thrashed.

Charlie T. only glowered in response, and the local women began to whisper to each other.

"I'm leaving," Fletcher said. "There's no problem. Thank you again for your help."

With a dubious squint, Charlie T. backed up a step, letting Fletcher's arm go, and Fletcher rushed, stumbling, to his car before any more unanswerable questions could be posed. He jumped into the driver's seat, slammed the door shut, and hurriedly started the car. As he peeled out of the parking lot, he broke into sobs, knowing he would never return. He was a pathetic, repulsive fool.

16

Celia

When Bianca pulled into the driveway and hopped out of her car, Celia took off running. "Bianca!" She lunged at her grinning sister, hugging her as they stumbled back together.

But then Bianca forced Celia away and brushed herself off. "Why are you all wet?"

"Just having some fun." Celia beamed. "What are you doing here?" She assessed Bianca's attire. Silken, undefined layer upon layer of clashing color and pattern, topped with a floppy, wide-brimmed hat. Bianca never used to cover this much skin. "What are you wearing? You look . . . different."

"No, what are you wearing? One of Mommy's doilies?" Bianca poked around at Celia's bikini top. "Where's the rest of it?"

"What," Celia said. "I've got shorts on."

"Barely."

"Why are you home?"

"I'm on my way down to LA to look for a new pad." Bianca's

smile faded a bit as she leaned close to whisper, "I need to borrow money from Mom."

"Mom's gone." The drugs had definitely burned through a good portion of her sister's brain cells. "And I'm broke. I'm not working at the Cannery this summer."

"She'll be home tomorrow." Bianca put her arm around Celia's shoulder. She steered her toward the front of the house where Moose and Jeremy stood talking. "I'm picking her up from the airport in the morning."

Celia snorted. "Your brain is like fried chicken. She doesn't come back until August seventh."

"Uh, Earth to Celia. Today's the sixth . . . Who is that?"

Celia did a little calendar math in her head, then gasped. It *was* the sixth! She pondered the date a moment before she looked up and realized that Bianca's attention was transfixed on Celia's most cherished would-be possession.

"That is Jeremy," Celia said sharply. "I told you he was back when you called."

"Yes, you did. But you never mentioned that he was all grown up."

Celia gritted her teeth. "I swear it on that stupid, floppy hat, I will gouge your eyes out with a spoon if you make a move on him."

Stunned, Bianca smiled. "Chill out. I'm only looking."

"Bianca!" Moose yelled happily from across the yard.

"Moose!" Slapping her hands together, Bianca let out a big chuckle. "I didn't know you'd be here tonight." She and Celia approached Moose. A few yards back, Jeremy rolled up the hose. Angie had gone inside to put on dry clothes, while Fletcher sulked in the kitchen, having returned upset, for some reason, from the grocery store. He wouldn't talk to a soul, not even Celia, and she felt useless.

Moose scooped Bianca up into a hug so zealous that she was lifted off her feet.

"I've come to check on my kid sister," she said, patting his arms as he lowered her to the ground. "I heard she's out of control."

"When isn't she?" Moose was enamored with Bianca, as usual, his smile that of a kid in a candy store.

Celia fluttered her eyes. She hated when the two of them got together. Their favorite pastime was to pick on her.

"You've got to catch me up on the Haight," Moose said, his expression turning serious. "I haven't been up in weeks. What's the skinny?"

Bianca groaned. "It's crowded. It's really bringing the heat." She looked at Celia, then back at Moose. Her eyes held a secret. "I have something for you," she said.

Celia knew what the "something" was. She was no dummy. She'd never smoked grass herself but was seriously considering it. Not because she craved the high—a high she had no knowledge of, except through Moose's many warped accounts—but because her curiosity had grown into a strong, persuasive voice that made some very valid points. The people around her who were partaking seemed to be enjoying themselves immensely, and life—*youth* more specifically—was short. Once she was married with children, experimenting with illicit drugs would no longer be an option. There would be too much to lose. It was now or never. If only she weren't so chicken.

Moose inspected the contents of a hemp satchel Bianca opened for him and smiled appraisingly. "Remind me why we haven't fallen madly in love yet?"

"Because I would break your tender little heart, and you know it."

He laughed, draping his arm around Bianca's shoulder. "Come on, we're having a cookout."

A few steps later, Bianca stopped, having come face to face with the past. She gave Jeremy a wide, toothy, movie star smile. "Jeremy," she squealed. "Do you remember me?"

"Of course, I remember you," he said, stepping over the hose to get to her. "How've you been?"

Screaming her delight, Bianca threw herself at Jeremy, surprising him, surprising both Celia and Moose, and hugged him tightly. When they separated, Bianca was shaking her head at him in disbelief. She slapped his shoulders twice. "Wow. Just far out! I have so many questions. God, you filled in. I can see why my sister's been throwing herself at you." Her hand made a sweep over his chest. "You're a little bit of a sexpot, aren't you?"

"Bianca!" Celia was mortified. Her sister put on this act with every man she encountered, young and old, because she could, and Celia was ready to knock her lights out. Jeremy was off limits, and she damn well knew it.

"Well, he is." Bianca dismissed her younger sister, then gave Jeremy a wink. "You are." Celia tugged on her sister's hair. "Ow!" Bianca yelped. "What is with you today?"

Rubbing the back of his head, Jeremy fought back a smile. "I should split. I've got work to do." He smirked at Bianca as he passed her. "I'll see you."

Bianca watched him go. "Not if I see you first, sexpot."

"Tramp," Celia bit, giving her sister a little push.

But Bianca only laughed as Celia trailed after Jeremy through the partially shaded orchard, quickly catching up. "Are you coming for dinner?" she asked him. "You never said."

"Oh." He stopped, letting her come around to face him. "No, probably not."

"But we're going to barbecue on the back patio," she said. "Steak and potatoes, your favorite."

"Yeah, I know, but I've got a lot to do. I wasted the whole day out here."

Celia was glad about that. He'd abandoned his own work that morning to spend the day helping her with her yard work. He'd never been so flirtatious, so generous with his attention. There was a moment, when they were breathless and wrangling with the hose, that she thought he might kiss her. His eyes had fallen to her mouth, then rose to make intimate contact with hers. She welcomed it, but it never came, and the moment passed. She'd smiled shyly afterward, and he'd smiled back with those same soft eyes. Whatever had passed between them was probably good enough, sweet enough to last her a lifetime, but she was greedy and wanted more, so much more.

"But everybody's here," she said. "You should come. There's plenty of food, and Moose brought beer—" The moment the word flew from her mouth, she realized her gaffe. "Or I can make more lemonade."

Jeremy didn't respond right away. His eyes simply drifted between hers. She must have looked pathetic and hideously desperate, but a smile crept across his lips anyway. "Yeah, okay," he said. "I'll be back later. I have some things to do first."

"Great! I'll wait with you."

"You don't have to do that."

"I want to."

Jeremy laughed. "You're really pushy. Has anyone ever told you that?"

"No."

He laughed again, walking toward his house. "You're pushy, and you're a liar."

He grinned back at her, his tone playful, so she started to walk with him.

"Well, I figure if I wait with you, we can walk back together," Celia shrugged, widening her own smile. "It'll be fun. We're friends, right?"

He stopped, his expression turning serious. "Celia—"

"Jeremy," she said in her sweetest voice.

His brows knit curiously at her. Any other boy and her hopes might have been dashed by the vinegary contortion, but this was her Jeremy. She didn't let the minorly skeptical expression deter her; she was too committed to the hope that at any moment he'd cave, pull her into his arms, and declare his undying love.

"Never mind," he said. "C'mon."

Once inside his house, Jeremy directed her to sit on the couch in the otherwise empty family room. "Wait right here," he told her. "I'm going to go take a quick shower and change. Don't move. And don't touch anything. There are loose tools all over the place. Sharp ones."

"I won't touch a thing," Celia promised, straightening her back and crossing her hands on her lap in mock obedience.

He turned on his transistor radio, to keep her occupied, she guessed. "I'm serious, Celia."

"You always are, Jeremy. It's one of my favorite things about you." Boy, was she laying it on thick.

Though he looked mildly suspicious, Jeremy left her there and disappeared up the stairs.

Legs crossed, the bare ball of her left foot slapping against the shiny wood floor, Celia waited with antsy impatience, deaf to the music meant to keep her entertained.

She'd never been inside this house before. The family room was eerily stark, aside from the couch she sat on and an old coffee table on which the radio broadcast a glum Animals song. What did he do here at night? There were no books or magazines, no television or telephone.

A sudden hiss startled her. The shower.

A memory came forward.

This room.

She *had* been in it before.

No. She'd been standing outside, looking in through the window. It had been night, and the only light in the room was filtered through a dingy lampshade. *The Adventures of Jim Bowie* on a TV set. Everything felt murky in memory, dirty. The memory itself, sinister. Upon its arrival, Celia caught a chill, wishing Jeremy would hurry.

Against his wishes, she stood and began to explore. Straight ahead were two large, wide-open windows, and to the right was another smaller window. The two large windows looked out onto the yard, onto the buckeye trees. Walking farther, Celia met up with the front door. The foyer flowed into another room—intended to be a dining room, she presumed—which had three additional windows that looked out onto the porch.

As she stepped farther inside the dining room, she followed the sight line of those porch windows back into the kitchen. He'd been hit there. A large, vicious fist had been driven into his young face, causing his head to bounce against the refrigerator door.

Allowing herself to remember for the first time in years, Celia brought her hands to her mouth and nose. She loathed this house. It didn't matter that it appeared new with fresh paint and a shiny wood floor. The past squatted like a toad here. Its ugliness percolated through the walls to touch her with ice-cold fingers. Another facet of the memory struck her as hard as that fist had Jeremy. He'd escaped his father to find her out on the porch. His eyes had been round with fear, his skin gray. Blood trickled through the tiny cracks of his lips.

Celia backed out of the dining room and tripped over a machine made of metal. Had he whispered her name with those bloody lips, or had she dreamed that part? Something tingled against the back of her neck in answer, making her pivot around.

Fear took over, pushing her up the stairs toward Jeremy, the urgency traveling like a shiver up her spine. The farther she got from the refrigerator, from that hellish room, the better.

She reached the upstairs hallway and found the bathroom door. Drawn by the dull, humid sizzle, she pressed her forehead against it, telling herself not to knock, that she was being ridiculous.

Taking a deep breath, Celia pushed herself away from the door and inched down the hall to peer into one of the bedrooms. A double-sized mattress lay in the far corner beside a window, a royal-blue blanket tucked neatly at the corners. Two clean, white pillows lay piled at the head of the bed.

Beside the bed, a lamp sat on the floor, and next to it was an open suitcase filled with clothing and other items. The reminder made her heart sink. His stay would be brief.

Celia surveyed the room. It had been his when he was young. She remembered from the position of the window against the house, remembered waving to him once when he was in trouble, him climbing out to see her, the beating he'd gotten for defying his father, the bruises that lasted weeks, turning from bluish purple to the exact olive shade of his eyes.

Her curiosity on fire, Celia burned to touch his things, inhale his pillow and clothes, but she was restricted by time and a bourgeoning sense of shame.

His warning loomed like a dark cloud over her head. "Don't move . . . don't touch anything . . . I'm serious, Celia . . ."

While her ears monitored the trickle of the shower, Celia calculated the amount of time she had. Her own showers took approximately thirty minutes. His shower would probably take half that. Fifteen minutes tops, and it had already been five.

She gave herself a minute or two.

Celia scooted over to the suitcase and knelt to examine its contents. Oh, this is wrong, wrong, wrong, she told herself. She was a horrible, nosy, unbalanced woman. Jeremy would be livid if he caught her. But there were so many questions he wouldn't address outright when she asked. Could he really blame her for seeking answers wherever they may be? The first thing she noticed was an unopened box of stainless-steel flatware. Next to that, a white undershirt hung over the edge of his suitcase, strewn there as if it had been peeled off and tossed down in a hurry. Celia picked it up and sunk her nose into the soft material, inhaling his scent and closing her eyes to the feeling it evoked inside her chest. It was him, the grown man, and the sudden contact—or at least the illusion of contact—made her ache to be close to him, not as her friend, but as a man to whom she felt an extraordinary attraction. She felt a pang of resentment toward the girls who had reached this level of intimacy with him, who had gotten close enough to breathe him in, taste him.

Celia dropped the shirt and squeezed her eyes shut. It would do her some good to get a grip on herself. What everyone said would fade with time had only become stronger, surer, and was now veering into infatuation.

When her eyes opened again, they landed on the filthy plasterboard wall a few feet away, and what appeared to be a series of etched grooves. It only now occurred to her that the other three walls were covered in fresh paint, while this one had been left sullied and intact.

To get a better look, Celia crawled onto the mattress. Eroded carvings decorated the wall, faded words and drawings notched in childish scrawl. Many simply said, *Celia*. A larger one said *Jeremy + Celia* in slightly neater script, framed by a clunky heart. Her index finger traced the plus sign between their names. A smile stretched her mouth wide. Two of the other drawings were of dogs—horses, maybe—while another was a rudimentary sketch of Superman: a prominent S snaked down the middle of a commanding figure's chest, his fists at his hips. A cape was caught in an invisible breeze at his back. Below that was row after row of tally marks. What had he been tallying?

Celia sat back on her heels. Light from the setting sun reached her eyes. Squinting, she peered out the window there. Her house was visible through the swaying tops of the fruit trees, her bedroom window in full view. Had Jeremy sat in this very spot as a young boy, carving, dreaming, wishing for a kinder friend? For her unconditional love? She thought of her own room, how warm it had been back then, how safe. The guilt she often felt when thinking about their childhood together came surging back with added force.

Feeling like a wretch, she climbed off his bed and stood up. What was she doing to him now? Was it not enough that she had been a monster to him while he etched her name into this wall with such care? Was it not enough that when he had needed her most, she'd deserted him, discarded him, dangled her affection in front of him like a treat to a starving animal? She was going to cause him more grief by spying on him? It was no wonder he seemed to hate her sometimes. She was an awful person who'd never deserved him or his love.

As she turned to leave, to go home and find Fletcher—who she desperately needed to talk to—Celia's gaze fell on something reflective and gold, shining from within Jeremy's suitcase.

Bending down, she pulled out a familiar metal canister.

"What the hell are you doing?"

17

Jeremy

1957

Six months he'd been here. Six months of feeding chickens and lug-ging hay. There wasn't time to be angry. Even at night, after his bubble bath and glass of warm milk, Jeremy never remembered his head hitting the pillow; he was so tired.

Caroline, his mother, was a quiet sort, like him. But the old man who called himself 'Granddad' clucked on more than those hungry chickens. Every event, no matter how trivial, had a story to go with it. With every mistake, a lesson. It was hard to say if any of the claims the old man made were true. They came off as outrageous but, at the same time, wise and practical.

It was Jeremy's first Easter Sunday in Tennessee when Granddad told him the first of many of life's secrets. Caroline had insisted the three of them attend church together for the holiday, and when Jeremy complained, Granddad gently shook his head. "Don't sass your mama. If she asks us to go to church, we go to church. She don't ask a lot."

At that baloney, Jeremy rolled his eyes. He thought a tie was quite a damn lot. As was his new church suit that itched like a son of a bitch. And the stupid, slippery, white loafers. It was a cold morning, too, so Caroline forced him to wear the cream-colored Tom Sawyer jacket that made him look like a doggone ice cream cone—specifically, vanilla, the worst flavor. The whole getup made him look like a sissy boy, and Jeremy was sure he was going to have to fight his way out of church.

Once there, he thought different. A dozen of his classmates were in attendance, and to his relief, every one of them looked like an ice cream cone. One by one, they glanced at him from across the pews and shrugged. Some made goofy faces to get him laughing. A few nearby passed him notes, letting on about places they'd rather be or baseball cards they were looking to trade.

When Easter service ended, everyone was directed to the potluck being held out back.

"You look very handsome this morning," his mother gushed, adjusting his tie.

"Caroline, stop," Granddad chortled. "The boy's head is already red as a cherry. Like a dandy little ice cream sundae, ain't ya?"

Despite Jeremy's sour puss, Caroline's proud smile never wavered. "You both wait here while I drop off this casserole," she said with needless excitement. "Then I'll put a few plates together for us." A wind kicked up, and she squealed at the chill, tightening her coat around herself as she scurried away from the table.

While Jeremy waited, he scanned the yard. He didn't want to sit here. He wanted to play, but the other boys were seated around their families as he was, looking equally miserable. Across the lawn, he noticed a girl his age with dark braids standing alone, swinging back and forth, her frilly dress swinging with her. He recognized her as Deidre, a neighbor from down the road who wasn't allowed at his school.

Another gust blew, and Jeremy watched Deidre hug herself, then rub at her skinny, bare arms.

"Go give her your jacket," he heard Granddad say.

"What?"

"I said, go give her your jacket."

"Why should I?"

Granddad turned to him like he had six heads made of stinky cheese. "Are those fancy little breeches o'yers on too tight?" he asked, making Jeremy self-conscious as he put on a show of inspecting the beige slacks. Wrinkled blue eyes pierced through Jeremy, straight to his guts. "You give that little girl your jacket because that's what a gentleman does, ya hear?"

"What's a gentleman?"

Granddad groaned. "Lord, help us all . . . A gentleman, Jeremiah, is what a real man strives to be every day of his life. He fails most of the time, but he always, always tries."

"That doesn't explain what it is."

"Let me explain it like this then. Every one of God's creatures has a knack, something it does better'n anyone else. Big or small, it don't matter. For instance, a horse can run for miles with a grown man on his back. A spider can shoot silk out its very butt and use it to build itself a house. Can you do either o' those things?"

Jeremy shook his head.

"I didn't think so. But does that make a horse or a spider better'n you?"

"No . . . ?"

"All right, well, a man's knack is his brawn, his ability to lift a bale of hay and hurl it wherever it needs to go without breakin' a sweat. Most women can't do that, y'see? Men are bigger, stronger. It's just how it is." Granddad leaned close and quieted his voice. "Now I like you, so I'm gon' let you in on a secret your daddy shoulda told ya already. A woman's knack is strength, too—Don't make that face. It's true! Women are strong in a way that only *real* men can see. It's in here," Granddad said, pointing at his own chest.

"You break a man's heart, he's a useless sack o' nothin'. But you break a woman's heart, my hand to God, she comes back ten times stronger. Like your mama. That girl's tough as nails. In here. Now you're a smart boy, so I reckon you already knew that. But what you may not know is that a long, long time ago, we men made a deal with women; a promise in front of God and all the angels. Y'see, women are delicate, soft on the outside, but strong as steel on the inside. For men, it's the other way 'round. So, we each pledged not to take advantage of the other's weakness. Women promised not to do harm to our tender hearts, and we men promised not to do physical harm to them. Now unfortunately, there are two types of men and women in this world: those who honor that promise and those who don't. So you, Jeremiah, can be either one or the other, a real man or a fake'un. There is no in-between. Men who hurt women cannot be real men, y'see, because a real man honors his promises. Go on, ask anyone. It's a known fact."

Jeremy frowned. He'd already broken that promise made in front of God and all the angels before he'd even known about it. His father had told him nothing! What did it mean? Would Granddad hate his guts now? Would God and the angels? How did he fix this? "What does this have to do with my jacket?" he asked.

"Right, well, women get cold easy." Granddad reached into his coat, grabbing a half-smoked cigar and a book of matches. "Their skin's soft, like a baby's. It's why it's so much prettier than ours." Lighting the cigar, Granddad sat back in his chair. "The cold, it bites harder at 'em. So if you sit there with your finger up your nose watchin' a woman shiver, and you don't do sumpin' bout it—pft!—well that means you're one of them phonies, the kind that can't keep promises."

Jeremy balked. He didn't want to be a phony.

Granddad pointed his cigar. "That little girl over there is cold—you know it and I know it—and you got a jacket just her size. But I'll let you decide for yourself what kinda man you are. It's about time we found out anyway, don't ya think?"

As Granddad puffed on his cigar, Jeremy watched the girl. She was shaking like a leaf in the wind, and he felt his shoulders sag. What kind of man was he? He wasn't sure. But he knew he didn't want to be no phony. They made Granddad's weathered face pucker with disgust, and Jeremy didn't want any part in it.

Standing up, he grudgingly removed his jacket, feeling that bite of cold, then dragged his feet across the grass to where Deidre stood.

"Here," he grumbled, pushing the jacket at her. "Take it."

Deidre made a face. "I don't want it."

"Well, you have to take it."

"Why do I have to?"

"Because we all made promises," Jeremy snapped. "Now take it and stop askin' questions."

When Deidre once again snubbed his offering, he glanced back at Granddad, who was watching him—and judging harshly, by the looks of it.

Jeremy turned back to Deidre, wondering why she wasn't holding to her end of the deal. Maybe she was one of *those* women. "Aren't you cold?"

The girl sniffled, dragged the back of her hand under her nose, and said, "Course I am. But I want folks to see my pretty new dress."

"You want to be the prettiest Popsicle at church?" Jeremy shoved the coat at her again, and this time, she took it. "The second you get warm, I want it back. It's my favorite, so don't wipe your nose on it."

"I wasn't gonna!"

"Good!"

Jeremy stomped back over to Granddad, slamming his backside down on his chair with a grunt. With big, hulking movements, so that Granddad would know just how put out he'd been by the whole ordeal, he folded his arms and produced a loud, disdainful huff.

Granddad leaned close, his eyes shifting conspiratorially. "Good to know you're on our side. I was startin' to worry. I don't trust that other kind at all."

Jeremy sat up a little straighter. "What does the other kind look like?"

"Oh, they're sly devils. They look just like er'body else. They can be tall, short, smart, dumb, rich, or poor. It's all kinds. That's how they fool ya. But I found the trick to spottin' 'em years ago. It's in the promise.

A fake'un can't keep one to save his life. It's like their kryptonite or sumpin'."

Jeremy gaped. "Really?"

Arching one grizzled eyebrow, Granddad said, "Really."

———

1967

Jeremy charged toward Celia, yanked his father's urn from her hands, and threw it onto the bed. "What the hell's the matter with you?"

He wanted to shake the truth out of her, for once, but she stared back at him with big eyes. Whether it was out of contrition or shock, he couldn't tell.

"Answer me!" he shouted, making her flinch.

"I—I don't know. I'm sorry."

Jeremy watched her. Her expression was agony to witness, rich with anguish and regret. And fear. Honest-to-God fear.

He needed to calm down. He spread his fingers to fight back the rage that had been threatening to boil over. The truth was: he feared him, too.

"I know it's childish, but . . ." Celia stepped toward him. Jeremy stepped back. "I got scared downstairs, so I came up here and—I shouldn't have come into your room. You have every right to be angry." Her expression oozed remorse. "I'm sorry, Jeremy. Really, I am."

Confounded, Jeremy wondered why she would want to snoop in his room anyway. There was nothing of significance in here—a "like new" mattress set he'd purchased through an ad in the newspaper, a suitcase full of stained work clothes, and the markings of a delusional, adoles-cent ego etched into a dirty wall. But Celia had always been this way, audacious to the point of foolishness. Nothing, least of all common sense, ever stopped her when she wanted something. He remembered an afternoon when they were young—four or five years old—and she'd stubbornly followed as he climbed up several branches of the ogre tree. He'd warned her, told her to get down—she wasn't strong enough—but she didn't listen—she never listened!—and she fell, coughing out a distressed gasp as she plummeted to the ground. The earth that met her body knocked the breath from her lungs, freezing her expression into an arrested howl of tears. He could still recall the horror on her face and the panic in his heart as he jumped down after her. He had begged God for her breath, bartered for it, offering his own, and rolled her into his arms as her sob broke free. She'd cried so hard, so much, that he'd cried, too. She was his only friend.

To Jeremy's dismay, he had that same feeling now, as though her anguish was his own, a joint emotion assailing them both. As she stood before him now, big, brown, waterlogged eyes continued to plead with him to react—to yell, chew out, or forgive. His instinct was to yell, but the more he thought about yelling at her, the more like a fraud he felt. *Real men don't yell or hit.* His mother and Granddad had pounded that into his head about a million times growing up, hoping to break the familial cycle or at least tame the monster they feared waited inside him. Did his father's barbarity and rage run through his veins? It felt like it sometimes. That rage had flourished upon seeing her in his room. His fists had tightened, prepared to do harm.

Jeremy shut his eyes and listened as the sounds of summer crept in through the open window, then inhaled a deep, satisfying lungful of the warm, salty air.

Feeling a little calmer, he opened his eyes. The low western sun was blazing like a fireball through the window behind her head. In its light, her hair, falling to her shoulders in wild, uncombed waves today, shone a bright honey gold. He was noticing the smallest details about her lately. The pattern in the headband that stretched across the top of her head matched her bikini top exactly. Her shorts were not white, but an insipid yellow, similar to the paint color he'd chosen for the bedrooms. The knobs of her shoulders were shades darker and much shinier than the rest of her skin. How smoothly this summer would've gone had Celia grown into an ugly woman. But it wasn't the case. Still, she looked defeated, and Jeremy knew the feeling. And in the quiet spaces between his distrust of her, he could remember loving her. He could see why, as a boy, he'd been unable to resist the inclination. She was all softness and warmth and everything good and clean in the world.

The good-for-nothing kid he'd been hadn't stood a chance against her.

Jeremy felt perfectly calm again, and Fletcher's voice grew loud inside his head. *Act like a human being.* He brought his fingers to his eyes and growled. "You really know how to make things difficult."

"I know," Celia responded. "We were getting along so well, and I ruined it."

"You didn't ruin it. Stop being dramatic."

Nodding, Celia wiped a tear away.

Now she was crying? "Goddamn it." Jeremy stepped toward her. "Look, don't get me wrong; I'm pissed at you for snooping. But I'm pissed at myself, too. I should've known you would." He sucked in a halfhearted snicker, and she surprised him with a hug.

After some hesitation, Jeremy put his arms around her but didn't tighten them.

Then into his ear, she said, "Thank you," and the sultry tremor of her breath sunk like an anchor inside his chest, then lower still. The opposing instincts to squeeze and to push away arrived simultaneously. In response, every muscle froze, and Jeremy was sure she noticed. How did he explain himself without sounding like a psychopath? What the hell would he even say? *You remind me of pain, rejection, and humiliation. Go the fuck away. But please, come back tomorrow.*

Letting her go, he took a step back, then another. "We should get going."

18

Angie

Angie was a listener, a watcher, mostly because she was uncomfortable with being the center of attention. This made her very, *very* unlike a certain gregariously annoying, dangle-on-your-last-nerve-like-a-yo-yo—you-can't-punch-her-in-the-face-or-you'll-go-to-jail-Angie!—human hurricane.

Namely, Bianca Lynch.

Stories circulated about Bianca. Rumors mostly. All were scandalous, some downright disgraceful. One involved a secret abortion. Another, communist affiliations. The maddening twit was beauty personified but irrepressible chaos at the same time. When she blew into town, on those very rare occasions that she decided to gift Pacific Grove with her presence, the quaint breezes that were its citizens found themselves slave to her storm, forced to ride her out and then clean up the destruction left in her wake.

The most taken with Bianca had always been Moose. He was the tidal wave to her hurricane, rising high as she approached, reacting with fervor to every shift she made. But it was always Angie he ran to afterward for comfort when Bianca inevitably broke his fragile heart by disappearing as suddenly as she'd arrived.

Angie was sick to death of it. And sick to death of Bianca Lynch, for that matter.

"You still hang out at Jerry Garcia's pad?" Moose asked Bianca now, starstruck, making Angie want to chew off her own tongue to keep from saying something she would later regret.

Bianca was Celia's sister, after all. Angie was forced into this pleasantness.

"When I'm in the mood," Bianca shrugged. "I did psychedelics with one of the Beach Boys there a few moons back. He and I dated for a while. If you want to call it that."

Moose gaped. "No way. Which one?"

"Doesn't matter now."

"I bet it was Carl," Moose guessed, turning to Fletcher. "I met him once. He's a cool cat."

Fletcher shook his head. "My money's on Dennis. He's the best looking. According to Celia."

"Dennis has his charms," Bianca murmured.

Behind Moose, Angie rolled her eyes. Across from her, Fletcher snorted, fully aware of what was going on inside her head.

"You're so full of it," Angie told Bianca. "The Beach Boys aren't into that scene."

Bianca appeared unaffected by Angie's vitriol. "Why would I make that up?"

"Because you get your kicks watching Moose's head spin," Fletcher interjected with a laugh. "Look at him."

Bianca grinned despite the charge. "Well, that is true," she said, winking at Moose. "But I don't need to lie. My life is full of the things dull people fabricate in order to sound interesting."

Angie flicked her eyes away. "Oh, please."

"You know, I'm thinking about taking this semester off and moving up there," Moose mused. He nudged Bianca. "Maybe I'll move into your pad."

"Keep dreaming," Angie laughed. "Your dad would never let you have that much time off work."

Moose plucked a cold beer from his Lucky Lager pack and held it out to Angie. "Take it," he said. "You need a drink."

"Your solution to everything," Angie said, snatching the offered can. Maybe he was on to something. She had been in quite a foul mood lately. Popping the can open, she took a few chugs and settled into her chair.

"She's not wrong." Moose flashed his smile at Bianca. "I'm fairly certain I could end the war with dope and beer."

Angie smirked at the night sky above them, raising her can. "Yes, just intoxicate the entire North Vietnamese Army, and hallelujah, war's over."

"Don't be ridiculous," Moose retorted, trying to save face in front of Bianca. "It's not that simple, dill weed. I would get the leaders together, from all sides, you know, even the Vietcong, then lock them in a room. I'd get 'em all juiced up, smoke their brains out, maybe hire a couple of skirts to dance, then get the leaders rapping about world peace—like really rapping. And *then* hallelujah, war's over." Moose grinned. "Durrr."

With a cynical shift of his eyes, Fletcher sat back in his chair, raising his arm over the seat back. "Very enlightening, Moose."

"Curtis," Moose corrected him.

Fletcher looked at Angie, but she could only shrug. Who knew why Moose, who had always seemed fine with the grade-school moniker (coined by his mother, incidentally), was suddenly insisting on being called by his given name? "I wonder why no one's thought of this sooner," Fletcher said. "Why aren't you in DC, again?"

"Because my mom's a fusspot and my dad's cheap."

The girls and Fletcher chuckled. "What does that even mean?" Fletcher asked.

"It means bite the big one, Fletch," Moose said as he plucked off another can and extended his arm. "You need a drink, too. Everybody's so damn uptight around here lately."

Fletcher waved the beer away, and Moose sighed. "Bianca, explain things to this kid. He's never going to get laid if he doesn't learn to appreciate the natural benefits of fermented wheat."

"You don't drink?" Bianca asked Fletcher.

"I drink."

Moose snorted. "Wine."

"My parents stocked a lot of wine in their cellar. What do you want me to do? I like wine."

"I want you to have a beer, princess."

"I don't like beer," Fletcher explained. "It tastes like crap."

"All alcohol tastes like crap. You drink it anyway. That's the point."

"Didn't you bring anything more flavorful?" Bianca asked Moose. "Or vodka? We could've spiked Celia's lemonade."

"Nah, I didn't think of it."

"It's all right," Bianca said with a devilish grin. "I brought my sack of tasty treats to share."

Moose sat back and shook his head in admiration. "I am madly in love with you," he told Bianca. "Marry me."

Angie knew he was only half-joking, but she wanted to hurl her lunch at the dumb grin on his face as he watched Bianca pull her long, dark hair into a ponytail.

"Easy, big boy," Bianca said. "My mother would kill me if I married a bartender named Moose."

"So, call me Curtis. I'm in college for accounting. And your mother loves me."

Angie was finishing another big, fat, juicy roll of her eyes when Celia and Jeremy walked out onto the back patio together. Celia's eyes and nose were red. Beside her, Jeremy looked guilty, but Angie wouldn't give him too much grief. Celia was stalking him, after all.

"Now we can eat!" Moose exclaimed, scooting out from the table to walk over to the barbecue. "I've got the coals nice and hot, dollface."

"The steaks are in the fridge," Celia said with a soft smile. "I'll get them."

"Hang on." Setting down her beer, Angie stood up and walked

over. "Everything okay?" she asked Celia while giving Jeremy a mind-ful glance. Angie loved her best friend, but sometimes there was not much she could do for Celia, other than blindly take her side, even when she was wrong.

Celia nodded. "Everything's fine. Why?"

"Good." Angie needed to get her alone. "Come on. I'll help you get the food."

Fletcher approached the trio. His suspicious, palpably jealous glare landed on Jeremy, whose guilt morphed equally fast into something akin to smugness. The two men were not on the friendliest of terms, and nei-ther bothered to pretend otherwise. Nobody else, meanwhile, bothered to inquire as to the origin of their rift, because everyone was certain that Celia was the answer. It was possible they were wrong, sure. Jeremy wasn't exactly one for emotional exposés, and Fletcher refused to even discuss Jeremy, other than to counsel Celia against him. But they all had eyes.

"You all right?" Fletcher asked Celia, throwing Jeremy another hostile glance.

Before she could answer, though, Jeremy whispered something in her ear and strode off toward the barbecue to chat with the always-affable Moose.

"Why do you look like you've been crying," Fletcher asked more pointedly now that Jeremy was out of earshot. "What'd he do this time?"

"Nothing," Celia responded with curt defensiveness. "It was my fault."

"Sure, it was."

"No, really. He caught me snooping around in his room." A sheep-ish wince—one Celia displayed way too often—crinkled her face. "And his suitcase."

Angie gasped. "Celia."

"I know. He was furious. But he forgave me. I think we might actu-ally be friends again, like we used to be." Celia was clearly jazzed by the idea. "Isn't that wonderful?"

Angie looked at Fletcher. "Fletch, honey, can I talk to Celia alone for a minute? Please?"

Fletcher sighed, then turned away, walking back to the table. Angie followed Celia into the house and closed the French doors to the patio behind them.

"What is going on with you and Fletcher?" Angie asked as Celia pulled grilling utensils from a drawer. "I had a talk with him today, and he's miserable."

Celia shrugged. "I think he's still mad at me." The blond began piling food to bring outside—a green salad with tomatoes and cucumbers, a chocolate tunnel cake, and a box of something called Fiddle Faddle that she dumped into a large serving bowl. "He thinks I'm wasting my time with Jeremy."

Angie grabbed a handful of the candied popcorn. "I'd have to agree with him," she said, shoving it into her mouth. "Jeremy's leaving soon. Fletcher's been here for you for years. You shouldn't turn your back on him."

"How am I turning my back on him? He's been avoiding me."

"He's in love with you, Celia, and he's hurt."

Celia guffawed. "Angie, please. I promise you, he's not in love with me."

"You're blind if you think he's not." Angie hesitated. What she was about to say would sound terrible, but Celia needed to hear it. "I'll be glad when Jeremy leaves. He's tearing you and Fletcher apart." Celia raised her eyebrows but kept silent as Angie continued. "He's going to keep being careless with your feelings and keep hurting you, and then he's going to leave. They always do."

Celia's expression veered into bewilderment. "What are you talking about?"

"I don't want to see you left a pathetic mess like my mother. Trust me when I say that Fletcher will never hurt you, Celia."

"I know he won't. He's my friend. I don't want to be just friends with Jeremy. I want more."

Angie went slack-jawed. Celia couldn't be serious. "Oh, come on, Celia. He'll never be your boyfriend." Angie turned from the indignation that spilled over Celia's face, feeling like an abysmal friend. "I only mean that he would make an awful boyfriend. Men are awful, with the exception of Fletcher. You'd be better off alone than with someone like Jeremy."

"How can you tell me not to want a boyfriend when you have one?"

Roger was the last topic Angie wanted to discuss. "I don't have one anymore," she confessed, stepping around Celia, who opened her mouth to speak. "And I don't want to talk about it." She hadn't seen Roger in over a month, and he wouldn't return her calls. Their relationship was dead in the water, as she'd wanted. All she could do now was keep herself from thinking about him, keep paying the bills, and be grateful that along with Roger, her father, too, had buckled to her demands. They'd all vamoosed (as she'd known they eventually would). But it was on her terms. And that demarcated the victory, as the pain, too, was of her own making. That, she could live with.

"But you want to talk about my love life," Celia said. "How is that fair?"

Angie sighed and turned slowly around. "I'm being a hypocrite, I know." Leaning back against the counter, she folded her arms and took a deep breath as she made a frustrating but sincere attempt to be a better friend, to neutralize her own prejudice and come at this as if her best friend's love interest wasn't a complete turd. It was hard, but she managed an impartial thought on the matter. "If you really want him," Angie said with a slight grumble, "you need to stop chasing him."

Celia frowned.

And Angie couldn't help but smile. "You have this . . . tendency . . . to chase down what you want, and that's great. For everything except men. If you chase a guy, even if you catch him, you'll always be chasing him. It's just the way they are. You've got to make him chase you. They're like dogs. And you need to be the grossest, most slobbery tennis ball in his yard, rolling away every chance you get."

Celia's brow furrowed deeper.

"Something to think about." Angie grabbed the steaks from the fridge. "Come on. Moose is starved. And you know how he gets."

19

Fletcher

Some go down slow, while others rush the line, extracting their
herbal spoils with damp, gluttonous lips. They pucker tight to its
delicate tip, thinning their smoke-filled eyes, crimping wary-but-
pleasured brows, as if it hurt, as if it hurt sooooo goooood.

Deep breath. Deeeeep breath!

"Hold it in!"

"Don't be a pussy, Fletch!"

A chorus of laughter, then Bianca's smooth arms slid around his
neck. "Come on, handsome boy, you can do this."

Across the table, Celia watched his reddening face with soundless
trepidation.

"Angie's got it," Moose declared, drawing everyone's attention to
the redhead.

The music warbled—*warble-warble*—and Fletcher became lost in
a train of thought about Captain Kangaroo's sidekick, Mr. Green Jeans.
That train left the station when he noticed how Angie's blue jeans
looked rather green in the yellowish light of Celia's back patio. Yellow

and blue made green. The lean queen was mean. She wears green jeans. Like Mr. Green Jeans . . .

Fletcher finally exhaled.

Holy cow, Batman! Angie was *Miss* Green Jeans! The Green Queen!

Moose held out a bright-red, glowing doobie and drew Fletcher's name in the air with it, like a Fourth of July sparkler, while Miss Green Jeans exhaled what appeared to be the sputtering smoke from the bowels of the Little Engine That Could.

Cough! Cough! Puht! Puht!

"That's it." Moose soothed the Green Queen by rubbing her back. "Take another drag, doll. You've got it. Hey, you sure you don't want to try it, Celia?"

Celia shook her head. Fletcher wondered why. His brain was clogged with so many unanswerable questions . . . Why wasn't Celia speaking? Why did she keep glancing toward the sky as if she were conferring with God? And if God created everyone, who created God, and did He ever sit around pondering His own existence?

Fletcher took another hit and held his breath. Why was his own face moving up and down? Was he nodding? Good God, at what?

"You told me you wanted to try," Jeremy said so quietly to Celia that Fletcher had to strain to listen. Had Jeremy's lips moved? Was he reading Jeremy's mind now?

"I do," Celia responded. "Just not yet."

A strange grin lifted Jeremy's cheek, and it occurred to Fletcher that he was staring at yet another man. Staring, staring. Damn it.

He hacked out the smoke burning his lungs. They felt atrocious. "Not yet," Fletcher said aloud and laughed, then coughed again. The words sounded . . . off. "Not yettt."

"Oh, yeah, he's flyin'." It was Moose. *Moose.* To himself, Fletcher laughed. It was a funny name. Moooooose.

"I think they both are," Bianca said, browsing between him and the eerily still Angie.

Feeling disordered, laggard in movement and thought, Fletcher focused on the quiet pair directly across the table from him. He watched Jeremy frown, then analyze Celia's discontented face for what seemed like hours. He wondered if anyone else would notice that he was watching Jeremy watch Celia, especially after learning today that he was such an incompetent starer. Now, if Celia would only look at him and complete this cozy circle of dysfunction. But she turned her eyes to Jeremy, instead, and Fletcher felt himself get ejected from the intimacy.

Bianca nicked the blunt from between Fletcher's fingers and took a drag. Smoke pervaded his field of vision, and when it cleared, Jeremy was pulling Celia toward himself. She moved easily as Jeremy sunk back into his seat, stretching one leg out before sitting her down carefully on his lap. He reached over to take a smoldering joint from Moose's hand.

Fletcher stayed enviously locked on the pair.

"Ever smoke a cigarette?" Jeremy asked Celia so privately that Fletcher had to strain again to make out the words.

Celia shook her head. It was the truth.

"Part your lips."

Celia obeyed, and Jeremy slipped the joint in.

Looking somewhat stoned himself, though he wasn't, Jeremy shaped his lips to match hers and sucked in the salty, night air for her to mimic. "Now suck. Gently."

His own mouth dry, Fletcher swallowed hard. He wondered where Charlie T. was right now. Was he holding someone like this, with strong, confident arms? Did he look upon them with seeing eyes, drowning them in his attention?

What a way to go.

Celia let the joint slip from her mouth, though it remained between Jeremy's fingertips. "I'm scared," she admitted. "Angie coughed so much."

"Because it's not filtered like her cigarettes."

"Angie doesn't smoke."

"Yes, she—"

Fletcher cleared his throat loudly. "Celia has asthma," he informed Jeremy. "She's scared for good reason."

In his typical fashion, Jeremy refused to acknowledge Fletcher's interruption. "You have asthma." It wasn't a question, but a revelation. Celia nodded. This seemed to intrigue Jeremy. "You probably shouldn't smoke then."

"But I want to try," she said, and Fletcher suspected it was only because trying meant holding on a bit longer to Jeremy's attention. God knew Fletcher would smoke an entire field of dope for it, to have that protective gaze for himself, to have those arms—no doubt warm and strong—wound around him. Fletcher ached for the sensation. Not necessarily from Jeremy, but from someone like him. It was a whimsy, like the many others he entertained. And, like the others, it would never materialize. The pain of that had begun to numb over the years, stinging only when a little oxygen slipped in, like a pinched limb in the middle of the night.

Like Charlie T., Jeremy Hill was fresh oxygen in this dark, stale closet, and Fletcher felt like he couldn't breathe.

A gull cried, and across the table, Jeremy sighed, his gaze soft on his admirer's pouting mouth. "How about just a little taste?"

"You'll show me?"

Jeremy nodded. "Watch," he said, bringing the joint near his own lips. "Pull the smoke into your mouth, but not your lungs. You can suck it into your lungs after, when you're comfortable. Watch." He sucked a swirling cloud of smoke into his mouth, showing it to her before it disappeared down his throat. Then, he blew it out in a long, slow stream right onto Celia's face. Her eyes closed, her chest expanded, and Fletcher felt a surreal rush of euphoria as Jeremy smirked.

"You ready?" Jeremy asked her.

Celia opened her eyes, her nod eager.

"Caution, young lady," Angie, Miss Green Jeans, mock-scolded Celia. "Not too much now, you mop-top degenerate you." Her subsequent giggle was infectious.

"Wow," Moose said, laughing. "You're loaded."

Angie continued to laugh, nearly falling into hysterics with Moose over God knew what. Behind Fletcher, Bianca chortled loudly, saying, "First-timers are the best. I live for the show."

"Oh, sit and spin, prom queen," Angie, the Green Queen, snapped, her mood swinging in the opposite direction. "Nitwit, twit, twit, twit—" Then the giggles returned.

"Angie!" Moose burst into breathless laughter, which sent Fletcher and Bianca into a fit of giggles, too.

Fletcher hadn't laughed so hard in his life, and he would be lucky if he ever stopped. He would die laughing, never knowing why. It wasn't even funny. Minutes passed, hilarious, nonsensical minutes, and his face hurt.

But then Celia started coughing and gasping. "Is she all right?" he asked Jeremy.

Jeremy, unsurprisingly, ignored him.

"Easy," Jeremy guided Celia as she went in for another drag, her second or third. "Good. Now hold it for as long as you can." She nodded and touched his face with both hands, her cheeks pinking. Between her palms, Jeremy looked proud.

Fletcher felt his jealousy ping and flourish, rising to scorch his foolish heart and sting his covetous eyes.

He'd never felt so alone.

"She's fine, Fletch," Jeremy belatedly answered him, never removing his eyes from Celia. "Now blow it out."

Celia followed Jeremy's direction by leaning in and releasing her smoke directly into his mouth, parting his lips wide with hers.

Eyes screwing shut, Jeremy breathed it in, taking her head suddenly with one hand, to bring her closer. Fletcher's own breath stopped, but then Celia sat back, proud of herself, unaware of what she'd done with that little move. She hadn't registered Jeremy's infinitesimal reaction, hadn't even considered the deep kiss he'd clearly anticipated before she pulled away. "It tastes so weird," was all she said.

Recovering quickly, Jeremy smiled. "It tastes good."

Fletcher thought he would celebrate the day Jeremy Hill showed this level of unwavering affection and kindness toward Celia, but he didn't. It bothered him, a lot. It piqued his suspicions and the ever-burgeoning, ludicrous envy that he felt toward the both of them equally. Eyeing the intimate placement of Jeremy's hands and arms—on her hips and lower back now—Fletcher found himself wishing for Celia's asthma to flare, for her lungs to seize, so he could scoop her up and say to Jeremy, "See! I told you! You know nothing about what she needs," if for no other reason than to separate them from each other. It hurt to watch them, yet he couldn't, couldn't, *couldn't* stop. Like a spoiled, irrational child, Fletcher wanted it all for himself: Celia's love and loy-alty, her freedom to publicly obsess over anyone she damn well pleased; Jeremy's attention, and the barefaced, unrepentant desire that rose like steam off his skin. Fletcher wished to have Celia all to himself, and yet wished to be her at the exact same time.

Fletcher hated himself.

He thought, for a brief instant, that they would all be better off without him around, without the bitterness and jealousy and deviancy that had consumed him.

The world would be better off.

The whole world.

The night unspooled, the hours passing in woolly, high-flying swells. Fletcher floated and brooded through a random series of trivial events—a roving, red June bug here, a puddle of spilled beer there—realizing himself lost in his own dark tunnel of introspection when Moose sauntered into view, half-draped in Helena Lynch's sable coat. Pearls adorning his neck and a martini glass swinging, he dished a monologue about the picket-fenced pigs of society and their hollow, middle-class excesses. The soliloquy ended rather climatically as Bianca joined in to dance her witchery under the glow of a black light that had Fletcher's mind in a never-ending state of disorder.

The only person who seemed to recognize this about him was

Jeremy, who was too sober—or was he?—his scrutinizing eyes too aware. Fletcher briefly wondered if "Jeremy Hill" was in fact a narc, or the emissary of some warped, alternate dimension bound on disrupting the harmony of this one. It would explain so much. The bastard knew things and had Celia under his spell. Had him, Fletcher, under an even greater spell or perhaps that ancient curse that made men crave what they couldn't have.

Sprawled on the lounger now, Jeremy licked his chops and slothfully stretched. The cramped space between his legs was now the whole of Celia's universe, the Eden from which she mulishly refused to wander. Oh, she leaned off the chair to grab luxuries for herself every so often, and later, moved down between Jeremy's feet to decorate Moose's face with DayGlo paint. But that was as far as she was willing to stray. If Jeremy stirred, adjusted his position in any way, greedy fingers verified his presence and then, once satisfied, continued with whatever activity had her rapt. "Your hands are rough," she told her would-be lover at one point, through lust and innuendo. She laced her fingers with his, studying skin, nail, and bone at length, inspecting every inch. And while he made no effort to evade her persistent touches, Jeremy did appear now, much to Fletcher's satisfaction, to be searching frantically with his eyes for a way out, like the black-and-white pussycat who'd been mistaken for skunk. But it was his own damn fault for getting her high. He was hers until she landed.

And everyone had someone.

Even Fletcher. Bianca was a terrible, self-absorbed little companion, dancing and drinking and cavorting about. It might have been fun had he found her interesting, if he saw her the way Moose did, but he had no such luck, not even now.

His vinegary transformation was complete.

The Mean Queen had Moose, who admonished her relentlessly for her waywardness, all while managing to circumvent her wrath. While everyone's high had served them exultation, through either quiet introspection or uncontrollable laughter, Angie's high made her into a tyrannical monarch. By and large, she was speaking her partially transcended, partially mad mind. Her red hair fanned like a blazing, California ridgeline as she loafed portentously on her Barcalounger throne made of sun-bleached wicker. Like Moose, Angie had slipped into one of Mrs. Lynch's fancy coats, which she'd styled with Bianca's old homecoming crown and sash—both "yokes of oppression," according to Moose. A long, smoking tube extended from thin, overworked fingers, joint ablaze at its tip. The Green Queen was unimpressed with everything, even Moose's energetic stab at a Jack Benny impersonation. This wasn't Angie. This wasn't the resentful waitress raising her orphaned siblings. This was truly Miss Green Jeans, the Mean Queen, in all her despotic glory. Free to indulge in excess. Free to pretend. To let go and fly. Fletcher feared her most of all, while Moose waited on her hand and foot between performances, laughing like a lunatic with the others. "Off with their heads!" was next to tumble from her lips. But when she instead commanded that Bianca "shut her hippie trap already," Fletcher felt a hard quake of laughter ripple through him until he could not stop, until he fell off his chair and that Mean Queen showered him with lemon peels and praise.

He was Fletcher! The Mean Queen's jester!

"All Hail Miss Green Jeans!" while the radio told them to feed their heads.

"Green Queen! Green Queen!"

Bianca laughed. "You won't know until you've truly freaked out."

That caught Moose's attention. "You brought some with you?" he asked Bianca.

"What, LSD? No, not this time." Bianca sat twirling her index finger around a lock of Jeremy's hair, thoroughly enjoying his discomfort. "But you two will have no problem finding it. It's more plentiful than water in the city." Appearing bored, she sighed. "Well, I'm beat. I'm gonna crash. I left the keys to the building and my front door on the kitchen counter. Do *not* lose them. It's my only set. I'll be back next week to get them." She dragged the nail of her index finger from Jeremy's nose to his bottom lip, most likely to make him squirm. "Have fun, sexpot."

Celia glowered at them both. "Keys to her place?" Drowsy, crimson eyes questioned Jeremy. "What's she talking about? Why would you be going to her place?"

Jeremy sought out Moose, who shook his head, repeatedly mouthing, *No*.

"Bianca?" Celia turned to her sister now, her voice thick. "What's going on?"

"They didn't tell you?" Bianca was equally confused. She tilted her head at Moose.

"Tell me what?" Celia asked.

"Moose and the sexpot are staying at my pad for a few days while I'm in LA. They told me you didn't want to go."

Beside her, Jeremy winced.

"That so," Celia said to Jeremy before eyeballing Moose.

"Oh, come on, you don't want to go to the city," Moose said. "It's crowded and dirty."

"And how would you know what I want?" Celia cut him off. "You certainly didn't ask . . . So, what, we're not hip enough to go to the Haight with you? This is exactly what happened with Monterey Pop."

"Monterey Pop is what we were trying to avoid," Jeremy said quietly.

Celia's crestfallen gaze fell on him. A hush fell over the patio. "I see." She pulled a blanket over her shoulders and stood, moving past Bianca into the house.

Fletcher settled deeper into his seat, feeling a small smile of vindication contort his cottony mouth. "Well, that didn't last long."

Jeremy set a hard glare on Fletcher.

"Oh, come on, we all knew you'd screw it up eventually." Fletcher wondered when he'd become such a vicious person. When had it happened exactly? Probably the moment he'd realized he had nothing left to lose.

Looking away, Jeremy said nothing.

The Green Queen chucked a half-full can of beer at Moose's back, unflinching as it exploded against the patio floor. "You can be a real ass sometimes, you know that? And you," she pointed at Jeremy. "This is *Celia's* home. We're *her* friends. That's *her* dumbass sister. Who the hell do you think you are?"

Bianca folded her arms. "I gotta say, the Mean Queen's right. That was a shitty move." Her eyes were pinned on Moose, twinkling with a stony mixture of mischief and disappointment. "How about this, sport. I'll let my baby sister decide who's worthy to stay with *her* in the city, and who's not." Her tone was stern suddenly. "Those keys and all this grass belong to Celia now." Swiping the brown paper bag off the table, she spun as gracefully as a ballerina. "Later gators!"

Bianca sauntered off the patio and into the house, approaching a dispirited Celia at the breakfast nook. Through the window, Fletcher watched Bianca kiss her sister's head, say something, and set the bag on the counter before disappearing from view.

Jeremy blew out a breath. "Well, there goes that."

"I hope she breaks your tiny reptilian heart," Angie told him. She stood, shedding her coat and crown. The serene hush of waves crashing in the distance did nothing to soften the chafe of French doors slamming shut as Angie made her exit.

"Damn!" Moose cried out. "Freakin' chicks killed my buzz. Man, we should've invited them. What do we do now?"

"Yep, well, good luck with that," Fletcher said, rising to his feet. "I'll send you a postcard from San Fran."

"Aw, don't be that way, Fletch," Moose said. "We would've invited you. We just knew you wouldn't go without Celia."

Jeremy snorted. "You're practically joined at the hip."

"You don't know the half of it," Fletcher said tauntingly. He eyed Jeremy, who was eyeing him right back after that comment. Moose and Jeremy were up to something. Probably had been plotting to find themselves an interchangeable set of easy girls in San Francisco, a plan that Celia's presence would've certainly spoiled. It was a simple plan for simple men.

Moose sat forward, his brown eyes pleading. "Man, I just wanted to show Jeremy a good time before he heads off to war. What's so wrong with that?"

"War?" Fletcher echoed. "What are you talking about?"

"Crap." Moose sighed. "I keep forgetting you don't know. He got drafted, man. That's why he's here, tying up loose ends. He reports for boot camp in, what, ten days now."

Fletcher turned to Jeremy for confirmation, but Jeremy only sat, contemplating the ground. Fletcher knew immediately that it was true. Feeling his throat tighten and his heart sink like a stone into his gut, Fletcher sat back down. "Jesus." He shook his head, then looked again at Jeremy, who had lifted his face to the night sky, looking oddly at peace. Why was he only hearing about this now? Why was Jeremy keeping this kind of information to himself? Fletcher felt like a monster. The Vietnam War was an unprecedented mess, and he wouldn't wish it on his worst enemy. But Jeremy was far from his worst enemy. On the contrary, there was a time when Jeremy had been his only friend, his white knight, when he had loved him like a blowball loved the sun. "I'm sorry," he said to him. "Why didn't you say anything?"

Jeremy lifted one shoulder. "People act different when I tell 'em. They talk to me like I'm on my fuckin' deathbed."

"Help me fix this," Moose said to Fletcher, who was still processing Jeremy's answer. "Celia listens to you."

"Not anymore, she doesn't." Fletcher jerked his head toward Jeremy, feeling lost. "Not since he showed up."

How was he supposed to act around Jeremy now?

Not different.

Not the same.

Moose shot to his feet. Fletcher could practically see the light bulb appear over his head. "Mr. Hill, I think it's you who can fix this."

Jeremy shook his head. "No, I'm out. I'm done."

"What?" Moose threw out his arms. "Why?"

"Man, it's fine. Go without me. Have a blast. I have work to do anyway." He looked at Fletcher. "And you're right; I screwed up. It's on me."

"Bullshit," Moose rumbled.

Fletcher rolled his eyes. "Oh, for Christ's sake, Jeremy, just apologize to her. I promise you, she'll fall right into your arms."

"Yeah, and I'm not going anywhere without you." Moose threw the discarded crown at Jeremy. "Go apologize. We're right behind you."

Grumbling to himself, Jeremy spun the crown around in his hand, thinking, fidgeting, huffing, then pushed off the lounger and tossed the crown. "Shit." He paced while Moose and Fletcher, like tennis spectators, tracked him with concerted interest.

When Jeremy came to a stop, he took a deep breath and pulled open the French doors.

Moose and Fletcher glanced at each other, then trailed several yards behind as Jeremy stalked into the family room, where all three girls now lounged in front of the television. Johnny Carson flickered in the dim lamplight, a turban on his head. Bianca lay sprawled on the long couch in a nightshirt, flipping through a magazine. In a chair, Celia sat on folded legs, filing her fingernails, while Angie watched the show from the floor.

It was three against three, better odds than they were used to, which was good, except Fletcher couldn't figure out how the hell he'd landed on the guys' side. The girls weren't mad at him.

"I'm worried," Moose whispered to Fletcher, "that he's going to make this worse."

"It's a talent of his, for sure."

Approaching the girls like they were a herd of grazing, pissed-off antelope, Jeremy glanced back at Fletcher and raised his palms in question, as if to say, "What now?"

"Is she crying?" Fletcher mouthed silently, pointing to his eyes and squiggling a finger down his own cheek.

Jeremy checked, then shook his head.

Fletcher waved him forward.

Testing the waters, Jeremy put one foot forward and waited. Angie did nothing, only stared at him with tight, bloodshot eyes and followed his cautious movements. Jeremy stepped in front of Celia, who kept her head down.

"So far so good," Moose whispered to Fletcher.

Obviously uncomfortable and aware of his audience, Jeremy squatted down in front of Celia. "Can I talk to you for a second?" He looked around. "Alone."

"No," Angie answered snidely for Celia. "You can talk to her right here."

Celia raised her head. Fletcher couldn't see her face, but he could see Jeremy's. His expression was gentle and surprisingly replete with remorse. "I'm sorry," Jeremy said, considering his words carefully before speaking again. "I'm not going, okay. But let Moose go. He had nothing to do with it. It was all me. It was before . . ." He watched Celia with earnest, telling eyes. Jeremy played dumb sometimes, but he knew exactly how to reach her.

Celia lowered her head again. "It's not your fault," she said, scraping the file repeatedly over her thumbnail. "I had no right to get upset. It's none of my business where you go." She opened her palm, revealing two brass keys. "Take them. I want you to have fun, even if it's not with me."

Jeremy appraised her, then leaned forward to whisper something only for her ears. She whispered something back.

"No," Jeremy answered quickly.

"Yes."

"What are they talking about?" Moose whispered to Fletcher, who could only shrug.

"How about you all go?" Bianca touted. "How about you all stop being such uptight, theatrical little babies and go to the city, get wasted, and enjoy your boring damn lives? God knows you all need it!" She stood up and stalked from the room. "You really know how to kill a girl's high."

Moose straightened his spine and grinned.

"Ugh, whatever." Angie stood up and walked toward the kitchen.

Moose followed her as she passed. "So can we go or not?"

Eventually, everyone moved into the kitchen where Angie warmed up leftovers. It took nearly an hour to convince her, but in the end, she agreed to take a few days off work. They were all going to San Francisco.

As they made quick, efficient travel plans for the next morning, Fletcher could only nod. He was too famished to object to anything. Food—leftovers at that—had never tasted so good.

Around one in the morning, deeply sated and ready for bed, Fletcher caught Celia's eye and gestured for her to follow him out of the kitchen. He left first and waited for her in the downstairs hallway, surprised when she arrived wearing a smile. He took her hand. "Come on," he said excitedly.

"Where are we going?"

"To bed." It'd been forever since they'd slept in the same room. "I want to talk."

Her smile widened. "Ooh, about what?"

Fletcher guided her into a shadowy corner near the bathroom, then pulled her into a hug. "I don't want to fight with you anymore."

"Me neither," Celia said, the relief evident in her voice. "I can't stand it when we fight."

Fletcher set a chaste kiss on her lips. They would never muster true passion for one another, but through the years, they'd perfected tenderness and love. "I was thinking about our talk back at school. About us getting married. I think we should do it. Soon."

Celia recoiled. "Where is this coming from? Yesterday, you weren't even speaking to me."

"I was thinking about us a lot tonight. About you." He felt as troubled as she looked. He hadn't planned this well at all. "I don't want to lose you, Celia. I want to make this work. You love me, don't you?"

"Of course, but—"

"And I love you. I trust you. I'd do anything for you."

"But you're not attracted to me."

Fletcher felt his stomach flip. "That's not exactly true."

"It's true enough. Married couples have sex. They build families."

"And we will." Fletcher leaned close to nuzzle her. "We've practically done it already, Celia."

"We tried and failed."

"We didn't fail. You weren't ready to go all the way yet. That happens with everyone. We'll do it when you're ready. I was ready, but I wasn't gonna push you for my own selfish reasons."

"What reasons?"

"The—" Fletcher stumbled over his own tongue. "You know what I mean."

"No, I don't. You were ready, why? Because you wanted me? Because you were attracted to me?"

Fletcher tried to swallow, but it wouldn't go down, and the more he tried, the more impossible it became. "Marry me, Celia. I love you."

"No." Celia pulled away from him. "No. I'm sorry, I can't. Things are different now."

"What's different?"

"I'm committed to someone now."

"Have you gone insane? It only counts when the other person is committed to you, too. You think Jeremy turns down girls for you? Well, let me tell you, he doesn't." Part of Fletcher regretted saying it, seeing the way her wistful expression collapsed. The other part of him was being selfish, and that part won out.

"Why are you trying to hurt me?" she asked, withdrawing farther from him.

"Hurt you? I couldn't hurt you if I wanted to. Nothing I say matters anymore. It's like I don't exist to you now. What happened to us? He doesn't want you, Celia. I do."

"No, you don't," Celia hissed. "You're just afraid of ending up alone."

Almost instantly, she stepped forward and wrapped her arms around his waist. "I'm sorry. I didn't mean that."

Fletcher hugged her tightly to himself. "We were happy before he showed up."

"But I wasn't." Her expression pained. "Don't you see? There was something missing, and I know what it is now. I feel it with him."

"Listen to me." Fletcher took a gentle hold of her face. "When he leaves—and he will; he has to, Celia—it's going to be just you and me again." He thought about Jeremy's news, about him being shipped off to Vietnam soon, and though he should tell her, Fletcher didn't want this to be about Jeremy. He didn't have the heart, anyway, not with the way she was looking at him, her entire face drawn downward. He bent his knees to catch her gaze more directly. "I'll wait. I'll wait for these feelings you have for him to go away. I'll wait however long you need me to. But please, promise me you'll think about marrying me after that." Leaning close, he nuzzled her nose, rolling his forehead over hers. "Please don't forget about me."

Celia remained quiet.

"I'll never hurt you," he added. "I'll never leave you. Not ever."

"I know."

"Are you happy right now?" he asked her, truly wanting to know. Because if she was happy, chasing a guy who didn't love her (lust wasn't love), who would be long gone in ten days, then he would concede. He would bow out without another word on the matter. But he knew she wasn't happy. He knew her better than he knew himself.

"I don't know," she murmured. "Sometimes I think I am. When I'm with him. Other times I feel pathetic. I'm so desperate to fix things that I don't even recognize myself. I think I love him, Fletcher, and just when I think I've reached him . . . when he's smiling at me the way he used to, I mess it all up again. I have no idea what I'm doing anymore."

Fletcher squeezed his eyes shut. "If it makes you feel any better, neither do I."

He felt lost and just wanted to go home to her, where he felt safe and loved.

Celia raised her head to smile at him, really smile at him, like before, when it had been only the two of them. Back when they were a team and he didn't feel so alone. "I'm so sorry, sweetie," she said. "I know this has been a lonely summer for you. I didn't mean for it to go like this."

"I know," Fletcher said. "I just miss you."

"I miss you, too."

"Would you consider trying again?" he asked her. "Please?" He bent his head to touch his lips to hers, tentatively kissing her, testing her will, and when he felt her hands rise to his chest, he closed his eyes. Maybe this summer had all been a bad dream. Maybe it was over, and their lives could return to normal. But pressure was the next thing he felt, her pushing him away.

When Fletcher opened his eyes, Celia's were wide on the other end of the hall, where Jeremy stood, demoralized.

Then he was gone.

"No!"

And she was gone, too.

20

Celia

"You're leaving?"

"Yeah," Jeremy said, walking away. "I was just coming to say good night."

"Wait! Are you still coming with us to the city tomorrow?" Celia's feet sunk into the cold grass of her front yard and padded her deeper into the darkness. "Jeremy?" She was already out of breath. "Please."

Before his silhouette could blacken any further, he swung around. "I'll be here in the morning," he said, "after I'm done painting my room."

Celia stopped several feet away, close enough to gauge his expression in the moonlight. He didn't seem upset—his general countenance suggested apathy—but he wouldn't make eye contact with her, either.

"If I get behind, you shouldn't wait for me."

"We'll wait," Celia assured him. "I wouldn't leave without you."

With a taut smile, he nodded before turning to walk away.

"*He* kissed *me*," she blurted out. "I didn't kiss him back."

Jeremy considered her words, then shrugged. "Maybe you should," he said in earnest, finally making eye contact. "Fletcher's a good guy."

Celia took a step forward. "I'd rather kiss you."

He offered no reply to that. His expression was stern as he stood there, looking at her.

Never in her life had she felt so vulnerable in front of another human being. Never had she experienced such craving. She wanted to leap at him, show him what it looked like when she rightly kissed a man.

"Thanks for dinner," he said, killing the few minuscule buds of hope he'd spent the night nurturing. But then, with a few steps, he bridged the distance between them and pressed a kiss to her cheek. Work-coarsened palms slid down her arms as heat spread from her ear to the corner of her mouth, sizzling where his lips sunk into her flesh. "Night."

Then he was gone.

Celia lay on her side, replaying that last conversation. He thought she should be with Fletcher. That, by itself, hurt. When someone wanted another person, they didn't want them with someone else, even if that someone else made more sense. Human beings, in general, were jealous lovers, too selfish for that kind of gesture. Jeremy, most of all, wasn't the sharing type. He was a possessive little brute. And with all her heart, Celia wished to be his possession.

Ostensibly, he didn't want her. Yet his kiss still burned her skin. His hushed good night still resonated in her ear. Her heart felt naked and exposed. Were these strong, agonizing feelings infatuation or real love? And what difference did it make?

"What do I do?" she whispered into the void between herself and Fletcher. "One minute, I think maybe he wants me, then the next, I'm sure he doesn't. But I can't stop hoping, no matter how hard I try."

"I don't think it's you he doesn't want," Fletcher said. "I think . . ."

He was quiet a moment before saying, "Do you remember my Great Aunt Lavinia?"

Now Celia was really confused. "The mean one that used to set her teeth on the table after dinner?"

"Yeah, with the wiener dog that . . ."

"Hiccups." Celia could recall the time they visited Lavinia, several years back, when they'd tried to startle that pitiful little dog, to rid it of its hiccups, which only succeeded in ticking off Lavinia and getting them kicked out of her house until dinner, when the teeth came out.

Fletcher had kissed Celia for the first time that weekend.

"She was married once." Fletcher interlaced his fingers with hers. "Long before you met her. She and her husband had a son named William. When he was three, he contracted polio. It paralyzed him. There was some problem with his throat or his breathing or something, and he ended up suffocating to death when he was six."

"Oh, God, that's awful."

"Lavinia and her husband blamed each other for years. They couldn't be around each other, because when they were, all they saw was their little boy. All they felt was the pain of what happened to him. And to them. They were constantly reminded. So, they divorced. Not because they didn't love each other, but because it was the only way to move on with their lives." Fletcher paused. "Do you understand what I'm getting at?"

"I think so," Celia said. "But I don't want to move on from Jeremy."

"But Celia, honey, I think he wants to move on from you. Or maybe from this place." Fletcher spoke the words very carefully, as if they might shatter her. "I think he already has, and that's what he's been trying to tell you in his boneheaded way. He's said, over and over, that all he wants is to fix up that old house and go home."

Celia didn't want to believe that Jeremy had moved on so finitely. "When we grow up," he'd said the night of his father's death, "I'll never hit you or our kids." Those were his exact words. He'd had plans for them. He'd wanted children with her. It was a silly memory to hold onto. But it was one of the only places she had left to go, a time when everyone she loved, everyone who loved her, remained. The very last time. And while Fletcher was probably correct about Jeremy moving on, Jeremy was here now. If she didn't at least try to mend their relationship or some fragment of the past, she would never forgive herself. She would fade with those memories.

Of course, Fletcher had always been there. He loved her unconditionally and accepted her for what she was and wasn't. She was not like the women of her generation who coveted autonomy and casual sex. As disgraceful as it was to the feminist cause she so publicly supported, she privately accepted that she did not want to live without a man in her life, could not. She'd spent her childhood admiring her mother and father, wishing for nothing less than their exact kind of romantic love, the kind songs and stories were written about. It was a flaw in her makeup, maybe, a weak trait to be shamed and scorned in these modern times. But it was the truth. Men made her feel safe, loved, though she couldn't understand why because when she really thought about it, it was also men who'd hurt and abandoned her, who'd made her feel unsafe and unloved.

Except for one.

Celia touched Fletcher's cheek, watching as he kissed her palm. He was a good friend, a loyal one. But they were losing sight of what that meant, and she had to take some responsibility for that. She'd been the one to suggest it, after all: giving her body, her innocence, to the experiment. And though they'd never gone all the way, the deep intimacy of the things they'd done made her feel as if they had. But that intimacy had lacked one very crucial component: passion. There was no desire in the acts, no hunger whatsoever.

Had that one feature been present, they would've made a wonderful match.

"How are you doing?" she asked him, realizing she'd been a terrible friend this summer. Fletcher wasn't a complainer. When he was depressed or upset, he did the exact opposite of what she did. He curled into himself, buried his feelings, and went silent. Summer was his favorite season. He should've been smiling nonstop, his white teeth shining against his sun-kissed face, being his jovial self, making comical assumptions about the tourists on the beach, doing their voices to make her laugh. But he hadn't been that way at all. In fact, he'd been telling her with his silence for a month now that he was far from all right. She'd been too focused on Jeremy and on herself to care.

"I'm all right," he said.

"No, you're not. Do you want to talk about it?"

"Yes," he sighed. "But not right now. It's late."

"I'll try again," she said a moment later. "If that's what you need."

Fletcher shook his head. "No."

"What do you mean, no?" Celia popped up onto her elbow. "In the hallway, you said—"

"I know." Fletcher rolled to his back with a huff. "I saw Charlie T. at the market." The words were barbed with shame and mortification.

Celia knew this wouldn't be good news but listened anyway, hoping. The stock boy at Purity Market was gorgeous. And very into girls. She knew because he'd asked her out about a dozen times over the years. But she couldn't tell Fletcher that. He'd be heartbroken.

Fletcher's face crumbled into sadness. "I stared too much this time."

"Oh, sweetie—" Celia laid her head on his shoulder.

"He noticed. He got angry and asked why I stare so much." Then he chuckled to himself, though there was no amusement in it. "How was I supposed to answer that? Because I find you incredibly sexy, and I would sell my right arm just to touch you . . . ? I can't figure out if he thought I was going to club him over the head with my Wonder loaf and drag him back to my homosexual lair, or if he thought I was looking for a fight. But I got out of there before he called the cops or hit me." Fletcher shook his head. "I'm so stupid. In what world would he . . . with me?"

"He'd be lucky to have you!" Celia exploded, fuming about that stupid jerk of a bag boy. Fletcher was the wonderful one, not Charlie T. But because of some cruel twist of fate, his wants and needs were an impossible fantasy that only served to break his heart again and again. She didn't know how to help him anymore.

Fletcher took her by the chin, his expression smoothing out into something she didn't recognize in him, something nearing peace. "Just listen," he said. "When you ran out after Jeremy tonight, I stood there thinking: What if that had been me? What if you kissed me and the stock boy saw? What if Charlie T. had that same look on his face that Jeremy did, after spending the entire day and night flirting with me? What if there *was* hope? Would I let anything stand in my way?" Fletcher laughed, this time a little more cheerfully. "No. I wouldn't, Celia. Not even for you. I would run after that man like an Olympic sprinter with my hair on fire. For the love of a complete stranger. Because he makes me feel alive just looking at him. I love you, but I will never be able to give that to you. I will never be able to feel that for you, that 'I have to touch you this instant or I'll die' feeling. You deserve that. You deserve someone who can't stop staring at you or touching you, who would chase after you when you walk away. Everyone does . . . Even me." Fletcher sighed. "I think he does want you, Celia. That was my point before. I can see it in his eyes. But that doesn't mean he wants to act on it. I understand how you feel—I really do—but sometimes we have to respect their wishes and love them quietly."

They stared into each other's eyes as Celia mulled over his words and nodded. She couldn't argue with any of it. And God, did she want to. But her friend was right.

Fletcher pulled her closer and gave her a squeeze. "I love you, Cee."

"I love you, too." Sensing her own exhaustion, Celia closed her eyes. "Fletcher?"

"Yeah?"

"When you kissed me earlier," she said, unable to swallow her guilt any longer, "I imagined you were Jeremy. I'm so sorry. You're right when you say you deserve better. We both do." Even as they lay together, her body throbbed for the other, the craving constant and overwhelming. "I'm in love with him. Or maybe I'm crazy. I can't tell the difference anymore."

"I was pretending you were Charlie T."

Her jaw dropped. Then they both snorted and burst into laughter. Celia hit Fletcher as punishment for waiting that whole long-suffering minute to admit it.

"Ow. Okay!" Fletcher avoided another swat. "Next time, we can both imagine Jeremy. Bring this craziness full circle."

"Fletcher!"

"What? I'm kidding," he said, laughing, blocking her next slap. "Ow!"

"Wait." Stilling, Celia had a sudden thought. "Do you find Jeremy attractive?" The possibility had never even crossed her mind before now. "Like sexually?"

Fletcher's smile disappeared. "Please don't make me answer that."

"Oh." Celia slinked under the blankets, pushing the image from her mind. "Good night."

———

When the morning sun streamed through her bedroom window, Celia hopped out of bed. She couldn't lay there any longer, unlike Fletcher, who still slumbered like the dead.

Downstairs, Bianca was already dressed, standing in the kitchen with a mug of black coffee.

"Morning," Celia yawned. "You look nice."

"Thanks. Hey, you might want to check around for paraphernalia."

"Paraphernalia?"

"Anything that might get us busted by Mommy," Bianca explained, grabbing a piece of buttered toast from her plate and biting into it. "I need to go get her from the airport right now, so you need to clean up."

Celia groaned. "Fine. But you owe me."

"No. You owe me."

"How do you figure?"

"Jeremy could be going into the city today without you. You don't want that. Trust me." Bianca, reeking of freshly smoked marijuana, stuffed the last of the toast into her mouth, grabbed a pair of keys off the counter, and kissed Celia's cheek. "I'll be back in an hour."

"Spritz some perfume."

"Yeah, yeah."

———

Celia spent a quarter of that hour cleaning up the kitchen and back patio. It was all the time she could spare. There was still packing to do for the Haight, and she had to shower, something she would've done the night before had she not been so stoned.

Reflecting on the previous night, she felt a pang of guilt for inserting herself into Jeremy and Moose's plans. Then again, Jeremy would be returning to Tennessee soon. She may never see him again.

After a speedy shower, Celia dried her hair and fixed her face. Her sister, a dark, natural beauty, had worn no makeup today. But with her freckled nose, pale-pink lips, and light-brown lashes, Celia wasn't sure she could pull off the natural look, so she settled on mascara, lip gloss, and a little blush. People would just have to deal with her freckles today.

She was slipping into one of Bianca's dresses when Fletcher woke up. The dress screamed of color. It was mostly yellow with little pink, white, and orange flowers. Celia wished it was shorter.

As Fletcher watched her from bed, she tried on that dratted floppy hat, too.

"Keep the hat," he said. "Makes you look hip."

"You think?" Celia admired herself in the mirror. The outfit did make her seem very *with it*, like she truly belonged in San Francisco, in the Haight. "Bianca's going to kill me."

While Fletcher dressed, Celia packed two small bags for them, sneaking in a few more of Bianca's clothes, then headed downstairs to grab a bite to eat.

Halfway through her bowl of oatmeal, the car rolled up.

Celia ran outside as her mother pulled a suitcase from the back seat. "Mama!"

"There's my sweet girl!"

Elated, Celia threw herself at her mother, hugging her tightly. "I missed you!"

"I missed you, too. Oh, you look so pretty," Helena noted, spreading Celia's arms wide. "What a nice dress. So feminine."

Bianca gaped. "Yeah, nice dress, Celia."

"Thanks."

Their mother pinched Celia's chin. "Your makeup looks lovely, darling." She turned to Bianca. "Bianca, honey, it wouldn't kill you to wear something feminine and put on a little makeup, like your sister. The girls these days," she tutted at Celia. "They want to look like boys."

Bianca made a face and grabbed another suitcase.

"She's still pretty, Mama," Celia said.

"Of course, she is. But a dab of rouge won't kill her." Her mother cupped her cheeks, probably noticing all her new freckles. "You got a lot of sun this summer."

"How's Aunt Flossie?" Celia asked, changing the subject.

"Wonderful," her mother said. "You should see the adorable little cottage she bought in the old country. I didn't want to leave, but I had to get back to my girls."

"Did you tell her?" Celia asked Bianca.

"About Los Angeles?" Her mother's face sobered. "Yes. Bianca told me. We're still discussing it."

"No, about our trip today." Celia smiled. "Angie, Fletcher, Moose, and I are staying in San Francisco for a few days. In Bianca's apartment while she's in LA."

"Is that so?"

Celia nodded, waiting for the backlash. No matter what her mother had to say about it, she was going. She would stand her ground.

"No, your sister didn't mention it. But it's the least of my concerns." Her mother's tone was reproachful as they lugged her suitcases toward the house. "Luisa called me. I'd like to know why you didn't inform me of Jeremiah's return. Did you think I wouldn't want to know about something like that?"

"Well, no, but—"

"But what, young lady? It was important news, and you kept it from me. Why?"

Celia sighed, setting a suitcase down on the porch. "I'm sorry. I've been busy." Truthfully, she didn't want her mother returning home early. There would be curfews and rules, even at her age.

"Doing what? I also heard you quit the gift shop this year."

Damn Luisa! Celia opened her mouth but couldn't think of anything to say.

"Well," her mother huffed. "Where is he? I want to see him."

"Oh." Celia bent her head toward the orchard. "Home. Painting."

"And how is he? Is he faring all right here? You're not misbehaving around him, are you?"

Celia pulled a face. "He's fine. And I'm not 'misbehaving.' I'm not a child."

"Well, I hope you've been making him feel welcome."

Bianca broke out into laughter. "Oh, she's making him feel welcome all right."

"You, zip it," Celia growled.

Her mother's eyebrows arched. "Celia?"

Celia was speechless again. Her lips parted, but the words wouldn't form. "I—"

"She chases him around like a puppy dog," Bianca taunted. "She's in looooove."

"Just wait till I get a hold of your things," Celia hissed at her sister.

"Don't you mean the *rest* of my things?" Bianca flicked the hat on Celia's head. "Thief."

"Celia?" Her mother appeared slightly amused. "Is this true?"

"I was going to ask her. It looks better on me anyway."

"You wish."

"I meant about Jeremiah," her mother said, taking a loose piece of Celia's hair between graceful, manicured fingers. "You're in love?"

"Oh. Him." Celia let her face fall into a pout, embarrassed. Oh, how she'd missed her gentle mother. "I don't know . . . You should see him, though, Mama. He's so handsome and wonderful. But he hates me, so it hardly matters how I feel."

"Oh, Celia." Her mother smiled. "I can't imagine that boy ever hating you. He adores you." She had to be forgetting that last day in the front yard. "You can be so melodramatic."

"I'm not being melodramatic."

"She is," Bianca cut in. "He's just as smitten."

"Is not!"

"Huh." Bianca tilted her head. "Well, maybe we should tell Mommy how you two were behaving last night and see what she thinks."

"I will burn everything you own."

"Just try it, thief."

"That's enough out of you two. My sister and I do not threaten each other." Helena Lynch turned to her youngest daughter. "Now take me to Jeremiah." With a nudge here and there, she guided Celia toward Jeremy's house before pointing back at Bianca. "We're not done with our talk."

"All right." Bianca's tone was petulant. "God."

"We're going right now?" Celia asked. It was a repeat of the Luisa disaster. But at least this time Jeremy was used to her barging in on his life. "He asked about Dad. He wanted to know how he died. But I . . . I couldn't."

Her mother sighed. "How are you doing? Have you spoken with Dr. Frank at all this summer?"

"I don't need a psychiatrist anymore, Mother. I was alone at a concert with fifty thousand people, and I was fine. No panicking or anything. I didn't use my inhaler once." A lie, but a trivial one.

"Alone? Well, Celia, that's dangerous for any woman."

"But I handled it fine is the point."

"It wasn't one of those flower hippie hair concerts with the mari-juana, was it? Did Bianca put you up to it?"

"No. Moose took us."

"Oh, my." Her mother laughed. She really did like Moose—he hadn't been fibbing about that part—despite his shaggy hair and the fact that he'd tried, on several occasions, to get her to see the advantages of herbal enlightenment. "Where is Curtis this morning?"

"He'll be here soon. He bought a new car. You should see it. It's so groovy."

Right then, Jeremy emerged from between the buckeyes with a small duffle bag slung over his shoulder, his forearms speckled with pale-yellow paint. His pace slowed when he caught sight of both Lynch women.

"Jeremiah." Helena began to jog in her heels, then pulled Jeremy into her arms. "My goodness, you're all grown up. Look at you." She stepped back, elation glittering her eyes. "Do you remember me?"

"Of course, ma'am."

She squeezed his arms. "I hope Pacific Grove is treating you all right."

"It's good. I've been busy."

"You're fixing up your father's house, I hear."

"Yes, ma'am."

"May I see?"

They walked together toward his house, chatting superficially. Her mother asked questions. Jeremy answered them. Celia followed a few paces behind.

"How's your mother doing?" her mother asked Jeremy.

"Uh . . . she's good. I spoke with her a few days ago. She's anxious for me to get back home."

"Of course."

Celia kept herself out of their conversation, and Jeremy barely looked at her while he showed his work. Was he unhappy with her? Or only distracted?

Her mother oohed and ahhed and continued the small talk with

Jeremy. Neither mentioned Thomas Lynch. Had he been alive, he would be admiring Jeremy's work right now, showering him with fatherly affection and praise. Tears pooled a little in Celia's eyes. Her father had loved his daughters, but he'd loved and treated Jeremy like a son. He'd been waiting on this moment for years, the day his son might return home, unaware that he would never live to see this quiet summer morning.

21

Jeremy

At close to ten in the morning, Moose roared up in his new-but-used, mud-spattered, left-front-corner-dented, flat-coal-black-on-black 1966 Chevy Impala SS convertible. It had a snarling, tire-shredding 425 hp, 427 cubic-inch, big block V8 engine, and yet he honked as if his arrival needed announcing.

The story of the car went like this: after saving for a full two years, Moose had purchased his dream car the previous week from a woman in Oakland. Her eldest son had been killed in action eight thousand miles away in South Vietnam, three miles north of the village of Con Thien. A sniper shot to the head. "At least it was quick, *su pobre madre.*" Moose had gotten a killer deal, so to speak. That Impala and Moose had vanished until yesterday, and according to Pacific Grove's resident fat mouth (Betty, whom Jeremy still ran into on occasion), Moose frequently did stuff like this on his days off work, going on spontaneous adventures. Where he'd gone this time would remain a mystery, though, because in a bizarre turn of events, Moose wasn't talking.

After loading the trunk, Jeremy walked around, palming the black beauty, passing her clean engine, absorbing her warm, thunderous purr as she revved and revved.

Behind the wheel, Moose sat happy and maybe a little stoned.

Jeremy opened the passenger-side door and flipped the front passenger seat forward so the girls could slide in back. "Ladies."

"Wait," Celia said while Angie slid into the car without complaint. "Why are we in back?"

"Because your legs are shorter," Jeremy responded with as much condescension as humanly possible. He had hit the sack the night before feeling mostly fine but awoke resentful and jealous. He couldn't shake the image of her and Fletcher in that dark hallway, joined at the mouth, or the fact that she'd lied to him afterward, claiming she hadn't kissed Fletcher back.

Jeremy knew what he'd seen.

The girl had played him like a fiddle, and to his surprise, it stung. Bad.

Standing before him now, taking his words as a challenge, Celia hiked her dress up over the smooth arc of her hip, presenting to him a lean, pretty leg.

Jeremy's focus flew to her thigh, then floated thoughtfully over the impeccable curve of her ass. He couldn't remember suddenly what had him so angry. All that seemed crucial suddenly was bunching that dress up to her tits and taking her good and hard from behind.

Jeremy pushed the imagery away. It made it easier to stay mad at her.

"Not so short, are they," Celia boasted, then turned her shoulder on him to slide in next to Angie.

Mildly amused, Jeremy snorted. Chicks loved to pull this kind of cutesy crap in order to win arguments, but Celia wasn't winning today. Pretty leg or not. He'd seen her body before anyway, laid out on his front lawn, goading his basest instincts. So he was familiar with the celebratory grin she wore as she settled into the back seat.

Too often, he found himself charmed by these little antics of hers. Had she been any other girl, she probably would've had him in knots at her feet by now. But she wasn't any other girl—she was her. So they eyed each other as Jeremy snapped the front seat back into place and got in the car. He wanted so badly to stay angry with her, but the smug grin she wore beneath that oversized hat made her so damn cute that he elected to grant her this single, provisional victory by giving her a smile.

Whatever. He still had shotgun.

Moose waited for Fletcher to get situated in back, then turned to ask the girls, "You okay with the top down?" Both nodded, and he clapped his hands together. "All right! Let's hit the road!"

Throwing the car into gear, he punched the gas, leaving a cloud of dirt in their wake.

Everyone held tight as he whipped around Sunset Drive, placing his new car side by side with the sunny California coastline.

Taking control of the radio, Jeremy twisted the tuner knob, stopping on a Kinks song he dug, listening as they made their way toward Pacific Coast Highway. That was when Celia got her panties in a twist about her windblown hair. She bent over the front seat, with the car moving at nearly sixty miles per hour, to drape herself over Jeremy's shoulder, her hand propped on the seat between his thighs, to roll up his window with an inspiring wiggle. She could've just asked, but Celia chose brazenness instead, and Jeremy couldn't help but enjoy it.

"What difference is it going to make with the top still down?" he asked her over the music and wind.

"What?" she yelled back, her hair lashing at his face.

He wondered where her hat had gone, but said, "Never mind."

Her hip at his ear, Jeremy stared up at the cloudless sky until she finished whatever she was doing with the window. A few accidental (totally on-purpose) glances revealed that she was wearing white silk panties with a lacy trim. God help him.

"Celia!"

A hand slapped Celia's exposed rear end. It was Angie.

"Ow! What?"

"You brought a head scarf. Sit your backside down. Jesus!"

Angie had a habit of scolding Celia like a mother would a misbe-having child, and the two began arguing in the back.

A few other mundane facts became apparent to Jeremy throughout the long drive. For instance, Moose had no patience for car lighters, and Fletcher harbored a soft spot for animals, particularly gutted ones in the middle of the road.

Fletcher, like Celia, also liked to sing along with the radio. His rendition of "Summer in the City" was more subdued than Celia's, though. She belted out the lyrics as though she were sharing a stage with John Sebastian himself. The girl was tone deaf but entertaining, something he'd learned well over the summer. Fletcher, on the other hand, could actually sing.

Moose's travel habits included playing finger drums on the steering wheel and pointing his cigarette at everything they passed, so he could spin another one of his bullshit yarns, every one of which translated as ludicrous and untrue. He'd run from the cops here, brawled with a band of territorial surfers there, stolen a street sign from this place or that, and on and on it went. Jeremy knew for a fact some of it was made up, or at least, wildly embellished. But he wasn't one to let the truth get in the way of a good story, so he let it slide.

Angie, in contrast, endured the trip with closed eyes, saying noth-ing except to explain that she gets car sick on warm days.

"Why are we stopping?" she asked halfway to San Francisco.

"Gas. Everybody better pitch in a whole buck this time," Moose said as he parked the car against the pump and hopped out. "Fuel ain't cheap, kitty cats." He threw the girls a wink before handing the teen-aged attendant a five-spot with a slap on the back. "Fill her up, small fry. Clean the windshield, too, and there'll be a shiny quarter in it for ya."

Outside the car, Jeremy stretched his arms over his head and watched as Fletcher and Celia climbed out one after the other. Bile rose at the sight. Catching them the night before had curdled his already-sour opinion of Fletcher. He'd suspected from the beginning that the two were messing around. Still, it had caught him off guard.

"Does Bianca live near the beach or what?" he asked, lighting a cigarette before he could give himself away with some caustic jab.

"No." Folding his arms, Fletcher leaned against the passenger door. "She lives a few blocks east of Golden Gate Park."

"You've heard of Haight-Ashbury, right?" Celia asked.

Jeremy avoided direct eye contact with her. "Yeah, I guess."

"She lives there." Celia moved toward him. "You'll like it."

Flirting in Fletcher's face, Jeremy noted as she sidled up closer to his side, her hip bumping his. She was always finding nonsensical reasons to touch him. Whether or not it upset Fletcher never seemed to matter to her. Though, at the moment, Fletcher was spacing out.

Stepping away from Celia, Jeremy leaned against the pump to face them both.

Celia leaned back against the car, propping her elbows back on the hood, winking away from the morning sun as she described the neighborhood where her sister lived.

Amid the noise, Jeremy's gaze sunk like a weight to her chest, where her small breasts managed to stretch the upper buttons of her dress to their limit, revealing slivers of bare skin. He shifted his concentration to a sign behind her head, but of course by then it was too late. What he assumed was a self-satisfied smirk was already plastered across her face. She'd been baiting him like this all summer, sunbathing in skimpy bikinis, staring hotly, scratching at his arms with willowy, painted fingers, making him crazy.

"You'll see," she said. "I visited last year. It was wild." Her smile disappeared. "My mom and I mostly stayed inside, though. She didn't like it."

More subtly this time, Jeremy watched her, transfixed as she bunched her lips sideways, then frowned in response to some private thought. Her freckled nose twitched, and he didn't know anymore how to slow the momentum of memories that flooded his head whenever she was around.

"I'm going to get a Coke from the machine," he said. "You want one?"

Fletcher shook his head.

"Sure," Celia said, straightening herself up. "Thanks."

She started to sing to herself as he walked away, the sound following him until the popular Left Banke tune slipped quietly from his own lips.

He bought his bottle of Coke (and Celia's) from the clunky machine beside the service station, and by the time he turned the corner to head back, Moose and Angie, who had set off together for the restrooms, had returned to the car with two men he didn't recognize. Several feet away, Celia clung to Fletcher, but other than that minor aggravation, Jeremy thought the situation seemed pretty copacetic. That is, until Celia's eyes darted fretfully to his as she nudged Fletcher forward.

Fletcher moved briskly toward Jeremy. Behind his approaching form, Celia found shelter behind Angie.

"Walk with me," Fletcher said when he reached Jeremy, spinning him in the opposite direction.

Planting his feet to the blacktop, Jeremy jerked his arm away. "What the fuck are you doing?"

"You don't want to see those guys," Fletcher explained. "Trust me."

"Why not?" Intrigued now, Jeremy squinted back at the car where Celia chewed on her fingernails, watching him, looking like a child from behind Angie's shoulder. And not just any child. But the very one he remembered. A burst of adrenaline made his chest throb, and he had to blink back a sudden bout of blurred vision. A memory of her mother scolding her for biting her nails—"Ladies don't eat their fingernails; that's for boys and monkeys"—knocked him back like a bowling ball to his gut.

"Do you remember Tommy Russo?" Fletcher asked.

Blinking free of the image, Jeremy turned to Fletcher with a frown. Tommy Russo. "Yeah." Some people could not be forgotten. No matter how many miles or years or mandatory family—fucking psycho!—therapy sessions were wedged in between, they were eternally, damnably trapped inside your head.

"Is the other one Kevin?" was Jeremy's first question as adrenaline charged him, muscle, blood, and bone.

Across the parking lot, Celia continued to gnaw on her fingers.

"No," Fletcher answered in an unexpectedly somber tone. "Kevin was killed last year in Vietnam. I don't know who that other guy is."

Sensing something akin to grief, Jeremy had no real response for that. Why had no one told him? Why did no one around here ever tell him anything of importance? The thread of his thoughts swiftly unraveled. His mind backed further away from Celia, from Tommy Russo, from the gas station altogether.

Kevin Donahue.

Dead.

Vietnam.

Jeremy struggled to remember the kid's face. Had his skin always been so wasted? So ashen? Had he always gazed on with inanimate eyes? For Jeremy, it was impossible to imagine. Nonexistence. Sea after sea of blackness with no internal dialogue to remark on its exact shade. What did this news mean to him? He figured he should feel some sense of satisfaction. It was retribution, wasn't it? Justice, after years of torment. Only it was the wrong kind. Delivered by the wrong enemy. He and Kevin had been cut from the same cloth. Two enraged little shits fighting for supremacy over nothing, when there was something much bigger coming for them, something that recognized them both as disposable bodies made for war. He suddenly felt sorry for the little prick.

"Moose is distracting Tommy till he leaves," Fletcher said. "I guess he works near here. I haven't seen that scumbag since high school. He was always hassling Celia back then."

This surprised Jeremy enough to jolt him once again from his own disordered thoughts. Typically, Fletcher was the composed one. But today, blood seemed to boil beneath the surface of Fletcher's pallid skin.

"Hassling her?" Jeremy's full attention returned to the pumps. "Why are we standing over here then? Let's go pound his face in."

"No." Fletcher positioned himself more squarely in front of Jeremy, where they stood eye to eye, but it did little to dissuade Jeremy's newest intention. "You can't do that, all right. You can't just go pound people's faces in whenever you get the urge. It doesn't work that way."

Confused, Jeremy glanced around. There were no kids, no cops . . . "Why not?"

"I don't know. Because. Because it would upset the girls."

"So?"

Fletcher gave him a look.

"All right." Jeremy peered around to check on Celia again. She looked terrified. "I'll just go say hello."

Fletcher laughed. "Why don't I believe you?"

"Get the hell out of my way, Fletch, before I move you myself."

After some hesitation, Fletcher stepped aside. "Have it your way."

Thrusting the two soda bottles at Fletcher, Jeremy managed about six steps before Celia became his next obstacle. Having run over, she set two palms on his chest. "Everything's fine." She put on a false smile as her eyes sought an audience with his. "Come take a walk with me. Please?"

He touched a thumb to her chin, surprised to find it trembling. "Relax, huh," he said. "I'm not looking for a fight." He didn't understand why this mattered to her. Did she have no faith in his ability to defend himself? He wasn't ten anymore.

"You promise?" she asked him, turning her ear to his chest in what felt like a search for comfort.

It felt nice having her against him, and he pressed his lips to her hair, then touched his cheek to its softness. "No."

"Jeremy fuckin' Hill!"

The jovial call dragged sluggishly from grinning lips that Jeremy had once dreamed about pulverizing, from a person he'd fantasized on more than one occasion about killing. Violent, brutal deaths this kid had endured inside Jeremy's aching head, late at night in his bedroom. Nightmarish cruelty, the likes of horror flicks. Bloodied, split faces. Flesh ripping from jagged, cracked bones. He, Jeremy, always the V-armed victor.

Jeremy tuned out Celia's gentle pleas and handed her over to Fletcher.

"Look what the tide dragged in," Tommy said, smiling, as Jeremy approached. "Aren't you supposed to be in prison?" Turning to his friend, Tommy broke out into laughter. "This cat right here is a Pacific Grove legend. Gimme some skin." Tommy stretched his hand out to Jeremy. "How are you, man?"

Jeremy ignored it. "Can't complain."

"Right on," Tommy nodded, eyes glinting with merriment as he lowered his hand. "I gotta ask, man, I mean, did you really, you know, kill your dad? 'Cause that shit was crazy. People still talk about it to this day, man."

"Yeah," Jeremy replied casually. "I did. Stabbed him right . . ." He flashed a quick look at Moose, warning him to be ready, then jabbed two fingers into Tommy's chest, startling him, "here in his lousy fuckin' heart. He went down after that first slice. Kinda took the fun out of it, you know?"

Following a moment of awkward silence, Tommy began to laugh broadly, with Jeremy following suit.

Uneasily, Moose joined in, his brown eyes dubious.

"Jeremy," Angie cautioned, trying to call him back from whatever trip she'd thought he'd gone on. But the redhead had it all wrong. He was cool as a cucumber.

"Oh, man, you had me there for a second," Tommy said. "You gotta admit, though, you were one crazy little guy back then. But killing your own dad, I mean, that's some heavy shit."

He seemed to leave a question hanging in the air for Jeremy to answer. All jokes aside, a man had died, and the rumor mill left little room for an innocent son, especially one like him. But Jeremy sort of liked that people were wary of him, never really knowing for sure.

"No," Celia uttered behind him, the words fuzzy, clipped, as though her mouth had been muffled. "Stop it, Fletch . . . They need to . . . Let me go . . ."

Jeremy refused to take his eyes off Tommy, though.

"Oh, that's right," Tommy said, peering around Jeremy. "The chick who flew over the cuckoo's nest was there, too. How could I forget?"

"Cut it out, Tommy," Angie warned him, her tone sharp, as Jeremy felt his own ire ballooning, gradual and steady. The motherfucker had "hassled" Celia, according to Fletcher. Jeremy wondered how and why. The adrenaline kicked up a notch, making his feet feel light, his fists tighten. "Let's go, Jeremy. In the car. Now."

"Bossy lady," Tommy said admirably to Angie. "I can dig it."

Jeremy wasn't listening to Angie. Nor to whatever was happening behind him between Celia and Fletcher. He was too busy sizing up Tommy Russo. Tall but thin and probably slow. His guard was for shit; he was too preoccupied with banter. And if memory served, the kid was a dirty fighter in school. A toady and little else. Only effective among his stronger, more capable buddies. His best work came when you were down, with the bruising toe blows to your gut and kidneys. Coward shit. Kevin had been the true opponent: fearless, resilient, controlled, but Kevin was off sleeping with the worms somewhere.

"Please, can we go," Jeremy heard Celia beg tearfully behind him. "Please, Jeremy . . ."

But he maintained focus and contemplated the force it would take to get Tommy to the ground with one hit, to minimize Celia's distress. "Hey, where's Kevin these days?" he asked Tommy, to get the fucker to stop smirking at her first. "I know he was dead set on being . . . What was it? A fireman?" Of all things, Jeremy could recall a construction paper patchwork collage from fourth grade—"Kevin Donahue wants to be a fireman when he grows up!" His own smirk followed. "How'd that work out for him?"

Tommy's smirk disappeared. "Real funny, man," he said, posturing, lengthening his spine. "I wasn't looking for a hassle. I just wanted to say hello. What's past is past, you dig?" Tommy moved to walk away then, his quiet friend a step behind.

It was difficult for Jeremy to relax enough to fall back a step, but he managed. Dredging up dead friends hit below the belt, but to hell with it. It got the son of a bitch to lay off Celia.

"Oh, and for your information, man," Tommy said, ambling back around, "Kevin and I, and well, most of the guys back in school, we felt really bad about everything after you left. So we made sure to take extra special care of sweet little Celia for you. If you know what I mean . . . Ain't that right, sweetheart?" With a sleazy grin, Tommy winked over Jeremy's shoulder to where Celia stood, and it became enough, a brilliant whitewash all around—

———

A full-page advertisement for the RCA Victor television set—with new Rotomatic Tuning!—circulates with the paper every Saturday morning in the spring of 1954. Illustrated in simple, monochromatic print, Mother smiles and directs Son to marvel in the wondrous, glowing box as Father bounces Daughter on his knee. The ad with Mother and Father and Daughter and Son is placed on a dusty television console airing an episode of *Leave it to Beaver* in which Ozzie Nelson—Father—scrambles to complete Sons' paper route because Harriet—Mother—insists they are ill. The kicker is that they are not ill. Mother is overprotective. But that's beside the point. The point is: RCA Mother is amazed.

"Darling, can you even imagine such a thing?"

Son cannot.

Because it's all fantastical. There are no Mothers. Fathers do not bounce Daughters on knees or tolerate idle Sons. They sit in the middle of smoke-filled dens and wave you over, squinting as Viceroys sizzle from their cracked lips. "Come on, boy! Come at me," they grunt, and you run at full speed until the blow from their fist knocks you clean off your feet and the wallop from the floor rips the breath from your lungs. "Get up," they say, Viceroy dangling. "Shake it off. That didn't hurt. Come back at me." You stand, and they are proud. A bizarre but pleasurable feeling washes over you, threading through the pain. You charge forward again until a blow to your stomach confounds you, and your head meets the floor with a thud. You climb dizzy to your feet before they can tell you to "shake it off."

That is the game. To "toughen you up" and "make you a man."

Your skin burns where the last Viceroy was snuffed out. Your stomach aches. Your throat becomes a desiccated inferno of need and regurgitated meatloaf, demanding relief while the blood, sweat, and tears touched by wind as you race at a red-knuckled fist are your only relief against the pain. You are raking at wood, praying for oblivion, learning the true measure of indifference. You are a man now. He is proud! It doesn't matter that he is killing you. *Shake it off.* There are no Mothers. No Fathers with bouncing knees. Ain't television just a fucking gas? The shit they come up with! There is only fight. And pain. The secret being in the total absence of fear, sowing the seed for your iniquity, your survival.

There is no protective Mother. No mercy. Not for anyone except Daughter. With her, you must be gentle. She is small and weak and disorienting. She cries if you tell truths and yells when you lie. Sometimes, she's no fun to play with. She never listens. She runs away to tattle—*SHAKE IT OFF*—and hurt you. She is not at all weak! She is formidable! She can cut you to dust with a single word! Her Father—with bouncing knees!—trusts you, and only you, to protect her. He pats your head and smiles down, saying, "Now take care of Daughter for me, Son."

Son!

I will, Father!

It matters not that Daughter hates you. She is life, cruel and unjust, in limitless Technicolor. She's cool wind and water, a reason to get off the floor and get knocked back down again. Father has charged you with Daughter's delicate arms and the umber eyes that look like perfectly round beach pebbles washed up on fine, white sand. You commit them to memory as she spins on that sweltering, dizzying merry-go-round, whirling and wheeling until everything disappears into stretched lines of blue and gold, and you cannot see anything but Daughter's unspoiled face. The game doesn't exist here. There is no fantastical bullshit. There is only her and that feeling she wields like a sword, that woozy sensation of spin when she smiles or laughs or chases you around the yard, when she holds your ruined face between soft, clean palms and shines her beach pebbles at you—

———

"Jeremy," he heard. Then tearfully, "Oh, my God."

But there was no Jeremy. No God. There was only rage—rage felt real—and exhilaration, fueled by the adrenaline and noradrenaline that bounded and pinged like an out-of-control pinball throughout his veins. It transformed every cell, every muscle, and every improperly healed bone into ceaseless energy. Into freedom itself. It flared gratifyingly with each thrust—the faster, the harder, the completer the rush—never entirely satisfying the building need. Like fucking. Marking little difference between his enemy's flesh and a soft, warm cunt.

"Fletcher!"

"What the hell do you want me to do?"

"Anything!"

Strong arms hooked beneath Jeremy's armpits and, abruptly, he was lifted, separated from the delicious rush and thrown in the opposite direction, then shoved forward.

When he turned, still pulsating with excitement, Fletcher was there with another forceful heave. Behind his head, Tommy lay bloodied on the oil-stained asphalt.

Again, Fletcher pushed him. "Hey, snap out of it! You won." Another shove, and Jeremy turned. "Walk." And so, he walked with Fletch at his back. "That was a dumb thing to do." Once they reached the other end of the gas pumps, Fletcher wedged Jeremy against one. "Stand here. Cool off."

After a minute or two of gnashing silence, of only his hammering heart registering behind closed, crimson eyelids, Jeremy felt a hard thump against his chest.

"You got him good." Fletcher thumped him again, not in anger or castigation, but praise. "I've always wanted to do that."

"Yeah?" Jeremy said. "Why didn't you?"

"I don't know. I guess, not to upset Celia."

"Horseshit."

Fletcher sighed. "All right, even if I could fight, I wouldn't want to. She's really upset . . . Hey, you've got blood on your mouth."

Confused, Jeremy touched a finger to his bottom lip, and it came back bright red. "Huh. I don't remember getting hit."

"Really? That other guy sucker-punched you pretty hard. That's when Moose jumped in," Fletcher said with a low chuckle. "Guy didn't know what to do. He got jostled around a bit, then just surrendered."

Jeremy wanted to laugh, but his head was pounding.

"*Vámanos*, Sugar Ray," Moose said with a clap as he strolled up. "Let's split before someone calls the cops."

The next thing Jeremy knew, he was back in the front seat of Moose's car. He closed his eyes and rested his head against the seat, wondering what the hell happened. An affront on Celia, and he'd completely lost it. Stupid.

The vibe in the car was tense.

"Damn," Moose grumbled as he plopped down into the driver's seat and shut the car door. "My bag these days is all about peace and brotherhood, and yet we've scrapped twice this summer. Over chicks. Both times. I may need to sit down and reevaluate my life."

Seated now directly behind Jeremy in the back seat, Fletcher chimed in. "Twice?"

"Yeah, you weren't home yet," Moose explained. "It was a few months ago. We brought these two skirts to the Point, and the one Jeremy was with—you remember that chick that used to go to Santa

Catalina's?" Moose asked Fletcher. "The cute brunette who used to run with Betty sometimes. With the big titties."

"Moose," Angie chided from the back seat.

"Sorry, Ang. Big brrrrreasts. What was her name?"

"Sheree," Jeremy answered. His jaw throbbed now, and he rubbed at it.

"Pointy-tits Sheree! That's right." Moose shifted into laughter. "Man, that chick looks like she's smuggling traffic cones."

"Sheree Humphrey?" Fletcher asked.

"That's the one! She'd just cut it off with some jock from CSU, and he followed us. We ended up in a hell of a brawl with him and three of his buddies. It was wild."

"Traffic cones," Jeremy chortled, still staring at the ruddy darkness behind his eyelids. Sheree had never even let him near those traffic cones, and still, he wound up with a week-long shiner.

"Neanderthals. Can we go now?" Angie was displeased, which seemed to tickle a few funny bones. Even Fletcher joined in on the sniggering. "Ugh."

"All right, all right, we're going," Moose said. "Hang on a sec." Reaching into the glove compartment, he grabbed a folded white rag and passed it to Jeremy. "Here you go, man. Clean up. I don't want blood on my new seats."

Jeremy eyed the dingy fabric in his hand. "This clean?"

"Of course. My mom did the wash this morning."

Satisfied with that, Jeremy wiped at his bloody knuckles.

"Your mouth, too, brother. That little guy clocked you good."

Jeremy could taste the blood, could feel the deep split in his lower lip.

"So, were her actual breasts pointy?" Fletcher asked from the back seat. "Or was it her foam domes?"

At that, Jeremy twisted around to smile at Fletcher, and it was only then that he was reminded of Celia's presence. She'd been quiet back there. But she was watching him.

Was it concern he saw on her face or repulsion?

A sense of betrayal struck him. Hadn't he done it for her? For her honor and all that shit? His body reflexively strained against the nauseating flavor of iron and salt as it seeped farther onto his tongue. Still, he stared into her dark, accusing eyes.

—*like beach pebbles*—

"Want to kiss me now?" he bit off, then turned from her scrutiny. He threw the blood-spotted towel at the dash, livid that he'd allowed her to get so far beneath his skin again. So, Celia was repulsed by him. What else was new?

—*shake it off*—

"Let's just get out of here," he told Moose.

The engine turned over, and there was a loud *thwack!* on the vinyl between them. Celia was climbing over the middle seat with ferocious intent in her eyes.

"What are you doing?" Moose asked her. "Your shoes are going to ruin my upholstery. What's she doing?"

Jeremy watched Celia clamber onto the front seat. Then she was over him, parting his lips wide until her tongue was hot and sweet in his mouth. Her weight sunk into his lap, and Jeremy coiled his arms around her, squeezing her tightly to himself. The abrupt thrill of her kiss, the violence behind it, plummeted fast from his stomach to his groin, which then jerked against her. When she fed him a faint whimper, biting his busted lower lip, he was sure she'd felt it, and he couldn't remember suddenly why he'd put so much effort into avoiding this. The many sides of him were warring. He was still angry at her for toying with him, for letting Fletcher touch and kiss her. But he couldn't move beyond the anxious beat inside his chest, beyond the assertion of her mouth, the very notion of her, romanticized by the lonely kid in his head, the one who'd hungered endlessly for any morsel of her. He'd gotten off on the pang of it for too many years. He'd never intended to set Celia aside from the others. Girls ignored him until high school. In the years between, she was *Girl,* with long, silken hair and soft skin, her image unfettered and wild until petting and kissing and gloriously awkward teenage sex arrived to set him free.

Masturbating at thirteen, he'd dreamed of what treasure waited between *Girl's* thighs. What raw, red vulgarity. Had they never parted, he'd started to wonder at that age, would she have wanted him the same way he would've wanted her? Or would she have scoffed at the idea? She'd let him kiss her once. What else might she have permitted once they were older? His pubescent fantasies had thrived from there, blossoming into lush, detailed pornography—her ripe body sprawled beneath his, naked and willing, while he suckled and fucked her into oblivion, his come lashing her tongue as crimson-painted fingers milked him. Or maybe he'd come inside her as she uttered some whorish string of vulgarities or "I love you, Jeremy," depending on his mood. She was everything he needed her to be, every time. The ultimate fuck. And when the daydream ended, when he was alone and unaided once again, when he'd contemplate writing to say hello, he'd remind himself that she'd shredded his worthless heart every chance she got.

Until the day he let her go, the day Pamela Conrad lavished on him a smile in freshman gym. Sweet Pamela became *Girl* then.

The memories chafed at Jeremy now, embarrassed him. Still, he slanted his mouth to drive his tongue deeper, finding pleasure in the hungry yet gracious way Celia took him, her melodious little moan, the slow burn that all at once ignited like a bomb. She was better than his thirteen-year-old, depraved self had ever imagined.

From somewhere far away, a female voice bellowed her name.

Jeremy tightened his arms, demanding she stay.

"CEEL-YA!"

At the brasher shout, Celia pushed away from him. "ALL RIIIIGHT!" She scrambled off his lap onto the center console between him and Moose.

Jeremy inhaled the abrupt blast of cool air as a hush fell over the cab of the car. Yearning thundered through his heart. His whole body ached for her. What was she doing to him?

Looking left, he caught Celia gazing dreamily at the dash, her lips—now haloed with his blood—spreading to form a gory smile.

Jeremy stared at her, dumbstruck, as Moose emerged out of Celia's profile to point at Jeremy's mouth. "Man, I think she missed a spot."

22

Celia

The five of them stood on a sidewalk in the Haight-Ashbury district, squinting up at a whitish Victorian row house on Clayton Street. It stood tall and lean and almost invisible between two adjoining homes. Its solitary carport was occupied, so Moose had double-parked alongside a blue Volkswagen bus.

"That's the one," Moose confirmed for Celia. "I'll go find a parking spot up the street."

As an impatient line of traffic honked, Fletcher and Jeremy gathered bags from the trunk.

Celia and Angie trotted up the front steps of the house, offering greetings to the colorful malingerers there, who greeted them back with two-fingered peace signs and lackadaisical nods.

"Bianca's going to kill me for losing her hat." Celia tried the door, finding it locked, then dug through her purse for the house key.

"Who are all these people?" Angie asked.

"No idea. But she warned me it might get crowded. It's part of why she's looking for a place down in LA."

"Who else lives here with her?"

"A few others." Celia jammed the key into the doorknob and wiggled it. It seemed stuck. "I only know Alan and, oh, Ted, a guy she dated last summer."

A man opened the front door, startling Celia and Angie. He was heavily bearded with wide-set eyes that shined an unnatural shade of blue. He smiled at them.

"Hey there," Angie said with a friendly lilt.

"Hey there to you." He held the door for them. "Come on in. Make yourselves at home."

"You live here?" Celia asked, injecting herself between their hot gazes. Maybe he was one of the newer roommates she hadn't met yet.

Peeling his eyes from Angie, the bearded man only shrugged. "I have no idea who lives here."

"Of course you don't," Angie said with a chuckle, drawing his attention back to her. "Why should you?" She leaned into Celia, her smile lingering on the man. "What is this place?"

Both Celia and Angie stepped around the man, who held his languid smile on Angie as she headed up the stairs.

"Did you see him?" Angie asked Celia. "I would do so many dirty things to that hairy freak."

Celia laughed. "You're the freak."

"You're one to talk, Bozo."

"What?" Celia was overcome by confusion as they reached the top of the stairs. The door to the apartment itself was wide open, and they could see that the second-story unit where Bianca lived contained more of the same love crowd from the steps. They flooded every corner of the tiny, four-bedroom unit, chatting, making out, and smoking. The air reeked of incense and pot.

Meandering through the vibrantly dressed crowd, Celia struggled to recognize any faces. "It wasn't this crowded last time," she said over the music.

"When was that again?" Angie asked.

"Last June."

In the kitchen, Celia and Angie bumped into a friendly fellow named Alan, who lived in the house with Bianca and five other people who were supposedly "around." Alan expressed his delight at "meeting" Bianca's little sister with a spirited hug. And like the other times Celia had "met" him, he smelled heavily of both stale and freshly smoked marijuana. He was chaotically dressed in a shapeless, homemade tunic made of clashing fabrics and colors. His blue jeans were decorated in higgledy-piggledy patchwork. Much of the crowd was dressed in a similar style, and Celia began to feel a little out of place in her fitted, A-line dress, despite its vivid colors. That morning, Bianca had told her she could keep the dress, saying it wasn't her style anymore, and Celia now understood what she'd meant. Bianca inspired trends, whereas Celia followed them. Fashion-wise, she often found herself one or two steps behind.

"Bianca locks her bedroom door with a padlock," Alan told them. "You can sleep in there if you can break inside. Hey, did she give you the combination?"

"No," Angie grumbled. "And one bedroom? There's five of us."

"Yeah, I know, you got lucky," Alan said, staring at Celia's mouth. He'd been doing it since they ran into him, and it was making her self-conscious. "It's the biggest bedroom."

"That's not—"

Celia nudged Angie toward the kitchen door. "Swell! Thank you, Alan. I'm sure Moose has the padlock combination."

"It's the last door on the right!" Alan called out. "Later, Banana Girl!"

"Banana Girl?" Angie asked.

"He told me last year I'm always wearing yellow, then started calling me that."

Angie eyed her friend. "You do wear a lot of yellow."

"I look good in yellow."

"Nobody looks good in yellow."

"I do."

Arms linked, the girls followed Alan's directions down the dark hallway to the last door on the right. The door stood open by an inch. No padlock in sight.

"Oh, what now?" Angie pushed the door open.

Inside, Moose lay sprawled on a large bed that was blanketed with an old patchwork quilt Celia recognized from childhood and a half-dozen tattered stuffed animals (one of which, Celia realized, was her Knickerbocker teddy, missing since Easter of 1955). On the floor below him, Jeremy and Fletcher sat with their backs against the mattress.

Angie dropped her satchel. "What the heck?"

Moose sat up. "Where've you two been?"

"Wading through about a hundred trippers beading necklaces," Angie said, scanning the room.

The first person to catch Celia's eye, of course, was Jeremy. But it was impossible not to notice him, considering he had, what looked like, a massive pink bruise encircling his mouth.

"Jeremy," Celia whispered, her hand inviting him forward. "C'mere."

"What's wrong?" Angie asked her.

"His face has blood."

"Celia," Angie laughed quietly. "Yours is ten times worse."

"Oh, my God." Covering her mouth, Celia ran out into the hallway, grateful to find the only bathroom empty. Checking her reflection in the mirror, she gasped loudly and twisted the knobs on the sink, thrusting her hands beneath the icy flow of city water to quickly sluice her mouth and chin. Pink water swirled around the drain and disappeared.

As her mind sifted through all the people she'd encountered in the last hour, Celia pulled her toiletry bag from her travel bag and dug around for a fresh bar of soap and washcloth. When she found them, she began to scrub her face clean.

Through dripping eyes, she saw Jeremy enter the small room.

"We must have looked a fright walking in here," she told him, rinsing the soap off. "Why didn't they say anything?"

With a slight smile, he said, "I think we freaked them out back in the car."

"Oh." Celia's freshly cleaned cheeks heated with embarrassment. "I'm sorry about that."

"Why?" Jeremy leaned against the door jamb as he watched her dry her face. "I'm not."

Celia, staggered now into nervous silence, grabbed another washcloth from her stack and straightened up. "You know," she said, trying to cool her cheeks with her palms, "in certain cultures, when you swap blood with someone, they say your spirits are bound forever." She promptly rolled her eyes. She sounded ridiculous.

"Yeah?"

Celia shrugged, and their eyes met through the mirror. "It's just something I read."

"We didn't swap though," Jeremy said.

"No, I guess we didn't." Sighing, Celia gave the bathroom counter-top a pat. "Come on. Let me clean you up."

Closing the door behind him, Jeremy squeezed past her and leaned back against the sink, watching as she stood between his feet and bent around him to saturate a fresh towel beneath the faucet. He was staring at her with an indecipherable expression, but Celia tried to ignore it. She tried to quell her trembling fingers as she raised them to his mouth and dragged the washcloth carefully across his cut bottom lip. The act felt intimate, and Celia struggled to swallow. She didn't know what had come over her in the car. *Want to kiss me now?* The words had tumbled irritably from his bloodied lips, and she hadn't understood why or what she'd done to make him so angry. Of course, she wanted to kiss him. More than ever. But the desire after his snarky invitation had transformed into a fury to rival his, then into pure grit, and there was no stopping her after that. She knew for certain now that he was attracted to her. Very attracted. It was wonderful news. But she was also pretty sure that she was in love with him. And those two things were nowhere near the same. She didn't know how to proceed from here, having started something she couldn't finish.

Standing before her, Jeremy looked primed, eager even, to resume the physical intimacy she'd begun. His hands came to her hips to draw her the slightest bit closer, and she steadied herself for another kiss.

Then he surprised her.

"How'd your dad die?" he asked for the second time this summer. "I want to know."

"I—I figured you would've asked my mother." Bewildered by the sudden change in subject matter, Celia returned to clearing the dried blood from his skin. "Or Moose. Or Angie."

"I want to hear it from you."

Dodging the intensity of his gaze, Celia leaned around him, rinsed the towel in the sink, then continued cleaning around his mouth. "I don't want to talk about my dad."

"Funny, I remember saying the same thing."

"And you never talked about him."

"Celia." Jeremy caught her wrist. "Please."

The uncharacteristic plea compelled her eyes to rise and meet his. Wearing a gaze that was as demanding as it was pitiful, he released her wrist and let her thumb return to its work.

"You're pushy," she said.

"So are you."

"Fine." Celia rinsed the towel again. "If you must know, he was killed in a car accident. A drunk woman ran a red light." Celia jerked her shoulders up, her typical punctuation whenever someone forced this topic on her. The words came out as frosty indifference because it had become the only way to say them aloud. "That's it." *That, and it was my fault he was out there that night.* "Now you know."

"Celia, look at me."

A summer spent in quest of his attention, and now that she had it, now that it begged her notice, she wanted nothing but to run from it.

"Celia."

Celia stuffed the washrag into a makeshift laundry sack. "There you are, clean and handsome again." She quickly gathered her things, powered a bright smile, and walked out.

———

Moose introduced his oldest friends to everyone he knew, and even those he didn't. Evidently, he spent more time here than either he or Bianca had let on. The crowd welcomed Moose's hometown friends, as well as Bianca's little sister, as if they were all long-lost pals returning for a grand reunion.

Beer and other homemade concoctions were offered freely. Marijuana was passed around in a glass pipe with a large, glowing bowl. Celia refused it all. At home, with her sister and friends, she'd felt somewhat safe to experiment. But she needed time to vet unfamiliar people, despite endorsements from Moose (she loved Moose, but he wasn't very discriminating with his company). And then there were the legalities. Getting caught by police in a house full of marijuana could ruin her life. If she wasn't stoned, she could argue naivete or ignorance. Maybe she'd say they'd come to visit with her sister, who turned out not to be home. Looking around, she'd probably pull it off. She stood out like a Muppet in a Hitchcock film.

Beside her, Angie swilled beer and became an instant hit. The hepcats of San Francisco didn't seem to mind her brashness. Her backhanded insults were met with laughter and intrigue. Celia suspected they thought Angie was putting on a show. If they knew she meant every word, they might not be laughing. But such was Angie's relationship with practically everyone.

Fletcher, a fellow Muppet, remained quiet and observant. Celia trapped his gaze with a grin, and he grinned back. Words were unnecessary. They responded similarly in this sort of environment, uncomfortably lame and dull around such vibrance. When she was young, she had been gregarious, a real show-off. She dreamed of reclaiming that comfortable feeling someday, that freedom to be outspoken like Angie, sociable like Moose, or at the very least, complacent with the unease, like Jeremy. He seemed to be enjoying himself, though, chatting easily with anyone who initiated a conversation.

Celia felt a tap on her shoulder.

"Hey, I'll be right back," Angie said, pulling on her jacket. "Moose wants me to go to the store with him. Fletch and Jeremy are still here."

Celia nodded.

Within seconds, a guy about her age took Angie's abandoned seat. "Hiya, sunshine."

23

Fletcher

Fletcher stared down at his new Romeo boots. There was a smudge across the leather of the left toe. He wiped it away with his thumb before sitting back and taking a deep breath. The house on Clayton Street was more than he could stomach today. It wasn't the crowd or the smoke. It wasn't the vibe.

It was him.

An hour before, Angie and Moose had run off to whereabouts unknown and were still not back. But Celia and Jeremy were still there in the same jam-packed living room as he was, seated on separate couches, talking with separate people, pretending not to care what the other was doing. Except, Fletcher had to hand it to Jeremy; he was far more skilled at the game than Celia. After being witness to their outlandish display in the car, Fletcher knew that he had made the right decision the night before to let Celia go. He would never share that kind of passion with her, and it had become painfully obvious that passion was something she desperately needed.

From a single make-out session, she glowed. It had looked almost excruciating for her, to kiss the object of her affection, while Jeremy, for his part, had soaked her in like a desert flower in rain. All Fletcher could think about now was how it must feel to crave someone like that, to finally drive your fingers through their hair and taste them, to pull them into your arms and hold on tight. Fletcher wanted so badly to know, and it made him incredibly sad to know that he never would.

Lovers were all around him, on full display, having no idea how lucky they all were. No idea at all.

Needing air, Fletcher stood. He tried to catch Celia's attention, but she was busy chatting with a long-hair in denim overalls who was doing his damnedest to hold her attention. Normally, Fletcher would need to stick around—to make her feel safe, to provide an excuse—but going by those covert glances, Jeremy had it under control. No one would harm a single strand of hair on Celia's head, not without it being the last thing they ever did.

Fletcher blew her a kiss and coasted out the front door, slipping through the crowd on the front steps.

A full-figured brunette, with a face painted in motley eddies of blue and green, smiled at him as he slipped past. She had flawless lips and teeth, set against a cherub's face.

"Hi," she said.

Skirting around her, Fletcher hopped onto the sidewalk and kept walking. A stone fox of a girl who was clearly interested, and he couldn't have cared less. He wanted to punch something at the unfairness of it all. He headed down Clayton Street, not sure where he was going.

Straight to hell, by all reports.

———

After several hours of Fletcher strolling aimlessly, the sun began its descent over the western horizon. To his dismay, his new boots had started to pinch his toes. He didn't know how long he'd been walking, but he was sure he'd gotten himself lost.

After buying his third Coca-Cola from a corner grocery, he rested on a bench off Market Street, pondering which route would lead him back to the Haight. He considered asking a passerby for directions but decided instead to retrace his steps and kill more time. Really, what was there to rush back to? It couldn't be too difficult anyway; the whole city was positioned on a grid, with a few exceptions.

The nearest street signs read Market and 7th.

Somewhere to the west should be the Haight, Fletcher guessed.

It was then that he noticed movement over his left shoulder. Two thirty-something women were tucked closely together inside the late-afternoon shadow of a recessed storefront.

French-kissing.

In public.

Both shocked and terrified for their well-being, as well as his own, Fletcher glanced around frantically, then fixed his glasses on the women again. Nobody but him seemed to be watching.

The taller woman noticed him and yanked the other away, plainly annoyed. "Mind your business, square," she chided as they hustled westward down Market Street.

Mortified, Fletcher pulled off his glasses and shifted his weight in the other direction to make a show of cleaning them. He hadn't meant to startle or upset them. He felt like a heel for staring. But what were they thinking? Kissing, where anyone could see. They were lucky it had only been him and not someone more . . . serious-minded. Were they lesbians? They had to be. He knew of their existence but had never seen any before now. Not that he was aware, anyway. Thankfully, there were no police officers around, and none of the sidewalk pedestrians had been witness to their very public display. At least he didn't think so. The women were safe for now, he determined as he slyly watched them disappear around a corner.

Not even a minute later, Fletcher observed more of the same. This time, it was two Black men—his age, maybe a little younger—across the street. Through the small crowd of a bus stop, Fletcher watched them gently lock fingers, check the small area around themselves, then dip into a bookstore together. Before Fletcher could put two and two together, someone sat down on his bench, and when he turned his head, he was shocked to find a face mere inches from his own.

Fletcher jolted backward and covered his heart. "Oh, good God. You startled me."

The tan-skinned man, small in stature with a round, feminine face and full lips, smiled at him. "Hello," was all the man had to say. The word, so simple, gave the impression of covertness with its delivery, so Fletcher scanned his immediate field of vision, feeling as though he'd been dropped into a spy film.

"Hello," Fletcher responded with the same air of secrecy. "Can I help you with something?"

"I don't know," the young man said, his accent unfamiliar to Fletcher. "*Can* you help me?"

"Pardon?"

Now the cryptic man appeared even more confused than Fletcher. "Are you lost?" he asked Fletcher, his tone leading yet cautious.

"Oh." Exhaling his relief, Fletcher smiled. "Yes. I am, in fact. I need directions to Clayton Street in the Haight-Ashbury District. If you'd be so kind."

"I understand." The man's expression descended into nettled disappointment. "It's over that way." He pushed his puckered lips westward, in the same direction the two women had gone, and slid to the other side of the bench, murmuring to himself in a foreign language.

"Thank you." Fletcher forced a smile. "Appreciate your help."

"Mm-hmm." The tan stranger rolled his eyes and twisted his body in the opposite direction, his leg crossing away.

"I'm sorry," Fletcher said. "Did I say something to offend you?"

"Of course not," the man said stiffly. "I thought you were someone else. It is my mistake."

Then it happened again. Two older gentlemen walked past in each other's arms, chatting and laughing together, and Fletcher saw one of them slide a hand into the back pants pocket of the other as they entered the corner grocery. It wasn't his sordid imagination, after all! He'd seen it! Again! His eyes grew wide. He felt energy and curiosity seep in to mix with his anxiety and fear. How was this occurring out in the open? Last year, he'd seen two sophomores necking behind the university dining hall at school, but he'd also seen those same two boys later get beaten to a pulp behind his dormitory for being "disgusting faggots." He'd never seen either boy again.

Aside from that unforgettable incident and the news special that he and Celia had watched earlier that spring, the subject matter never touched his own world. The question prodded at him now, demanding he react. How was this "criminal behavior" happening in broad daylight, on a major city street, while nobody flinched? He wanted to know. Needed to know. He remembered the documentary talking about a gay subculture in big cities like San Francisco and New York, but who could have imagined it being this bold? This open.

His mind reeling, Fletcher returned his attention to the stranger beside him, who sat staring at him with what appeared to be anticipation. Or was that fear on his round little face? Had this man noticed the pair, too? What to say? Fletcher wondered if he should get up and walk away. Was he supposed to feign disgust at the couple that walked by? Pretend he hadn't noticed them? What was the etiquette here? He had no experience with this.

"Are you sure you're lost?" the man asked him with a cock of his well-groomed eyebrow.

Fletcher considered that question carefully and, after a moment, felt his concern slip away into something he didn't understand. This new sensation expressed itself through an uncontrollable smile, and then he burst out into laughter. The idiotic, nervous kind. "Oh." Frantically, Fletcher covered his mouth to stop himself. "Oh, I'm sorry."

His bench friend held only concern in his eyes. "Are you all right, honey?"

"Yes," Fletcher answered, relaxing into the bench. "I mean, I think so."

"Could I get a sip of that pop you've got there?" His new companion scooted closer while lighting a cigarette. "Please," he added in response to Fletcher's hesitation.

"Uh, sure." Fletcher handed over his bottle of soda, uncertain about what to do or say next.

The man pointed his long, unfiltered cigarette at Fletcher, a silent question in his eyes.

Fletcher waved it away. "Oh, no, thank you. I don't smoke."

"Do you have a name?"

"I do!" He was excited to finally have a solid answer to something. "It's Fletcher."

"Fletcher . . . I like it." The man offered Fletcher a petite hand, much darker than his own. To Fletcher's astonishment, the nails at its tips were painted a glossy, fire-engine red. He hadn't noticed it until now. "I am Michael," the man said. "It's a pleasure to meet you, *Fletcher*."

His name had slithered out of the stranger's mouth like sex. Fletcher gulped at the slight tingle in his chest. "It—It's nice to meet you, too, Michael."

Satisfied, Michael stood, taking a large, yellow canvas bag and Fletcher's soda with him. "Fletcher, sweetheart," he said, slipping on a pair of red sunglasses. "You might be the handsomest boy I've ever met on this corner, so I'm going to risk life and limb to ask you one very crucial question. Are you ready?"

Heat rushed to Fletcher's face. He averted Michael's pointed gaze. "Uh . . . sure."

"Would you like to take a walk with me?" Michael smiled, clearly tickled with himself. "Breathe, Fletcher. I prefer you better alive."

"Oh." For a second there, Fletcher had been afraid Michael was about to ask him something personal, perhaps something about what they'd just witnessed. The relief he felt was followed by a great surge of energy. "Then yes."

"It's settled then," Michael said, his straight teeth gleaming. "We will walk."

Fletcher got to his feet.

"Holy matrimony! Fletcher, how tall are you?" With piqued interest, Michael snatched up Fletcher's arm as the two began to walk, the late afternoon sun shining painfully bright in their eyes. Fletcher wished he had his sunglasses. "Six three? Six four?"

"Six feet," Fletcher said, knowing it was more like five eleven and a half.

The touching was making him nervous. He scanned his surroundings to see if anyone was watching them, but nobody on the streets of San Francisco seemed to care that he was walking, arms linked, with another man, so he didn't pull away. But he remained vigilant.

The two of them received barely a glimpse, though, as they made a right onto Hyde Street.

"I ask because I once had the dishiest mannequin fellow who stood six feet two inches tall," Michael recalled whimsically. "I'm a seamstress, you know. Every night, I would imagine that Paul Newman—that was my dishy mannequin's name—was a tall, beautiful boy such as yourself. Three weeks before our wedding, I put a cinder block at Paul Newman's feet. I had to know if I would be able to kiss my prince charming in the heels I had put on layaway and—"

"Heels?"

"Wouldn't you know it, Fletcher, darling, we were a perfect match! We danced all night." Michael caught Fletcher's confused expression. "I've lost you now, haven't I?"

"Maybe a little."

"Didn't you ever try on your mother's heels, sweet boy?"

"No," Fletcher said, bemused. He'd never met a person like Michael before and wasn't sure how to behave around him. Regardless, he would not be rude, no matter how uncomfortable or confused he felt. "Can't say that I have. Sorry."

"Oh, it's all right." Looking up at Fletcher, Michael beamed. "Fletcher, you might be my prince charming after all. A real man's man."

Fletcher tilted his head. He'd never been accused of that one before.

A man's man, he was pretty sure, he'd never been. Hell, Angie made a better man. Perhaps he'd heard Michael wrong, as his accent was incredibly pronounced, so much so that Fletcher had to strain to listen to every word.

Michael's eyes flew toward the sky. "Thank you," he mouthed before turning to Fletcher again. "Are you a religious man, Fletcher?"

It was an odd question for a stranger to ask another stranger, but Michael was odd. "No."

"Well," Michael sighed, "nobody's perfect. But let me tell you this, darling, you're close enough for me. Your eyes are mesmerizing. Bewitching. I saw that color blue once when I was a little girl back in the Philippines. I loved to swim in the ocean. But you would never catch me in a swimsuit now. I don't go a day without my waist cincher. My lola raised me right. Anyway, I can't wait to show you off to the girls! Are you a banker?"

"A what? A baker?"

"Bank-er."

"Oh, no," Fletcher replied, wondering what he'd gotten himself into as his companion steered him farther and farther away from the direction of Haight-Ashbury. "Why do you ask?"

"An accountant?"

"Pardon?"

"Are you an accountant?" Michael repeated, more slowly this time.

"No."

"Do you see where I'm going with this, Fletcher?"

Fletcher shook his head. "No," he said, offering a shamefaced smile. "I'm sorry."

"What do you do?" Michael asked, spiraling his hand. "You know, for a living. What is your occupation? You are something official, no? You're quite the straightlaced fellow. But I like it very much."

"I'm a college student."

"Of course," Michael said. "Silly me. How old are you then?"

"Twenty-one."

"Ooh. Well, I am twenty-eight, though people say I don't look a day over twenty. They also say I don't act a minute over twelve, the cows."

"Where are we going?" Fletcher asked as Michael came to a stop and posed.

"We're here!"

24

Angie

After grabbing a bite to eat at a hamburger stand and taking a stroll around Bianca's circus of a neighborhood, Angie and Moose stopped at the market to purchase themselves a drink. Angie had yet to learn why Moose had insisted she accompany him. He'd spent most of their time together chatting with strangers on the sidewalks and steps of row houses. When Angie asked why he hadn't included Celia, Fletcher, or Jeremy, his answer was vague and dismissive. He was up to something, she knew, but she would be patient. He would spill the beans eventually. There was plenty on these streets to keep her entertained in the meantime.

Moose pulled a small glass bottle from an ice box inside the store.

"Orange juice?" Angie asked him. "In the middle of the afternoon? I'm getting a soda."

"This isn't ordinary orange juice." Moose dropped the ice box lid shut, twisting the bottle this way and that, to flaunt his prize. "This is special juice. Well, it's going to be." He grabbed a soda for Angie, then headed for the cash register. "We're going to go unwind in the park for a while. Just you and me. I want to show you something."

Moving farther away from Bianca's row house, the pair strolled northbound up Ashbury Street toward the panhandle of Golden Gate Park. Once they crossed the last busy street to reach it, Moose told her that he wanted to stop there instead of heading into the main park. The panhandle was perfect for what he had planned. Or so he said. There were people everywhere, but it was nowhere near as crowded as the Haight.

"It's perfect." Moose settled down into the grass. "Now sit."

"I wish we had a blanket," Angie said, doing as he asked. "The ground's a little damp."

"You won't even notice it soon," he replied with a grin.

But Angie was no fool. "I am not getting loaded in this park, Moose. In front of all these people. You can forget it."

"Why not?"

"Because someone will see, like—oh, I don't know—the police."

Moose laughed. "Give me a little credit, will you? We're not going to smoke out here. I'm not that stupid. You need to mellow out, and stop being so uptight."

"I'm not uptight. I'm smart, adorable, and practical. I shouldn't even be here right now. I should be home, keeping an eye on my brothers. My mom's been a complete basket case. I'm only here to look out for Celia. And Fletcher. Speaking of . . . we should get back."

"Should, should, should." Moose scrutinized her, part amused, part concerned at whatever he saw. "You know what you should do? You should relax. You've got all these hang-ups. And Celia's not a child."

"That's arguable."

"Wow." Moose shook his head. "Man, why are you even worrying about Celia? And Fletch. And your brothers. Your mom. And me." He flopped back onto the grass, throwing a forearm over his eyes as though the list had exhausted him. "It's no wonder you're so tense all the time. I've got a bigger uphill battle than I thought."

"You want to know why? Because none of you worry about your-selves. My mom's . . . my mom. My brother's still missing. Celia's out of control over Jeremy, who's hot one minute and cold the next. Fletcher is miserable and won't speak to anyone. And don't even get me started on you. Where have you been all week? Your dad said you disappeared with that car. You didn't tell anyone where you were going. You missed four shifts at the bar. And when I asked you about it, you made a joke."

After a few casual blinks, Moose popped onto his elbow. "Angie, doll, I love you more than life itself, but what everyone else does with their lives is their business. Not yours."

Angie huffed. Funny, coming from him, the guy who ran to her whenever Bianca upset his delicate heart, or whenever his dad was pissing him off, or when his two older sisters upset his mother. "I dis-agree," was all Angie said. As irritated as she got by Moose's intrusions, and everyone else's for that matter—always seeking her help, her opin-ion, her outrage—deep down, she didn't want the intrusions to stop. It felt good to be needed. Good and frustrating and draining as all hell.

"Listen to me." Moose sat up. "You are a free inhabitant of this earth . . ."

"Here we go."

"A child of nature. You're not a mother. Not a wife. You're not even a waitress. You are a smart, independent, beautiful woman who has a lifetime of endless choices ahead of her. Think about all the people we met today. Are they stressing about some nine-to-five, or their best friend's dysfunctional love life, or the rat race our parents created for us? No. They're experiencing life, Ang. The blue of the sky. The love in their hearts. The wind in their hair. Do you feel that?" he asked as a cool breeze made perfect contact with her skin, as if on cue. He looked at her like she had no inkling it was there. "We're all experiencing the moment right in front of us, feeling the pleasure or the pain of it for ourselves. Just *being*. Everyone except you."

Angie looked away, extremely annoyed suddenly. Was that why he'd brought her out here? For a stinkin' lecture? That was her thing.

"Angie, I'm worried about you."

"About me?"

"Yes. You're too young for all this pressure you put on yourself. It's taking its toll on you, and we all see it."

"All? Have you all been talking about me behind my back?"

He hesitated. "We're concerned about you."

Angie couldn't believe what she was hearing. And who exactly consisted of "we"? "This is ridiculous. My mom can't even take care of herself, and Celia's the one who—"

"Stop it."

"Stop what?"

"Just stop." Moose's tone was serious. "All these people you keep mentioning are adults, and they can handle their own shit. And if they can't, it's not your job to handle it for them. Your mom needs to own up to her own mistakes and her own solutions to those mistakes."

"But she'll—"

"She'll have to figure it out for herself, Ang. And she's not ever going to learn how to do that if you keep doing it for her."

Folding her arms, Angie looked away. Her jaw felt rigid, tight. The sensation was spreading outward from there.

"You know what I think?" Moose said. "I think you don't want to let go and focus on yourself. I think you're afraid of what you might find."

Angie rolled her eyes. Oh, for the love of . . . "And what's that? Do tell."

"Freedom. An open road."

"Are you psychoanalyzing me? This is because of that psychology class you took, isn't it? It's gotten into your head."

Moose sighed just as a shirtless man ran up to a group of people nearby and began helping them to their feet. Whatever he was saying had everyone excited. As the group moved swiftly in the direction of the main park, the man yelled out, "Hey, everyone! George Harrison's in the park! This way! Come on!" Many more rose to follow, some more reluctantly than others, not totally buying the rumor.

Moose raised an eyebrow at Angie. "Want to go see?"

Angie tittered. "What would a Beatle be doing in this park in the middle of a Monday afternoon? Don't be so gullible."

"Okay." In a surprise move, Moose simply slumped back down onto his elbows. She'd expected disappointment from him, a remark about what a drip she was being, but his expression remained untroubled. "You truly are the most impossible woman I've ever met," he said, almost impressed. "I've never had to convince a girl to let go and have fun before."

"Because you date airheads with no responsibilities in life."

Moose huffed. "Responsibilities. You're always using that ugly word. You're overstrung, woman. Life's too short to be miserable for even a minute. And for your information, I date delightful women who are in tune with themselves and the universe. If you smiled more, I might try dating you, too."

Angie laughed so loudly several people looked over.

"There you go," Moose said. "A smile. I'll be damned. And it didn't kill you."

Angie pressed her lips together, and so Moose hopped up from his spot in the grass, said, "Scooch," and squeezed in behind her to lean against the tree, his long legs flanking hers. He slipped his arms around her waist and took both of her hands in his. It was a captivating visual, the dark, warm shade of his skin against hers, which was virtually translucent. "Now we're making some progress," he said. "Look around. What do you see?"

Angie frowned. "Not much."

"Don't be difficult. Just answer the question. What do you see?"

"Um . . . high school dropouts."

"Try again, smart aleck."

Angie laughed, cursed herself for leaving the house with Moose, then opted to play along with him in order to get past this arduous conversation. She was sure he meant well. "All right, all right, I see a park," she said.

"Very good. And . . ."

"And what? It's a park."

"Aw, come on, look deeper than that."

"You're a major pain in my neck, you know that?"

Moose grinned. "Keep going. What do you *see*?"

"I don't know." What did he want from her? "I see a park with trees and grass and people."

"Good. And what are those people doing?" Moose flipped his hand in front of her face, urging her to continue. "They're . . ."

Angie blew out a frustrated breath but let her eyes land on several of the people out in front of her. "They're talking, and laughing, and singing . . ." Tilting her head, she pointed straight ahead. "Oh, okay, that couple right there is swapping spit while those weirdos over there are taking Polaroids of them." Angie gawked. Wow, people had nerve. It occurred to her as well that she hadn't noticed any of these people twenty seconds before, yet they were directly in her line of sight. She had simply acknowledged generic figures in the distance and had given them no additional thought, not even to identify their ages or genders or basic coloring (hair, skin, clothing) until Moose forced her. Was she that unobservant? Was that the point he was trying to make? And if so, why did it matter? It wasn't a crime to have your head up your ass. Not yet, anyway.

Scanning the park more carefully this time, Angie absorbed the scene. The population around her consisted mostly of young adults her age, mostly male, and she told Moose that. There were few children, even on this nice summer day that she now noticed was cloudless with a slight breeze. Also, it appeared as though a few homeless men had set up camp nearby, their personal belongings and trash scattered around them.

She continued, "Those people way over there are dancing and playing . . . are those drums?"

"Bongos."

"Oh."

Why had she not noticed any of these individuals until this very moment? In fact, the more Angie looked, the more she comprehended the scandal that surrounded her.

Moving her attention to a nearby cluster of trees, Angie squinted. "Hey, you can't do that out here!" she yelled loud enough for the overly affectionate couple to hear. "Get a room. There are children. Be ashamed!"

Near her ear, Moose chuckled. "I was wondering when you were going to notice them."

"They're breaking the law. That's indecent exposure."

"Never mind them then."

"Kind of hard to ignore—"

A young voice interrupted their conversation. "Ain't that the truth," a grinning teenaged boy, who couldn't have been older than sixteen, commented to Angie. The smoke from his lit joint caught her attention. Was that beer at his feet?

"Where are your parents?" Angie asked the kid.

"Angie," Moose said, squeezing her waist. "I can handle you ruining my good time, but try not to ruin everyone else's, too."

"Oh, fine."

"You lookin' for a little grass, Red?" the kid asked her, opening his palm to reveal a small baggie of dope. "It's Acapulco Gold, cloudy and fresh. Harvested it myself."

Angie was flabbergasted. "How old are you?"

"Your friend's right, you know," the youngster added. "You're way too tense. I've got just the thing to mellow you out."

"Is that so?"

"Thanks, sport," Moose winked at the kid, gesturing for him to back off, then raised his bottle of orange juice. "But we're focusing on one trip at a time right now."

"Right on, man," the kid said, and then gave Angie a once-over. "Just know I think you're beautiful, Red. I would enjoy making love to you."

Though peeved, Angie had to laugh. "Groovy. Thanks." Then she said to Moose, "Can we get out of here now?"

"We're not moving a muscle until you learn to unwind a little." He placed his chin on her shoulder. It was heavy there, but she didn't mind. "Look, doll," he said with his usual diplomacy, "you know I worship the ground you walk on, but I can also read you like a book. You'd love nothing better than to beeline it back home and continue on with the *Old Woman in the Shoe* gig until you die. But I can't watch you do it anymore."

"Old Woman in the—Excuse me, but that Old Woman had a mound of obligations. I don't think smoking dope in the park with Eddie Haskell over here would've fed all those kids. I mean, for God's sake, she lived in a shoe, Moose. Give the poor woman a break."

"It's not the shoe, Ang. I could live in a shoe if I had to."

"I feel you, man," the teenaged boy leaned closer to say. "I once lived in a school bus. I could live in a shoe."

"Neither of you have children to care for," Angie snapped at them both. "I do!"

"Your mother has children," Moose reminded her. "You do not."

"Moose—"

"Give me one night, Ang," Moose pleaded, turning her face toward him. "You can go right back to your shoe tomorrow. I know you will. And I love you for it. I know your family is going through some heavy stuff right now, but they'll be okay tonight. I stopped by your house this morning and gave your mom enough cash to take the boys to dinner and the drive-in. They're fine. I promise."

Stunned, Angie stared at her friend. "You did that?"

"Yes. And I promise you that Celia is fine. Fletcher, too. Will you please give me this night to show you?"

"Show me what?"

"What's out there."

"Out where?" Angie watched as Moose pulled something from his pocket, a tiny purple satchel made of crushed velvet. "What is that?"

"Hang on." Scooting around to face her more directly, Moose pulled the satchel's string and dumped its contents into his cupped hand. A dozen or so capsules rolled around in his palm. He selected two and put the rest back. He grabbed the glass bottle purchased at the market, popped off its cap, then broke each capsule in two, dumping their white, powdery contents into the orange juice.

Angie knew what it was. She'd seen a news report about LSD on television. The state of California had just made it illegal, but that didn't seem to be deterring anyone. According to the reporter, it was fast becoming as commonplace as the orange juice it currently transformed. Even in the suburbs where she lived. Among mothers as well as their teenaged children.

Angie grabbed the bottle he was shaking and eyeballed the concoction inside. "I don't know, Moose."

"Come on, don't be square."

"I happen to like being square," Angie said, sniffing the juice. "I—I don't want to freak out in this park," was all she could voice as she searched her mind for a sounder excuse. She read once that LSD made people go mental, and they were never the same after. Then again, Moose had taken it and seemed fine. He was no crazier than usual. "It's not my scene. I've never done anything like this."

"I know," he said. "And that's why I'm going to take full responsibility for your trip. You've got to trust me though."

"I trust you'll be stoned by sundown."

"Not tonight, I swear it." Raising a hand, Moose pulled a twisted brown paper bag from his other pocket and handed it to the kid. "Here you go, Buster Brown."

"Thanks, man."

"That was all my dope," Moose said to Angie. "Do you trust me now?"

Angie laughed. "No."

"Oh, come on." He looked hurt now.

"Fine," she grumbled. "But why can't we do this at home?"

"You would never do this back home. Home has bad vibes for you anyway. You need to do this somewhere tranquil. Somewhere free of negativity. Somewhere you don't know anyone, and they don't know you. I want to show you what's on the other side."

Angie grimaced. "There's another side?"

"There's always another side. Welcome to life."

Movement cast a shadow over them suddenly. Long, brunette hair tickled Angie's face as a young girl knelt beside her. An untidy bouquet of wildflowers danced in the wind from the girl's fist, and Angie found herself lost in shining, russet eyes. Without warning, the girl freed Angie's hair from its tight ponytail. Before she could complain, a tiny, pink flower was gently slipped above her ear, followed by a tender kiss on the cheek. "You looked so sad," the girl explained, then turned to Moose, angling her chin toward his pocket. "Could you spare one of those, Daddy-O?"

"*Lo mio es tuyo.*" Moose gave the brunette a capsule, earning himself a kiss and a flower in his hair as well.

Once the girl had moved on to another group, Moose touched his thumb to the flower in Angie's hair. "Much better," he said and gestured to the jar of juice still in her hand. "Now, will you please trust me? You know I would never let anything bad happen to you. You're my best girl."

Angie studied the foamy orange liquid. She hated to think that Moose's cockamamie charms could work on her, but she had to admit that they sometimes did. Not to mention, he'd been her friend for as long as she could remember, and he'd never once let her down.

"All right, you win. This time. But if I turn into a homicidal maniac, I'm coming for you first."

Moose smiled. "That's fair."

Closing her eyes, Angie made a quick appeal to Jesus, then guzzled down the warm contents of the bottle before she could change her mind.

Moose was lighting a smoke when she finished. She snatched it away and lay back onto the grass to savor the summer sky and swaying leaves before it all twisted and warped in front of her eyes. She took a drag off the cigarette, hoping to exhale her anxiety away. It was too late to turn back. For some wacky reason, she'd ceded power to Moose for God knew how long, drinking God knew what at his request.

Angie closed her eyes. "Now I lay me down to sleep. I pray the Lord my soul to keep . . ."

Moose stretched out beside her and lit himself another cigarette. "If I should die before I wake," he joined in, and they finished together, "I pray the Lord my soul to take."

"Thank you," Angie exhaled.

"Any time, doll."

25

Jeremy

Keeping an eye on Celia was a piece of cake, even in the crowded apartment. In her figure-hugging dress, with her wavy-yet-tidy strawberry-blond hair, she stood out among the litany of planned chaos.

Moose had teased him once, asking why, if he hated Celia so much, he consistently guarded her the way he did, like a sentry being paid his weight in bullion. The answer he'd given Moose was twofold. One, he didn't hate Celia. Two was harder to put into words. When a man you respect, Jeremy had explained, commissions you with the duty to protect his youngest daughter in his absence, you do it. It didn't matter to Jeremy that he'd been only five and a half years old the day her father took him by the shoulders and made him swear to keep Celia safe. A promise was a promise. He didn't make them lightly.

On a nearby sofa, one bare foot tucked beneath her thigh, Celia chatted up a long-haired houseguest wearing overalls (and only overalls) who had squandered forty long minutes working to convince her to drop acid with him. Like any decent salesman, Farmer Feelgood displayed for his prospective consumer a small ampule full of liquid LSD, regaling her with stories of psychedelic acid tests that lasted weeks and resulted in copious life-altering epiphanies. Celia appeared enthralled as she listened. Both were oblivious to Jeremy, who had absolutely no intention of letting the dipshit drug Celia.

"Soft," cooed a female voice as fingers pushed their way into Jeremy's hair. He twisted right to find the woman attached to those fingers. Gently, he pulled her hand from his head and appraised her. He'd noticed her earlier, smiling at him. She was cute, petite but full in the right places, with a colorfully painted face and tiny, white flowers scattered throughout a long, chestnut braid. Normally, he would encourage this kind of touchy-feely attention—girls were extremely forward out here in California—but he was preoccupied at the moment.

"Sorry, honey, not interested." Unable to help himself, Jeremy added, "What's with the paint?"

"It's art," the girl answered, turning her cheek to show him the left side of her face where a long grapevine of flowers had been painted. "It's how I connect with nature."

"Huh?"

The girl sighed. "Mystics in India and the Middle East paint their bodies with symbols of the earth, of love and sex. It increases fertility, cleanses the body, and rouses the subconscious mind."

Jeremy stared at her, trying to process what she was saying. A small part of him wanted to smile and nod and take her into a dark corner, but the rest of him had shit to do. "Right," was all he said before resuming surveillance on Celia and Farmer Feelgood.

"Right," the brunette beside him parroted. "Why don't you go talk to her already? The staring is going to get real creepy after a while."

Turning to the painted girl again, Jeremy said. "I'm not staring. I'm keeping an eye on her."

"What's the difference?" she laughed.

"I don't know."

The brunette narrowed her eyes at him playfully. "You're cute, but you're a little dumb."

Jeremy had to smile. "I know that chick, okay," he explained. "I'm just making sure Farmer Feelgood over there keeps his dope to himself. He's offering her LSD."

"Oh, the poor thing." The painted girl's smart mouth twisted as she gestured to the cozy pair on the other couch. "She doesn't seem to mind his attention, if you ask me."

"Well, no one asked you."

The girl's smile broadened. "You know, if you focused on yourself and stopped being such a stick in the mud, you'd probably be having a good time, like her."

"I'm having a fine time."

Jeremy watched the brunette sink two fingers between her full breasts and pluck out a thickly rolled joint.

She slipped the marijuana cigarette between her lips, lit it with a match, then held it out to him. The sharp stink of sulfur was quickly replaced by the promise of quality pot.

"Friends?" she asked with a well-crafted pout.

Amused by the girl, Jeremy went to accept her gift but first glanced over to notice that Celia's seat was now occupied by a young mother nursing her baby. Farmer Feelgood was gone, too.

Jumping to his feet, Jeremy caught a flash of Celia's yellow dress disappearing around the bend of the bedroom hallway. "Shit," he said, hopping over several people to get to her.

"Good luck, dummy," the brunette called out behind him.

Jeremy's heart raced as he dodged the bodies in his path, his thoughts consumed with twisted, agonizing images of Celia and that overalled moron getting it on.

Halfway down the hall, he jolted to a stop, recognizing how insane he was acting. The way this day was going, if he walked into Bianca's bedroom to find Celia and that hillbilly-looking meathead pawing at each other, he was likely to go apeshit. How had he gotten back to this place? In only a month, he'd regressed into a destructive ten-year-old with a crush. He'd spent the last hour trying to catch her eye, telling himself that he was guarding her from dopers in overalls, hoping she'd come to him. And when all he'd gotten was a few placating smiles, he'd been disappointed and jealous.

Drawing a deep breath, Jeremy pressed his eyes shut and waited for his agitation to subside. He had no right to feel possessive. Celia wasn't his, and it was her own business who she let paw at her.

Grudgingly, he forced himself around and took a few sludging steps back down the hall. As he reached the living room, he watched Farmer Feelgood saunter past with his arm around the painted brunette from the couch.

Slumping down, Jeremy dropped his head into his hands, laughing at himself over the incredible relief he felt. "Oh, fuck me."

"What was that?" he heard Celia ask.

He looked up to find her standing over him, slipping into a light jacket. She was dressed more casually than before, in yellow capri pants and a white blouse. "I'm going for a walk. Want to come?"

"Yes," he breathed, still absurdly grateful to see her alone.

Celia breezed past him. "Well, come on then."

Feeling beaten and cuffed, Jeremy got up to follow. Then something occurred to him. "Hold on." He scanned the living room for Fletcher and, when he couldn't find him, his eyes sought Bianca's roommate Alan.

Dragging Celia behind him, Jeremy found Alan in the kitchen, cross-legged on the floor, passing around an elongated pipe wrapped tightly in leather straps and adorned with feathers.

Jeremy squatted down. "Alan?"

"Hey! Curtis's friend. And Banana Girl!" Alan thrust the pipe at Jeremy. "Hit this. It's real heavy, man. It's laced with peyote."

"No, thanks," Jeremy said. "But could you do me a favor?"

"Sure thing, brother."

"If you see Moo—Curtis, can you tell him that Jeremy and Celia went for a walk and we'll be back soon?"

Alan promptly drifted off, the pipe continuing to burn a sweet-smelling smoke.

"Alan," Jeremy prompted.

"Oh, hey, man," Alan said, opening his eyes. "Judy and Carlos went for a walk. They'll be back soon."

"Perfect," Jeremy said with a smile. This had been pointless. "Thanks."

"Pleasure's all mine, man."

———

The midday sun shone bright as Jeremy and Celia strolled through Haight-Ashbury. The air simmered with a fresh, youthful energy. The entire population of the city, it seemed, meandered through the summer streets and loitered on the steps of row houses, offering salutations and a welcoming stoop on which to rest. Tour buses rolled slowly down the boulevard. Guides barked into microphones about the "flower children" milling about, while gawkers on foot and nearby media crews snapped photos of the misbehaving hippies who were making headlines around the world.

According to Moose, the city's psychedelic scene had gotten uglier since its utopian beginnings. And Jeremy could see it between the mirth. He stayed mindful of the harder elements of these lurid streets, of the sallow faces pushing harder drugs that he wanted nothing to do with. He would stick with pot and maybe a little acid here and there. But nothing too crazy.

Jeremy held onto Celia's hand as they walked. Music permeated the neighborhood, most of it coming from open windows or car radios as people cruised, but some of it came from the people themselves, gathered in intimate clusters along the sidewalk, experimenting with guitars and beat drums, providing the public a rhythm with which to dance.

Out of courtesy to Celia, Jeremy pretended not to notice the dancing woman across the street who had freed herself of her blouse.

To his surprise, Celia pointed her out anyway. "She has nice breasts," she said.

"Uh-huh," Jeremy replied, staring at anything but, and they shared a laugh.

Celia nudged him. "Like you didn't notice."

"I noticed."

"I sort of admire her," Celia mused as she watched the woman. "How liberating that must feel. Men get to do it whenever they want."

"Please don't take your top off out here," Jeremy said, rubbing his sore jaw. "The last thing I need is another knuckle sandwich."

"We should get you some brandy or something to ease the pain," Celia said, then went lax with realization. "I keep forgetting you don't drink."

"No, but this'll help." Jeremy pulled a clear sandwich bag of joints from his pocket. "Thank you, Bianca." He realized quickly, though, that he'd left his cigarettes and lighter back at the house. Maybe it was for the best. Celia often complained when he smoked, claiming to hate the smell, and he was hoping to get another kiss.

Approaching a group seated on the front steps of a green-and-white row house, Jeremy shook his baggie. "Anyone got a light? I'm in a sharing mood."

"Hell yeah, brother," one of the young men said, handing Jeremy a gold Zippo lighter, then his hand. "Steve."

"Jeremy. This is Celia."

Celia gave the stranger a shy smile, staying close to Jeremy, who squeezed her hand and directed her to sit down beside him on the steps with Steve and company. Celia took his arm and used it to keep him close.

"I don't want any," she whispered to Jeremy. "Last night was fun—Angie was a riot—but we were home where I felt safe."

"I'd keep you safe." Checking past the crowd for police or media, Jeremy lit the joint, sucked the warm afternoon air through to get it going, then offered it to Celia. "You sure?" He wanted her to take it. He wanted them to get past this awkwardness. The night before, getting stoned with her had been his favorite of the summer.

Until he found her and Fletcher sucking face in the hallway.

To his surprise, Celia took the joint and gave him a smile that made him feel warm and light on the inside. That or the dope was quick to kick in. But he was pretty sure it was her and leaned in to kiss her.

"You two from the city?" Steve interrupted.

"Oh," Jeremy tore his eyes from Celia to hand over a few joints from his bag, as promised. "No. We drove up from the Monterey area."

"Groovy. I was just down there for the Pop Festival. Got any plans up here?"

"Not really." Jeremy turned and watched Celia put the joint between her lips and close her eyes, its cherry sizzling brighter and brighter. "Hey, easy, tiger. Take it slow."

"Sometimes, the park's got stuff goin' on," another guy chimed in as he lit one of the gifted joints. "Here. Take these." He reached behind himself and handed Jeremy a six-pack of warm beer.

Jeremy didn't want to be rude, so he took it and set it down between him and Celia.

"Just look out, if you go," the guy continued. "My brother got mugged there two nights ago. Lotta weirdos out here now." The guy shook his head. "The city's gone too commercial."

Jeremy and Celia passed their private joint back and forth. She still looked uneasy, and he had an idea in his head that hadn't left him alone since the night before. He wanted to cave to it now because he was starting to notice that when he did, when he fed this desire for her rather than starved it, he felt an unfamiliar but powerful sense of freedom.

Then Celia smiled at him, and all doubt slipped away.

Sucking a large cloud of smoke into his lungs, Jeremy pushed his fingers into her hair and sealed his open mouth over hers. He exhaled, and as she had hours before, she kissed him deeply and didn't let go until the smoke cleared from both their lungs.

With the music flowing through them as smoothly as that dope, they passed the time idly kissing, talking, and watching strangers move throughout the lively neighborhood. Some panhandled, approaching cars full of rubber-necking sightseers, asking for change. Not every traveler responded in a friendly and generous manner. One of the hippies asked a young teen in the back seat of a station wagon for her loose change. As the excited girl dug through her purse, her father realized what was happening, shouted at the "long-hair" to "get a job!" and peeled away. A minute later, the same station wagon returned with a red-eyed, teary teenager and a handful of quarters for the hippie. Triumphant, the hippie raised his fistful of change into the air, and everyone cheered as the defeated father sped away. Beside a clapping Jeremy, Celia whooped, and the hippie bowed.

Jeremy felt a hard tap on his shoulder.

"Hey, man. From me to you. Merry August." It was good ol' Steve, the lighter man. He opened his palm to reveal several sugar cubes to Jeremy. "They're potent, so take it easy."

"Thanks." Jeremy took the sugar cubes and inspected them before turning to Celia. "Hey, how do you feel right now?"

"Good," she replied, her grin languid as she took a swig of warm beer. "Hungry."

"Go easy on that," Jeremy said, pointing to the beer. He presented her with a sugar cube.

"That sugar?"

"Laced with LSD," Jeremy explained.

"Oh." A frown formed over Celia's brow as she stared at the small, white cube between his fingers. "Wow. And you're going to eat that?"

"*We* are. If you're up for it." He assumed she was, having witnessed her fascination when Farmer Feelgood had waxed poetic about the drug. If she was going to experiment and fry her brain, Jeremy decided, it was going to be with him, not some numb-nut loadie looking to diminish her capacity for his own benefit. "If not, it's okay. We'll just give 'em to Moose."

"I want to try," Celia said, taking the sugar cube and turning it over a few times. "But I don't want to go crazy like they say."

Jeremy chuckled. "It won't make you go crazy if you're not already there. I promise."

"You've tried it before?"

He nodded, wondering if she would judge him. "You don't think I'm crazy, do you?" Maybe he didn't want her to answer that. He wasn't the sanest person alive, but that had nothing to do with drugs. If anything, drugs evened him out and made him kinder, more tolerant of other people's bullshit.

Jeremy watched Celia inspect the sugar cube and chew her bottom lip, captivated by both her innocent exterior and the devil that he knew lurked beneath. He wondered which was the truest version of her.

"I swear," he said, "if you don't like it, I'll take you back to Bianca's pad to sleep it off."

"You wouldn't be taking it with me?"

"Not if you don't want me to."

Her eyes danced between his for a moment. "I want you to."

Jeremy smiled. "Let's do it then." He separated his two remaining sugar cubes, dropping one inside his shirt pocket. The other remained in his palm. He tapped his sugar cube against hers and popped it into his mouth. As he worked to dissolve the gritty, sweet cube with his tongue, he watched Celia do the same and made a promise to himself to take good care of her.

A promise was a promise.

He didn't make them lightly.

26

Fletcher

With a reassuring smile from his new friend, Michael, Fletcher lowered himself onto an ornate footstool in a dressing room full of men who all leaned toward their respective mirrors, caking makeup on puckered faces.

"This color is shit," one man with a darker complexion than the others said, slamming a small glass bottle onto the vanity. "Anyone have Bastard Amber Number Two?"

"I do. But I'm not handing it over to you. Last time I lent you one of my brushes, it came back looking like a dead sewer rat."

"One time, Dolores!"

"One time was enough!"

A tall Black woman with large eyes and plump, red lips sauntered past Fletcher and then swiftly returned, stopping directly in front of him. "Well, hello," she said, flipping thick, blond hair over her shoulder. Fletcher could tell immediately by the voice that she was not a natural woman, but she would have had him fooled otherwise. "Whose vanilla milkshake?"

"Back off, Loretta," Michael said as he fitted a flesh-colored wig cap to his head. "The milkshake's with me."

"I'm only saying hello. Don't want to be rude."

Michael flipped his eyes. "Bit late for that, hussy."

Unfazed, the Black woman smiled flirtatiously at Fletcher. "I'm Loretta. What's your name, baby? Don't mind Michael. She's always bringing back the yummy strays and is too much of a greedy tart to share."

"Bite me, Loretta."

Fletcher was experiencing such sensory overload that he'd already forgotten Loretta's question. "I'm sorry, ma'am, what?" he said.

"Ma'am. How darling. I'm not that old, honey. My father's *ma'am*. Call me Miss Loretta. And I asked your name, sweetheart," Loretta prompted lovingly. "Do you have one? It's all right if you don't."

"Go ahead, love," Michael said to Fletcher. "These hookers don't bite unless you've got the right amount of scratch."

Hookers? Fletcher was terribly confused. "Um . . . It—it's Fletcher. My name, I mean."

"Well, okay." Loretta's wide smile returned. "So, what's your story, Fletcher?"

"Oh," Michael cooed, standing up and sashaying over to Fletcher to comb through his hair. Though Michael's nails felt amazing on his scalp, Fletcher bent his head away, suddenly self-conscious as so many watched Michael gush. "He's just your average college dreamboat, studying to become, get this, a civil rights attorney. My baby boy's going to save the world!"

"And you're a queer?" Loretta asked Fletcher, somewhat dubious.

Fletcher glanced around the room. Every painted eye was on him. "Uh . . ." He felt his throat parch and his stomach sour. He'd only ever admitted it aloud to Celia. But down deep, on an instinctual level, putting aside all the obvious cues in front of him, he knew he could trust the people around him. They awaited his next word with the utmost patience, some of them with smiles so soft and welcoming that he wanted to buckle and cry at the sight. "Yes," he whispered, swallowing down the huge lump that had formed in his throat.

Everyone delighted and squealed, and he was flooded with a strange, sickly kind of relief.

A middle-aged woman walked over in a modest pair of cream pumps that Fletcher recognized from his own mother's wardrobe. Her baby-blue dress was classy, matronly, something Jackie Kennedy might wear. "Oh," she crooned in a motherly tone, her countenance replete with sympathy. "He's in the closet, the poor thing. Look at him, he's shaking. He's petrified."

Loretta seemed pleased. "Michael, you've struck gold once again."

"Oh, you. Get," the older woman snapped, batting Loretta away. "All you vultures, quit your salivating. Give the boy some space to breathe. Don't you remember how hard it was before coming here? We need to be supportive."

A young man scootched closer, shirtless and not yet having donned his wig. "Raquel is right. Every baby gay needs a mama to love and guide them. It's a jungle out there." He touched Fletcher's hand. "You're safe here, sugar."

"Precisely." The older woman took a seat beside Fletcher with the poise of an aristocrat. "By the way, I am Raquel, and this is Li," she said, pressing a hand to the shirtless boy's chest. "Where are you from, Fletcher? Do you live here in the city?"

"N—no, I'm from Pacific Grove."

"Oh, the little town with the butterflies. Next to Monterey," Li said to Raquel. "It's very quaint. I spent a whole week there once with Stan."

"Yes," Fletcher managed, swallowing the newest lump in his throat. He felt sweaty and dizzy. "That's the one. Next to Monterey."

Loretta squeezed back inside the tight circle that surrounded Fletcher. "Are you okay, baby?" she asked him, then turned to Michael. "He's getting whiter by the minute."

"I'm just . . . thirsty," Fletcher said, his mouth and throat desiccated. He adjusted his glasses. Sweat, as always, had them sliding down his nose, and it was becoming harder to catch a satisfying breath. More than ever before, he sympathized with Celia and her asthma attacks.

"I'll get you a glass of water," Li said, dashing off.

"Why are you here, if you don't mind me asking?" Raquel asked him. "In the city, I mean."

"Visiting." Fletcher fixed his glasses again. "I came with friends," he said as Li returned and handed him a tall glass of cold water. "Thank you." He guzzled half of it down immediately. His thirst was quenched, but his heart was still hammering inside his chest. The sound sloshed inside his ears. Had he actually said out loud that he was gay? Was he really safe here? Any one of these people could easily expose him. He knew none of their characters. He glanced around to see who else was in the spacious, well-lit room, listening, judging him. A dozen strangers in various stages of undress gawked at him as he panicked and perspired through his clothing.

Concern splayed over his freshly painted face, Michael squeezed in on Fletcher's other side and touched his arm, stroking gently with those pretty red fingernails. "It's going to be all right, honey. Where are your friends?"

"I—I don't know."

"Do these 'friends' of yours know you're gay?" Michael asked gingerly.

Fletcher shook his head. "No. Well, yes, one of them does. Celia. But not the others." He wondered how Michael had known about him. Was it obvious in Fletcher's own mannerisms like it was for Michael? Or had it been a lucky guess on Michael's part? He had only been sitting on a bench. The question had him suddenly terrified. If Michael had figured it out so quickly, what chance was there that others wouldn't eventually find out?

Oh, God, Charlie T. had probably seen it, whatever *it* was. It would explain his hostile reaction the day before.

At Fletcher's trembling silence, Loretta raised an eyebrow at Michael. "Who's this Celia person?"

Fletcher struggled to swallow as he said, "My best friend."

"Ah, the best friend." Loretta tilted her head knowingly at Li, who offered a sorrowful nod.

"The beard," Li said, bringing a hand to his chest.

304 | FLIGHT OF THE MONARCHS

"The beard," Raquel echoed sympathetically. "Of course."

Fletcher was confused. "Beard?"

"Yes, you know," Michael said, combing his fingers through Fletcher's hair. "The darling girl who may or may not know your little secret and either doesn't care or thinks she'll 'fix' you with her delightful lady parts. So, you go steady with her, thinking she'll either change you and, if not, her presence alone will stop people from suspecting that you actually have the hots for the boy who works the popcorn stand at the drive-in."

With a quiet tsk, Li sighed, "Or the boy at the garage you keep returning to, claiming there's still a rattle in your engine." He cupped the side of his mouth to whisper, "There was never a rattle."

"Or the hunky postal worker who lived next door," Raquel hummed, gazing dreamily into the void. "Gosh, was he a fine-looking man. Like a young Gary Cooper. But more in *The Texan*. Not *A Farewell to Arms*."

Wearing a slanted frown, Loretta sighed. "Or the sexy waiter with the big, brown eyes at the Greek restaurant below your apartment."

"Or Paul Newman." Michael turned a dreamy grin to Fletcher. "Fletcher?"

Fletcher looked down at his boots, guessing it was his turn. Faintly, he said, "The bag boy at the market."

"Oh, yes," Raquel said, rubbing at Fletcher's back. "There's always a bag boy at the damn market. You sit tight, honey. It'll all work itself out. Like Li said, you're safe here, so just relax and enjoy the show." With that, she stood and clapped her hands together. "Back to work, ladies. Fix those gorgeous faces. And I want those titties on straight this time, Greta! Show starts in ten!"

Fletcher looked at Michael. "Show?"

"Oh, yes. You're going to love it. Have you ever been to New York City?" Michael asked.

"No."

"Well, that's too bad, because we blow those amateurs out of the water."

The performers around Fletcher applied makeup, wigs, and costumes in a frenzied, excited rush, save one quiet boy who occupied the vanity bench next to Michael's. He stared into his mirror, judiciously blushing his high cheekbones, his wig and costume on a metal rack at his side. He couldn't have been more than eighteen. His eyes met Fletcher's, and Fletcher realized, once again, that he'd been staring. He really, really needed to work on that.

"I'm from a 'quaint' little town, too," the boy said to him, giving him a half smile through the mirror. The chaos of the room continued around them. "Pooler, Georgia." Fletcher took note of the Southern lilt as the boy continued. "Quaint doesn't mean the same thing for everyone, I've learned, especially not for fairies like us."

Fletcher listened, not knowing how to respond.

"My family are devout Christians," the boy continued, smiling. "Myself included. It was the one thing we shared, our love for Jesus and for our church." He set down his blush brush and grabbed another just like it, dipping it into a little pot before tapping it gently against the side. Powder dusted the air as he set the brush to his nose. "When I was fifteen, I confessed my secret to my parents. I was terrified, obviously, but they're my family. Unconditional love and all of that. I didn't know anything else." His smile fell. "But instead of supporting me, they opened a Bible and used it to justify their newfound hatred for me."

"I'm sorry," Fletcher said.

"Oh, no, don't be. I still have my faith. I don't blame Jesus for my family's sins. I may be separated from them, but He's still right by my side." The boy lit a cigarette and blew a cloud of smoke. "Have you ever read the Bible, Fletcher?"

"No."

"Well, in the Bible, Jesus runs around with repentant thieves and whores, and I think, if full disclosure of the word had been permitted, he probably kept company with us faggots, too. He was a beat, a hippie. Like all the hippies flooding this city who have been decent enough to us, I suppose. Granted, they're all baked out of their heads." The boy laughed, then became contemplative. "I like to think that dope brings the soul to the surface for everyone to see."

After finishing his cigarette and the last touches of his makeup, the boy from Pooler, Georgia, adjusted his wig over his skullcap while Fletcher watched. It was a brunette bob that made him (or her now) appear older, more sophisticated.

The boy twisted in his seat to face Fletcher. "How do I look?"

"Very nice," Fletcher said.

"Nice," the boy parroted, disappointment embittering his features as he returned to his mirror. "And I took you for a gentleman, Fletcher."

"Pardon?"

The boy sighed. "When a Southern lady asks you how she looks, you're expected to fawn and tell her she looks more beautiful than Ava Gardner. Now, how do I look?"

Fletcher relaxed into a smile. He didn't know how he'd missed the resemblance. "You look beautiful tonight, more beautiful than Ava Gardner."

He received a hefty wink for the remark. "Why, thank you, sugar."

The next thing Fletcher knew, he was being hoisted to his feet by Michael. "Follow me, baby," Michael said, pulling Fletcher down a narrow hallway into a dark backstage area. Parting a beaded curtain, Michael pointed beyond the stage. "There, do you see? An open seat at the bar. Get a drink, relax, enjoy the show." He grabbed Fletcher by the shirt, pulled him down to kiss his cheek, then shoved him through the curtain and into the main room.

Men watched Fletcher, their curiosity evident, as he made his way to the bar. He lowered his head, his jitters taking hold again. But this time, they were accompanied by a slight, budding thrill.

Finding several empty stools at the bar, he sat down and ordered a soda from the bartender.

The house lights dimmed, and Fletcher swiveled around to get a view of the spotlighted stage. A robust redhead, her face caked with garish makeup, sauntered up to the microphone, while the throng began to hoot and holler. Fletcher hadn't seen her backstage, but he assumed she, too, was a man. If not, she was an unsightly woman. Regardless, as an entertainer, she was delightful, uplifting the mood of the room with dirty jokes and flirting unabashedly with the rowdy tables of men up front. They all seemed to know and love her, and she them.

"Hello."

Fletcher turned to the man now seated on the barstool to his right. He had thick, black hair, sable-colored eyes, and a jaw that could cut glass. His skin reminded Fletcher of perfectly creamed coffee, and God help him, he was instantaneously attracted. It was becoming clear to him, too, that he had a very specific type, and this man was *it*.

"Hello," Fletcher responded, annoyed at the timidity evident in his voice.

The man thrust a hand at him. "I am Sérgio."

He had an accent. An inherently sexy one. Spanish or Columbian or something. Fletcher could only guess as he had insufficient experience with people from other cultures and nationalities. He'd been sheltered from birth up to the present in a very homogenous area. Moose and Luisa were as exotic as Pacific Grove got. And Fresno, where his college was located, wasn't much different.

"Do you have a name?" Sérgio asked, bemused by Fletcher's silence.

"Oh . . ." Fletcher felt his face scald with embarrassment. Had he been ogling, staring again? Argh! "Fletcher. Sorry. My name is Fletcher."

Sérgio smiled, sprouting deep, bottomless dimples beneath a five o'clock shadow. Fletcher knew he was ogling again, but it was hard to act cool in the presence of such a face. He could barely act cool in the presence of homely ones.

"It's lovely to meet you, Fletcher. Would it be all right if I bought you a drink?"

"Uh, sure, yes," Fletcher managed through a gulp. "Thank you."

Sérgio pointed to the glass in front of Fletcher. "What have you got here?"

"Coke."

"Coca-Cola? Plain?"

Fletcher nodded.

"Oh, no," Sérgio grinned. "We can do much better than that. Do you like beer?"

"Not really."

"Probably because you have been drinking the wrong beer." With alluring confidence, Sérgio called out his order to the bartender: two glasses of a beer Fletcher had never heard of. "I've noticed that about Americans. You know very little about beer."

On stage, the host raised her voice. "Put those big, beefy, moan-inducing hands together—yes, I'm talking to you, Rodney—and welcome to the stage, in all her bodacious Black beauty, Miss Diana Gloss and the Wet Dreams!"

Three voluptuous, caramel-skinned women sauntered gracefully onto the stage, hips swinging with sensual panache, each dressed in glittering, white chiffon. The one in the center, Miss Diana Gloss, Fletcher presumed, wore a tight-fitting bell gown made of black and silver sequins and sparkling, six-inch heels. The eyelashes hooding her eyes were inches long, thick, and jet black. Below a prominent beauty mark, her lips shimmered in pale pink.

Watching her, Fletcher was reminded of Marilyn Monroe singing to JFK during his forty-fifth birthday celebration, the only difference being that this woman was Black and not a woman at all. A man was somewhere beneath all that grace and chiffon. A grown man with man parts and the societal expectations that came with them. Miss Diana Gloss began a rapturous cover of "I Hear a Symphony" by Diana Ross and the Supremes, and Fletcher found instant rapture. This "woman" had more poise than any woman he'd ever met in real life or seen in movies. Fletcher had to admire her confidence, grandiosity, and, to an ever-greater degree by the minute, bravery. He wished he could be that brave. Granted, Fletcher didn't want to be a feminine man, but he did want to be something equally loathed by the world: himself. And what struck him even more than this woman and her courage was the crowd that adulated her. The room contained around forty men in total, and not one ridiculed or pulled Diana Gloss off stage to beat her or have her arrested. Rather, they praised her performance with hoots and hollers and joyous dancing. Fletcher realized his own smile had grown so strong and his heart filled with so much hope that he was on the verge of crying tears of joy.

He was so caught up in the merriment that it took him a minute to register that Michael was one of the other two entertainers on stage. A pair of stilettos added at least five inches to his height, the bouffant wig with perfect pin curls added several more, but Michael's petite stature and cherub face were dead giveaways. He was stunning.

Grinning from ear to ear, thoroughly enjoying himself, Fletcher clapped his hands to the beat, feeling like a child at his first parade. He danced in his seat and sang and, when a strong arm tugged at his waist, he jumped.

"You all right, friend?" Sérgio asked, dragging a callused thumb across Fletcher's cheek.

"Oh." Wiping the tear from his cheek, Fletcher smiled. "I'm wonderful."

With a curious smile, Sérgio took Fletcher's face in both hands and leaned tantalizingly close. Fletcher's throat closed on him. He swallowed hard against the discomfort as he registered what was happening. Sérgio was close enough for a kiss, his every exhale affecting Fletcher's lips, which parted to accommodate the sudden change in his own respirations, now coming in cumbersome pants that seemed to emanate from deep within his belly. Above that, his chest ached where his heart kept him alive with rich, heavy booms. The hands were warm on his face, and those dark-sable eyes dropped to his mouth, then rose again.

"May I?" Sérgio asked.

Through his panic, Fletcher nodded. From the time he was a boy, he had fantasized about this kind of intimacy with other boys, yet he'd never imagined that any of those fantasies could ever come true. They had been just that, he'd assumed, fantasy—a dangerous fantasy that degenerates had and criminals indulged. Right now, though, with this beautiful man holding him, the scent of Aqua Velva making his head swim, sending his heart into a tailspin, all that had only ever existed in dreams was coming true. But he never could've anticipated the feeling that beset him when Sérgio's lips touched his. The firm softness, the warmth, the heavenly taste of liquor and intimacy. To Fletcher's amazement, it felt natural, more natural even than the oxygen that entered through his nose as he inhaled deep. Fletcher vanished into the feeling and let it carry him away. Never had he suffered such consuming sensations, such profound desire, not even on those obscene, experimental nights with Celia. No, *this* was desire. This was what it meant for a heart to race, a need to burn, a stomach to swarm with butterflies. This was what human beings had lusted after since the beginning of time, what had them all going mad.

Tilting his head, Sérgio slipped his bourbon-warmed tongue into Fletcher's mouth, and Fletcher moaned at the delicious rush of pleasure. Life itself pumped hot and healthy through his veins for the first time. He was alive, human with all its lovely flaws and weaknesses, its possibilities, and resplendent, God-given freedom to sin as one sees fit.

The music throbbed all around them, the crowd open and pliant. Nobody in the bar seemed to mind two men kissing each other, and with such passion. Many others did the same, enjoying the night and each other, like anyone else in the world on that splendid midsummer's night. They were in a small-scale paradise, where spiteful laws about love were spurned, and as Sérgio ended their kiss, Fletcher wished he could stay forever.

Sérgio appeared amused as he let Fletcher go and sat back on his barstool. "I know I'm a good kisser," he said, his tone playful, "but you are overinflating my ego."

Fletcher laughed, realizing how he must look, for he felt downright delirious. "That was my first kiss. I'm just . . . happy."

"Your first? No," Sérgio said with skepticism. "It can't be. You are a very good kisser. Sensual, but assertive. I enjoyed it."

"No, my first with . . . a man."

"I see." Without inhibition, Sérgio gazed into Fletcher's eyes, admiring, seducing, though it may not have been his intent. "My God, you are gorgeous," he said, making Fletcher's face burn through his bashfulness. "And so shy. How come? I am not complaining. It is charming on someone so beautiful."

At a loss for words, Fletcher cleared his throat. "Do you live here in the city?"

Sérgio smiled. "Yes," he said, bending close to nuzzle Fletcher before giving him a gentle kiss, first on his lips, then his jaw. "I moved here three years ago from Buenos Aires." He moved around to bite softly at Fletcher's earlobe, whispering, "Beautiful and soft," before kissing his neck with an open mouth.

Fletcher thought he might die, it felt so good. He gasped and panted through Sérgio's hot, drifting tongue. "Is it always this free and open here in the city?"

"In certain areas." Sérgio pulled back to look at him. "There are many of us, you know. More than they want you to believe."

"I'm noticing."

The beers Sérgio had ordered were sitting on the bar in front of them, and Sérgio handed Fletcher one of the weighty glass steins.

"To freedom," Sérgio toasted. "And first kisses." They clanged glasses, laughing as the foam erupted and spilled onto their laps. Normally, Fletcher would be concerned. He would clean up before the beer stained his slacks. But tonight he felt like a new man, a daredevil and risk-taker. He chugged his beer, relishing how delicious it tasted, how gratifyingly the ice-cold liquid quenched his throat, and then thumped the stein down on the bar, empty, to Sérgio's delight.

"Oh, that was good," Fletcher said of the beer. "Let me buy you one now."

The bar grew livelier and more congested as the night grew late and the stage acts more salacious. Fletcher drank and danced and kissed Sérgio until the night grew wild around him. He danced with several men in the middle of the revelry, letting them kiss and touch him wherever they pleased, his body writhing against sweat and muscle and heat, finding the succor it had always longed for.

At one point, he peered through the hazy room to find Michael swaying with another, dressed once again in suede and striped polyester. Their eyes met, and Michael shot him a wink and a smile.

Back at the bar, Sérgio planted a hard, impassioned kiss on Fletcher's mouth. "Now, that's what I like to see," he told Fletcher. "Use this freedom to dance and drink and fuck. You are young but once." Sérgio passed Fletcher a shot glass filled to its brim with a dark, amber liquid. "Drink with me."

They threw back the shots and enjoyed a wet, liquored kiss. Afterward, warm and flushed, Fletcher sat back in his seat to scan the room. So much bliss and debauchery, and it was all his for the taking. All he had to do was stay in the city and take it. Could it really be that simple? Would it all look different tomorrow, in the light of day, when he was sober and surrounded once again by conventional society?

"Two more," Sérgio told the bartender.

The music stopped suddenly, and everyone turned toward the stage, where Michael ran out and grabbed the microphone. "Pigs!" he shouted. "Go out through the back!"

"Quickly!" Sérgio yanked Fletcher free from his barstool. "This way." The bulk of the crowd moved swiftly in one direction.

"What's going on?" Fletcher asked, his vision spiraling from the alcohol.

"A raid!"

27

Jeremy

Jeremy was inside a carnival of endless wonder. Faces painted neon blue with marbled eyes and shiny, electric smiles stared back at him, each pristine and beautiful until time revealed the human disease beneath. Color blasted from their mouths, as if out of a cannon at a big-top circus, into a cosmic starburst of light and geometrically flawless shapes.

To keep trudging forward, he carefully placed one foot in front of the other. But when he looked down, he saw that the soles of his shoes no longer touched the sidewalk. Cement slabs fractured, rising to float away, a thousand steely balloons on a breeze. The way his body moved was all wrong. Thoughts sprang backward. Time retreated, and Jeremy had to work to physically steady himself against the increasing velocity. He wondered how Celia was handling this change in gravity.

With that thought, he spun around.

Celia?

Bodies marched in a northward pilgrimage. But none were hers.

Celia?

An arbitrary memory answered. When Jeremy was fifteen, Granddad had insisted he join his bowling league, the Lucky Strikes. One of its members, a wiry old grouch named Jack Johansen, had been forced by his wife, Margery, to quit the team on account of his newly discovered heart condition. The Lucky Strikes needed a replacement fourth, someone young and strong and able to roll a level ball without grabbing for his chest.

For his first practice, Jeremy was given Granddad's prized "Greased Lightning," a champion sixteen-pound rubber ball, credited with bowling a perfect game in the 1961 Germantown league tournament. It was a demonic thing from the armpit of bowling ball hell that had a magnetic, almost sexual attraction to gutters. He quit the team after one game, but that didn't matter now. What did matter was that, in the middle of this San Franciscan orgy, on this cool August afternoon in the summer of 1967, each of his eyeballs felt as heavy as that monstrous, black bowling ball. And yet, he managed to roll them around in their desiccated sockets, in sync, left and then right, in hopes of finding his lost companion. In doing so, Jeremy discovered that time did not move backward but in fact careened forward faster than his cumbersome eyeballs could keep pace with.

Two alien beings, twin blurs reeking of patchouli and pot, zipped past him like runaway trains, leaving magnificent trails of color and light.

Maybe they could tell him where to find Celia.

He took a few more slanted steps through the mass of pedestrians, panicking at the thought of having misplaced her forever in the chaos.

"Are you Rick?" Jeremy heard, while fingers gripped his shoulders and swiveled him around. A friendly face greeted him. Then a soft mouth made contact. Its warm, velvety tongue slithered like a snake over his. Pink lips parted to laugh before something was lowered onto his head.

He touched it.

A hat.

"Take this, Rick," the girl said. "My old man doesn't need it anymore."

Jeremy reached out until her light disappeared into a fine streak of laughter. He covered his eyes, conscious of the trip and yet not. Color, touch, and sound were all at once vying for his attention. He backed himself flush against the red, writhing wall of a laundromat. Red conveyed warmth. The wall felt safe, a friend at his back, so unlike his traitorous shoes or that generous serpent of a woman who had left a minty, sweet taste in his mouth.

His eyes opened again, only to be assaulted by another kaleidoscope of light. Had Celia ever truly walked beside him? Or was she part of a dream he'd once had? He half-expected to find himself back in Tennessee in that miserable, old bowling alley. But his body remained in San Francisco, his mind wandering far and wide for the girl.

He willed himself to focus.

It took a few uneven steps to find her gazing into a storefront window, palms flat against the glass.

"Celia."

She turned. "Jeremy!"

Colliding with her, Jeremy buried his face in her sun-warmed hair, appreciating its silkiness, its alluring perfume. "Where were you?" he asked, squeezing her tightly to himself. "You left me."

Celia patted his head. "Whose hat is this?"

"Rick's," he replied, transferring the thing to her head.

"I think that sugar was rotten," she said.

Laughing, Jeremy took her face in his hands. In that instant, she was a flawless, raving beauty. He'd never seen a woman so spectacular. The late afternoon sun lit her hair into a halo of fire, illuminating her face and transforming her into an angel. "It's not rotten. Just strong."

"Please don't leave me again."

"Never." Jeremy was astounded by the comforting baritone of his own voice. He hunched close to speak to Celia, feeling a warm pull of intimacy. It would be so easy to succumb. "I thought I'd never find you," he whispered, serenity pulsing through his polluted veins. After the pot, and now this, he felt connected to everyone and everything.

No wonder these damn hippies never went looking for a fight. Make love, not war. It made so much sense to him now. "I'll take you to the ocean," he told her, taking her hand and pressing a kiss to the tip of her middle finger, the act smoothing out the tiny worry lines marking her forehead. "It relaxes you."

Celia smiled. "You remember."

"I remember everything." He kissed her mouth then, the pace languid to better experience the lips that yielded so softly to his and the lazy, dillydallying tongue that had him fumbling for more.

Together, they wandered in a fog while the summer sun shot like a rocket across the sky, blazing tail and all. Navigating the craggy, bubble-gum streets only grew more difficult with time. In one minute, Celia got lost. In the next, it was Jeremy. People floated in and out, offering assistance, rebukes, more drugs. A few wanted in on their gaiety. Jeremy shooed them away, but the undulating, misshapen road signs and slanted sidewalks often distracted him. When Celia dropped to her knees to pluck a Marigold from someone's garden, a spider web of cracks in the nearby sidewalk blew his overwrought mind. It was all there in that blacktop fractal and in the blades of green grass that broke free from their concrete prison: the answers to all his questions about life. He considered dropping to his own knees to read the map inside them, but Celia lured him away.

"We need to find the ocean," she reminded him as he pulled her into his arms.

Her fingers raked through his hair, and he closed his eyes. "Okay."

"Where is it?" she asked.

"I wish I knew."

When Jeremy discovered a kindred spirit in an old man with a guitar, singing a song about a dead father, Celia preened between his legs, keeping him tethered to the ground.

"Drink," she insisted, offering him a glass bottle that sloshed with warm pineapple juice. Where she'd gotten it, he didn't know, but he sucked the bittersweet, LSD-laced nectar from her tongue and drifted with her into a dream.

When the sun crouched low against the western sky, she laid him across a shady bench and lifted her face to the canopy of leaves above, bathing herself in a cleansing breeze. The whole of the earth's population surrounded them, chattering and singing songs of love.

"Which aside shall I give you?" she asked him.

"I don't know what you mean," he answered, reaching out to touch her. Her hair was on fire again. But she slipped away, and Jeremy sat up as she climbed onto an elaborate cement stage. In the visible distance, a Japanese pagoda rose out of the trees. Where the hell was he?

Then she spoke. "The jewels of our father!" The words echoed; the quad grew silent. Every eye landed on her, his lunatic companion disturbing their innocent afternoon. "With wash'd eyes, Cordelia leaves you . . ."

Cordelia, the faithful daughter of King Lear. Her favorite play. She'd told him about it when they'd lounged like big cats on a shaded hill, necking and tripping, unearthing a long-buried language.

"But yet, alas, stood I within his grace, I would prefer him to a better place. So, farewell to you both!"

———

After the long ramble through the city, keeping each other shackled to reason while erupting into hysterics over the unreasonable—namely a censorious, old fist-shaker who'd accused them of trampling his azaleas—Jeremy and Celia hitched a ride and finally found the elusive Golden Gate strait.

The sun had set an hour before, but even so, Celia squealed with joy when her toes sunk into the fine salt-and-pepper sand of Baker Beach. "We made it," she sighed, taking off her sandals. "That's the Golden Gate Bridge. Isn't it pretty all lit up?"

Jeremy followed her toward the black water, then plopped down several yards short of the tide line. Supporting his elbows on raised knees, he watched his vivacious companion romp amid the bridge's rippling reflection, darkening the bottom few inches of her pants. At the sight, he had only enough energy to smile.

Exhausted, he spread out Celia's jacket and lay back to breathe in the cool, briny air and ponder the universe. The LSD they'd taken had been strong, persistent, and though it had faded, it continued to alter his perceptions, transfiguring the dearth of stars above into a revolving, dizzying wealth. Constellations of his own making animated themselves into stories of comedy and tragedy, some virtuous and dull, others warlike and droll, daring to take sides with the wicked. But each spectacle, no matter how riveting his brain's translation, only served to highlight his own solitude.

Then Celia was crawling over him, and with a ready smile, Jeremy welcomed her tongue into his mouth. Wrapping his arms snugly around her torso, he felt the loneliness recede.

Though a small group of individuals amused themselves at the far end of the beach, Jeremy and Celia were essentially alone, free to indulge in what had been building all afternoon and, if Jeremy was being straight with himself, all summer long. The awareness had him clutching her back and hips, while she kissed him with the abandon he'd come to know as distinctly hers. He didn't know where or with whom she had learned to kiss—and he didn't want to know—but he was intoxicated by the mix of raw, turbulent passion and molten seduction that she poured into every caress of her lips. Her soft mouth hunted as it incited and soothed, seeking all the ways it could fit with his, pushing, pulling, and twisting until he felt crazed with want. The shape and pressure of her surging body, the rising vitality of her kiss, drove him to roll over and dry hump her like an inexperienced, oversexed teenager, blurting the kind of accolades that would've embarrassed him sober.

No matter, though, because Celia responded favorably, using her warm palms to clutch his face, her icy, wet heels to tug him close, whispering equally senseless utterances with the gravity of a Shakespearean sonnet. In tacit agreement, they kissed and whispered and rolled a few more times, collecting sand and other coastal finery in their hair and clothing while the heavy wind helped to clear it all away.

Slowing for a moment, Jeremy and Celia both smiled at each other, laughing a little at the sandy mess. But Jeremy's smile faded as he looked down at her. She'd never looked more beautiful, smiling brightly at him in the moonlight. His heart beat with elation, his stomach fluttered, and it gave him pause. The thought of leaving and never seeing her face again . . .

Celia's smile fell a little, her palm touching his cheek. "What's wrong?"

Jeremy shook his head. His thoughts were rife suddenly with warning, his mind deciding cruelly to present for him once again the image of her kissing Fletcher the night before. He flattened his hands against the sand and lifted his face away.

"What about Fletcher?" he asked her.

"What about him?"

He searched her face for lies. "Are you together?"

"What? Why are you wondering about Fletcher all of a sudden?"

"It's not all of a sudden." Jeremy rolled off her and sat up, dragging in a salty lungful of oxygen. "Just answer me. Are you with him or not?"

He watched surprise awaken her features as she sat up. "You *are* mad about last night," she said. "You're jealous."

"Yes." Hearing himself admit it took some of the edge off, but Jeremy also knew he'd just screwed up. She wasn't his, and he had no intention of making her his.

Her expression shifted into sympathy. "Jeremy . . ." Celia crawled over to settle herself between his splayed legs. "Fletcher and I have tried dating, but it never worked out for us. Then last night . . . I don't know. He's lonely, so he asked me to try again."

Jeremy examined her closely, then pushed a hand through her hair to fish out a dried piece of seaweed. All he could read in her was sincerity. "What'd you say?"

"I said no. Then I chased after you, remember?"

"You're forgetting something."

Celia rolled her eyes. "Yes, he kissed me. *Then* I chased after you."

"Let me get this straight," he said, skeptical. "You said no to dating him . . . so he kissed you?"

"Yes, but—What do you want me to say, Jeremy? I can't control how Fletcher feels. Just 'cause he wants to get married doesn't mean I want to, and I told him that. And frankly, I don't see how any of this is your business." Celia cocked an eyebrow. "Unless you plan on making it your business . . ."

"No . . . Wait . . ." Jeremy's brain sputtered. "He proposed?"

Quickly, he checked her ring finger. It was bare. Guilt flashed in her expression, nevertheless.

"I said no this time. Because of you."

"This time?"

This shitshow was messier than he thought. But it wasn't his problem. It wasn't his shitshow. He had to remember that. What could he do from the other side of the planet, anyway, while Fletcher was at her side in college? Fletcher was good looking and smart, his family rich, and evidently, he wanted to make a damned housewife out of Celia. What chance did he have against that? And what the hell did it matter? What was his big plan? Make out with her a little, fuck her if he was lucky, then peace out to Southeast Asia? Ask her to wait? For what? He wasn't coming back here. And what was her plan? Though they'd never discussed it outright, she knew he was leaving for war. Was it her intention to make him fall for her so he could go die in a jungle, lovesick and alone? Why bother? Did she actually give a shit about him? Or was it all a game to her?

Celia slid closer, her tone stern. "His proposals never mean anything, Jeremy. They're not real."

Jeremy rubbed his fingers over his eyes. He had to remember that they were both high and not in their right minds. This discussion was going nowhere.

"It's hard to explain," she added.

And the vague remarks were really starting to piss him off. "Just tell me something . . ." he said, bearing the weight of his dread as he chided himself for being such a sadistic, self-sabotaging prick. "Did you let him fuck you?"

Celia's jaw dropped. "How dare you ask me that." Her voice both trembled and strengthened. "I am not that kind of girl. Fletcher and I have never done . . . *that*. Not that it's any of your business!" Moving away, Celia pulled her knees to her chest. "Jerk."

Regretting the question, Jeremy's spine sagged. His head fell. And that lambasting fire of jealousy turned quickly inward, becoming self-hatred, a more familiar and comforting sentiment.

He sighed. Crawling over, he slapped the sand from his palms before taking her face between them. "Look at me."

Cold, brown eyes rose to condemn him.

"You're right," he said. "I am a jerk. I'm sorry." He'd been coasting from minute to minute, free-floating through the summer, and now he'd hit a barrier. Things with Celia had gone about as far as he was willing to take them, but he also itched like crazy to tell her how beautiful she was, to take what he wanted from her, to consume and use her. He trapped the impetuous words inside a sharp inhale. "I don't know what I'm supposed to be doing right now," was the only confession that escaped.

"You're supposed to be kissing me," she said through squished lips, her frown deepening.

Jeremy let go of her face so she could speak.

"It's a beautiful night," she went on grimly. "And we seem to like kissing each other. A lot. When you're not being a jerk."

Jeremy gave her a weak smile, feeling exhausted suddenly, and nodded.

Her arms wound around his neck, her lips coupling with his at a slow, controlled pace.

"See?" she whispered, nuzzling him and stroking his hair.

Opening his eyes, Jeremy watched her, noting the hard crease between her eyebrows as her mouth seduced.

"If he's offering to marry you," he started to say.

"Shh. Stop worrying about him." She punctuated the end of each sentence with a frustratingly delicate kiss. "He doesn't really want to marry me. It's all for show."

Jeremy pulled back. "What?"

"It's complicated." Her fingers gripped his hair to bring him back, ruffling out sand as she puckered against his lips. "It's an arrangement we have."

"Celia." Jeremy removed her hands from his hair. "Sweetheart, conversations go a lot smoother when you try making sense."

Celia sighed. "Fletcher's gay."

28

Angie

Angie and Moose strolled through Golden Gate Park, past its meadows, museums, and botanical gardens. It was all very picturesque. Flora covered nearly the entire landscape. Trees and plants of every breed wobbled in the brackish summer wind, while rolling hills of grass gleamed such a deep green that they seemed false somehow, like out of a magazine.

But it was while exploring the winding paths of the Japanese Tea Garden that Angie found delight, becoming entranced with a koi pond there.

Falling to her knees, she watched as plump, orange-and-white fish swam smartly around one another. Each individual koi showed off its unique personality for her, some shoving while others cavorted about good-naturedly. One, in particular, contemplated her with suspicion, and Angie made a point not to startle it with any sudden movements.

Thoughtful as always, Moose bought crackers from a food cart for Angie to toss at her new acquaintances. Excited over the purchase, the koi fought each other for her consideration. The smartest of the bunch, a thickset, refined sort of fellow, elected to smile and say a courtly hello, earning his treat with simple charm.

"Here you go, fat fishy," Angie cooed, releasing the last of her crumbs to him, appreciating his genteel bow of gratitude. She repaid him with a curtsey.

It did seem a little peculiar that a fish would have manners enough to bow, so Angie decided that the LSD was likely kicking in. If she thought about it, she did feel a slight head change, her reasoning the tiniest bit disjointed, but otherwise, she felt quite orderly and fine.

"I'm ready to go," she told Moose.

One tier above the pond, beyond a stairway made of stepping stones, a bronze Buddha sat cross-legged, a gold-plated sun fixed behind his head. All around the statue, foreign tourists with cameras snapped photos of several long-hairs who loitered nearby, imploring the young hippies to stand alongside the Buddha, finding providence in the matchup. But Angie sympathized with Buddha, who asked them all, twice over, to please keep it down so he could hear himself think. Sadly, they all ignored him, and she could totally relate to his frustration.

People.

Moose bent toward Angie. "And we're the weirdos."

Walking through the park afterward, she and Moose came across hundreds of young people dancing and making music. The scene was like a dream, bizarre and carefree.

And naturally, Moose fit right in with the peaceniks, making friends of them with ease. He was fascinating in that way and so confident in his ability to charm others. Being with him was effortless, and Angie realized that everyone had that same easy feeling in his company.

The energetic group with beat drums and acoustic guitars quickly claimed Moose for their own, involving him in every aspect of their revelry. One of the peaceniks offered him pot. Another offered magic mushrooms for a small donation. Moose accepted both and fed them to Angie, who remained close by his side. The people were kind and hospitable but preoccupied on various levels by whatever phenomena they were experiencing inside their own heads. Their weirdness put her on edge. That said, it didn't take long for Angie to become one of them, becoming weirder than weird. Whatever polluted her system now was more potent than the orange juice mixture Moose had given her earlier in the afternoon. And by the time twilight descended, Angie was just another pulse inside the heartbeat of humankind, having liquesced into the phantasmic flow.

Aimless and wandering, Angie discovered a crowd seated near an Acacia tree with a trunk split into five distinct pieces, each piece more multifaceted than the last. She folded her legs over an available stretch of grass that writhed and twisted beneath her and realized with some astonishment, when Moose sat down to her right, that he was sticking to his word to stay sober.

The crowd, containing both men and women, was in the throes of a heated discussion about societal constraints, particularly for women. When an attractive college girl mentioned sex, Moose's ears perked up, and unsurprisingly, he joined the debate.

The instant Angie heard that same, recurring phrase, the one he'd been spewing all summer long to anyone who would listen, she laughed broadly. "There you go again with that Free Love crap," she said, causing a hundred eyeballs to abruptly turn on her.

"Why is it crap?" Moose asked.

Looking around, Angie realized the attention was on her. The crowd had gone quiet. "Don't get me wrong," she said after a nervous puff. "Free Love would be an interesting idea had women thought it up." That seemed to titillate a pair of young women nearby. They glanced at each other with intrigued puckers, giving Angie the boost she needed to continue. "But all I hear is men telling women to hand their bodies over in the name of 'women's liberation' and not to worry about pesky little matters like pregnancy or disrepute. It's a dream come true for men, but a dangerous game of Russian roulette for women."

Moose's face crumpled. "That's bleak."

"The truth usually is, my friend." Angie lay back onto her elbows and flicked the seat of his pants.

Moose raised his eyebrows, then laughed. "Watch out, Ang, you're letting your anger toward men show again."

Angie huffed, indignant, then snorted. She did not have anger toward men. And even if she did, it didn't make her wrong. "What's your outlook then? Shock me."

"I'm a man," Moose said. "No matter what I say, you're going to say I'm full of crap and only thinking with my penis." Around him, the crowd chuckled.

"Eh, you're probably right," Angie admitted, gesturing to the pretty blond whose comment about sex had caught Moose's attention in the first place. "Let's get another woman's opinion then." Angie grinned, praying the girl took the attention off her. "What's your take?"

Blondie tilted her head, almost bashfully. "To be honest, I think Free Love is a groovy concept," she said, and others nodded in agreement.

"Groovy how?" Angie asked, unable to help herself.

"Well . . . I think about my mother's experience as a woman. She was pregnant at eighteen and expected to marry a boy she barely knew. I love my dad, but marriage signaled the end of her identity as a free-thinking individual. In society's eyes, she's just a wife and mother who's expected to fulfill everybody's wishes but her own, otherwise she's considered selfish and inadequate. As far as the law is concerned, my father owns her body and every asset they've ever acquired together. Pregnancy enslaves women. But with the pill, we're free to live as we choose now, and I think we should."

Angie sat up. "Having sex with that boy she barely knew was her choice, though, wasn't it? You wouldn't be here if she'd made a different one."

"In their case, yes, that's true. But it doesn't change the fact that if she'd had the pill, she would've made a lot of different decisions for herself. She might've enjoyed my dad for a time or for a lifetime. She would've had that choice. Our generation has that choice. Women have true freedom finally, and we owe it to the women who came before us to use it."

"Okay, so options are a good thing," Angie said. "I think we can all agree that men have dominated women for way too long. But doesn't it bother you that most of the men here supporting your right to Free Love are only looking to get into your pants? Isn't this just another ploy for control over us? I mean, of course they're going to support female sex that's free of commitment and responsibility. It benefits them. But what happens if your pill fails? Will these free-wheeling, free-loving men then accept responsibility for their part, marry you and help you raise a kid? Or care for the kid if you want to work? How far does their support for Free Love actually go?"

"My point is that you don't have to marry them," the girl replied, "if you don't want to. There's still a choice."

Angie frowned. "What if I want to marry them? What if I want to have children? How many men will commit to a family when there's a generation of women giving their 'love' away for free?"

Quite abruptly, Angie pinched her lips shut. Now she was just arguing to argue, something she did from time to time, for no other reason than to be defiant. The last thing she wanted was to marry and have kids, and arguing on its behalf was starting to make her queasy.

"Come on," a young man jumped in. "Give us more credit than that."

"Why should she?" another guy joined in. "Women had to invent marriage to tie men down. It's not a natural human arrangement."

"... exactly the point ..."

"... humanity is one big family ..."

Everyone jumped in on the conversation, and Angie lost track. Her brain was turning to slop. Dropping back onto her elbows, she stared at the evening sky while the chatter grew spirited. Not a single star was visible here. In Pacific Grove, several would've peeked out by this hour.

"... Free Love is the natural state of humanity ..."

"Of humanity or of men? What's the natural state of women?"

A deep, silken voice pierced through Angie's fog. "Do you really want to marry and have a bunch of rug rats?" a man to her left asked, and she turned her head. The question had roused Angie, but she was far more galvanized by the powerful attraction she felt toward the stranger who asked it. Not because he was classically handsome, but because he oozed a barbarian level of masculinity: hirsute, broad-shouldered, tall, and muscled. "Or are you following the path society brainwashed into your psyche before you could even talk?"

"What?" she asked.

His eyes narrowed. His voice turned gruff. "You heard me."

Oh . . .

Sufficiently provoked by his insolence, Angie cocked an eyebrow, then narrowed her own eyes. "Fine. You're insinuating that women aren't capable of recognizing the difference between their own desires and the wishes of society. How daring of you. I'm so impressed I think I feel the vapors coming on."

His smirk grew. "You're a little hellion, aren't you?"

"What's it to you?"

He leaned toward her, not stopping until his lips touched her ear.

The heat of his breath spread across her skin, and a shiver clambered up her spine. She was both annoyed and beguiled, and the brew was intoxicating.

"I fear you may be severely sexually repressed," he said against her earlobe.

Angie's stomach clenched involuntarily; then she choked a little on her own spit. Quick as a swallow, she pulled herself together. "Excuse me?"

"You should be climaxing several times a day." He spoke with such deadly serious, measured leisure that she was forced to listen more carefully than usual. "Deep, full-body orgasms," he went on. "Have you read Wilhelm Reich?"

Twisting her neck to face him, Angie probed his dark, collectivist eyes, gleaming with visions of violent government overthrow and nonconformist retribution. She then glanced farther down to his enticing, pink lips, half-shrouded by an unkempt bushel of wiry beard hair. He was like a big, radicalized grizzly bear. One making some very excellent points.

"Not yet," she told him, damned if she wasn't going straight to the library tomorrow.

"All this sexual tension you're harboring is concentrated deep inside your loins," he whispered, his mouth so near that their breath coalesced, the air between them stifling. "It needs release. I could help you reach orgastic potency. Make you come so hard you see God."

"Oh . . ." Angie shuddered, then gulped. "I—I read something recently that said, 'God is dead.'"

With that same measured leisure, the man shook his head. "Would you like to meet Him?"

Panting now, she nodded. "Yes, please."

They lunged at each other in a lecherous kiss, and he was every bit as indecent as he looked. His lips were supple but aggressive. His arms beefy and strong. His hands like battered baseball mitts at the back of her neck and on her hip, yanking her close. Hot and sweet, his tongue penetrated her mouth, tasting like a heady mix of fruit juice, liquor, and pot. It made Angie feel hot on the inside, tingly, like she'd been drugged. Then again, she had.

As the beat moved over her, pushing her back onto the grass, she forgot all her scruples and woes. There was only this thick stranger between her legs and the searing hot mouth that latched onto her neck, to suckle and lap at her neglected flesh. Her head lolled back. Her hands clutched his disheveled head. He was a lover underneath the maddening mix of chauvinism, muscle, and hair. She wanted to cry out, he felt so good. "Oh, God, yes," she whispered instead, dragging his mouth back to hers for another taste.

But then he was gone.

"All right," she heard Moose say as she was lifted off the ground. "Upsy-daisy. Here we go. Sorry, Paul Bunyan. No hellions for you tonight."

"No," Angie pouted. "He's teaching me about Free Love. I think I get it now." Her bushy lover winked at her from the ground where he still lounged. She flapped her fingers at him as Moose dragged her away. "Bye, you."

"I promised I wouldn't let you do anything stupid tonight," Moose reminded her. "I don't need sober Angie all over my ass tomorrow."

"But he was so sexy, Moose."

"Uh-huh. Let's get you some water."

"I don't want water; I want to climax several times a day. Full, deep-bodied orgasms."

"Yep." Moose set her against a tree. "Stay," he demanded, turning away briefly.

Angie plucked a beer from his shoulder bag and popped it open.

Spinning back around, Moose snatched it from her hand. "No more drinking either. You can't drink, trip, and smoke at the same time. It's overload. I don't know what I was thinking. You can't handle it."

"Can *so* handle it."

"Can you promise me you won't make it with every beat who comes on to you?"

"Who can promise such a thing in this vast, unpredictable universe?"

Moose growled at her use of his phraseology. "We're going back to Bianca's so you can burn all this dope off."

"I still think you got jilted. I don't feel a thing."

Moose's plan to leave the park never materialized. There were way too many distractions. The park teemed with every vibrant complexity the world in its infinite wisdom had to offer. If people weren't making music, they were making it with each other or dancing alone. Angie experienced it all in short clips of time. Moose had been right; the mixture of intoxicants made her head spin like a top. Deep within the recesses of her mind, the drugs continued to wipe away the old notions, providing her with new, more stimulating ones.

Despite Moose's objections, Angie continued to guzzle beer and anything else she was handed. She smoked whatever grass got passed her way. She was having a great time, talking and flirting and making out with men she found dangerous and exciting. It was becoming clear to her that she had a type: intelligent barbarians. Bedraggled beatniks. They spouted their avant-garde philosophies, and she argued to the contrary, whether she disagreed or not, until the heat building between them blistered and turned sexual. Then it was all mouths and hands and dirty, carnal covenants in her ear.

And every damn time, Moose jumped in to ruin her fun.

"Damn you!" Angie bellowed as she was dragged away from a flaxen-haired beat who had worked industriously to convince her that all women had an evolutionary need to ingest male ejaculate. Science had always intrigued her. "I am officially giving you permission to buzz off, Moose!"

"Not happening, angel."

Angie whined. "But he was saying such filthy, yummy things to me. I miss that. I miss sex. I miss Roger. I'm so lonely."

"So, what, you want me to let my high, drunk friend suck off a stranger in the park after she explicitly told me to stay sober and make sure she doesn't do anything stupid?"

Excitedly, Angie nodded. "Yes, yes, do that."

"Are you out of your frigging mind?"

"Yes," she said. "Wasn't that the point of all this?"

Sighing, Moose kissed her on the forehead. "You'll thank me tomorrow."

"No, I wo—" An errant thought struck Angie, one that had never entered her mind before now and wouldn't have in a million years if her mind wasn't so open and stretchy. "You know . . ." Pushing to her tiptoes, she slinked her arms up Moose's chest and tightened them around his neck. She kissed his mouth with less chastity than usual. "I'm not opposed to Free Love among friends."

Moose unhooked her arms and set them back at her sides. "Say that again when you're sober, and we'll talk."

Angie flopped her head against Moose's chest. "Oh, come on, don't you miss sex? How long has it been for you?"

"A week."

"A week! Well, don't you have some nerve! With who?"

"You don't know her. Her name's Delilah."

"Oh, well, la-di-da. Deli-i-i-i-lahhhh." Peeved that he dared to make a nun of her while grabbing Delilah by the horns, Angie plopped herself dramatically onto the grass, folded her arms, and began to people-watch.

The hypocrite plopped down beside her and lit himself a cigarette.

Every gesture made by the people around them was followed by a fine streak of light. Faces morphed. The very air pulsated. While over the entire assemblage, trees fluctuated, tall and valiant. But Angie saw the trees for what they truly were: noble protectors, guardians of the young people of the park who toiled under the spell of varied intoxicants. Like the several young women who, one by one, removed their blouses to dance around a trash can fire that sent heat in Angie's direction, its flames like huge, orange tongues lashing at the darkness. A twosome, a man and a woman, stripped down entirely. Angie stared, transfixed, at all the frolicking bodies, the jiggling breasts and buttocks, the nimble, outstretched limbs. How beautifully they moved through the night air, impervious to climate or shame, their faces triumphant in the light.

A magnet to steel, Angie drew closer, climbing to her feet.

"What are you doing?" Moose sounded so far away.

Angie pulled her blouse over her head. Chilled air caressed her exposed breasts, constricting her nipples into stiff, aching points. Oh, the freedom, the welcoming night. They enveloped her, embracing her like a mother welcoming a wayward child home.

"Mother of God," she heard Moose snarl as he struggled to get to his own feet.

Before he could once again thieve her precious liberty, Angie sprinted toward the dancing women and joined them inside the warm firelight. She waited for shame and embarrassment to come as she let her limbs slacken, as she let the music guide her body, but they never did. Their absence was an invigorating presence. She felt weightless and . . . Oh, yes-s-s, so sensual. Her arms curled against the moon-shine. Her hips and belly rolled, bare breasts jutting toward the fire that felt like warm hands cupping her fondly, easing the ache. There was a whimsical, erotic gratification that came with every movement her body made. Her every nerve ending blazed with ecstasy, and she made love to the sensation, to the elements, to the loving human energy that surrounded her.

Polyester fell over her shoulders, and she openly rejoiced as Moose dragged her back into the darkness. "I'm orgasm itself," she crooned to him, running her hands over her naked flesh. "Touch me, Moose. You might be able to feel it."

"I'll do no such thing," Moose grumbled, struggling to put her shirt back on. "Stand still."

The next thing Angie knew, she was being pushed down a pathway through the park.

Moose informed her, quite brusquely, that they were heading back to Bianca's—"for sure this time!"—to eat, rest, and smoke enough weed to put down a horse—Angie being the horse. And to ease his rattled nerves.

"Celia will sit with you till you sober up," he said. "I can't be alone with you right now."

"I love Celia," Angie sighed, thinking of her oldest female friend, one of the few women on planet Earth that she could actually stand. "She's swell."

Most of the park's walkways were lit, and as Angie glanced around, she observed lovers everywhere, necking in the dark or having, what looked like, crucial, earth-shattering discussions.

Near a giant oak, two people embraced, their mouths caught in a stormy kiss, and Angie thought the acid must have toasted her brain because it looked to be two men. What made this trip even freak-ier was that one of the men could've been Fletcher's identical twin. He was built exactly like him, well-proportioned and slim, with a sharp, handsome jawline and clean-cut, sandy hair. He even sported Fletcher's signature black-framed Browline eyeglasses . . .

Angie tipped her head. "Fletcher?" she called out. "Is that you?"

"What?" Moose stopped. "Where?"

"There," Angie pointed, giddy at her find.

Brash amusement tumbled out of Moose, a true belly laugh. It was a lovely sound. "That's not Fletch, Looney Tunes. That's two guys sucking face. Welcome to the city." His expression and tone turned uncharacteristically bitter as he watched them. "Let's get out of here."

"No, that's Fletcher," Angie insisted, staring at the couple with sharper eyes. The whole of the planet seemed to spin on an axis directly between her and that oak tree, where the men enjoyed each other, where Fletcher (or Not-Fletcher) slid his hands into his lover's dark hair, looking beautiful as always as his appealing jaw stretched open for a great, yawning kiss.

Besotted, Angie couldn't look away.

"Well, at least we know the LSD is good." Moose's hand pressed to the small of her back, redirecting her. "Told you it wasn't junk." Then—maybe to humor her or perhaps he saw it, too—he took a step toward the couple who were going at it like it was their final hour on earth, like they were burning alive with their passion for each other. Moose frowned. "Wow, that one guy really does look like Fletch."

Angie stuck two fingers in her mouth to blow her infamous, ear-splitting whistle. "FLETCHER!"

The pair of men separated and turned.

It *was* Fletcher. And a good-looking, older man.

"Oh!" Angie pointed a finger at Fletcher, then at Moose, masking her mouth with the other hand. "Oh!" She hadn't expected to be right.

"Do you know these people?" the handsome man asked Fletcher with an accent Angie didn't recognize. Somehow, he was more handsome than Fletcher, and Fletcher was the most beautiful boy she'd ever known. Fletcher was so gorgeous, in fact, that Angie ogled as he pulled off his glasses and wiped at his mouth (which was a phenomenal feat of God's engineering all by itself).

Then that perfectly formed face evinced distress, and her shock dissolved into concern.

"They're my friends," Fletcher said, then brought his hands to his head. "They were."

"Fletcher?" Angie moved toward him. Was he high? Drunk? She didn't understand. "Honey, what are you doing?"

"Hello." Extending his hand, the striking foreigner stepped toward Angie and Moose. "It's very nice to meet the both of you. I am Sérgio."

"Curtis," Moose said, paying no heed to Sérgio's hand.

"Um," Angie forgot her own name and, evidently, her manners. She didn't know how to respond to a simple greeting suddenly. "I'm, um . . . um . . ."

"Don't mind Angie here," Moose said. "She's considerably incapacitated."

"Hello, Angie." Sérgio smiled sweetly but cautiously now. He glanced back at Fletcher, who was staring toward the heavens, his hands on his head. "It's very nice to meet you both."

Nodding dismissively at the stranger, Angie waved Fletcher over. "Fletcher, can we talk to you, please? Alone."

Fletcher huffed, lowering his arms. "Excuse me," he told Sérgio and followed his friends several yards away. The three of them formed a loose circle and began to whisper.

"So," Angie began, clearing her throat in a lame attempt to clear her head, "uh, is there anything you want to tell us or . . . ?" The query was absurd, but it was all that would leave her mouth. Her teeth felt soft, pliable. Her tongue, enormous.

Fletcher's expression hardened. "What's there to tell? You saw us. Am I supposed to spell it out for you, too, humiliate myself further?"

"Whoa." Angie raised her hands. "I figured I'd give you a chance to explain yourself. I mean . . . he's a man, Fletcher."

"Yes, I'm aware," Fletcher whispered, every part of him tensing. He pinned Angie in place with blue eyes that told a tale of emotion: fear, anger, pain, resentment . . . "You can leave now."

"Why are you getting so bent out of shape?" Angie asked. "We're just . . . we're . . . we're in shock, okay? Why didn't you tell us? Is this . . . Is this new? Are you—What about Celia? Where is she?" Her head whirling and woozy, Angie leaned against Moose, who was reticent for the first time in his life. The scene around her started to darken, twisting to rot before her eyes, and she had to squeeze them shut to dislodge a few stinging teardrops. "I don't like this anymore."

Moose gave her a squeeze. "It's all right. I've got you."

"I can't believe this." Fletcher's voice sounded wrong, shaky, as he peeked back at Sérgio. "I came this close to being arrested tonight," he told Angie and Moose. "Arrested! I refuse to have to answer to you, too. I'm so drunk I can't even think straight, and you're embarrassing me."

Stunned by the hostility in his voice, Angie straightened up and suffered the dizziness. "*We're* embarrassing *you*?" No matter what was transpiring, she couldn't believe he was being so nasty to them, his oldest friends. "That's rich."

Fletcher shot daggers back at her, and Moose finally jumped in. "Angie made out with four different guys tonight."

Angie gaped at Moose.

"What?" Moose responded, clearly stressed. "I figure that makes you both even. He's . . . And you're . . . well, kind of a tramp," he said, shrugging. "I'm sorry, okay! I don't know what to say right now."

"I'm a tramp?! Earlier, it was Free Love and my earthly right and responsibility as an enlightened woman. Chauvinist jerk!"

"I'm just trying to ease the tension here!"

"Oh, and you're doing a real bang-up job, aren't you?"

"I'm leaving," Fletcher said, walking away.

"Wait." Angie watched Fletcher disappear into the shadows with Sérgio. "Fletcher, come back!" she called out. "I'm sorry!" But he was gone. "Damn it, Moose."

"The one night I stay sober."

29

Jeremy

Jeremy woke up in an unfamiliar house that teemed with strangers. Some of them sat in large gatherings on the floor while others sprawled on bean bags or makeshift sofas, ingesting various substances or just chatting. The three closest to him helped one another inject a pale fluid into their arms. One or two wandered with, seemingly, no purpose at all. Music, rich and resonating with a rapid drumbeat, charged the hazy air. He couldn't tell how long he'd been watching them all or whether he'd passed out at some point and dreamed their activities.

Short, wispy trails followed the slender fingertips of a young Black girl nearby. She couldn't have been more than fourteen or fifteen. Her face, round and pleasant at first, elongated and warped, and Jeremy knew he was still high.

"Are you all right?" the girl asked him, her mouth stretching her into the uncanny valley, making her appear demonic, scaring him a little. "You aren't going to be sick, are you?"

"No."

"Keep your eyes closed," she said, draping her jacket over him. "It'll pass."

Sometime later, Jeremy became hyperaware of his solitude. The girl—Marion had been her name—eventually left him, and without another person to keep him grounded, it was hard to maintain a grasp on the real world.

Then there was Celia. It felt as though he hadn't seen her in days. Last he could recall, she had scored them a lift back into the heart of the city while he'd popped the last sugar cube into his mouth and smoked another joint, thinking that if he got high enough, he could stop his mind from racing, from fretting about Fletcher and mooning over Celia.

Climbing to his feet, Jeremy waited for the dizziness to pass, determined to rejoin the tactile world. He would need it to navigate the dark, crowded duplex. Even sober, the place would be disorienting with its strange blue tint and doors at every turn.

He stumbled through a swinging door into a kitchen, where a dozen people loitered. Someone pushed bacon around in a pan, and the scent activated Jeremy's appetite. He was starved.

"Have you seen a girl with reddish-blond hair?" he asked another passing stranger and then another. "She doesn't like to be alone." No one answered him. "Move." He pushed a few more people aside. They did nothing, the damned pacifists. "Move it."

He saw her colorful dress first, then her hair. It fell over her shoulders, that shining ruddy gold. She was standing by the sink, and Jeremy celebrated his discovery until he noticed the hands on her. Coming around from the front to knead at the small of her back.

He ambled over, not understanding.

She wouldn't. She wouldn't do that to him now.

Mouths twisted together, like two gaping wounds in a wrestling match. Those hands roamed. Celia was kissing someone else, and he didn't like it.

She, however, seemed to be thoroughly enjoying herself.

The grief that accompanied that thought hit him like a sledgehammer to his chest.

"Celia." The word barely left him. He pictured her face when she was young. In the past month, it had grown into something welcoming, something attainable and warm. And now there was only agony again. And a petulant, backsliding rage.

Not knowing what else to do, Jeremy nudged himself between the pair.

"What the hell, man," Celia said. Only it wasn't Celia. This girl was taller. And not as pretty.

"Oh, sorry." Jeremy staggered away, twice as disoriented as before, until he was lost again. "Celia?"

Another door opened into a narrow hall. At the far end of it, an unfurnished bedroom glowed a deep, dark blue, and in the far corner of that bedroom, three girls sat. One braided the hair of another, a strawberry blond wearing yellow pants and a white blouse.

Celia looked up and smiled. "There he is." Her hands reached for him. "Come here. I missed you. You were out cold."

Flooded with relief, Jeremy dropped into her waiting arms and sunk his head into her lap, wrapping his arms around her.

"Are you hungry?" she asked, stroking his hair.

Jeremy nodded.

Celia handed him a grease-splotched, brown paper bag. Inside, a semi-warm cheeseburger and cold fries waited.

Rolling onto his back, Jeremy lay beneath her, head still in her lap, and got to work on the food. It was lard-filled ecstasy.

When he was done eating, she cleaned ketchup and mustard from his face, then stroked his temple with the back of her fingers. And when her fingernails began to scratch at his scalp, Jeremy closed his eyes and thought about third-grade science. He had been assigned a report about a deep-sea creature called the anglerfish. In his library research, he discovered that the male anglerfish bites into the skin of the preciously rare female anglerfish, releasing an enzyme that works to dissolve his own flesh so that the pair can fuse. The male is then absorbed into the female's body to become a part of her forever, living inside her, wasting away as she lives on.

He was that stupid male fish when it came to Celia Lynch, Jeremy realized as he drifted off to sleep.

———

Jeremy awoke feeling much better. He was no longer hungry and more of the acid seemed to have burned through his system. Above him, Celia chatted with two girls.

"I'm hoping I can convince him to stay," she whispered.

"You think he will?"

"I don't know. Maybe?" Her voice, while doleful, projected hope. "If I can just convince him that we belong together—"

"My old man—fiancé now—took off to Chicago a month ago," one of the girls cut in. "His wife lives out there. I'm trying to convince him to come back here. The baby's due in December."

As Celia stumbled through a response, Jeremy sat up.

"Hey, sleepyhead." Celia brushed his hair back. "How are you feeling?"

"Better," he said, rubbing his eyes with his thumb and index finger. "I've gotta go. What time is it?"

"A little after midnight," Celia answered. "Where are we going?"

"Back to your sister's pad." Standing up, Jeremy pulled Celia to her feet. He lugged her from the room as she waved a rushed good-bye to her new friends. "I need to get back to Pacific Grove," he said as he hunted for an exit to the maddening house. Door after door got in his way.

"I'm sure Moose can take us home first thing in the morning."

"No, I mean right now," he said, opening another door to find only an empty closet. "By myself. I'll hitch a ride." He slammed the door shut. "Damn it."

"What do you mean? Why?"

In the dim hallway, Jeremy twisted around and held Celia at arm's length. "I don't know what you think is happening here, but I'm leaving on the seventeenth."

"I know that. I was just hoping, maybe, you'd consider rearranging your flight so you can stay a little longer. Or maybe . . . not go at all."

Jeremy squinted at her. "Are you insane? They'd arrest me." He watched her expression plunge into disarray. "Don't look at me like that."

"I don't understand," Celia said. "Why would someone arrest you? I—If you'd just give us more time . . ." She reached up to take his face in her hands. "You could come back and then—"

Jeremy pushed her hands away. "Don't you get it? I'm probably not coming back."

"Never?"

Letting her go, Jeremy laughed darkly. Was she playing games? He didn't even know if he would be alive in six months, and she was concerned with her love life, clearly unaccustomed to not getting her way. Maybe she was as self-absorbed as he'd originally assumed. It wouldn't be the first time she'd fooled him into trusting her.

"Look," Celia said, wringing her hands. "I know it's hard for you to be around me. But we had a good time this past month, didn't we? Maybe I could visit you in Tennessee, and we can—"

"Celia, that's years away. Stop—" Turning, he stepped away. He couldn't look at her anymore. He tried another door. "Where the fuck is the way out?"

"Please just listen to me!" Celia called from behind him. "I could enroll in college there, and if all goes well, I'd stay."

"If all goes well?" Jeremy scoffed. "You mean if I don't die or come back a stump?"

"What? I—I'm just saying, I know we could be something. We were meant to be something. I could move there for the fall semester. It'll give us more time. And if it's not working . . ."

As she rambled on and as his bewilderment grew, it finally struck him. "They didn't tell you," he said. It would explain so much about Celia's behavior the past month. He'd assumed she'd been told about Vietnam, by Angie or Moose, and was too wrapped up in her little game of chase to give a shit. And when Moose had told Fletcher the night before, it had surprised Jeremy that Fletcher didn't already know. But he'd been too concerned about Celia's anger, and too damn high, to put together that if Fletcher didn't know, Celia probably didn't know. As Jeremy thought back to every disgusted reaction he'd had to something she'd said or done, actions that came off as uncaring or even cruel to someone about to go off to war, he began to pace. "Fletcher didn't even tell you last night? I thought you two told each other everything."

"What didn't Fletcher tell me?" Her voice sounded so cold suddenly, the pitch deep and guttural. He didn't like that voice on her. Her eyes, so dark in the dim light, narrowed. "Jeremy?"

Jeremy ceased his pacing to look at her. "I was drafted." In that instant, his frustration with her disappeared. Any residual disgust or anger vanished altogether, having been misguided from the start. The expression she wore confirmed for him that she genuinely hadn't known. He took a step toward her, took her face, and exhaled with relief. Her frown coarsened. "I report for boot camp next week."

He studied her face, weary after the long day together, and her frizzy, knotted hair that she was always trying to smooth with her palms. She was beautiful.

"That's where I'll be," he said with a smile. "Not Tennessee. That's why we can't—"

"Oh," Celia exhaled, "God." She lowered her head and forced his hands away. "You really hate me, don't you? I knew you did when you first got here, but I thought we—I thought—"

Jeremy shook his head. "No—"

"I'm so awful that you would lie about getting drafted just to get away from me?"

"I'm not lying."

"I thought—" Tears pooled in her eyes. "I thought we'd gotten past—"Then her face hardened. "I made you lemonade! I got up at four in the morning for a month to put your favorite snacks in that stupid wagon. I tried everything to make you like me."

"I do like you."

The words had barely left his mouth when Celia dissolved into tears.

Instinctively, Jeremy reached for her, but she pushed him away, and he'd forgotten how painful her rejection could be.

"Celia, listen to me. I'm not—" As he spoke, he reached out to touch her again, and again, she pushed him away. With much more force.

"Don't touch me!" Red, watery eyes tightened on him. "Drafted. You are so mean!"

Jeremy flinched. "It's the truth. I thought you knew—"

"Shut up!" The words expanded into a sob as she held tight to her stomach. "Oh, God, I wish you'd never come back here. Why couldn't you have stayed gone?"

A torrent of lousy feelings knocked Jeremy back a step, and he suddenly felt the need to throttle something, anything, before he imploded. Grabbing the nearest object, he hurled it into the wall behind him, the tension in his chest easing a bit as the cheap, yellow vase shattered apart.

Celia let out a startled cry and retreated from him. He wanted to tell her she had been right to hate him all those years ago. Right to hate him now. He wasn't good like Fletcher or like her father. He wasn't worth anyone's tears. But another long-buried sensation, built of self-preservation and ego, bubbled up into his throat, strangling the words.

Jeremy watched her kneel to pick up shards of yellow glass from the dirty Berber carpet below their feet. "Stop it." Dropping to his own knees, he shoved her hands away. "I'm the piece of shit who broke it. I'll do it."

"Don't say things like that." Through waterlogged eyes, Celia searched the carpet for stray fragments of glass. "People are barefoot. We need to hurry."

Lacking the energy to argue, Jeremy let her help him clean up his mess. And when they finished, having dumped every findable shard into a nearby trash can, he sat for a long time on the floor, appraising her distant, tear-stained face.

"I need to get out of this house," he said gently, feeling trapped within the dingy, empty walls. "Will you come with me?"

They walked in silence down Masonic Avenue in the direction of the Haight, and when they reached the panhandle of Golden Gate Park, Jeremy stopped to rest against a tree. He'd worked an entire summer, nonstop, and he'd never felt so depleted.

Noticing he was no longer beside her, Celia turned around, her eyes tender again, contrite. "Did you really get drafted?"

He nodded.

"I didn't know," she said.

Jeremy felt the smallest of smiles lift one side of his mouth. "I know."

"Can't you get a deferment?" she asked, taking a step. "An extension?"

"I already got one. I was originally supposed to report for duty in May."

"You could register for college courses," she said, inching closer. "They can't send you then."

A silent chuckle shook Jeremy's chest. She sounded like his mother. "I barely graduated high school, Celia. I'm not smart like you."

"Yes, you are." Celia stopped in front of him. "You could go to Fresno State with me and Fletcher. We would help you study. Please, Jeremy."

"Celia, it's all right. I've accepted it."

"We could take it slow. I wouldn't push. I swear."

Jeremy squeezed his eyes shut. "Celia, this isn't some convenient excuse I'm making. Even if I hadn't been drafted, I wouldn't stay here. I spent a decade trying to forget Pacific Grove and three years avoiding this trip. The last thing I meant to do was get into a thing with some-one." At the change in her demeanor, he grabbed her hand. "Look, I'm starting to understand why you're so set on making things right between us. I'm glad our childhood was wonderful for you. Really. But I don't remember it that way, and that's fine with me."

"Wonderful for me?" Celia scoffed. "In case you forgot, I watched him die, too."

Jeremy shook his head. "I didn't watch my dad die, Celia. I *wanted* him to die. I was tired of being afraid."

"You were protecting me."

"Is that what you think? Is that what this is all about? You think it was some grand romantic gesture?" Jeremy wasn't trying to hurt her, but he had to laugh through his exhaustion. "I was ten. I was trying to head off another beating. You got in the way."

"So, what, it was my fault?"

"No. Of course not. I'm saying, forget about me. Forget all of it. We both should do that."

Celia shook her head. Sorrow returned full force to cloak all her prettiest features. Her lip quivered. Her eyes shone with tears, a light beckoning him home.

He watched her, wondering how to put it into the right words. Everything that popped into his head sounded childish and weak, and he never wanted to sound that way to her. Cruel, angry, indifferent, but never weak.

And some things were better left unsaid.

"Whatever it was . . . it's over," he said gently. "And I need it to stay that way."

The statement rattled her, though it hadn't been his intention. Her face and shoulders crumbled. More sorrow welled up around her. It took all his willpower to sidestep her pain and continue.

"Not because you were a brat, Celia," he said, tipping her face by the chin. "And not because I blame you. I moved on, and I won't go back. Not for you. Not for anyone."

They stared at each other, trapped in the middle of a conversation that had nowhere else to go, the tension of it growing around them like a cancer. But he had nothing left to say.

Then she spoke.

"I don't think I can move on."

A placid tear dropped down her cheek.

When he was a boy, brand new to Tennessee, he'd erected a wall around himself, bigger and better than the one he'd built in Pacific Grove. It was as heavy as his hatred and as durable as the belief that he was a mighty Goliath capable of killing his own father. That fresh identity had given him strength against the pain. It had gotten him through to the other side, where he'd found a little peace. But now he understood that she was still back there. He'd left her there. A scared little girl alone in the dark.

Jeremy pulled Celia into his arms. "I'm sorry." He wondered how this would end between them. If it ever would. Then he cupped her face in his hands. Beach pebbles shined up at him, and he considered telling her to become a mighty Goliath, too, to raise her own impenetrable wall. But he could see now that it wasn't in her. She was not an angel, nor some devil sent to torment him forever. She was not all-powerful. She was just a girl.

Bending his knees, Jeremy lowered himself to the ground, bringing Celia with him. He set his back against a broad elm tree, his legs spreading apart to make room for her as she folded down between his thighs, crossing her knees against him.

He wrapped his arms around her when she lowered her head to his shoulder and said, "Where did the police take you that night? I never knew."

Jeremy blew out a breath. He still didn't want to talk about that night but now felt like he owed it to her. He'd never spoken about it to anyone, not even his mother. He had no clue where to begin. A lot of it was embarrassing, and as much as he didn't want to admit it, what Celia thought of him still mattered.

He decided the beginning was as good a place as any. "The cops took me to their station."

He didn't add that he'd grinned like a lunatic as they questioned him about his father's death, creeping them all out, something he now found funny. Back then, he'd wanted them all to hate and fear him. And going by their treatment of him that night, he had succeeded in his mission.

"Then they took me to juvie," he went on. "I tried being a tough guy when I got there, and this fossil everyone called Old George knocked my lights out. When I came to, he said something like . . ."—Jeremy altered his voice to match the memory—"It's those soulless little fucks out in the yard you gotta fool, boy. You walk around wearing them sissy school clothes and that mule stare o' yours, you'll wind up as bloody as the day your mama shit you out."

Celia raised her head. "He said that to a little boy?"

Jeremy laughed, then guided her head back to his shoulder. "He told me to 'kick a few teeth in' my first day to avoid becoming the yard kickball. It was good advice. Then he made me put on a uniform that stunk like piss and showed me to my bunk."

Peering down to check Celia's reaction, Jeremy decided not to mention that part again.

"Anyway, like he said they would, the other kids stomped me good that first night, but after I 'kicked a few teeth in', like Old George said, they didn't bother me again."

Celia pressed herself closer. "I'm sorry, Jeremy."

Smiling to himself, Jeremy kissed her head. She'd never understand. He'd been glad to prove himself. Yeah, it stunk getting kicked in the gut, but a good payback ass-kicking was always worth the pain.

"A few days after that," he continued, "this woman came and got me and drove me to an office where my mom was waiting." Jeremy winced at the memory. "I was such a prick to her. I hated her back then. They tried explaining what my dad had done, keeping me from her. But I didn't give a damn. I didn't know her. They made me stay in a motel with her while they filed custody paperwork with the court. I refused to speak to her. And then there was the day of my dad's funeral. I was so pissed at you for not being there. Your parents said you chose to go to school instead."

Celia jolted upright, her eyes wild. "No! I didn't know about the funeral. Nobody told me."

"It's all right." Jeremy stroked her back. "It doesn't matter."

"It matters to me. I didn't know. I would've chosen you."

"Okay," he said, pulling her closer. "I believe you."

Clearly, Celia wanted to say more, but after every emotion in existence passed over her face, she snuggled down against him again and mumbled, "Keep going."

It took Jeremy a minute to refocus. Her distress had affected him. His heart thrashed against his rib cage; his throat was so thick with anxiety that he had to clear it. He preferred her happy. "After . . . afterward, my mom and I drove to Memphis." It all came flooding back, that road trip, and Jeremy had to shake his head at the dumb kid he'd been. "I took off on her a few times. I felt like absolute shit for hitting you. I had this brilliant plan to get back to California. I was going to beg your forgiveness, then convince you to run away with me."

Celia raised her head again, an energized little smile on her lips, but he pulled her head back down.

"Don't get any ideas. Anyway, Oklahoma state troopers started a full-blown manhunt and found me easy enough. After that one, I gave up."

Celia snuggled deeper against him, taking his hand to lace their fingers together. She gazed up at him, and he got lost in the structure of her face, in her every feature, each perfect to him, together forming a face he found beautiful. He wondered if he was in love with her, if that's what this heavy sizzle inside his chest was.

Jeremy pressed his lips to hers, making the sizzle flare, recognizing it as intense desire. Not the animal lust kind. He'd felt that plenty in his life. This was different. This roiled deep inside his psyche, this incredible need for conquest, for her complete submission. For her obsession and her desire. For her love. But he had no idea what he would do with those things if he ever got them.

"I'm still listening," Celia whispered.

Jeremy raised half a smile to her. "She took me home. She lived with her dad, my granddad. He was a real hard-ass at first, but I couldn't blame him. I was being a real shit to his daughter. I made her cry a lot in the beginning. A couple days in, he sat me down and told me he'd be damned if I was going to become my father. He wasn't going to let me treat his daughter like Dennis had. But he never hit me. Not once. He put me to work instead. He ran a farm, and every morning at five o'clock, he'd barge in my room with a bucket of cold water. I got soaked four mornings in a row before I realized he wasn't fucking around."

Celia raised her eyebrows. "Oh, you must've been mad."

"Yeah, but I got up," Jeremy said. "I milked the cows and fed the chickens and pigs. I cleaned the coops and the stalls and did a hundred other chores, all before seven. Granddad and his crew worked the fields, and I was put in charge of the animals. I didn't have the time or energy to stay mad. He's how I learned how to fix up a house."

"Where's your grandpa now?" Celia asked.

"He died last year."

"Oh, Jeremy, I'm sorry." Her palm went to his neck, her fingers dancing lightly against his skin. Her eyes were warm with affection, and the feeling they invoked in him was one he remembered chasing a lot as a kid. It was all he ever wanted at any given time: her affection. And when he got it, when her eyes and her voice liquified this way, he'd felt like somebody who mattered.

Rising to meet him, Celia pressed her lips softly to his, and his heart constricted so painfully that he deepened the kiss, needing to assuage and feed it.

Letting her go, Jeremy cleared his throat. "It's cold," he said. "We should get back to the house." He gave her nose a nuzzle. "We can smoke a little grass and keep each other warm."

"Listen to you." Celia nudged a teasing poke into his ribs. "Is that how you got the girls in Pacific Grove all aflutter? With sweet talk and pot?"

Jeremy gave her a shallow grin and slid an appealing curl of her hair between his fingers. "I'm not trying to seduce you, Celia."

Her eyebrows crumpled. "Why not?"

"Because I have more respect for you than that. Anyway, I don't have to try. You're making it super easy."

Giggling, Celia smacked his chest. "How dare you, Jeremy Hill," she said as he stood and pulled her to her feet. "I am far from easy." Raising her chin, she brushed the loose earth from the seat of her pants. "Kevin's brother found that out the hard way."

In that instant, Jeremy's mood swung in the opposite direction. "What?"

All her flippant buoyancy gone, Celia blinked. "Oh, no, it's—it's just a stupid joke. Ignore me. Come on, let's get out of here. It's cold."

Jeremy stayed put. Earlier in the day, at the gas station, Tommy had said something similar. "No, what did it mean? Tell me."

"We can talk about it at the house. I'm cold."

Jeremy could see that Celia had no intention of clarifying her statement back at the house. "All right," he said, tucking it away for later.

It was well past midnight when they reached Bianca's house, where stragglers from the earlier crowd continued to loiter and listen to music.

Sitting among them was Alan, who gave Celia and Jeremy a nod as they passed him on their way to Bianca's bedroom.

Celia tossed her jacket on Bianca's bed. "Where are they?" she grumbled, referring to Angie, Fletcher, and Moose.

"I know Moose had plans to take Angie to the park." Jeremy sat down at the foot of the bed and kicked off his shoes, his insides stirring as Celia began to undress behind him. He listened intently to the quiet rustle of clothing and bedsheets, then the soft woosh of her limbs sliding beneath them.

When he twisted around, she gave the mattress a pat, a shy smile playing around her lips. "Lie down with me."

Hesitating only briefly, Jeremy crawled to her and slid beneath the covers, where they curled around each other in a blatant embrace, accustomed to the position after the long day together.

Clad in flannel pajamas now, Celia felt soft and warm against him.

She made a contented hum. "Now would be a good time to kiss me," she whispered, smoothing her cheek against his jaw.

Jeremy chuckled at her audacity. Sometime in the last twelve hours, there had been a tipping point. With his defenses down, Celia had taken the opportunity to crawl inside his heart and make herself at home. Even if he bothered to think much about it, he no longer minded. Time was slipping away so fast, and it would all be over soon.

"How do you want it?" he whispered back.

Being given the choice seemed to thrill her, demonstrated by an excited little wiggle. "Mm . . . Kiss me like our first kiss."

"In the car?"

"No. When we were kids."

"Was there tongue?"

"No," Celia said, indignant. "We were kids. It was an innocent peck on the lips."

"I distinctly remember tongue."

"You must've been dreaming."

Shrugging, Jeremy gave her a chaste kiss with closed lips, the way he thought a nervous ten-year-old might. He couldn't remember the actual kiss; the real thing had probably gotten muddled within subsequent fantasies. But none of that mattered. What mattered was that he was enjoying her company immensely and would take any excuse to kiss her. "How was that?"

"Perfect," she said, touching her thumb to his lips, watching as he gave it, too, a kiss. "Tell me about your second kiss, the first girl you kissed after me."

With a groan, Jeremy rolled onto his back. Why did chicks have to ask these kinds of questions? They were always so damned determined to ruin a mood.

Undeterred by his melodrama, Celia snuggled up against him to wait patiently for his answer. In a leisurely (or possibly masterminded) move, she slid her hand across his lower stomach, her pinky finger grazing the skin above the button of his jeans, stirring the erection that had to be clear as day beneath the thin bedding. "I'm waiting."

Jeremy couldn't think straight. "All right," he breathed. "It was . . ." He swallowed hard as that same pinky finger swept back and came into brief contact with the waistband. His hips bucked faintly toward it. "Um, Pamela Conrad. I was thirteen."

"Was she pretty?" Celia whispered in his ear, her teeth nipping at the lobe, making his dick jerk again.

"Jesus, Celia." His hand moved to her thigh and squeezed. Then Jeremy forced himself to let go. He knew where this kind of bedroom play was going, and he had to remember that girls like her didn't handle casual sex well. Once a dumb, impulsive teenager, he'd learned that lesson the hard way. "Of course, she was pretty," he said. "What do you take me for?"

Celia breathed a quiet laugh, her roaming hand finally settling on his chest. "Well, pardon me, Casanova. Tell me about Pa-a-a-a-mela."

Jeremy groaned. "This is stupid."

"I want to know."

"You want to know everything, all the time." He hated these kinds of information-mining conversations. He liked it better when she was asking for kisses.

Celia lifted her brows at him.

"Fine."

Pleased with herself, she hitched her thigh over his, tucking her foot between his calves, and got comfortable as she waited for him to speak.

Uncomfortable suddenly, Jeremy had to reach down into his jeans and adjust himself. That brief contact made things worse. His erection was straining, aching for relief as he took hold of her thigh again. With each passing second, his body had to fight harder to maintain control, to not roll over her and seduce his way inside. At this point, he was almost positive she would allow it.

"We'd been flirting at school," he said, trying to focus on the words and not the underside of her thigh or the manicured fingernails that scratched so softly at his neck and jaw. "And one day, Pamela invited me and my friends to her house to swim with her and her friends. Of course, we went. A bunch of chicks, half-naked in a lake, we'd have been stupid not to."

"Sure," Celia agreed.

"Anyway, she was splashing and giving me the moon eyes, but nothing happened until we got inside the house. Her parents weren't home, and one of my friends got the idea to play Seven Minutes in Heaven. Like the song. Ever play?"

Celia shook her head, and Jeremy found himself pleased by that.

"You spin an empty soda bottle," he explained, "and whoever it points to, you take into a dark closet to make out. For seven minutes. Hence the name."

"And your bottle landed on Pamela."

"Yeah, I made sure of it. We had no idea what we were doing. Tongue. Slobber everywhere. It was great."

"Well, I don't want that kind of kiss."

"Aw, come on." He lunged playfully toward Celia, his tongue dangling, dog-like. "Pamela dug it."

Celia squealed and pushed him away. "No, thank you."

"Your loss," Jeremy shrugged.

"What about your third kiss?"

"I don't remember that."

"Then tell me about your greatest, most passionate kiss ever," she said. "The kiss to beat all kisses. You had to have *one* that really knocked your socks off."

Since Celia had gotten herself so worked up about it, Jeremy decided to be a good sport and consider her request. He thought back to every pair of lips he'd ever tasted, from the inexperienced Pamela to his skillful, widowed neighbor Constance, and every pair in between.

"There was this one chick," Jeremy said, lolling his head to face her as she listened, a glint of trepidation in her eyes. "A space case like you wouldn't believe. But a total fox. I'd just gotten into a fight, defending her honor, and my mouth was a bloody mess. But she didn't give a damn. She planted one on me anyway, in front of everyone. Knocked my socks clean off."

Blushing, Celia sunk down in his arms, giving him a smile that walloped him square in his heart.

"Maybe she was grateful," she whispered as he touched his nose to hers, her breath turning fraught against his mouth.

He slid his hand up the back of her thigh and squeezed. "Maybe."

"Kiss me like that."

"Why don't you tell me about Kevin's brother first?"

30

Moose

On a clear afternoon in January, in the year of our Lord 1967, Curtis Francisco Mousseau Camarena, widely known as "Moose," was reborn. And that was precisely how he explained it to anyone listening because it was the truth and nothing but the truth, so help him God.

Prior to the Human Be-In, Moose had been sleepwalking through his parents' ticky-tacky existence. That very existence had been carved out for him since his first birth, twenty-one years before, in postwar America, where consumerism, gluttony, and facsimile became human aspirations. He'd nearly followed that long, pedestrian road right into the afterlife. But then one winter night, via a copy of the San Francisco Oracle (left on his bar atop a puddle of warm Schlitz), the universe called out to Moose. As it instructed, he brought flowers, incense, feathers, cymbals, drums, and the love in his heart, and merged with the sea of young humanity in motion, all moving as one toward a kinder, freer future.

Moose's father, Vital Mousseau (who escaped the Nazi occupation of Southern France in 1942, at the age of sixteen, with assistance from a second cousin living in Monterey, California), and Moose's mother, Petra (who at seventeen immigrated, as a contracted bracero, to Monterey from Hermosillo, Mexico) had met at a movie palace and fallen in love. Within a month, they married two very dissimilar cultures into one loud and convoluted household. Three ankle biters later, the ticky-tacky split-level full of love was a minefield of warring languages and expectations. One minute, Vital was hollering at his children *en Français*; the next, Petra chided woefully *en Español*. And those were the good days when both languages weren't screaming bilingually to *¡limpia tu chambre!* On those afternoons, Moose didn't know whether to explain his messy room or clean up his shit-talking ways. The best of days dwelled in an exclusive place where English, French, and Spanish fused into an unparalleled but lovely bastard language that only Moose and his sisters could understand with any fluency.

But beyond those crucifix-covered walls, his parents conveyed the appearance of seamless American assimilation, and they demanded their children pursue the same cookie-cutter, middle-class American dream that seemed to serve their counterparts well. Moose was respectful of their attitudes—he loved his parents—but he didn't hold those attitudes himself, nor did he plan to rigidly follow in their footsteps.

He had his own ideas, far-out ideas, about love, individuality, and freedom of expression, the latter being the foremost important in his mind, the rest following in natural order. Freedom to be oneself, to find love and happiness in whatever manner one saw fit led to inner peace (and thus, outer peace) and thus, success—his only personal constraint was that his pursuits never needlessly harm another.

He'd had that moral argument a thousand times with his father (and other belligerent old fuddy-duddies who got philosophical after a few beers). People were bound to disagree—it was human nature—but that was what made the world such a groovy place. Three billion unique minds made for some fascinating conversation if one only took the time to listen. It was why, Moose argued to his father, the First Amendment was so essential and fought for so boldly in places like Berkeley and San Francisco. It existed explicitly to protect unpopular speech (like his), since popular speech (his father's) hardly ever needed protection. How could Vital not see that?

"Freedom of speech exists to defend the everyday grievances of the political minority, the institutionally powerless, and those reviled by society at large. Not just those fighting imperialism or fascism or communism. You can't destroy fascism by becoming a fascist, Dad."

"*Les enfants de nos jours,*" was how his father put an end to every tête-à-tête, grumbling the words before walking away. *Kids these days.*

Moose told his father once, after a separate, heated discussion about morality and censorship, that if he, Vital, was so sure of his convictions, if his convictions were truly flawless and infinitely moral, then he should have no qualms about defending them to skeptics. He should have no fear of debate. In fact, he should encourage it.

"Like panning for gold, debate is how humanity separates the treasure from the dirt."

His father didn't want to hear that manure either. New (therefore, wicked) ideas were barred, atypical (therefore, wrong) thoughts forbidden, based on some decision made a century before—by total strangers—about what was and wasn't acceptable.

A lot had changed in the last hundred years.

"The most dangerous kind of fascism doesn't have a little mustache or goose-stepping army, Dad. The most dangerous kind of fascism lives inside the heads of people who are so convinced of their rightness that they stop listening."

At that, what Moose thought was a pretty damned good argument for a C-student in his first year at community college, Vital Mousseau had switched on the TV.

"Come on, Dad. Every generation thinks they've got it all figured out, but then the next generation comes along and shows the world a new way. Not better, necessarily, just new. The same will happen to me and my kids, and then their kids and so on. That's the beauty of life. But you have to be open to it. You have to be willing to see beyond your own time, your own experiences. It's the duty of every human being to decide which way of living is best suited for them, and it's equally our duty to step aside for others to find their own way." Moose had smirked then, aware that he was about to really piss the old man off. "Be a humanist, Dad. Live and let live."

Vital hated slogans almost as much as he hated fascists.

"*Casse-couille*," his dad growled.

"Aw, I love you, too, *Père* . . ."

And yet, for all that lip service he'd given his poor ol' dad, for all the homilies and late-night high-piphanies with his more enlightened friends, Moose could not accept this news about Fletcher. Not even a little.

A self-purported free thinker and humanist, he wondered if he was also a hypocrite. He wondered, as his father often did, where the line of morality was to be drawn and by whose tenet. God's tenet (damn, he *was* becoming his father) seemed a good place to start. But as someone who spent every Sunday Mass cracking jokes to make the Santa Catalina girls giggle, Moose wasn't clear on what God thought of homosexuality. Oh, he knew what people thought God thought, but it wasn't the same. People were flawed. They didn't listen. Especially when, as noted, they were convinced of their own rightness. Or when pretty schoolgirls giggled.

Why did Fletcher have to go and make everything so complicated?

But Moose had to wonder, too: Could loving another human being be a sin? Did it rank above or below eating shellfish? Were sins ranked? Didn't Jesus die for them all? Or was there a Jesus-approved list out there somewhere? What Moose knew for absolute certain was that Vital and Petra were good people. They were raised in a different time, in different cultures, with varied influences and religious practices, but their hearts were good. And so was Fletcher's, for that matter. He also knew that if Fletcher's secret ever reached Vital's and Petra's ears, they would insist Moose terminate the friendship. His oldest friend in the world would no longer be welcome in his home or place of work, deemed a pervert, a heathen, and a molester of children. And not by his parents, but by the community at large. And to a pair of immigrants desperate to assimilate into said community, its approval meant everything.

Hell, even Moose's friendships with Celia and Jeremy had once been admonished by his skittish parents. It was only Jeremy's long absence and Celia's polite manners (along with a few offerings of banana bread) over the years that had placated their concerns. If Fletcher's secret was exposed, then Celia, by association, would be banished as well.

Moose couldn't fathom any of it. He didn't want to.

The morning of the Be-In, his mother—while once again needling Moose to cut his hair, his precious freak flag—packed him a killer lunch, with every food group represented, and kissed his cheek. His father, after a long lecture on work ethics, had handed him the keys to the family Plymouth, a crisp twenty-dollar bill to fill the tank thrice over, and a roll of dimes for the pay phone in case of a flat.

They were good people.

Amazing parents.

"You are your own salvation, man!"

A speaker had chanted the words at the Be-In. They stuck like peanut butter to the inside of Moose's skull.

Happiness was in his own hands.

"Thank you for sharing your day with all the people here. And please, please take it home . . . and realize the beauty that can come forth if you'll just open at one time that wondrous thing called your mind . . ."

Moose had left the Be-In a changed man. The gathering had been populated by an affable mix of flower children and student demonstrators. He knew he belonged somewhere in the middle of the two—not as fancy-free as the love crowd, not as militant and politically minded as the students. He valued both, as both had important roles in this new world. But Moose held his own nuanced views that couldn't be boxed in or labeled. Political activism got violent at times—the violence was sometimes justified, but many times not—and he had not a single violent bone in his body. He was more lover than fighter. And as to the radical peaceniks (a bona fide oxymoron, to be sure) . . . well, the freewheeling commune life they lauded held no appeal for him. He felt too much responsibility toward his own family. The family business was important to Vital and, when Moose was being genuine with himself, important to him, too. The Blue Pelican, aside from being a source of familial pride, meant financial freedom, to be one's own boss and make one's own rules. He wouldn't give that up for anything. He had to admire those who could liberate themselves from all possessions and live off the generosity and cooperation of a loving collective. It was a noble goal, but not for him.

From the day of the Be-In on, Moose lived out the words of the man on stage. He went about life with an open mind, imploring anyone within earshot to do the same.

And yet it was here in this same city that he was forced to once again second-guess everything he believed.

Watching Angie, through the clarity of a sober mind, it became clear to Moose that Free Love had a downside that couldn't surmount its benefits, especially when one loved a person as much as he did Angie. Years before, he had claimed both Angie and Celia as surrogate sisters. Neither had an older brother or father to protect them, so he'd assumed the role for himself, and Fletcher had, too. Proximity being a factor, Fletcher focused on the care of Celia while Moose looked out for Angie. He couldn't remember exactly how the arrangement had been decided, but he knew exactly when and where: a bus ride home in the fifth grade.

On that summer night in 1967, in Golden Gate Park, after Moose had dosed his favorite girl with LSD, hoping to expand her tightly wound mind, the plan had gone awry. It was, regrettably, *his* mind that had been altered, *his* thoughts and positions that had come full circle, bringing him back around to the place where his parents stood. He couldn't stand watching Angie give herself away. He couldn't stand watching men disrespect her. And it was what he saw. Disrespect. Not sexual freedom or biological truths. Not anything so enlightened or plugged in. He saw the woman of his dreams being treated like a slab of meat, and what really broke his heart was that she had enjoyed it exactly as he'd wanted (back when he thought he knew what he wanted).

It wounded him, and that wound cut deep. Angie Martin deserved better than an anonymous romp in the park, better than a stranger's momentary gratification. She was so strong, so crucial to the world, and the world needed to know it, needed to respect it and respect her. Her body was not mere flesh to be mounted and used, and her exceptional mind was not a toy to be played with or manipulated. The night made Moose question everything he thought he believed, everything he'd been preaching for months.

And then they'd come across Fletcher in the park . . .

Moose didn't know anymore what to think, who he was, or where to go from here.

———

He woke with a start and, after a few blinks to clear his bleary eyes, he checked his watch. It was twenty past ten in the morning. And cold. Looking around, he was reminded that only hours before, he'd lain down exhausted on this rug in Bianca's bedroom, meaning to get up and get a blanket and pillow. Clearly that had never happened.

Sitting up, Moose pressed his palms to his face to rub moisture back into his eyes. Other than having dry eyes, though, he felt great. To his right, a massive window gleamed with morning light. This type of light, so harsh and white, was normally headache-inducing punishment for a decadent, drug-addled night. But today, he found the light beautiful.

If he lifted his chin high enough, he could see Celia up on the bed. Her hair could've hosted a small family of sparrows. Her exposed cheek was marred by sheet creases, the rest of her skin pale. The room had been too dark to notice her appearance when he and Angie had stumbled in hours before. She was a bit of a mess, and that made Moose smile, hoping it meant she'd had herself an eventful night.

Stretching his chin a little higher, he caught a glimpse of auburn curls splayed across the pillow beside Celia's. The two little hoarders had slept beneath a thick heap of blankets while he'd frozen. He slipped his hand beneath the warm pile of bedding and found Angie's foot, giving it a sharp yank.

Angie groaned and kicked outward. "Stop."

Moose laughed. "Get up. Let's go get breakfast."

He climbed to his feet. His hair, he noticed in the dresser mirror, was as wrecked as Celia's. He pushed it back, grabbed his matches and crushed pack of Pall Malls off the dresser, then lit one with a sigh.

"I'm starving," Angie said, reaching for Moose's matches. She pulled a cigarette from her bag and lit it. "I saw a diner a few blocks over. They better have pancakes."

"There's my girl," Moose said, wincing through the smoke as he scratched himself.

He watched the two girls, wondering when Angie was going to notice Celia gaping at her, waving the smoke away.

"You're smoking?" Celia yipped.

Angie started and turned. "No."

"Wait a second . . ." Her spine going ramrod straight, Celia peered around the room. "Where's Jeremy? He was in the bed when I fell asleep."

"Ohhh, is that so?" Angie took another drag off her cigarette. "Do tell."

"Nothing happened," Celia said, her spine sagging. "We talked. That's all."

His cigarette dangling between his teeth, Moose slipped on a pair of clean socks. "I haven't seen him since yesterday."

"What about when you came in last night?" Celia asked. "He was here then, right?"

Angie swung her head from side to side. "Nope. It was just you in here."

"That can't be." Celia's eyebrows crumpled with concern. "What time did you get back?"

"Three, maybe?" Angie looked to Moose for confirmation. "Four?"

Rifling through his overnight bag for fresh clothes, he only shrugged. He'd been too emotionally shaken down by Angie and Fletcher to notice.

"Oh, my God."

In a flurry of movement, Celia threw back the covers and hopped over the corner of the bed, landing on Moose's toe, compelling his yelp.

"Sorry!" Not slowing at all, she bolted out the bedroom door, calling out for Jeremy.

Angie and Moose exchanged questioning frowns, making a joint, halfhearted decision to follow as Moose finished massaging his mangled baby toe.

"What's your deal, blondie?" a female voice groused from another bedroom. "Find your own old man."

"That's what I'm trying to do!"

Moose made it into the other room in time to watch Celia nudge a dark-haired man on the floor. The man smiled and lifted his blanket in invitation. He was very nude and very not-Jeremy.

"Oh! No, thank you . . . Jeremy!" she bellowed again, making every sleeping body groan. "Jeremy!"

"He's probably in the bathroom," Angie said as they followed her manic journey through the house. The other two bedrooms overflowed with people, but none were Jeremy Hill.

And the bathroom was unoccupied.

In the smoky and stale air of the main part of the house, more bodies slumbered. Celia checked the kitchen first, but it was empty.

"Jeremy!"

In her rampage, she tripped over a body that turned out to be Fletcher curled into a ball on the shag carpeting beneath a vividly colored beach towel.

"Fletcher!" She bent to shake him. "Fletcher, wake up!"

One blue eye stretched open wide enough to identify his assailant. He switched eyes to see Moose and Angie beside Celia, hovering. "This better be good," he said.

Moose took a step back, finding himself unable to interact in any manner with his oldest friend. He'd known Fletcher since kindergarten, but the kid was a stranger to him now. He'd been lying for years, keeping secrets about who he was. Moose felt hollow where trust had once existed, knowing that, for Fletcher, it had never really existed at all. That fact burned. A deep rift was forming. His friend, his *brother*, didn't trust him. Never had.

Kneeling, Celia combed through Fletcher's hair in a most intimate way, and Moose was so damned confused. He and Angie both would've bet their lives on a love affair between the two. He wondered now if Celia knew about Fletcher. Was he lying to her, too?

The night before, on the walk back to the house, Moose and Angie had discussed whether or not to tell her what they'd seen, deciding in the end to revisit the question after Jeremy's departure. Celia still had no idea about Vietnam—nobody wanted to be the one to tell her— and Moose felt his stomach churn with guilt, ready to upchuck every betrayal and lie that polluted his heart. He was equally culpable.

"Have you seen Jeremy?" Celia asked Fletcher, who looked up at her, as always, like a man deeply in love, and Moose shot a frustrated glance at Angie, who only shook her head. Was Fletcher manipulating Celia? Toying with her? Or was he truly in love? But how to explain what they'd seen the night before. Many men loved one woman while dallying with another on the side . . . But to do that to Celia? Moose could not abide it, would not.

Fletcher kissed her wrist. "Not since yesterday."

Without another word, Celia ran back toward Bianca's bedroom.

Quickly this time, Moose and Angie followed.

Back in the bedroom, Celia gathered clothing from her bag. "Everybody, get dressed," she said. "We need to find Jeremy."

Hearing the stress in her voice, Moose unzipped his bag and grabbed the first outfit he saw.

"What's going on?" Angie demanded.

"Have any of you seen Jeremy since last night?" Celia asked again, the sense of burden in her words mounting. "Anywhere? Think!"

"He's probably just out getting breakfast, dollface." Moose peeled off his shirt. "We'll find him."

"Will you tell us what's wrong already?" Angie rumbled. "My head hurts."

"I can't."

"Celia, if you want their help, you need to talk." Entering the room last, Fletcher dropped onto a chair near the window, the beach towel draped over his shoulders.

With a blustery exhale, Celia flopped down onto the bed. "Fine. Last night, I let slip about Kevin's brother. Jeremy made me tell him everything."

"Kevin Donahue's brother?" Angie asked while sliding into a clean pair of pants. "What about him?"

"About the night of the dance," Celia whispered, her manner turning to one of shame.

From his spot on the chair, Fletcher rubbed at his face. "God,

Celia," he groaned. "Why would you tell him, of all people? You had to know he'd go ape."

"Tell him what?" Angie asked.

When her question was answered with silence, Angie turned her confusion to Moose. But he could only button up his new shirt with an irritated shrug, wondering if the friendships they thought they had with these two had been superficial baloney all along. How many secrets were they keeping?

The redhead glanced between Fletcher and Celia, looking like she was wondering the same thing. "What happened?" Angie pressed. "Why does no one tell me anything anymore? I am a very supportive friend, damn it!"

"All right." Celia winced. "You remember the freshman spring dance? In high school."

"Yeah," Moose answered.

"No," Angie snapped at the same time.

"Well, there was a dance, you hermit, and I went with Kevin. After the dance, we ran into his brothers in the field behind the school, and his brother . . . Will . . . He . . . Well, he tried to . . ."

"He tried to rape her," Fletcher interjected.

"We think," Celia added quickly.

Trying to contain the fury that rose like bile into his throat, Moose crossed his arms. "You think?"

"Celia," Fletcher growled. "He held you down. He tore your underwear. He put his hands and mouth on you without your permission."

"But I got away," Celia argued, her voice thick with anxiety. Taking a deep breath, she continued. "Fletcher's right, though. He probably would've . . . you know . . . if I hadn't kicked him in the giblets and run."

"He would have," Fletcher growled. "Remember Mona Bradley?"

Celia slouched. "Yes."

"What happened to Mona Bradley?" Angie asked, indignant. "And why is this the first I'm hearing about all this?"

His muscles rigid with frustration, Moose yanked on his shoes. He remembered the Mona Bradley situation. Everyone in school (except Angie, apparently) knew that Will Donahue had taken her to senior prom, then raped her in a hotel room afterward. Mona had refused to press charges, though, and eventually moved away, having been mercilessly shamed into self-imposed exile. She'd been the talk of the entire town that summer. *"What was she doing alone with him in a hotel room? What did she expect, a tea party?"*

Across the room, Celia hid her face in her hands, and Moose knew immediately why Celia had kept her story a secret. Mona Bradley had been well liked and popular prior to her scandal . . . His dollface wouldn't have stood a chance. But that didn't explain why she'd kept it from him and Angie.

"What was Kevin doing during all of this?" Moose prodded, growing increasingly agitated.

Celia lowered her hands. "Nothing."

"Nothing?" Angie cut in. "I'm confused. Kevin and his brother tried to rape you, or Kevin didn't help when his brother tried?"

"Kevin didn't do anything wrong. His brother . . . Kevin tried to stop him but couldn't."

"Is that why you two broke up back then?" Angie asked, her voice breaking. "Why you took all those pills? Why you ended up in that mental hospital the rest of the school year?"

Celia nodded.

"Bastard," Angie hissed.

Moose couldn't hold it in any longer. "Why didn't you tell me, Celia? I would've knocked his teeth out for you. I would've murdered that piece of shit."

"Me, too," Angie said. "I would've made his life a living hell."

"That's exactly why I didn't tell either of you."

Moose couldn't listen to any more of this. He strode out of the room and went into the kitchen to get a drink of water. There, he found Alan counting pennies on the kitchen table.

"Hey, brother," the hippie said with a sleepy grin. "I'm supposed to tell you something."

"What is it?"

"Now let me think. What was it? Oh, yeah. Jessie thumbed a ride back to Partridge Orchard. He said . . . what did he say . . . he said, 'I'll see you when you get back.'"

"Jessie?" Moose turned on the faucet and stuck his mouth under it, swallowing down cold gulps of city water. As he stood and wiped his mouth on his sleeve, he finally comprehended the message. "You mean Jeremy? Jeremy hitched a ride back to Pacific Grove?"

Alan pondered the question. "No, that's not it."

"Thanks, Alan." Moose patted his friend's back. "What time was this at?"

"Before you came in. Man, he looked like he wanted to kill someone." Alan seemed to rethink his statement. "It's possible I hallucinated him."

Moose returned to Bianca's room and started repacking his duffel bag.

"Where are you going?" Angie asked.

"Home." Moose grabbed his wallet and keys. "Jeremy hitched a ride out of here this morning around three." He turned to Celia. "Alan said he looked like he was about to kill someone."

Angie threw her arms up. "Well, that's just great."

"Oh, what's he going to do?" Fletcher posed skeptically. "Murder Will Donahue? Come on."

The room went silent.

Would Jeremy really murder a man over Celia? Moose wondered with the rest of them. He'd done it once, hadn't he? Or had he? And he might've beat Tommy Russo to death the day before for merely taunting her had he and Fletcher not intervened. Moose could hardly blame him, though. He was close to punching Tommy himself once he saw the fear on Celia's face. He hadn't known what it was about at the time, but now he suspected he knew, considering Tommy had been Kevin's best friend. The scumbag.

What could be going on inside Jeremy's head right now? He was being shipped off to war soon. Would killing a man seem so wrong, when not long from now, killing a platoon's worth would be government sanctioned, the murder weapon handed over with a hefty slap on the back and a "Go get 'em, soldier"?

"Why did I tell him?" Celia murmured to herself. "I should know better by now."

"Yeah, you should. He's incredibly defensive of you," Moose said. "You saw him yesterday with Tommy."

Celia cringed. "I know."

"Did you tell Jeremy that you were dating Kevin at the time?" Angie asked.

Celia nodded.

Eyes wide, Fletcher leaned forward in his chair. "Was he mad?"

"He wasn't thrilled," Celia relayed, her gaze far away. "But he seemed fine. He held me while I cried. I must've fallen asleep."

"So, what now?" Fletcher asked everyone. "He's been gone seven hours at this point."

Moose flung his duffel bag over his shoulder. "I'm going to drive back and see if I can find him. I'll come back and get you guys tomorrow."

"No." Celia got to her feet. "I'm coming with you."

Moose knew she would only argue if he said no, so he nodded. "We leave in ten minutes. Do what you gotta do."

"Crap." Angie grabbed her sneakers. "I'll go, too."

Fletcher remained quiet.

Everybody turned to face him, their stares expectant.

"What?" he said in response. "I like it here. I have plans with . . . I have plans, okay?"

"Plans with who?" Celia asked. "Where were you last night?"

Fletcher looked around at all the judging, questioning eyes. "Oh, fine, I'll go. At least give me a minute to call and explain that I can't go because my violent childhood friend may or may not be murdering an old high school rapist as we speak. I'm sure they get that excuse all the time."

Angie rolled her eyes. "Drama queen."

"Park tramp," Fletcher muttered.

Angie gasped.

"What?" Celia watched her two best friends glare at each other.

"Nothing," both said simultaneously.

———

Two hours later, Moose pulled into a gas station in Monterey.

As planned, Celia leaped out of the back seat and bolted for the diner attached to the gas station.

"You could wait for the car to stop moving first!" Moose yelled after her as he brought the Impala to a full stop and shifted into park. "Why is everyone so determined to bloody up my new wheels?"

"There's blood on it anyway, Moose," Angie said. "That poor boy who died in Vietnam. You wear his sacrificial blood wherever you go now."

Moose gaped at her. "Jesus, Angie."

"I'm kidding," she said, her tone mocking. "I'm just trying to ease the tension here."

"I told you I was sorry about that. Cut me some slack."

"Uh-huh."

Rolling his eyes away, Moose snapped the pack of Pall Malls from his pocket. Angie was on one today, but he would overlook her attitude, as usual. She was hungover, after all, and that was one hundred percent his fault. He lit a cigarette as they waited for Celia.

Beside him Angie started to fidget and tap her feet. With an impatient sigh, she opened the glove box and started rifling through it with increasingly nervous energy.

"You got ants in your pants?" Moose asked. "What are you looking for?"

"I don't know," she muttered. "What's taking her so long?"

"It's been thirty seconds."

Pulling out a Fotomat envelope that Moose had forgotten about, Angie sat back. She pulled the photos out and absently rifled through them. "If Jeremy does something to Will, and we know about it but don't turn him in, are we accessories?"

Moose lifted his face to the graying sky and blew his smoke out. "Probably."

"Marvelous . . . What's this?"

He looked over to see what "this" was, and his heart plummeted fast. *Shit.* He was such a forgetful idiot.

"Why are you going through my stuff?" Moose snatched the little square photograph from her hand and shoved it beneath his thigh, then snatched the rest of the stack from her grip and shoved them into their envelope.

"When did you and my brother take that photo?"

"It was a long time ago, before he ran away."

"He looks so much older," she said, her breath growing heavy as her eyebrows pinched together. "And you're wearing that brown vest with the stupid dangly things. You got that a few months ago."

Moose said the first lie that came to mind, no matter how lame. "I got that years ago."

"Liar."

"I'm not—"

Angie bunched his shirt in her hands and yanked him hard to the right until he felt the deep rumble of her next words on his cheek. "You know where my brother is."

Moose swallowed back the lump rising in his throat. This was the last thing he needed right now. Why didn't he take those photos into the house?

"Tell me, Moose! Now!"

"I can't," he admitted calmly. "He made me promise not to."

Angie shoved him away. "You asshole. That's my brother. You know how crazy I've gone trying to find him."

"I'm sorry."

"Where is he?"

"I promised him, Ang."

Angie didn't respond, but Moose could feel the white-hot fury coming from her direction. His muscles tensed as he waited for a strike of some sort. But none came. She'd never hit him before, but she'd also never gone silent like this, which meant she was well and truly pissed. No way was she going to let this go. He had no idea what to expect from her, for once. He'd known that she may never forgive him if she ever found out. But the day he first discovered her brother Robbie in a drug den five blocks from the Haight in San Francisco, the teenager had pleaded with him not to tell his sister his whereabouts. They both knew that she would come looking for him, and though Robbie could fight it, in the end, Angie would win. Moose also knew that if he betrayed Robbie's trust, the kid would never confide in him again. He was wrecked on every drug imaginable, about to be a father, and living in the worst shithole in the city. But people liked the low-level street dealer they called Red Robbie, and they liked Moose. For the moment, it was enough to keep the dumb kid safe.

"Looks like rain," Fletcher said from the back seat, and just then Celia slammed into the car.

"Watch the paint!" Moose cried out.

"The phone book was gone," Celia said, out of breath as she tumbled into the back seat and poked her head between Moose and Angie. "But I dialed the operator, and she gave me Will's address. He lives on West Franklin in Monterey."

"Grab the map out of the glove box." Tossing his cigarette, Moose shifted into first and peeled out of the parking lot.

When they reached the address, he parked across the street and down a few houses, giving them space to snoop and time to add some detail to their slapdash plan.

"So," Angie said when all was said and done. "Who's going over there?"

"I'll go," Moose offered.

Behind him, Fletcher said, "Me, too."

The two of them walked together in silence, and when Will's front door opened, a girl of maybe eighteen stood holding an orange cat and smoking a cigarette. A bluish-purple bruise underlined her left eye, and Moose could only shake his head. "We're looking for Will. Is he here?"

"Who wants to know?" she asked.

"We're old friends of his."

"I'm his wife. Will doesn't have any friends."

The girl looked them both up and down, her gaze finally relaxing on Fletcher. She smiled approvingly, directing her next words at him, even though he hadn't said a word so far.

"He went out last night," she added, leaning against the doorjamb, giving Fletcher another lingering once-over. "Never came home. But he does that. He'll be back when the money runs out . . . It's starting to rain." At that, the girl shut the door.

"Crap." Rotating around, Moose flipped his palm and perused the leaden sky. The rain was light but picking up. "Let's pull the top up and try Jeremy's."

"You think he found Will?"

Moose sighed. "Well, if he did, he's going to need help digging in this weather."

31

Celia

By the time the Chevy pulled into Jeremy's driveway, the rain fell in thick sheets, and the air was chilled like winter. On a count of three, everyone in the car jumped out and made a mad dash for the porch, where they found Jeremy rocking on his swing, looking freshly showered and clean, eating an apple with a steak knife.

Celia was overcome with relief. "There you are!" Rushing to him, she wrapped him up in an awkward, grabby embrace that made the swing creak and moan. "I've been so worried."

An understatement, really. Wiping the water from her face, she squeezed in next to him, never taking her eyes away, looking for signs of distress.

He looked exhausted but so unbelievably handsome to her.

"Hey," was all he said.

Celia lifted her palm to his freshly shaven cheek as her own smile stretched so wide that she had to bite her bottom lip to contain it, the butterflies in her belly already swarming as her terrified heart began to settle into its usual race for him. "Hey."

An exasperated voice broke partway through the spell that his green eyes had cast on her.

"Hello!" Angie shouted. "Earth to Jeremy! Where is he? What'd you do to him?"

Then Fletcher. "Look, I've been thinking about it, and you can say it was self-defense—"

"Whoa, whoa," Moose joined in. "Hang back, Perry Mason. Let's all calm down before we start the interrogation."

"You can tell us," Angie spoke in a calm, calculated voice. "Is he alive at least?"

Jeremy's expression soured as he broke eye contact with Celia to finally acknowledge his accusers. "Is who alive?"

"Kevin's brother, Will," Fletcher answered. "Who do you think?"

"Oh." Jeremy settled back into his seat and returned to his apple. "Him."

"Yeah, him," Fletcher said. "We were just at his house, and he's conveniently missing. His wife is waiting for him. What did you do? Do you ever think? Does it ever occur to you that—"

"Let him talk!" Celia interrupted. "You're not giving him a chance to answer."

With a grin that hinted of surprise, Jeremy offered her a slice of his apple.

Celia took it, asking, "Why did you sneak out last night? You've had me worried sick."

"I needed to get back here." He shrugged like it was no big deal.

"Get back here for what?"

"To kill Kevin's brother," he said, tossing another sawed-off hunk of apple into his mouth.

Celia tensed. "Stop it, Jeremy." A gust of wind made the cold bite harder at her exposed skin, and she pulled her hands deeper inside her damp sleeves. "You did no such thing," she said through clenched, chattering teeth.

With a huff, Jeremy unbuttoned his shirt, leaving himself in only an undershirt, and draped it over her shoulders. Celia pulled it tighter around her neck. It didn't do much as it was thin and short-sleeved, but it was warm from his body heat.

"I might as well have," Jeremy said to her previous remark, picking his knife back up and waving it at Angie and Fletcher. "Sherlock and Holmes over here have already convicted me of the crime." He cut another slice of apple. "What about you, Moose? You think I killed someone last night?"

"Nah," Moose said. "I bet you cleaned his clock, though."

Jeremy grinned at his friend.

Angie took a step forward. "So, if you didn't kill anyone, what did you do? You didn't come all the way back here in the middle of the night to eat that stupid apple."

"It's a really good apple," he said.

Angie folded her arms.

Sighing, Jeremy slapped the knife down at his side. "Fine. Kevin's brother is alive and well and secured to the fence at Lovers Point. In his *chonies*," he added for Moose, who barked out a laugh. "I'm sure he's enjoying this lovely weather we're having." He bit directly into the apple. "Go check for yourself if you don't believe me. Sooner the better, though. I doubt he'll be there all day."

"Oh, thank God." Fletcher flopped down to sit against the front door. "I'm not going to pretend I wasn't assuming the worst. Especially after yesterday and, you know . . . back then."

Jeremy grimaced. "Back when?"

"Don't play dumb. That night. With your dad." Fletcher bared the confrontational pluck that Celia knew well. She hated when he got like this. He was a sweetheart down to his bones, but when his hackles were up, he could be insufferable. "We all know what happened."

"Oh, really," Jeremy said, his dark tone matching Fletcher's now. On Jeremy, however, it was far more intimidating. "Tell us, Fletch. What happened?"

Fletcher's tone dropped an octave and his eyes hardened. "You killed him."

Celia's jaw snapped open. "Fletcher!"

"What? We're all thinking it." He shot a quick look at Angie, then Moose. "Don't act like you aren't. We've all just been too afraid to ask him outright. Well, I'm done being afraid." He turned to Jeremy again. "You killed him, right? Your dad."

Jeremy sat motionless, his body language rigid and coiled as if he was about to spring at Fletcher like a snake.

Celia set her hand on his chest. "You know he didn't," she told Fletcher with censure. "I already told you what happened."

Contrite now, Fletcher looked away. He could snap his teeth at Jeremy, but not at her. She knew him too well. "You were vague, at best," he muttered. "You've always been holding something back, and we've never wanted to push. You had enough to deal with. But I don't trust him."

"I wasn't vague." Celia regarded her other friends. But like Fletcher had, Angie looked away while Moose ruefully lowered his head. She gritted her teeth.

"See," Fletcher said softly before returning to Jeremy. "She'll say anything to defend you. The rest of us . . . We've heard things."

To Celia's shock, Jeremy burst out laughing. "Let me guess," he said. "I stabbed him? Lit him on fire? Shot him out of a cannon? Am I close?"

"Mostly the stabbed one," Angie said with some shame. "People around here talk. A lot."

"Oh, I heard he shot him," Moose said with some enthusiasm. "With a bazooka. Though, looking back, that does seem a bit far-fetched."

Jeremy grimaced. "A bit? Where would a ten-year-old get a bazooka?"

"There are places."

"So, what did happen then?" Fletcher pressed Jeremy, motioning toward Celia. "She won't talk about it. You won't talk about it. So, we're getting most of our information from the gossips who love talking about it."

"Betty?" Celia sneered, and Fletcher nodded. She growled. "Why would you listen to her? And why would she date him if she thought he was a murderer?"

"It's Betty," Angie answered for him. "Why does she do anything she does?"

A moment later, Jeremy set his eyes back on Celia. They pierced her with a subtle request, and somehow, she understood.

"Fine," she said to everyone. "I'll tell you what happened . . . again. I won't be 'vague,' whatever that means. But if I unintentionally skip over anything, I'm sure Jeremy will fill in. Okay? But then you have to accept it and never bring it up again. It's not fair to Jeremy. Deal?"

Everyone nodded.

Jeremy held his tongue while Celia retold the events of that fall evening of 1956 in superfluous detail, including their argument and kiss. When she reached the point in which his father had begun choking her, her throat constricted, feeling those muscular hands still at work to silence her. It was probably where Fletcher had deemed her vague. Her parents told her that Dennis Hill's heart had simply stopped against that tree, but she hadn't witnessed it firsthand. It had been dark, and her head had been down as she'd fought to catch her breath. And given what Jeremy told her the night before about wanting his father to die . . . she found herself unsure now—of the official story, of her own memory—and didn't know how to continue without sounding "vague" again.

"It was my fault," Jeremy mumbled at her silence. His head was down, his gaze focused on his right thumb as it rubbed the calloused pad of his left ring finger. "I thought he was going to kill her, so I socked him in the stomach. I thought I could knock the wind out of him, but . . ." Jeremy pinched his lips and shook his head. "So I pulled my knife. One more second and I would've used it, but he grabbed his chest and went down before I had to. It's the only selfless thing he ever did for me." Jeremy bent his head toward Celia, his voice quiet as he said, "They're right. I probably did kill him. I caused that heart attack." He gave her the gentlest smile she'd ever seen him give. "But thanks for the confidence."

"No," Celia breathed, a dreadful pain in her chest. She ached to comfort him but wasn't sure what he would accept from her, sober and in the light of day. "No, it's not your fault." Steeling her nerves, she nestled her head against his shoulder and hugged his arm, meaning every word. "I should've listened to you. I should've gone home."

A kiss was deposited on her head then, and the porch grew quiet, save for the steady drum of rain. The other three on the porch, silent now, looked as guilty as Celia felt. As exhausted, too.

It converged on her all at once as Jeremy began to rock the swing: the cold, the hunger, the dull ache of her head. As much as her body desired to go home and crawl into bed, her mind wanted to stay, still burdened with uncertainty and worry. Yesterday, she and Jeremy had been thick as thieves, as familiar as lovers. But today, in the crispness of sobriety, it all presented like a dream. The distance between the two of them had returned. Not fully, but enough to make her wonder if everything he'd said and done the day before had been only a result of the drugs. She wanted so desperately to resume that level of intimacy with him. But how, without the risk of rejection?

Something else occurred to her, and she lifted her head. "What happened with Will? What did you say to him?"

The question renewed the energy of the porch. Moose, Angie, and Fletcher perked in synchronicity.

"Oh." Jeremy cleared his throat. "Yeah, I, uh, hitched a ride here last night and found his address in the phone book. I was going to pay him a visit, but I needed breakfast first . . ."

"Breakfast," Moose moaned longingly, shutting his eyes as Jeremy went on.

"I went to that all-night diner by the Cannery. When I walked in, the place was in chaos. The waitresses were trying to boot some drunk asshole that had grabbed one of them . . . An asshole," he said with some punch, "named Will Donahue." Jeremy nodded at all their expressions. "Yeah. Kismet, right? He was acting belligerent, and they were about to call the cops. But I offered to take that rapist motherfucker off their hands real quiet-like, before any tourists could show up."

A chill ran up Celia's spine. It put her on edge to think of Jeremy coming face-to-face with the worst of her nightmares and to hear his voice turn cold from it. He must've sensed her unease because he took her hand and held it with a firmness that comforted her almost instantly.

"They were so grateful," he went on with a grin, "they gave me a plate of hotcakes and sausage to go. On the house."

"Oh," Moose groaned, "sausage."

"I put him in his car, and we drove to the Point where I could beat the shit out of him without anyone hearing. The sun hadn't come up yet, so the beach was still empty. But I made sure he knew exactly why we were there."

"Oh, no," Celia said, pressing her free palm to her face.

"He's not going to bother you again, Celia," Jeremy asserted. "I promise."

"But you won't be here. You'll be in Vietnam with your own problems."

Angie straightened up. "You know about that?"

"Now. No thanks to you or Moose or Fletcher. We'll all be talking about that later."

"Hey, I only found out two nights ago," Fletcher argued in his own defense.

"You had plenty of time then."

Fletcher lowered his head as Moose chimed in, his teeth clenched. "Celia . . ." She thought he might apologize or defend his asinine decision to withhold the news of Jeremy going to Vietnam, but instead, he very bitterly said, "You come to me if you need help. I don't want to hear any more of your excuses."

After a moment, Celia nodded, unwilling to argue with him right now. He looked more distraught than she'd ever seen him. It was a disturbing sight. He was their big, beaming guiding light. The one who knew how to lighten a mood or keep any situation from becoming too serious, too glum. Which was a big possibility in the presence of herself, Angie, and Fletcher, who could be (though she was loathe to admit it) a rather miserable lot now and then.

Reading the porch, Celia realized how much had changed in the last two months. When she'd arrived in June, Moose and Angie had been their usual, polar-opposite selves. Theirs was an unlikely friendship, and yet they fit together like yin and yang, one providing what the other lacked. And Fletcher had been her dearest friend in the world.

But now Moose sulked within a cagey air of melancholy, offering none of his usual gaiety. Something was going on between him and Fletcher and possibly Angie, too. Celia saw that the two boys would not even look at each other, their faces turned subtly away, both looking to their own right. A frigidity existed between them—they who had behaved as brothers since kindergarten. Bigger opposites they couldn't have been, but both having been targets in grade school, they'd learned to take care of each other. Moose, with his bright, sunny nature, had won everyone over by high school. He'd even been nominated for senior prom king (though he lost to Brian Simmons). He could've abandoned his oldest friends in favor of the popular crowd, but he never did. He'd stuck by the three of them.

But something had come between her friends when she wasn't looking. Something was very, very wrong. Celia turned to watch Fletcher. His expression was swinging from one extreme to another. One moment he was scowling and then, in the blink of an eye, joy seemed to strike him, and he was grinning like the Cheshire Cat. Then he was scowling again, looking angrier than she'd ever seen him.

Very wrong, indeed.

Fletcher got to his feet. "I'm going home," he announced. "I need to take a shower and get that apartment floor off me." He offered Jeremy his hand to shake, and Jeremy took it with great hesitation. "Sorry I thought you were a murderer," Fletcher said with a flat smile. "Though I still think Celia can do better."

"Fletcher," Celia reprimanded, but he ignored her, jumping off the porch into the rain. "What has gotten into him?" She aimed the question first at Angie, then at Moose, but neither acknowledged her. "What is going on with all of you?"

"Breakfast time." Moose climbed to his feet with a grunt, eyeing Angie. "Want to see if Will's still tied up, then go eat?"

Her mouth twisting, Angie rose to her feet. "You going to tell me about my brother?"

"No."

"Then take me home."

Celia frowned. Her brother? Was that the source of the tension between them? She wanted to ask but instinctively knew not to. She wondered if they expected her to leave with them.

"Well, I don't want to see Will," Celia said, pulling her knees to her chest.

"You should stay here with Jeremy then." Angie had surprised Celia with that pronouncement, then really threw her for a loop by bending to give her a stiff, awkward hug. The last and only time Angie had ever hugged her was the day after her father died.

"You didn't take your pill this morning," came the whisper into her ear.

Before Celia could reply, the redhead skittered off the porch and ran out into the rain to catch up with Moose.

Celia glanced over at Jeremy, afraid he'd heard, but he was in his own world, staring down at his hands.

Alone now, they rocked the swing forward and aft, absorbed in the frenetic pit-a-pat of summer rain.

"Are you okay?" Celia eventually asked him.

"Yeah, why?"

"What happened last night? You seemed fine after I told you."

Jeremy watched as she laced her fingers with his, saying only, "I'm sorry I wasn't here to protect you."

"I handled it."

"You shouldn't have had to handle anything like that."

"No. I shouldn't have . . . I am sorry I didn't have your shoulder to lean on." Celia made her point by setting her cheek to it, reminding herself how sturdy and reassuring it had always been. "I'm sorry about

Kevin, too." She still couldn't decipher Jeremy's thoughts on the topic. His initial reaction had been contradictory. By his countenance, he'd been annoyed, and maybe a little hurt, but his words had been kind and consoling. "I was young and stupid."

"Was he good to you?"

Tripped up a bit by the question, Celia had to pause and think about her time with Kevin, something she tended to avoid, especially after news of his death. She'd cried that gray February morning, and the grief had surprised her.

"Yes, he was," she decided. They'd never spoken again after the night of the dance, and she couldn't remember the last time she'd seen him or his brother around town. "He really did try to protect me that night. He fought so hard. But he was no match for his brother."

Jeremy tsked. "Yeah, well, his brother's not so tough when up against someone his own size."

With a smile on her lips, Celia clutched his arm and gave it a cuddle.

The rain picked up. Torrents of it cascaded off the roof, hammering water onto the edge of the porch, where it bounced up and splattered everything within reach. A shiver rippled through Celia's torso. Her dress, taupe with little blue and white flowers, was damp and cold against her skin, and her teeth chattered. The crisp air smarted at her nose. She wanted to go inside his house, where it was almost certainly warmer, but Jeremy seemed content to sit outside. In the last hour, he hadn't invited any of them to come in and get away from the weather. And the last thing she wanted was to extend herself another unsolicited invitation.

Releasing his arm, Celia grabbed her overnight bag and stood. "I should probably get home," she said with a stiff grin. "Change into warmer clothes. I'm freezing."

Jeremy answered with a detached nod.

Disappointed by his response, Celia sauntered across the porch, stopping short of the dense onslaught of rain that hampered her path home. Down below, at the bottom of the newly built porch steps, water swamped the immature sprouts of grass planted weeks before, creating a sea of green-speckled mud. She looked down at her feet, wrapped in damp sandals, and sighed. She wanted Jeremy to stop her, to ask her to stay, but he held silent behind her.

"That's it?" she said, turning to face him. "You're not going to ask me to stay? You're not even going to say goodbye?"

Jeremy looked up. "You can stay if you want."

"What do *you* want, Jeremy?"

"Christ." His fingers rose to pinch the bridge of his nose. "Just do whatever you want, Celia."

"I want to know what you want. Why won't you tell me?"

"Why do you have to make everything so complicated?" he asked her. "Stay if you want to stay. Or don't."

I don't care. That was the logical end to that response, and Celia felt a palpable shift inside herself, compelling every frustration she'd ever had with him to spew like a geyser straight out of her mouth. "That is it! This is where I draw the line with you, Jeremy. I am not pushing myself on you anymore. I'm not chasing! It's time you do something. Tell me you want me here. Ask me to stay. Right now. Or I'm leaving and never coming back."

Jeremy grimaced like he'd been presented with a spoon and a dirty toilet bowl. "You're making threats now?"

Celia thought about it. "Yes. I guess I am. I'm making threats."

"Then go home."

Her shoulders falling, Celia couldn't bring herself to respond. It had all gone sideways in a matter of seconds when all she'd wanted was a little effort on his part. A gesture, a word, anything to tell her she wasn't fooling herself. But it was clear that she was, that he intended to keep their relationship—if it could even be called that—one-sided, ambiguous, confusing, and hurtful.

Oh, he was willing to reciprocate a few kisses and hugs, but nothing more and nothing real.

Well, that was just fine. Celia felt heartbroken and embarrassed but strong enough to turn her back on him. For the briefest of moments, she contemplated hollering, saying something hurtful to make him feel as awful as she did, but she had no real desire to hurt him. And if this part of her life was going to end, she was going to at least try to see it out with some modicum of dignity.

Peeling off her sandals, Celia stepped out into the storm, walking as briskly as was possible without breaking into a full run, as she couldn't see two feet in front of her. The rain soaked straight through her clothing, making her even colder and tremendously uncomfortable. Her wet hair fastened against her cheeks. Her days-old mascara was probably running. She thought she must look a fright, like a sodden raccoon, and laughed.

So much for dignity.

Her prideful stride quickly gave way to a jog, and that was when Jeremy snatched her up. He grasped her slippery hand and began lugging her back toward his house.

Her smile widened, hurting the muscles in her frozen cheeks, while Jeremy cursed and complained.

"You've got to be the screwiest chick I've ever met." The sound of his bellyaching rose above the thunder. "Nothing's ever good enough for you. If it's not one thing, it's another."

When they reached his porch, where the rain stopped prodding at them, Jeremy swung open his front door, directing her to step inside. "I'm glad this is so amusing for you," he said, dripping wet and mad as a bull. "Well, go on."

Planting her bare feet to his porch, the scent of damp wood filling her nostrils, Celia continued to stare at him, her smile fading as she tried to blink the river of water from her eyes with some poise.

Waiting.

"Will you get inside the house already?" Jeremy said. "You won."

Celia raised her eyebrows and waited some more.

After a bitter chuckle, Jeremy let his shoulders slacken and dropped his head back. He was prickly and stubborn and wonderful, and Celia couldn't help but love everything about him, bellyaching and all.

Say it.

"Fine," he said softly, lowering his head to look at her. "I want you to stay. I always do."

Bliss flooded Celia's veins and made her beam.

With a faint smile of his own and a shake of his head, Jeremy followed her inside the house and shut the door.

32

Celia

"Don't move. I'll get a towel," Jeremy said, kicking off his shoes before heading upstairs.

This time around, Celia abided by his request and didn't move except to place her shoes neatly beside his on the doormat.

The little house was complete, modernized, and tidy. And she understood with sadness that Jeremy's time here was truly done.

He returned holding a large, pink-and-red towel. "It's clean," he told her, handing it over. "But we'll have to share."

Celia made sure to keep the sticky, upper portion of her saturated dress covered as she cleared rainwater from her skin and hair. When she was done, she handed the towel back to him, careful to keep her arm crossed over her chest since, in her haste that morning, she hadn't taken the time to put on a brassiere.

"You can change in the bathroom if you want," Jeremy said, drying off. "It's right back there."

"Thank you. I will. I'm freezing."

"I noticed."

"Oh, I knew you were looking!" Celia stole the towel back, fighting to suppress her smile. "Pervert."

"Not a pervert, a man."

"I don't hear a difference."

Jeremy only smirked at that.

Inside the downstairs bathroom, Celia cleaned herself up, brushed her teeth again, and combed the knots from her wet hair. Digging deeper into her travel bag, she found her favorite paisley dress and then put it on, wishing she had packed a pair of socks. Her feet were freezing.

Finally, with a silent thank you to Angie, Celia located her little, round pill dispenser. She hoped the pills actually worked. She'd never personally tested their effectiveness but hoped to today.

Dropping the Tuesday dose onto her tongue, Celia scooped water from the sink to wash it down, then stared at her reflection in the mirror. She wondered, watching her own anxious eyes, what kind of pain awaited her on the other side of the bathroom door, the good kind or the bad. Would he refuse her? Had she misread him? And if he didn't refuse her, how badly would it hurt? What if she disappointed him? What if he disappointed her? Would she feel different after? Look different? Would he?

It was time to find out.

Tucking her hair behind both ears and taking a deep breath, Celia reentered the living area to find Jeremy also in dry clothes, switching on his transistor radio. It was already tuned to her favorite station. "I like this song," she said.

"Me, too."

The butterflies bristled in her belly as she followed Jeremy to the couch.

Flopping down, Jeremy propped his feet up on the coffee table.

In an effort to appear as self-possessed and unflustered as he did, Celia sat down and put her cold feet up too; then she sat back to take in the sparsely furnished room. It was the same room that had creeped her out two days before. It still smelled of fresh paint and wood lacquer.

The single source of lighting—an old lamp ornamented with sea-shells—still made the room feel dim and small. But with Jeremy here, it looked safer, warmer. A perfect, cozy place it would have been, if not for the wide-open window that had her shivering.

Jeremy dropped his feet to the floor. "You're cold?"

Celia nodded.

Jumping up, he closed the window and grabbed a colorfully embroidered blanket from the back of the couch, draping it over her lap as he reclaimed his seat. "My mom made me bring it," he explained. "You know, because summer in California . . . I might freeze to death."

With quiet amusement, Celia raised the blanket to her chest. "Thanks."

The silence that followed made things awkward. Yesterday, the two of them had been perfectly at ease with one another, rambling about the city, chatting, dancing, and French-kissing until their tongues ached (which they found hilarious). They'd giggled about it, then French-kissed some more. It was the drugs, she told herself, wishing they had some now.

Beyond the refurbished walls and windows, the thunderstorm continued its assault on the town. The additional noise coming from the radio—the DJ's remarks on the rain and advertisements for instant coffee and antacid—lessened the disquiet some.

The sky rumbled just before a deafening crack of lightning gave the house a jolt. With a pop, the lamp went out and Celia yelped.

It was the middle of the afternoon, and the overcast sky still held the bluish haze of daylight, so she could see Jeremy perfectly well as he chuckled silently to himself.

Her hand was still resting on her chest from the shock. "What's so funny?" she asked.

Jeremy exhaled. "I was just thinking we shouldn't be alone like this." He twisted to face her more directly, half of him obscured now by darkness. The other half watched her with contemplative interest. "But then I thought I should kiss you, and the lights went out."

Celia's heart rioted against her rib cage as he bent toward her.

Unlike the day before, the press of his mouth was cautious and lingering but so wonderfully soft and warm.

He took his time with his second kiss, testing her reaction, still watching as he parted her lips with his own and touched his tongue lightly to hers. A quiet moan seeped out of her, and she was pretty sure she saw him smile before their eyes closed. Another pucker, another deepening slide of tongue, and he rose higher, laying her back until his body grew heavy between her thighs and pinned her to the couch.

Motionless for a moment, Jeremy said, "I'm sorry I ruined the trip."

With a shush, Celia pulled his mouth back to hers, and for the better part of an hour, they explored with increasingly fevered hands and mouths.

When she could no longer satiate her hunger with kisses and hugs, she brought her fingers to Jeremy's sides to clutch at the thin material there, pushing and pulling until he rid himself of his shirt and tossed it aside. As he did that, she shrugged the oppressive blanket away.

A gasp slipped out of her at the sudden feel of his bare skin, smooth and hot against her palms. Celia grabbed up every available inch, blurting her pleasure out to God, while Jeremy's hips rocked her into the couch, his mouth setting blistering little pools of fire over her throat.

But then that was no longer enough, and in a delirious, impatient flurry, Celia moved to unfasten the petite buttons at the front of her dress. Her mouth open and wild against his, she wrestled with the blasted things, yanking and tugging, desperate to feel his flesh rubbing and sliding against hers. It was suddenly the most dire, immediate need to ever plague anyone in the history of the world and, frustrated beyond measure, she growled at him, "Help me get this off."

"No, Celia." Jeremy refused her another kiss, restraining her lips by pressing his winded mouth hard against her cheekbone. With one hand, he trussed both her wrists to her chest, as though he were trying to tame a snarling cat. "We can't do this."

"Why not?" She pushed her face to the right, trying with all her might to catch his mouth, but he was stronger. "Jeremy, kiss me."

"I'm leaving next week," he panted. "If we go any further, you'll hate me."

"No." Celia made her voice soft, breathy, for seduction's sake. "No. I could never hate you. Please, Jeremy." She arched her hips. "Take me. Don't you want to?"

"Yes." With a curse, Jeremy bit at the edge of her mouth, then kissed her hard, his delightful, reflexive thrusts returning with gusto.

Celia smiled as he released her hands, feeling triumphant, loving the tortured little groan he made when she slipped her fingers into his hair. Yes, her seduction was succeeding nicely.

"Oh, God, don't make this harder on me," he complained between deep, restless kisses. "We can't do this."

As he ground against her, she wanted to remind him that he was the one on top of her but decided against it. "Listen to me," she said, letting her touch wander with tantalizing softness over his skin. "The reason I almost made love with Fletcher . . ." Feeling Jeremy freeze, she spoke faster to get to her point. "Was because I wanted my first time to be with someone I felt safe with. Someone I knew wouldn't hurt me. But—"

Now she'd done it. Jeremy was pushing off her, a faint growl rumbling through his chest.

Celia coiled her arms and legs around him and talked even faster. "No, listen, whenever we tried, I couldn't do it."

With a cautioning look, Jeremy pinned both of her hands down again, this time on either side of her head. He was listening. For now.

"I didn't want to just feel safe. I wanted to feel wanted. I wanted to feel hungry and hot and bothered like I do right now." She stretched her neck, desperate for his mouth. "Bother me, Jeremy."

She got her kiss then, a rough, full-mouthed plunder that robbed her of breath, the kiss breaking as his mouth moved down her throat.

"Please," she gasped. "I want you so much it hurts."

At that, Jeremy's head fell to her shoulder, not at all the response she was expecting. There was only the sound of his heavy breathing until he said, "You understand I won't be coming back?"

"Yes." She clutched at him and kissed all the parts of him her lips could reach, paying special attention to the strange little round scars on his shoulder. "Yes, I understand." She understood too well, and it hurt—God, did it hurt—but it was even more reason. "Make love to me." She took a chunk of his shoulder between her teeth and fought the urge to bite down and create more scars. "Please."

Something drastic changed in him then. Heaving her upward into a sitting position, Jeremy stripped off the troublesome dress and gripped her bare torso firmly with both hands, the suddenness of it causing her to cry out in surprise. His fingers bit into her flesh, his thumbs sweeping the undersides of her breasts before he seemed to collect himself.

Celia swallowed down her pounding heart. Aside from her underwear, she was naked, and he was guiding her back down.

Having never gone this far, not even with Fletcher—their intimacy always centered on him—Celia cloaked her breasts with one self-conscious forearm.

Jeremy's manner softened. His free hand moved up her side to nudge her fingers away and cup the breast they'd been shielding. He pushed it upwards with a rewarding squeeze while his mouth brushed over the sensitive skin below her ear, tickling, whispering of perfection.

Unfettered by his desire for her, so raw and true, so unlike her previous experiences with Fletcher, Celia curled her arms around his head and strained toward him the way he strained toward her. Her breasts and stomach mashed against his hot skin, getting stroked and tantalized as he moved.

The hard bulge in his jeans pressed into her, over and over, while his lips and tongue continued to drop kisses down her throat, ripping a cry from her lungs when the tip of her breast was pulled into his mouth. Every balmy tug, together with the sharp twinge of pleasure that his hips created, electrified her flesh. Her breathing grew erratic. Celia worried fleetingly that he might trigger an asthma attack, but she felt wonderful. Oxygen flowed freely into her lungs, giving her life enough to reach down and plant her palms over his energetic rear, urging him nearer.

"Take me to your bed," she said without thinking, though she meant every word.

Without argument this time, Jeremy pulled her off the couch and steered her backward up the stairs, his mouth never leaving hers.

After a brief and fiery tryst on the floor of the landing, they staggered into his bedroom, where Celia yanked on his belt, enjoying the growl that rumbled through him and the playful, brutish way he dropped her back onto his bed. With wide, captivated eyes, she watched him jerk the belt free and step out of his jeans. The room was duskier than the living room had been, but there was still light enough to see him in striking detail. Bashfulness made her look away. They were really doing this. Her skin flushed with nervous sweat. Her heart palpitated and throbbed.

Then he was between her legs again, trapping her between his naked body and the mattress.

Rain pelted the roof above them. The tight space between his mouth and hers echoed with breath, the rough smacking of their lips, and the occasional cry that would escape her lungs whenever he made the sensitive tip of her breast slide tightly between his fingers or bucked his hips too eagerly against her. Celia could feel every inch of him, hard and distinct, rubbing against the thin cotton strip of her Maidenforms, which now shamed her with their dampness.

His kisses deep and frantic, Jeremy never stopped moving, his hands roaming, hips grinding and bucking until they were both whimpering and simulating the act that Celia had only ever fantasized about in the privacy of her bed. She almost panicked when he peeled the last of her clothing off her legs, anticipation surging like lightning through her veins as he kissed her belly, as his calloused palm delivered a long, adulating stroke up her thigh, then with shrewd simplicity, urged her thighs to spread wide.

"Jeremy."

He rose to kiss her mouth and, through gravel and lust, said, "Tell me to stop," while the narrow space between them grew stifling.

"Don't stop."

He held her mouth in another agitated kiss and moved his palm over her bare sex, making her stomach clench with alarm. Still, Celia didn't stop him. She endured as gentle, pleated fingers began a slow massage that moved in ever-tighter circles over her most intimate flesh. One finger ultimately separated from the pack and pushed between the folds to penetrate her, going deep.

Celia gasped. It was startling at first, unpleasant, but Jeremy opened his mouth over hers to muffle the complaint. That distressing finger, longer and thicker inside her than it had ever seemed on the outside, punctured her with slow pumps, then left her to clench on the emptiness.

To her relief, it rejoined the others to rub in slow, firm strokes until the discomfort gradually became something else.

Celia gasped his name this time, and with a slow smile, Jeremy pushed two fingers back inside, pumping cleverly, reaching deep. At her distressed whimper, he crushed the heel of his hand in, creating a delicious friction, while those invading fingers began snapping upwards, instead of spearing her like before. A jolt of pleasure surprised her.

Squeezing her eyes shut, Celia whispered nonsense, earning herself a soothing sweep of his lips. She couldn't tell if she liked what he was doing, as the sensation dallied between pleasure and pain. Then a new, deeply gratifying sensation began to pool, tormenting her with the sudden need to grind against his hand, to hunt for more.

She whined her confusion. Embarrassed by her own undulating hips, but so curious, she opened her eyes. Her skin was flushed and sheened with sweat. Between her thighs, his wrist jerked roughly upward, lifting her bottom a little with each thrust. Jeremy was minding her face, though, his green eyes glassy with lust. And while she should have been enjoying this intimacy that connected them, jealousy whispered in her ear. His manipulations were tender yet confident and devastating—a learned skill, no doubt, born from trial and error. How many other women had he primed this way? Had they, too, dissipated against the palm of his hand? Had he loved any of them? Did he still?

His kiss overwhelmed the possessive musings, and Celia's hips truly started to buck, chasing those swelling shocks of pleasure. The fact that she was humping his hand like some frenzied animal in heat made her dreadfully self-conscious. But she couldn't stop. Something was twisting inside her, coiling tightly, and it needed release.

"Jeremy," Celia whimpered. "Please." Not entirely sure what she was begging for, she reached down to cuff her fingers around the part of him that lurched fitfully against her thigh, appeasing it with willowy, practiced strokes.

Jeremy's deep groan filled her mouth, and the sound delighted her. Oh, how she loved him. That truth, if it was ever in question, was obvious to her now. He could truly do with her whatever he wished, take her wherever he wanted. To the deepest depths of hell she would follow.

With that thought, she watched him settle over her.

Angling her hips to cradle him, Celia kept her eyes glued to his face. She had to remind herself that it was *his* weight that held her down. *His* mouth that moved in to suffocate her. *His* silken head that slid along the seam of her bare sex. Between her legs, she was unnervingly slick. He would surely slip inside if he kept moving the way he was. The suspense had her whimpering with each of his fruitless thrusts, gentle as they were. His erection was a much bigger protuberance than his fingers, which meant there would be more pain.

To settle her nerves, Celia tried to focus on the sweet taste of his tongue, the irregular tempo of his breath, the changing shape of his musculature as he moved over her. Why was she so frightened? She was a grown woman, far from an angel, and he was the one she loved, the one for whom she would suffocate and drown. He should be her first. Of that, she was certain. She had to wonder, though, if she was ensuring said drowning. He hadn't made a single declaration of love. He'd not even hinted at a relationship. Quite the opposite, in fact.

Yet still, deep down, she hoped that making love would change things.

Jeremy stilled. "What's wrong? Should I stop?"

"No." Celia hugged him tightly. "I'm just scared it'll hurt."

"It will at first. Tell me what you want me to do," he whispered through an affectionate nuzzle that all by itself soothed most of her fears.

"Go slow." It was more question than answer. "Please."

Jeremy nodded, said, "I'll go slow," then lay one honeyed kiss after another on her skin as he pushed inside. "I promise. Oh, fuck, Celia, I promise . . ."

————

At some point in the night, Celia woke in Jeremy's arms, feeling like a brand-new woman. She felt sophisticated now, worldly. But more than anything, she was starved.

With the rapt fascination of a new lover, Celia watched Jeremy sleep, taking note of every alluring line that formed his face, which was even more attractive now that they'd been intimate. She resolved to remember forever the severe but helpless expression he'd worn at his climax. It was the most beautiful sight she'd ever seen.

Then her stomach growled at her to stop her staring, so she climbed out of bed. It took her a solid minute to find the light switch, which made the bulbous lamp on the hardwood floor come to life. "The electricity's back."

Draping a forearm over his eyes, Jeremy groaned. "What time is it?"

"Don't know." Still naked, Celia hopped back beneath the covers and wrapped herself around him to steep herself in his body heat. "But it's freezing in here."

She watched as Jeremy took something small and brown from his suitcase. He blinked at it several times, then said, "Half past ten."

"What is that?"

"This? It's my Roy Rogers watch." When he saw the look on her face, he added, "I found it in the floorboards. I stole it from Holmans when I was a kid."

"And it works?"

Jeremy put the watch to her ear, and it ticked a perfect little beat at her. "Hell of a machine, huh?" He lay admiring the thing until Celia began to nibble at his earlobe, hoping to steal his attention away.

It worked, and he tossed the watch aside.

"Are you hungry?" she asked as he rolled over her to place kisses along her neck and shoulder before inching down to her breasts.

"Starving," he mumbled, sucking a nipple into his mouth.

Closing her eyes, Celia slipped all ten of her fingers into his hair and stumbled through her next thought. "Oh, there's—there's, ah—food—Oh! At my house. That hurt."

Wearing nothing but a self-satisfied grin, Jeremy took hold of her and rolled until she was on top of him.

Setting her knees down on either side of him, Celia suspected that she now sat directly atop his so-called hunger. It was stiff again and bobbing between her legs, prodding her like a needy little beast, while Jeremy wound his right arm around her waist, his mouth still plucking at one breast while his left hand pawed at the other. She watched, captivated by his doings. Her fingers gripped his hair by the roots to pull him nearer, urging him to suck harder. She whimpered wantonly when he did. Her body felt so alive, her heart so wondrously full. She'd never felt such happiness and hope.

Jeremy's hands moved to her hips, pushing her down on his erection, then slid over her rear for a firmer grip as he rocked her over himself. He was like an octopus, his hands everywhere at once. He was getting himself riled up, with hardly any participation from her.

"Okay, you," Celia heaved before things could go any further, recalling that he hadn't eaten since very early that morning. "Food or sex. Pick one. You can't have both."

"Of course, I can," he said, squeezing her rear and rocking her harder. "But if you're making me choose, I choose sex."

Celia growled as his mouth clamped down on her breast again. "Oh, I was so sure you were going to say food. I'm too sore for relations."

Looking quite titillated, Jeremy released her. "Relations, huh? I like your dirty talk." His hands went to the small of her back to pet it in lulling circles. "I forgot you'd be sore. We'll get food."

"Thank you."

He pulled her upper body flush against his for a hug, then rolled her to his side. They stayed there, idly cuddling and kissing, until their hunger would no longer wait.

To save time, they showered together but spent more time necking than bathing.

And when at last they reached Celia's house, it was exactly midnight, as heralded by the low hum of the national anthem coming from the television set. They found Fletcher seated on the kitchen floor, talking on the telephone, his fingers buried inside the coils of its cord.

Jeremy mussed Fletcher's hair on the way to the fridge.

Fletcher fixed his hair. "Where've you been?" he asked Celia.

"Jeremy's house." She squatted down in front of Fletcher to give him a telling smirk.

He responded with intrigue and an unintentional blush of his cheeks.

"We're just here for food," she added. "Where's my mom?"

"Asleep." Fletcher covered the mouthpiece. "I told her you went to the drive-in with Moose and Angie."

"Good. In the morning, tell her I decided to spend the night at Angie's."

Fletcher gave her a thoroughly scandalized look. His blue eyes darted to Jeremy, who was busy rifling through the fridge, then back to her. "You're sure?" he mouthed.

Celia nodded, then said aloud, "Did Moose go to the Point?"

Fletcher's index finger shot up at her. "Could you hold on another minute?" he asked his caller amiably. "Thanks." He covered the receiver again with his palm. "Will was still there." He turned to Jeremy. "Was it you who wrote "rapist" on his forehead in permanent ink?"

"Yep," Jeremy responded, still ransacking.

Fletcher seemed to ponder that a moment, then said, "Well done." He then turned to Celia and said, "Anyway, a few kids were throwing seaweed at Will, making a game of it, so Moose joined in. But some lady threatened to call the police, so they had to release him, but not before Moose threatened to eat Will's future children should he ever come near you again. But then Will said he can't have children thanks to you, so . . ." After offering a conflicted shrug, Fletcher reluctantly returned to his caller. "Hi, again."

Celia's hand came to her mouth as Fletcher watched her, concern in his eyes. She didn't know how to feel about what he'd just said. Will couldn't have children? Had she stomped his groin that hard? Should she be feeling guilty? Worried? Had he given her any other choice?

The kitchen was filled once again with Fletcher's discreet chatter— Who was he talking to?

On the other side of the room, Jeremy looked pleased as he slapped a chunk of cold meatloaf between two slices of bread and shot her a wink.

But Celia was left wondering if Will would choose to heed these sudden threats or, alternatively, seek retribution for them, especially if he blamed her for his supposed inability to have children. That was not something a man easily forgot or forgave, especially one like Will. How did he know he was sterile? Had he gone to the hospital that night? Or had he found out after trying with his wife and failing? She wished she could talk to Kevin.

While fretting over these and other thoughts, Celia put together a few more sandwiches and another overnight bag that contained a gift for Jeremy.

"I have something for you," she announced later, rummaging through her bag on the floor of his bedroom. She pulled out the gift and forced a smile, choosing not to think about Will anymore tonight.

Jeremy took it. "It's a plumb bob."

"It's from my dad. You left before he could give it to you."

Celia didn't know what to make of the expression that beset his face as he examined the golden device. It was pensive but otherwise indecipherable.

"Thank you," he ultimately said, giving her a preoccupied peck on the lips.

With the level of care Jeremy seemed to give all his tools, he shined his new plumb bob, wrapped it scrupulously with one of his shirts, then tucked the neat little package into the inner pocket of his suitcase.

When it was done, he came to sit beside her. They ate cold meatloaf sandwiches, talking and laughing until three in the morning, at which time Celia drifted off to sleep in his arms, decreeing to herself that, though it started out rocky, that rainy August day in 1967 had been the best of her life.

The eight days that followed proved even better. Each afternoon, after finishing their various chores, Celia and Jeremy met up and either headed to the beach to laze together in the sun or retreated into Jeremy's house to exert themselves over one another.

Each night after dinner, Celia would daydream through a long, soapy bath before heading off to bed alone. On the nights she couldn't sleep, she went to Fletcher who, against his "better judgment," would facilitate her escape. On quiet feet, she would sprint through the dark yard toward Jeremy's unlocked house, then clamber into his open arms.

In the case that her mother discovered her absence at daybreak, Fletcher had a simple cover story ready about Celia waking early to watch the sun rise over the dunes. But the story was never needed. Not a single query of her whereabouts was ever made. She'd been set adrift with Jeremy to discover truths about herself.

Intimate, chastening truths.

Nearly a week into their love affair, while the descending sun painted Jeremy's bedroom in tawny radiance, Jeremy and Celia lay tangled, recuperating after a spontaneous fit of passion that began with Celia spread over his kitchen table like supper and ended with her face mushed into his mattress, sobbing from orgasm, her wrists manacled inside his fist at the small of her back. When he slumped against her sweaty back, she realized that none of it had taken any coaxing or sweet talk on his part. Through every stage of her debauchment, Jeremy had simply posed her how he wanted by way of rough, authoritative jostling, and like a deviant, she'd liked it. Fed off it. The thinking, civilized part of her considered the acts they'd performed, the vulgar things they'd said, shameful. But the feeling, primal part of her was aroused by the shame, by his tempered sadism, and sent that civilized girl straight to her room to cover her eyes and ears until the grownups were done talking.

Now, after a week of being laid bare, Celia felt a terrible, possessive ache ripping through her chest.

She made eye contact with Jeremy, this woman-flinging savage who now yawned like a blameless kitten, and dared to ask him, "How do you know what to do?"

His thumb swept lazily across her cheek, and she shut her eyes as the ache expanded.

"About what?" he asked.

"How do you know what to *do*?" Her eyes flared, her voice falling into a whisper. "What I'll like?"

Deep grooves formed between his brows. "Why are you asking?"

"I don't know." If she could hear the anxiety-ridden tremor in her voice, so could he. Her plan to sound cultured and unaffected was failing—quite spectacularly, Celia suspected—but she went on regardless. "Just tell me. How do you know what to do, with a woman?"

"Jesus, Celia." Jeremy's manner, by contrast, was mostly composed, colored slightly by apprehension and a touch of sympathy. "How do you think?"

The ache in her chest bloomed into a throb. "How many have there been?"

"Don't do this," Jeremy groaned. "You're not going to like it."

Celia gaped. "What does that mean? Why won't you answer me?"

"Celia, it's not like I've been walking around tipping random girls over in the street and having my way with them. I've had . . . girlfriends."

"Girlfriends . . ." A fresh torrent of questions materialized, and she finally understood why ignorance was bliss. "Who—who was the first?"

Exasperated now, Jeremy rolled flat onto his back and rubbed at his eyes, then after a long pause said, "I already told you."

What? No, he hadn't. By name, he'd only mentioned . . .

"Pamela," Celia recalled with quiet resentment. The girl he'd taken into a dark closet, who lived by a lake. Jeremy blinked his confirmation, activating in Celia a whole new level of masochism. "Do you still see her? Talk to her?"

"I don't see her. She hates me."

"Why would she hate you?"

If Jeremy didn't want to talk about girlfriends, he definitely didn't want to talk about this one in particular. It was clear in the stiffness of his mouth, in his demoralized stare. Celia knew rationally that she should stop, but she had to know. Her sordid imagination would conjure far worse than whatever had him so tight-lipped. Even while Jeremy delayed answering the question, she could feel the anxiety creeping in, crowding her throat. If she didn't soothe it soon, her diagnosed "nervous condition" would take possession of her, and if its nastiest manifestation, a panic attack, decided to enter the equation, her asthmatic lungs would seize. They always did.

Celia's eyes jittered around in search of her travel bag where her rescue inhaler waited. Her mind worked to recall where exactly her clothes had landed downstairs, wondering if she could get to it all, to Fletcher or her mother, in time. Whichever of her self-destructive behaviors had managed to land her here, Celia couldn't let Jeremy be witness to one of her flare-ups. They were embarrassing, and it's what he would remember about her. It's what everyone always remembered.

"I didn't want to marry her," Jeremy finally said.

The answer shocked Celia from her thoughts. "Marry?"

"I didn't knock her up," he said sharply. "We were always careful about that. But she wanted me to 'prove I loved her.' We were still in high school, for fuck's sake."

"So, what, you took her innocence, then refused to marry her?" It came out with a sharp note of accusation, making it sound as though she were finding some parallel between herself and Pamela. And maybe she was. But before Celia could fully consider it, she saw that she'd taken it too far.

Jeremy was furious. His brow leveled. "You begged me to. You said—"

"I know what I said!"

They were in a battle of wills now, glaring at one another, and if Celia kept his infuriated face in her line of sight much longer, she was going to lash out in embarrassment again or maybe cry like the foolish, young Pamela probably had. Another silly girl who couldn't handle casual sex. She would bet money, though, that Pamela had at least had enough sense not to beg for it.

Disentangling her limbs from Jeremy's, Celia yanked the sheet above her breasts and rolled to face the wall, where notches of broken dreams and pinky swears remained visible beneath two layers of yellow paint. She needed a moment to pull herself together.

After several cathartic breaths, Celia inertly traced the outline of Superman's cape and started Dr. Frank's *Internal List of Self-Responsibility* . . . She could apologize. She could change the subject. She could get dressed and leave and come back when she was feeling less anxious . . .

Her hand fell back to the bed as Jeremy's smoothed up her arm, his lips landing softly on her shoulder with her name. Celia shrugged him off, not ready for him yet. "Don't."

A shiver coursed through her at his expletive. Behind her, he moved away with irate abruptness, and when everything went still and quiet again, she worried that he'd left the bed.

A gruff exhale told her he hadn't.

Celia closed her eyes and drew another collection of calming breaths. She hated this aspect of herself, this part of her that still hadn't learned how to properly process her emotions. There was so little time left with Jeremy, and she was wasting it sulking, thinking herself into a jealous snit when all he'd done was exactly as she'd asked—no, begged. And all he'd done in the days since, when he wasn't bending her into enjoyably shocking positions, was dote on her. It had astounded her, in fact, how obliging and affectionate he'd been over the past week. He'd made her *feel* loved, whether she was or not.

Wasn't that enough?

Prepared to act like the mature, rational woman her mother had raised her to be, Celia flipped back over and propped herself on one elbow. She could see that Jeremy had been terrorizing the ceiling with his most serious glare, both arms slung over his head in exasperation.

Celia sagged. "Honey?"

With a single blink, his eyes were sidelong on her. "What?"

"I want to apologize. I . . . I have a habit of overthinking things. Fletcher says I get myself worked up over situations that I've concocted inside my head, and sometimes I think he may be right. It's just . . . this is harder than I thought it would be, this 'not caring' business. I want to be a worldly woman who can have relations and not care, not care that you don't care, but I'm realizing—"

"I never said I don't care," Jeremy interjected.

"I know you care about me. You must, or you wouldn't have gotten so mad at Will. You wouldn't have done a lot of things." Her tone retreated into antipathy. "But that's not the kind of 'caring' I mean, Jeremy."

"I know what you mean, Celia, and I never said I don't care."

Celia was taken aback. "Well, you never said you do either. You haven't said anything."

"What would be the point?" Jeremy replied through a rather nasty sneer. "To make us both feel worse later? I have no idea what I'd be doing or saying if I wasn't leaving, but the fact is: I am. How many more fucking times do I have to say it?"

"Don't be mean!"

Jeremy sighed. "I'm not trying to be mean. I'm not trying to hurt you, Celia. I'm trying like hell *not* to. For the next two years, I'm going to have zero control over my life. I can barely wrap my head around what's coming, let alone what I'm going to do after. If there even is an after for me."

The pause before his next words felt excruciatingly long, but Celia waited it out, understanding from his expression that they were important to him.

"I can't give you what you want, Celia. I'm sorry."

Another full minute of heavily burdened silence passed, during which Celia found herself with nothing to say and absolutely nothing to overthink. Both her heart and mind had reached an impasse, frozen in grief. And she'd done it to herself, as always.

Then Jeremy, having spent the entire minute in deep contemplation, his gaze faraway, said, "The way I used to imagine my future, there was this blank—I don't know what to call it—canvas, I guess, of time stretched out in front of me, with years of possibilities to fill in. Faceless wife, nameless kids, some job I complain about at the dinner table, maybe a trip or two to Hawaii if I'm lucky. But when I got that draft notice, it all disappeared. There's this huge wall now where next week should be. I can't see past it. I can't think past it. It's all just . . . gone."

Jeremy seldom displayed vulnerability, but whenever he did, Celia felt gutted. It had happened on occasion when they were kids. On those days when she was cold or indifferent to him, he would expose his soft underbelly, hoping to inspire her affection, unable to cope otherwise.

"Jeremy . . ." Celia crawled onto his lap and buried her face in his neck. "I'm sorry. I'm being selfish." She kissed the warm skin there, just kissed and kissed. "I'm so sorry."

She felt his arms come around her. "It's all right."

"No." Celia rose to look at him. "You've been trying to tell me, and I haven't listened. I wanted you so badly, I seduced you and didn't stop to think how you might be feeling about everything."

"I thought I seduced you."

Celia blew out a laugh, her mood bolstered by the fresh tranquility in his smile, the warmth behind it. Lowering her head to his shoulder, she let her weight drape him. "I don't regret it. I'm just sad you're leaving, and I'm not handling it very well." Strong arms gathered her closer and squeezed. A safer, warmer place couldn't exist. "And you're not going to die, if that's what you're thinking. I can see past your wall, even if you can't. There's a future with so many possibilities. One right here, if you ever want it."

On his last afternoon in town, Jeremy announced that there was something he needed to do.

He grabbed his father's urn and Celia's hand and took a walk down the road to the largest tide pool at Asilomar Beach, where enormous rocks withstood the crashing surf.

A northwest wind blew as he unscrewed the gold-plated lid.

"You're going to toss him?" Celia asked, though she knew the answer.

"I can't carry him around anymore," Jeremy said. "I don't want to. My mom told me he loved the ocean, so much he practically kissed your father's feet when he agreed to sell him the land for the house." His expression vacillating, he asked, "Am I supposed to say something?"

"Do you have something to say?"

"No."

Celia sidled up behind him and wound her arms around his waist, his back warm against her cheek. "Maybe find a good memory and focus on that."

Seabirds culled. Waves crashed against the rocks below. Another moment passed, and Jeremy flung the hand that held his father's urn. Gray dust went flying, stolen by wind.

The parallel of the situation struck Celia at once. Her mind evoked for her the very instant in time that Jeremy had comprehended his father's death. She remembered it clearly: Dennis's final breath, Jeremy's broken sob, herself crawling toward the sound, crushing her cheek to his back and squeezing him the way she did her teddy during thunderstorms. Jeremy made her feel safe, even then.

Standing on the rocks of Asilomar, Celia smooshed her cheek to his sturdy back, wondering if Jeremy remembered these things, too, praying to God he didn't. She couldn't imagine the horror of seeing her father's dead eyes staring at her in accusation. While she had been the cause of her father's death, she hadn't been a direct witness to it. She would never know if it occurred to Thomas Lynch, as he took his final breath, that she was the reason why.

"Are you all right?" Celia asked.

Jeremy pivoted around. "Yeah." His voice was easy, untouched, his smile a tad come-hither as he bent to kiss her. Considering the circumstance, she'd expected melancholy or irritability. But he seemed truly fine. And while his lack of sentiment troubled her, she chose to disregard it. People grieved in different ways, and Jeremy was a mystery on his best day.

"What'd you think about?" she asked him.

"Oh . . ." He turned thoughtful. "When I was seven or eight, my dad barged into my room and asked if I wanted to play a game of catch. He'd never done that before. We stood in the yard for an hour, tossing a baseball back and forth, talking about Willie Mays and the '54 World Series."

His bright disposition had dimmed midway through his answer, and Celia wondered if she shouldn't have asked. She pressed herself closer. "That sounds nice."

"I guess."

That night, since it was Jeremy's last in town, Celia invited Moose, Angie, and Fletcher to join them at the Cannery in Monterey for a bite and a stroll. All three, however, made excuses for why they couldn't go, and not one of those excuses came off as genuine.

Over the line, Moose said he had to help his dad inventory the bar, but it was Wednesday, and Celia knew inventory occurred on Mondays. Evidently, Moose had forgotten that Celia had moonlighted at the Blue Pelican the summer before. She supposed the schedule could've changed . . . Odd that it would change to one of Moose's nights off . . . But she didn't say that. She wished him well and hung up.

On the next call, Angie claimed she had to babysit, saying her mother was sick, but Celia had seen Rosemary Martin that morning at the market, and the woman had looked perfectly healthy. Celia wasn't about to argue with Angie, though, as she would never win against the redhead. So once again, she wished her friend well, then ended the call with a purposeful slam.

Fletcher, the only semi-honest one of the bunch, had declared boredom with the tourist-laden Cannery, having spent a lot of time there this summer. And considering his relationship with Jeremy, which was still relatively tense—and bearing in mind that there would be no Moose or Angie to buffer that tension—Celia found herself grateful for his refusal.

When Fletcher offered the use of his car, however, he was immediately forgiven without prejudice.

By the end of the night, Celia was glad for their lies. She and Jeremy had strolled the Cannery alone and stuffed their faces with burgers, taffy, and ice cream, chatting about films and politics and the purpose of plumb bobs.

It felt like an honest-to-goodness date. Jeremy treated, opened doors, and held her hand, even when Betty Jean Finnegan, with her own date, sauntered past and practically burned a hole through their laced fingers with her glare.

Celia waited until the other couple was out of earshot to whisper, "Can I ask you something?"

"I didn't sleep with her," Jeremy said.

"How did you know I was going to ask that?"

"Because you're a jealous little monster," he said and then chuckled at her show of indignation. "Oh, come on, I'm no better. I was ready to thrash Fletcher over you last week. And that dipshit in the overalls."

Overalls? A giddy, inquisitive smile pulled hard at the muscles in Celia's face. She didn't know to which "dipshit" he was referring, but that wasn't what had her so tickled. "You know," she said, sidling up to Jeremy, "if you're not careful, I'm going to start thinking you're sweet on me."

Jeremy smirked, his eyes sleepy-soft. Then he kissed her, slow and deep, right there on the sidewalk beside the outdoor dining court in front of about a hundred aghast tourists and one Betty Jean Finnegan.

Back at his place, Celia lay on his bed, trying to prepare herself for the inevitable as she watched him pack his belongings by the light of a few dinner candles taken from her mother's sideboard.

His flight home was scheduled for the next morning. He had disconnected the utilities that afternoon, and while the lack of electricity and running water rankled, the candlelight made his skin appear golden and godlike, making her feel even more lovesick. There were so many things she'd wanted to do, wrongs she'd wanted to right, but it had taken her nearly the entire summer just to get him talking. Time had run out.

Celia left the bed, went over to the little radio on the floor, and searched between the static for something suitable, stopping at an Otis Redding song and raising the volume.

Meeting Jeremy where he stood in the middle of the room, Celia took the shirt from his hands and tossed it aside.

With puzzled amusement, he watched it land on the bed.

"Ask me to dance," she said. "The way Ms. Pratt taught you."

Jeremy wilted at that, but when he opened his mouth, his tone was gentle. "You don't have to do this, you know. You think I didn't notice you over there, overthinking yourself in circles?" He gripped her jaw in his hand and planted a kiss on her mouth. "You have nothing to make up for."

"But I do."

"Like what?"

"Mistakes."

Releasing her, Jeremy snorted. "If you can forgive me for my mistakes—and I made some whoppers—I'm pretty sure I can forgive you."

"You were a child."

"So were you," he said, kissing her more gently this time. "It's going to be all right, Celia. I promise."

Who could know that those words would affect her so much? She wasn't even sure of their meaning. It was the tenderness in his voice or maybe his touch or the warm sheen of affection in his gaze. Without warning, tears smarted at her eyes. Celia pinched her mouth shut, trying to hold them in, but they burned straight through and trickled out, flooding her vision.

"Do you remember that last day on my driveway?" she asked his blurry face, trying not to think about how childish and ugly her blubbering must've made her look. "On the—the—"

"Damn it," Jeremy sighed, then drew her close. "Please don't cry. I can't take it."

"Did you hear me yelling after you? Do you remember what I said?"

Swiping her wet cheeks with his thumbs, he looked sympathetic but reluctant, and Celia couldn't fathom what was going on inside his head. "I told you," he said. "I remember everything."

"Ask me to dance."

For one excruciating moment, he watched her, not saying a word.

Her hand went to her mouth as she waited. Biting at her thumbnail, she hoped she hadn't ruined their last night with her fretting.

A strange little grin tugged at Jeremy's lips as he pulled her thumb from her mouth, smoothed his fingertip down her nose, then offered his hand. "May I have this dance, Miss?"

Celia marveled at him, at his eyes, in particular—there was something boyish about them that heightened his appeal. He looked so young reaching out to her, so exposed. How had she ever pushed him away?

"Yes." Taking his hand, Celia rested her cheek against his chest and rocked with him as one ballad blended into another, her eyes clenched shut against the candlelight and the ticking timepiece inside his breast pocket, bidding the night to stop its unfolding, the earth to stop its infernal spinning.

"Look at me," Jeremy whispered, then met her with a rich, languid kiss.

Usually, his mouth, so clever and self-assured, sent her into rhapsodies. But tonight, Celia was too aware of every bend and twist his body made as he lay her back on his bed, of every thud made by her heart. Her head ached with the pressure of it. Her ears rang, the sound cutting through her skull like an emergency broadcast. There was no pleasure as Jeremy kissed her, undressed her, and made love to her. The despair, a bitter, creeping sludge throughout her veins, had already wormed its way inside and made a home.

A teardrop rolled down her temple and leaked into her hairline. His breath burned hot against her ear, his body heavy and suffocating, tunneling into hers with calculated rhythm. His hushed words of praise were squandered in the ringing. How many times had she been lectured by Moose to live in the moment? And yet as she tried, self-preservation had her falling further and further behind, making her numb. For all her efforts, Jeremy still forbade any talk of the future, refused to make any promises or even listen to hers.

Celia knew in her heart that she would love him regardless. The emotion had grown steadfast, immortal. It thrived as Jeremy's mouth drifted over her skin with reverence, his lustful, unbridled whispers trailing so delicately behind. She had his attention, however single-minded it was, and a keen awareness of his every mood. His lovemaking varied in nature, sometimes rough and tumble, other times deferential, but always in extremes. He was in a tender mood tonight, his lips branding her flesh with unhurried heat, a zealot in worship.

Now was the time.

"Jeremy," Celia gasped as he pushed deep. "I love you."

Stilling, Jeremy rose enough for eye contact.

"I love you," she repeated, timidly this time, a response to his crippling scrutiny. Was he stunned, winded, angry? All three? His thrusting resumed. All gentleness gone. His mouth covered hers, the resultant kiss grave and turbulent, suggesting either pleasure at her words or castigation.

Fearing the latter, Celia held his face away and forced him to look at her again, taking note of the new vigor in his thrusts. "You don't have to say it back," she grunted. "I'll love you anyw—" A startled gasp flew from her lips as her head was tugged back by the hair, a chunk of it twisted up inside his fist.

"Stop it," Jeremy hissed, his kiss clinging, hot and livid, against her mouth. "I don't want to hear it."

Another grunt rattled her throat as his aggression escalated. But he could be as angry as he wanted. These words weren't only for him. She was weary of regrets. People left her, people she loved, and every time, she suffocated beneath an avalanche of remorse for all the things said and all the things not. "Please," she said. "Please stay with me."

His mouth mauled, moving down her throat to bite and suck. "God damn you, Celia. Don't do this." His hands slid beneath her, raising her hips as his plunges came down in rough, fleshy slaps.

More of Celia's heart was ripped from her in broken, air-deprived sobs. "I'll wait for you then. Forever if I have to." Having unburdened her mind, she capitulated to sensation, his thrusts too punishing, too unrelenting to ignore, engorging tissue and invigorating nerve until her tightly coiled flesh screamed at her for release. Jeremy's mouth joined clumsily with hers, and pleasure gushed through her with disabling severity. The relief was rapturous and warm as all sensation dissolved into a soft, buoyant fizzle, returning for the delightful signaling of his orgasm: clenched muscle and erratic breath, the desperate grunts that devolved into soft, fevered whimpers.

Celia clung to him. "Please don't go."

<hr/>

The next morning, visibly sapped of energy from the late night, Jeremy packed the rest of his suitcase without folding a thing. When everything was closed inside the case, he grabbed his Roy Rogers watch off the windowsill and called Celia over. "Keep this for me."

She was so tired she could barely keep her eyes open. "You don't want to take it with you?"

Jeremy shook his head, then fastened Roy Rogers and his horse, Trigger, to her wrist. "It's safer here." He raised her hand to his lips, then to his cheek, looking as though he might fall asleep.

"Will you want it back after?" she asked, hoping he understood the underlying question.

Opening his eyes, he turned his head as if hearing something, then touched her chin and said, "The realtor's here," before leaving the room.

Celia huffed.

Outside, the agent hammered a "For Sale" sign into the front lawn. Celia watched from the window as Jeremy rolled up the garden hose and chatted with the older gentleman.

Moose was probably already on his way over to drive them to the airport, so she hastily scribbled her college mailing address onto a scrap of paper from her purse. She shoved the note inside his duffle bag and whispered into the empty room, "You better write."

The only response came in the form of a light, steady tick.

The small airport in Monterey bustled with travelers. Summer was nearing its inevitable end as tourists with happy, sunburned faces caught flights home. A few of the travelers wore military uniforms, and Celia wondered which were coming back from war and which were going. But the distinction became apparent when she saw a legless man in a wheelchair wearing a dirty, green jacket, his stare full of torment and horrors that she would never know.

Tears threatened her eyes, but she refused to cry again. It was bad luck, her mother had told her that morning, parleying wisdom earned a quarter century before. "If you want a man to return from war, you must put on a brave face and believe with all your heart that he'll come home in one piece. The thought that he might die can never cross your mind, or you'll jinx his fate."

"Gee, thanks, Mom."

At Jeremy's gate, a handsome airline agent greeted passengers with a bright, welcoming smile. Behind him, twenty yards away on the tarmac, the TWA aircraft sat parked and awaiting its human cargo.

Jeremy turned to Moose and offered his hand. "It was fun, man."

But Moose wasn't that kind of friend. He pulled Jeremy in for a bruising hug as if trying to squeeze the life out of him. "One hell of a summer," he said. "Here, take this." Holding back manly tears, Moose stuffed a tiny pouch (probably crammed with pot) into Jeremy's bag as he kept one eye on the gate agent. "For the road. Go kick some Commie ass while we work on gettin' you out of there."

Once the gate agent accepted Jeremy's ticket and wished him a good flight to Memphis, Jeremy took Celia's hand and pulled her past the gate onto the tarmac.

Celia wondered if it bothered him at all that Angie and Fletcher had once again declined invitations to come. Her three friends still weren't speaking to each other, but she was sure the rift had nothing to do with Jeremy—as the missing two had communicated a suitable farewell to him that morning. So Celia opted to save her questions for the three secret keepers for after Jeremy's departure. She had her own goodbye to give.

"I have something for you," she told Jeremy. From her purse, she pulled a small photograph of herself. "If you'll take it."

Grabbing it, Jeremy studied the picture. "Why wouldn't I take it?"

It was a candid that her mother had taken of her the New Year's Eve before on Lovers Point beach. She liked the way she looked in it, so at peace, like she had not a care in the world. It was how she wished she could be, how she wished people saw her.

Jeremy slid the photo into his wallet, then thanked her with a chaste kiss on her cheek.

"When do you leave for boot camp again?" she asked, biting her bottom lip to contain any renegade tears. He wouldn't look at her.

"Sunday," he said to some spot over her shoulder.

Her arms wound around his neck. "Promise you'll be safe."

After several seconds of his silence, the gate agent informed Jeremy that he needed to board the plane and Celia had to leave the tarmac.

After giving the man a nod of understanding, Jeremy detached

Celia's arms from around his neck and finally made eye contact with her. He pushed his fingers into her hair as she waited for him to speak. With her eyes, she pleaded with him to say something meaningful, something to keep her warm at night. Anything that might ease her mind when it was going mad with worry, the verbal equivalent of the luscious, burrowing kisses he'd given her in the warmth of his bed in the darkness when she was feeling anxious. She loved those kisses.

So faintly that she almost missed it, she heard only, "I'm sorry."

Jeremy pressed his lips to her forehead, then walked off before she could stop him.

"For what?" she asked as he moved farther and farther away. "Jeremy! For what?"

Celia watched him climb the steps of the plane, praying for him to at least glance back before disappearing inside, but he didn't.

Minutes later, after a short puff off her inhaler and a long hug from her friend, she watched the plane carry him away.

Moose moved in behind her and looped his arms around her waist.

"I don't think he's coming back," she said as tears fell.

"Aw, sure he is, dollface." Hooking his chin over her shoulder, he watched the sky with her. It was going to be a beautiful day in California. "The monarchs always find their way back. Why shouldn't he?"

"He's not a butterfly."

"No. But this is his home." Moose sounded so sure. "He'll come back. They always do."

Acknowledgments

A heartfelt thank you to my wonderful husband, Daniel. I don't know how you remained so patient. Not once did you so much as sigh in annoyance at my procrastinating and endless questions, and I love you for it.

To my children: See? Mom really was working on something. I love you. Yes, *now* we can go.

To Suzie Q: Thank you for all the late-night laughs and fun insights into the '60s. Sundaes with Sue, soon.

To my one-time agent Rossano Trentin: thank you for believing in this novel when many in the industry didn't.

I also want to thank everyone who did read-throughs for me and offered advice, not knowing if it would ever matter: my fangirl soulmate Amanda K., author Brenda Marie Smith (*If Darkness Takes Us*), my mama, and of course, my amazing husband.

Thank you to Terry Miller at the University of California Fresno Theater Department for his assistance.

Thank you to the beautiful town of Pacific Grove, California, my favorite place in the world to just *breathe*. Please don't ever change.

Thank you to Renee Crocker at the Pacific Grove Chamber of Commerce for her help.

Thank you to the town of Monterey, California, and its famous Cannery, for always having the most amazing saltwater taffy (and for not judging me).

Thank you to everyone at Greenleaf Book Group, especially Brian and Tess. You're all amazing and attentive, and I couldn't have asked for a better publishing experience.

To my copyeditor Jeanette the Writer and proofreader Matthew Baganz, thank you both for being so eagle-eyed and good at your jobs.

To Jared Dorsey for designing the coolest cover ever and for your patience: Thank you!

Dad, I wish you were here.